B. CATLING

The Erstwhile

B. Catling is a poet, sculptor, painter, and performance artist. He makes installations and paints portraits of imagined Cyclopes in egg tempera. Catling has had solo shows at the Serpentine Gallery, London; the Arnolfini in Bristol, England; the Ludwig Museum in Aachen, Germany; Hordaland Kunstnersentrum in Bergen, Norway; Project Gallery in Leipzig, Germany; and the Museum of Modern Art in Oxford, England. In 2015 he was made a Royal Academician. He is the author of *The Vorrh*.

The Erstwhile

The Erstwhile

➤ A Novel

B. CATLING

VINTAGE BOOKS
A Division of Penguin Random House LLC
New York

A VINTAGE BOOKS ORIGINAL, MARCH 2017

Library of Congress Cataloging-in-Publication Data
Names: Catling, B. (Brian) author.
Title: The Erstwhile / B. Catling.
Description: First American Edition. | New York : Vintage Books,
a division of Penguin Random House LLC [2017]
Identifiers: LCCN 2016030228 (print) | LCCN 2016037343 (ebook)
Subjects: | BISAC: FICTION / Fantasy / General. | FICTION /
Historical. | FICTION / Literary. | GSAFD: Fantasy fiction. | Science
fiction. | Occult fiction.
Classification: LCC PR6053.A848 E77 2017 (print) |
LCC PR6053.A848 (ebook) | DDC 823/.914—dc23
LC record available at https://lccn.loc.gov/2016030228

Vintage Books Trade Paperback ISBN: 978-1-101-97272-4
eBook ISBN: 978-1-101-97273-1

Book design by Jaclyn Whalen

www.vintagebooks.com

Printed in the United States of America
10 9 8 7 6 5 4 3 2 1

For Alan Moore, who lit the fuse.

And for Ray Cooper and Terry Gilliam,
who fanned the flames.

The tree of knowledge has been fossilised into an island of coal ready to consume our earliest historical trace (a biological fact or a mythological belief). One is old, the other is new. But both exist side by side in the present.

UNKNOWN

Woe to Europeans if they do not remain conscious of their unity of culture and race in the African bush. Woe to them.

LEO FROBENIUS,
Paideuma. Umrisse einer Kultur-und Seelenlehre

The Erstwhile

PROLOGUE

To-bruized be that slender, sterting spray
Out of the oake's rind that should betide
A branch of girt and goodliness, straightway
Her spring is turned on herself, and wried
And knotted like some gall or veiney wen.—
Dayspring mishandled cometh not againe.

RUDYARD KIPLING, *"Gertrude's Prayer"*

LONDON

*T*his is where the man-beast crawls, its once-virtuous body turned inside out, made raw and skinless, growing vines and sinews backwards through the flesh, stiff primordial feathers pluming in its lungs, thorns and rust knotted to barbed wire in its loins. Guilt and fear have gnawed the fingertips away to let the claws hook out into talons. Sharpened by digging a home in a shallow grave. It is seen on all fours, naked, and worse across the broken ground on sharp knees that are red raw from chiseling the earth to gain some purchase. Prowling inside a trench blinded by stark glares of explosions. Another bellowing flash sculpts the rippling muscle of its back and arms and the thick prophet's hair that has become soured by warfare into itching dreadlocks, mud-filled like the beard of dribble and tangled ginger grit.

But it is the face that alarms, skinned alive by shock.

The eyes terrified in the sudden phosphorus glare. Ultimately lost and forever in a gutter of staring that has emptied its skull.

The small balding artist makes a further adjustment to their expression, widening the pupils, setting them in a squint, looking in different directions to give insight into the mind cleaving.

He then steps away from the table where the picture had been made and nods to himself, his ink-stained fingers rubbing his chin. Yes, it was almost ready to be finalised for printing. A small noise on the other side of the room made him look up and drag his thought into the open: "I say it's almost ready to be finalised."

Someone or something was draped against the shabby curtain that was saturated in the stink of London. The artist took the picture from the table and held it up to show his subject and emphasise his words.

"I never looked like that!" came the reply. "You have caught me between worlds, upriver before I left the great forest and downriver after. You have gone and left me here alone and all the other Rumuors have sailed over to the Dauphin's land to be torn apart in the mud, in the first of your world wars of which there shall be many."

It was difficult to understand the model because he had been speaking in a vocabulary of shadows. He had not yet learned language. Instead he spoke into the artist's mind telepathically, without words, which made the artist's mouth work unconsciously, trying to shape the sounds in his mind. For anyone else, this manner of communication could be shocking, but for this painter, it was just another day communing with the angels.

The model said he was of the Erstwhile, but this made no sense to the painter. He also referred to humans as "Rumours," with a capital "R." It all seemed a bit delirious and the waning day outside was blurring the edges of their meanings. The model's statement about a French trench in a future world war had not been understood.

The night closed slower back then, the eye calibrated to dusk and all the nuances that have since been removed and exiled by electricity. The city in these days was encrusted in an ancient gloom—the small wicks of the whale-oil lamps glowed in every tarry hutch, doing little but adding a smoked glitter to the polished coral of London's darkness. A blind man, and there were many then, could tell of night's arrival by the change of smell, as the whale oil's stench rose up against the departing light. The river held the tides in its deep ragged throat for a moment before reversing its might under the command of a hidden moon. On the banks of the Thames thousands of stacked wooden rooms creaked and shuddered.

The painter protested: "But it is you, exactly as you described it. As you looked before. Before you found me. It's you leaving that forest. Fleeing that Vure you speak of."

"V-O-R-R-H! And I did not flee."

This was transmitted in careful curves with a new insistence in its pressures, forcing the artist to drop the picture and hold his head.

The abruptness surprised the last particles of day.

"Do *not* write *my* name on this. If you must show it to others, say it is someone else."

"But who? What?" asked the confused artist. "Nothing else looks like this."

"Then hide it, bury it under others, show no one, burn it."

"But it shows another face of God," the artist said. "God in the beast and man declining, falling from grace."

The model maintained his clarity while dissolving in the gloom.

"An ancient king," he thought, tossing it back in the wake of his leaving, and the wisp of it undid the pain in the artist's temples. He took his hands down and looked at his stained fingers as if trying to match the same darkness in the pigment with that which was growing in the room.

"I will call it Nebuchadnezzar," he quietly called out, in the way one speaks to the final closed door of a departed lover, the fleeing absence of a once-attentive listener.

It became one of William Blake's greatest works.

Part One

CHAPTER ONE

*T*he old arrow was forgetting. The air had worn it thin, so many harsh landings, so many directions. It had sailed across time and place, slayed some men and saved others. The bow, however, stayed constant and vital. Its maroon-and-black curve was made of the flesh and bones of a divine woman, a priestess who had been born in the Vorrh. She had told her husband how to divide her flesh and remake it. To separate and shave the long bones, realigning their strength and grain, and how to bind their splints with her muscle fibres and tighten them with sinew and skin. Now the great Vorrh and all that dwelt within it watched as the undergrowth parted and the bow glided between the trees, twisting to avoid the hanging vines.

Any human would have seen only the bow and arrow travelling by themselves, yet they were being held by Tsungali: slayer of men, warrior of the True People. The man who had led the Possession War uprising. He who had hunted the English bowman Williams and been slain by the monster Sidrus in the process. These days Tsungali was a ghost. A battle in this very forest had made him so, but those moments felt dim in his mind, receded because ghosts have poor memories. They have only purpose, which for Tsungali was finding the final destination of the fatigued and last arrow.

He travelled now with the spirit of his grandfather, who had guided him thus far and encouraged him on. Their journey was circular throughout the Vorrh. The process had taken many months. Tsungali shot the arrow forward and they followed it to places no human, or ghost for that matter, had ever set foot. Now it had taken them to the forest's edge.

Tsungali's grandfather stopped before they made the next shot. He sat wheezing on a low rock. Tsungali felt him dissolving and turned towards the ancient man, who like him was a waft of his previous life. Then the old one summoned up a strong whisper, and spoke again.

"Little son, we have done our duty and I will stay now. The last part of this is yours alone."

The grandson did not argue. He bent and hugged the great spirit who had been so much to him. The ancient man faded as they embraced. In the mottled sap-green sunlight, he was barely there. Tsungali turned and loaded the arrow and bent the bow. He let the next shot fly and felt the suction of separation as he left the Vorrh forever.

The Vorrh did not recognise or want men trespassing its vastness. And any who did suffered a dismal erasure of mind. The Vorrh had its own time, its own climate, and its own mind. It was ancient before Adam was a supposed twinkle in God's eye. And so had few dealings with this troublesome species. The fabled monsters and ghosts that were permitted access to its core had a purpose and function that ran in opposition to the dreams and ambitions of humanity. And every other living thing inside its protection had a stronger version of the same natural distrust and suspicion of *Homo sapiens* that is exhibited everywhere on Earth.

He continued to shoot and follow the arrow for days and nights. Each flight and each stumble taking him farther and farther from the shadow of the Vorrh. He was moving south and a great tiredness was settling over him.

He knew his journey was nearly over because the bow was twisting in his grip, straining towards its destiny. It was late evening when he passed through a village. The honey-coloured stone of the simple houses kept the sun's warm glow after it had set. The day's heat was gradually released from deep inside the stone's fossil stubbornness. The bow brightened in the warmth as it bobbed and leaned forward.

As night fell, the bow pulled Tsungali into the star-clad fields beyond the village's perimeter. Here, he again found the white arrow. Together, they waited for the moon to rise, late and solemn, swollen and ponderous in its appearance. As the moths danced in the moon's glare, Tsungali sent the arrow on its last flight, high in the direction of the sea, and followed in its trajectory towards dawn and the oceanic roar of the coast.

He had never experienced so much water. Among the crumbling cliffs and booming waves, he would have been afraid if he were still alive. The land felt hollow beneath his feet, he heard the deep voice of its concavities. The whole cliff full of caves and tunnels, potholes and chasms. The sea sucking air and water through them all. Breathing in resounding echoes in the first warmth of his last morning.

Perched high, Tsungali saw the remains of a house. The bow writhed, almost alive in his hand, straining, pulling, yearning to enter the small patch of domestic ruins. It seemed aware it had returned to the place of its origin, where it was made.

The fence around the plot had long since fallen and there were signs of animal intrusion everywhere. There was not the faintest trace of any personal effects. It had all been picked clean. Scavenged by thieves, weather, and wild dogs. The garden plants had overgrown and died back so many times that a thorny tangle of wiry undergrowth covered everything. Its mass had kept all recent predators and foragers at bay for many years. He passed through it with ease. He found the splintered arrow and knew the journey had ended.

He summoned and focused his last strength of being into his hands and cleared the weeds and dead brambles away to make the arrow's grave. For that is what he knew to do. To bury the shards and splinters here in this exact spot of arid soil where it had landed. He clawed away at the yellow earth, making a shallow trench. Then he felt something under his hands, something different. He dug down, now like a dog pawing at the earth, his face almost in the hole. A bundle began to emerge. He uncovered the burrow and its occupant. He dug more carefully, pulling the roots and crawling flecks of transparent beetles away from the thin rotting cloth, revealing the tiny body of a baby. He put his black ghost hands under it and hoped he had the substance left to lift it out.

It was not dead. It was not alive. It was human, but it was both black and white. Its pale skin being mottled and patched with blue-black pigment. He lifted it into the sun and brushed the earth from its limp, naked body. He picked its ears, eyes, and nostrils clean. Its mouth was firmly shut. He estimated that the child was no more than a few weeks old. Then it opened its eyes.

There was no uncertainty in the action, no resistance . . . they worked perfectly. Its eyes were the colour of opals and he had seen them before. He sat down and sank deeper into the wiry undergrowth. The precious bundle in his hands. The baby looked at him. Looked with the eyes of Methuselah and told his body what to do. He cradled the child in his lap and put one hand over his head, the other over the child's. He then made a circular rotation over both, as if smoothing something down. After a minute or two the milk started to flow. First in drips that splashed against his belly and thighs, then in rivulets running down his chest. The white lines against his black, nearly invisible body were dramatic and agile. He lifted the child to his breast and the tight mouth undid and refastened on his nipple. An enormous pleasure pumped through him as the greedy baby drank and he drained. All he had been was now converted into another substance. It was more than he could ever become, greater than his tribe and sweeter than all his gods. With an overpowering joy he was pulled inside out to nothing in a resounding pop that let the child roll down to fall quietly among the plants, its eyes glazed in delight and its mouth still sucking.

A light wind came in across the sea and woke the child. With energy in its limbs and its eyes wide open it crawled towards the broken house. The terse grasses and low thorn shrivelled in its path. Nothing dared scratch its painfully slow progress. The bow waited and squirmed in the shade where Tsungali had propped it. It slid down and gave itself up, loosening into sprung sinews and lashed shaved bone.

The next few days were mercifully mild and the piebald remained sheltered and kept warm by the dry breezes both night and day. The bow now had lost all its consistency and had given up its rigid form to become a greasy paste of a high nutrient concentration. No other animal or insect went anywhere near it. It was for the baby alone to feed on. Sometime around the third or fourth day after its exhumation it started to cry. Whether this was instigated by some awakening of the fluid motors of equilibrium—the plumbing of the deepest emotions, or a working of consciousness sucked animate and oily after the mindless sands of hibernation—or a sensing of a change in the wind: an edge of water lipping the heat, the sniff of a distant storm. Whatever it was that opened the child's mouth did it with an increasing urgency. So out on that remote bluff with the waves crashing so far below it grew in volume and audacity until it was caught in the hollow limestone ventricles beneath. It echoed and slid between all the chambers, growing into a pulse that began to rival the reverberations of the sea.

>→

In one of the rotting fields nearby, Carmella Salib was bent double and working. She was a venerable woman, wiping the dusty earth off her shrunken collection of colourless melons. Her field hung midway on the stepped side of a narrow valley wall. In the rainy season the floods would torrent below, taking a yellow milky stream down into the clarity of the blue sea. It would lie under the surface like a slow, shadowed spectre until a rougher tide came to churn and blend them into one. Now the wadi was arid and empty. All water was precious here and her well, two fields higher, was protected by signs and warnings and occasionally by her hiding in a rag tent with a dented bird gun when she suspected that her water was being stolen. There was nobody to do these things for her. These young people's jobs. They had all left for Essenwald or Berlin or Australia or other places she had never heard of.

When the day ended, she tended the animals in their straw-laden courtyard at the centre of her bare stone house. She prayed for them. She prayed that their heat and their flesh would keep her another year. She prayed often because she knew that something else lived in this forgotten land, where the sea was gigantic and restlessly eroded the coast, making the thin crust of fields tremble in insecurity. She had seen them. Heard them. She prayed that they belonged to the God of her fathers and were under his benediction and control. Because in her heart she knew they didn't.

She had told Father Timothy about them and where she had seen or heard them. He had agreed to meet her and listen as well. They now stood and looked at the parched yellow ground, and only the sound of the sea at the end of the narrow wadi could be heard. The priest stood like a silhouette, or a fissure. His black weary clothing in contrast to the bright weary earth.

The light breeze caught the sea and the twittering of distant small birds and crickets rasped against the day, but no voices spoke.

It was a long way from Rome and sometimes the stoic faith of these people seemed as harsh and as blinding as their land. He wanted to be back inside before the sun got any higher. So he pushed against the endless time of waiting.

"What time of day do you normally you hear them, Carmella?"

"Just before siesta, Father."

His heart sank. He had no intention of sitting out here sweltering in his thick itchy clothes. Of course she heard it at that time, her brain had been simmering under the rock-cracking heat for at least two hours. Even her mummified resilience could not endure that.

"Has anybody else heard them?"

She looked at him, her eyes slitted against the glare and his contrast.

"Who else is there to hear it? I am the only one here. That is why they are faint. If they had more ears to listen, their voices would be louder."

"But what do they say?"

"I cannot understand, they speak in the words of a long way or a long time off."

"So you don't understand what they mean?"

"I don't know the words, but I can taste their meaning and know that they have come as a warning."

Father Timothy had removed his hat and was wiping the wet inside with a small grey piece of cloth.

"What kind of warning do you mean?"

"It's difficult for me to tell because of their anger."

"What makes them so angry, are they angry with you?"

"No, Father." She lowered her eyes and looked at the glaring soil. "They are angry with God."

Father Timothy had been interested when she first came to him. It was not every day that a visitation was reported. Once he got past the sticky business of her sanity and the fervency of her religious devotion, he could ask real questions. He knew she had been a respected but aloof member of her little community. But this revelation worried him and broached on blasphemy. He needed to escape its disturbance and consider its implications.

The priest arose and quickly brushed the dust of the fields from his trousers.

"Carmella, I must go now; I have duties to perform. We will talk of this again, it is a complex matter."

He found the narrow scuffed track, no more than a slender overturning of stones, and walked up and out of the enclosure.

"I will be at matins," he called back down.

"Yes, Father," she said and turned back to the melons.

She doubted the priest trusted her visions. He probably thought her mad, as others did. Those who left her here. Those wicked, spiteful people at the other end of the village. They had always whispered against her family. Now they were gone. She would prove them all wrong anyway. She knew what she had seen and heard out here in the hot hard fields. If they ever returned, she would drag one of them here to listen and see, their hair standing up on their heads, as hers had done the first time. The wailing under the wind making her heart stop. "There," she would say, "clear as day."

Then it was. It was here now. Here. Perhaps Father Timothy was still nearby. She called out to him, out of sight above her, walking back to the sanctuary. But he had gone and her voice

squalled aimlessly. But today the sound was unmistakable—
somewhere a child was crying. She looked in all directions.

This was something new. This was unlike the voices she had
heard in the past. It was like it was calling *directly* to her. There
was a spindle of ought at the core of its distance and it gleamed
and turned and wound her in. It pulled like steel gossamer.
Honeyed and biled. Threading through and bringing a taste into
her mouth that had been astray for forty years of motherhood.
She stepped down the goat path and out of her sliver of land.
Small stones, lizards, and crickets leaping aside. She zigzagged
down into the wadi and found the track on its other side that
hurried towards the sea. With a movement that looked like accelerated hesitation she paced in the direction of the resounding
bluff and the rising wind.

The path forked. Down towards the sea and up towards the
cliff and the broken house that she knew had been empty for
years. She took the upper path until she was at the boundary of
the fallen house and the scuffed garden. Some of the stones of a
low perimeter wall still were in line, making a stitched outline
of ownership. Inside, some of the walls of the house were still
standing. Its windows and doors had long since rotted away.
The roof had fallen through. The reeds, mud, slate, and ossified
beams lay in a shuffled heap across the once active floor. Carmella saw the remnants of the garden. She was thinking about
how it had been in its most vital point. Her family often talked
of its folly.

Then, without warning, a parched and slumbering mite of
her brain uncoiled, dampened, and squeezed a memory out:
a scent, an essence of the garden itself. Its scent jolted others
awake and fervent bleeds turned into a flood that rewrote her
little history. She had been here before. She had seen the garden
once as a child and remembered its violence of colour and form

crammed and spun into organised enclosures of overpowering beauty. There had been colours here that she had never seen before or since. For a moment she saw them again and began to understand something else. Then she noticed that it was quiet. The sound that had drawn her here had stopped as if waiting, giving her time for her reverie and the gift from her past.

Then another small cry came from the broken corner of the house. Carmella's fingers opened slowly like new flowers on a very old vine. She stepped over the stones and walked through the rubble towards the mewling. A child. Its skin an intense patchwork of black-and-white piebald. She faltered, before the quivering antennae of her hands pulled her onwards, twitching for touch. The baby rolled around to look at her and its opal eyes arrested everything when they focused for the first time.

She picked it up, pulling it away from a mess of maroon fibres. A red drool bridge yolked between the child's mouth and the sticky remains on the stone. A dead animal, she thought, some part of its leg or hindquarters. She wiped the child's mouth with the worn, soft sleeve of the shirt that she wore under her dress. She stepped carefully out of the corner, bringing the child into a harsher light. It blinked and turned its patched face into her dress. She held it tighter and looked up. Out at sea clouds were gathering, the breeze now running in advance of the rain. Her sturdy nipples tingled under the layers of wool. It had not been the wind that stirred them. But the sensation was coming from inside. The first spits of rain rolled in on the cooling breeze high over the cliff. She had saved the child just in time. By night the storm would have shaken and flooded the little hollow. She quickly turned to the path and scurried the child back, swaddled and hidden, to her edge of the village.

She did not think about who its parents could be until she was in her courtyard, the venerable, solid door severely locked behind her.

She felt relieved that the houses on either side of hers in the twisted alleyway were now empty.

Carmella unlocked the door into the interior of her home and put the child on her bed with a pillow propped against it so that it could not roll off while she busied herself opening the shutters, heating water, and trying to find something to dress it in.

How long had the child been abandoned up there? In that place of desolation. She tried to remember what she had heard about it. Vague thoughts, scraps of detail of a couple living alone. Keeping themselves to themselves. Mutterings of infamy and ungodly behavior. An Englishman named Williams, and she a tribal shaman named Irrinipeste. The strangeness of a white man living with a black girl. There is nothing more suspicious to a small isolated community than anyone who chooses to live in greater isolation. Then they vanished. He was last seen walking towards the Vorrh with a bow in his hands. But there was never a word about a baby.

Carmella thought of her own children. Two sons eaten by a great war in Europe that meant nothing to her or to them. The colonial forces had simply collected them to die young and elsewhere. Her daughter lived in the mountains on the other side of the world. Such notions were problematic for Carmella; she had once visited Essenwald. Even though the colonial city was only a week's walk away, it had been the longest journey she had ever made and she had hated it. The size and foreignness of the German infestation she found impossible, troublesome, and chaotic. Her domain at the end of the village and the scattered slivers of fields were enough for her. She needed no more.

As she washed the child, it occurred to her that she might keep it. Who would really care? Certainly not those who had abandoned it. Nobody else would want another mouth to feed, especially such a strange one. While bathing the child she became aware that it was difficult to be sure what sex it was. Its tiny genital cluster was unlike anything she had ever seen. She had seen malformation in animals. She knew that humans were different, but not that different. She dressed the child in a smock that she had kept from her daughter and carried the precious bundle back into her bedroom. The naphthalene and the embroidery brought tears to her eyes.

She did not see them when she entered the room, but she felt them behind her. The wet blurs and the careful steps. This time there was no fear. All the voices, all the visions were now crowded in her bedchamber. They were all smiling. The child sat up in her arms.

"Gentle mother," she heard, as if the bedroom had said it, "we have come to praise you for taking the little one into your sanctuary. The little one has been sleeping for too long. Sleeping under the earth, waiting for a returning to make it wake and sing. Gentle mother, protect and feed. We will speak with your priest. Benediction is yours."

Then they left in a great whooshing that was silent and without a breath of air.

Carmella and the child fell into a deep sleep across her iron bed.

Father Timothy had finished matins and was hanging up his gown in a long narrow cupboard that smelt of incense and cobwebs. When he heard someone enter at the other end of the empty chapel. He quickly looked up to see Carmella standing there.

He quietly groaned inside and decided he would be gracious and give her a few minutes, while he was still in the aura of ministration.

"Ah, Carmella, you missed the service but not me, I see. Do

you have more to tell me about those visions you have in the fields?"

He put on his civil coat and turned to leave, intending to brush her into the dusty street to finish their discussion. Then he realised that she was still silent in the shadows.

"Carmella, is something wrong?"

After a few seconds, he became irritated with her silence.

"Carmella?"

Then, as he pissed uncontrollably into his trousers, twenty voices gushed and squealed out of what he thought was her. Their pitch and timbre bellowed and hit Father Timothy like a tidal wave. The broken octaves found every resonance in him and the thin room. Repeated and shook them until a booming moan was the only thing left.

"Little pastor, listen. We have much to tell. *Listen* and take heed. The child that was unburied is the hand of God. Made for the Vorrh. She will be the seeing eye in the blind storm that is coming to threaten everything, she will grow beyond the constraints of time. She is already older than you, but it will take a year for her to become whole. During that brief span, you will protect her and the woman who keeps her until they are called away. You are watched and you will obey."

CHAPTER TWO

*I*n Essenwald, another child was coming into the world.

Ghertrude Tulp was fiercely proud that she would be its only parent. Mistress Tulp was proud about most things. Her independence and her determination being the guiding elements in her unusual young life. From the moment that she had broken into the shuttered house on Kühler Brunnen, it had increased exponentially. Her intense curiosity had led her to the house that concealed impossible things.

She was a tad younger then, and most would have run screaming from what she had found in its basement: the sight of four artificial humans nurturing a cyclopian boy-child. But the stealthy Bakelite machines and their unique ward fascinated her and turned her instinct to flee into that of fight. And in that she would triumph, for a short time. So she took the house and the one-eyed boy who was called Ishmael and watched in amazement as he flourished and strengthened into a man. A man whom she would possess. She put her hand across her belly and felt her baby move. Was it because she was thinking of him? There was a strong possibility that he was the father and that was her only dread, that her baby would be born with the same deformity.

All else in her self-willed existence she thought she could control, even her parents, who had been forced into understanding about her pregnancy and the lack of a father. After all, the conception had been during carnival, when most of the morals of the occupants of Essenwald wore masks. Any indiscretion or minor crime that occurred during those few days was carefully overlooked. So nothing was said and the Tulps' family wealth and position were aligned to her needs. But there were other reasons for their sympathetic response that were not spoken of. Ghertrude also had the enduring friendship of Cyrena Lohr, one of the richest women in Essenwald. Cyrena had sworn her support and allegiance. Even after Ishmael had turned his sexual attention to Cyrena, which came as a concealed blessing. Ghertrude's affection for the freak had been exhausted by his demands and his increasing dissatisfaction and peevish cruelty. Her attention was now entirely locked on the growing baby. Cyrena was welcome to Ishmael's overbearing sexuality and his need to sample and own every aspect of his new life. After all, he had supposedly cured Cyrena's congenital blindness, miraculously "taken away" the affliction that had guided her life before he crawled into her bed.

During Cyrena's last visit she and Ghertrude had talked again about the possibility of the upcoming child being Ishmael's.

"Is Ishmael interested in me anymore, does he show curiosity about the baby?" asked Ghertrude.

Cyrena hated lying to her best friend, but the truth that he never mentioned her was too hard to say.

"He occasionally talks about the birth when he asks after you, when I return from our meetings." In fact, he had never once asked after her and had little or no interest in Ghertrude or even in anything that Cyrena did when she left his side. Their relationship had grown tense, though she did not tell this to Ghertrude either.

"Shall I be with you at the birth?" Cyrena asked.

Ghertrude narrowly shook her head while tightening her

lips and closing her eyes. She then looked deep into her friend and said, "It's best I do it alone. The Kin know the way and you would distract each other."

Cyrena was about to protest when Ghertrude said, "You are my dearest friend and we have been through so much together. You are the only one who knows of their existence and you must not know any more than that. Of course I want you with me, but these circumstances are extreme."

There was a moment's stillness, then she continued.

"Also it might be his, and if it was born like he was, then I don't want you there. I am sorry to be so harsh, but I really think this is the only way."

Cyrena guessed at her meaning but did not dare question it. To interrogate such motives and turn over such painful soil could plant, invest, and nurture more pain than any of the realities that might lay cotted on the other side of the birth. So she agreed to visit after word of the event had been sent. She kissed her friend and tried to smother the fluttering panic in her heart.

Ghertrude had seized the opportunity of stepping out of Ishmael's influence and passing him on to somebody with more wealth and compassion than she would ever have. She had boasted to her parents about her closeness to Cyrena and her other "friends" in the house and for that reason they need not be concerned, and they were happy to be as little involved as possible and asked no questions. Had they known that the "friends" were not human, they might have changed their minds.

The Kin had lived in 4 Kühler Brunnen before Ghertrude had arrived there. They were machines of unknown origin, artificial humans, sleek and powerful with rudiments of care and commitment, and when she first met them they each had a single eye in the center of their heads. But now the Kin looked anew, changed.

Not the half-human-sized Bakelite cyclopes she first discovered. Before, they had been the same size as Ishmael when he was a child and like him had only one eye. Now they were the same size as her, and they all had two eyes. Something somewhere had changed, but Ghertrude did not know what exactly yet.

All of that was academic as Ghertrude stood on the cellar stairs and her waters burst. Each waddling footstep sent twists of pain and exhilaration through her body.

By the time she reached the cellar door she was panting hard and gripping the banisters until she heard them creak and move, and saw their sweat on her hands. She pounded on the door and opened it. The Kin were already there. They gripped her arms and held her cautiously about the waist, guiding her to the secret places below. Their Bakelite bodies were strong and hard and gave solid resistance to her faltering uncertainty.

Luluwa, the one that had seemed most responsive to her needs, had turned her shining head towards Ghertrude and said, "It is close, the great moment of expulsion is near. Your child wants the world in its lungs and in its eyes, and we are here to be with you at that devouring." Ghertrude smiled through the contractions and gripped the warm ridged plastic of Luluwa's slender, powerful wrist.

In the cellar kitchen Aklia and Seth undressed her and stroked her onto the prepared bed, which Luluwa had made from the table. The Kin had adapted the whole cellar area in preparation for this moment. They had even made a small bathroom area by the preparation sinks. Towels, bowls, a mirror, and a wash bag had been gathered from the rooms above to give the area an intimate, personal quality. Aklia came close, clasping her hands like one about to whisper or shout. She brought the cave of her hands to Ghertrude's mouth and shed a soothing wave of breath into her being. Ghertrude's spine flooded with an intense sunlight. Like the glimpsed light during a storm, which heightens the whiteness of gulls flying against the black and blue clouds.

Suddenly, a hefty contraction pushed the astonishment out of Ghertrude's body with a gasp. The Kin went into action. Another parcel of their specialist breath was given to her and they started to examine the progress of the journey.

Fourteen hours later Luluwa was explaining to reassure Ghertrude and to instruct the others, because animal anatomy was not their specialisation.

"All humans are corkscrewed in the womb, it's one of things that makes them all different. They have to struggle against the twists of their mother's anatomy to escape."

Seth was turning to look the other way, he had become distracted by the wind that in some way had got into the house, and he could hear it increasing between the floors.

"The bends they make now will stay in their bodies forever, a unique deformity like the lines on their fingers or the memories in their bones."

Ghertrude heard only part of this because the pain and the pressure increased her blood in spasms, pushing against her eardrums, while the baby nuzzled out.

"Here it is," said Luluwa. Her strong brown fingers were enclosed in thick red rubber gloves and they were engaging around its head.

"Push and I will pull," said Luluwa, and between the contractions Ghertrude had a terrible fear that those brown mechanical hands were too strong. She had never done this before and the tugging that she so violently felt might be too much. She imagined the head coming off in Luluwa's hands and the spinal stump of the neck still struggling to be born between her legs.

Just as she was sure she could feel its thrashing blood pumping onto her thighs, the baby twisted and came out into Luluwa's careful grip.

"It is born!" Luluwa cried, her fluttering voice reaching a new crescendo.

The pain crashed through the floor and all of Ghertrude's senses came home.

"Is it alive?"

"Yes, *yes* and well, it is a female."

"Give her to me . . . *no*. Wait, how many eyes does she have?"

"Two, and they are beautiful like yours."

Luluwa lifted the slippery-wet joy into her mother's dry arms and the Kin watched what happened next with an incomprehension that made them wish for a larger organ of understanding or at least tear glands, or something like them.

Seth was the only one who experienced something else that night. Perhaps because he had been shaped in the fashion of a male. He heard the wind reach the attic and the cellar at the same time. He felt the meeting tides of air turn off an unknown switch in him and turn on one in the eyes of the nuzzling baby who was glued to her mother's breast with perspiration, blood, tears, hope, milk, and terror.

CHAPTER THREE

*I*shmael was looking out of the high north-facing window of the Lohr mansion's library. Twilight was settling over Essenwald, drawn as if by a night magnetism to the great black shadow of the Vorrh that seemed to swallow the isolated city. It was in that forest where the Englishman Williams had saved him and had even given Ishmael his last name and the living bow. Once Ishmael found his way into the Lohr household, he left the bow behind; the palms of his hands tingled at the thought, but his heart felt nothing. His hunting days were over then, but something was stirring.

As he stared out he touched the scars of his face and felt the blind eye that had been sewn into his face to rectify what he always felt was nature's curse against him. He was no longer a cyclops and he had Nebsuel, the shaman, to thank for that. He had not seen Nebsuel since. And even though it had been almost a year, the memories seemed to ache deeper and longer than that, as they slid between attraction and disgust. As if reading his mind, a distant storm flickered on the other side of the Vorrh, sending jolts of lightning into the purple clouds.

Ishmael knew he was unlike any other being he had ever met. He stood alone in this shivering uncertain world. A young man with a face as old as sin. Nebsuel's operation had not removed his uniqueness, just disguised it for others. The second eye was a prop. It was there and alive but it was not connected to his brain. Humans could never understand the power that his single eye gave him. His vision had never been a twisted slingshot like theirs. Their optic nerves crossing over in a perversity of creation: right eye to left brain, left eye to right brain. He had no such entanglement. His was a singular clarity, a straight line from his vision to his uncloven mind.

The storm was getting closer, the flashes sped through the trees, towards the skulking city, looming over and encroaching on Essenwald's cathedral, which was modelled after Cologne's, smaller but just as imposing given its surroundings. His reflection flickered in the window. The first murmurs of thunder rumbled outside the thin glass and a warm jeering wind shook the pale eucalyptus into a ghostly flutter.

Ishmael knew what he wasn't but not what he was. He had entered the Vorrh because it was known that other one-eyed creatures lived there. But mercifully he had no kinship with the so-called anthropophagi, the squat cannibalistic horrors that roamed the endless forest. He had now met and dwelt among men, women, monsters, machines, animals, ghosts, and some things in between, but knew that he was not clearly one of them. Everything around him knew its lineage. Understood its place in the world. The forest and the city were both structured maps of generational organisation where everything knew its place and relevance in the food chain. He was outside it all.

The overpowering magnitude of Cyrena's need was becoming suffocating. Surviving the Vorrh had given him a taste of challenge, the need for an edge, and this seemed the only tool available to excavate his unknown origin. There was nobody to talk to about him. He wanted to see the Kin, but he did not want to venture to 4 Kühler Brunnen for fear he would have to see Ghertrude. He was truly beginning to despise the day-to-day pettiness and lack of purpose of the life he thought he wanted.

All these people so drenched in inevitability, so locked in the comfort of their families that they lived a flat and mechanical existence. His origins must be far more exotic and dynamic than this. He was unique and needed a life to match it.

He had, however, been collecting stories of another kind of life that supposedly sheltered in the Vorrh. They were called the Erstwhile. Nebsuel knew the most about these evasive entities, but his knowledge was tainted with distrust and suspicion. During the time of his postsurgical healing in the old sorcerer's house, Ishmael had read something about their mythology and sightings. He had discovered more pictures than words in the old man's dense library. Every time he brought the subject up, Nebsuel would grunt and adopt a position of cautious distaste. Only a few basic facts ever escaped the orbit of negativity. So he knew that legend said they were the angels that God put on earth to guard the tree of knowledge in the Garden of Eden. And when Adam committed the first sin God was furious with them for their dismal failure. He turned his back and forgot them.

Over the centuries of despair, they devolved or gave up and were taken over by a wanton decay. Transforming in form and meaning, trying to die or become nothing. Some of the illuminated drawings in the books showed them with feathers and quills. Bark and twigs under their skin, knotted vines and thorns in their fur and hair. One thing Nebsuel did say was that no two of them were alike. Part of their curse of exile meant that they were alone and growing strange in many different ways. The only constant thing about them was their desire to vanish. To hide in the wildest parts of the Vorrh and sometimes bury themselves underground, in a vain hope that sleep might breed hibernation and that hibernation might encourage death.

Cyrena walked in from the other side of the library. She examined the pensive figure at the window, trying to read the contours and depths of his unique body and his unfathomable strangeness. His oscillation between passion and aloofness. She did not know and could not predict either of their responses to the other, which perpetually tipped and lurched between the lush exotic and the doldrums of ennui.

Ishmael's sexual appetite had increased again. He had exchanged intensity for endurance. She feared he was seeking weakness in her and he was terrified of finding the boundaries of his imagination and his senses. Secretly each wished for the fear of the other. Both their bodies ached among the books and the silence of mental concentration. It gave them a pleasant, bruised, and rewarding space apart. She took Herodotus off the shelf. Seconds later a new sensation seized her womb. It was contradictory to the rolling unbalanced ache that their lovemaking had caused. Different from the ovarian pains that sometimes roared and clamped at her core. This one was a thrumming from elsewhere. A message sent by the deepest of drums. An understanding that no man may hear. She knew it must come from Ghertrude and why. She left the library without a word and went to her balcony.

The storm smelt of the Vorrh and it separated her from everything. She stood on the ornate parapet and took in the wilderness that contorted and thrashed below. The swelter of the tribes and their meanings, of the animals that thrived beyond the trembling lip of this artificial city. Of the Vorrh, itself vast, primordial, and without the slightest interest in anything that walked upright.

She circumnavigated the balcony, directly into the wind where her hearing had always taken her when she was blind, to face the spires of the cathedral. She examined their visual property and knew them to be out of place and quaintly vulgar to everything else that lived here. Her belly twitched again and she imagined the old house under the shadows of the spires. Imagined Ghertrude and her struggling with the birth, the future and all its implications. She wondered why the man she lived with had never asked about the growing foetus, which might well hold his blood. Cyrena held the ache in herself for her friend. She held it more against the deeper ache and the questions, but mostly she held herself against the future. But not against the storm.

The rain was near and behind her and threatened her thin dress. She turned and came back towards the door. On the other side Ishmael was undressing, ready to embrace her, unpredictable and relentless. The part of her that wanted to refuse him doubled in strength, but then inverted. The storm broke over the cathedral spires; they arched into strident opposite parallels.

CHAPTER FOUR

*T*haddeus Mutter had taken the ring of keys from his father, who had painfully wheezed out his instructions about the warehouse. The Mutter family had been employed by the owners of the warehouse and 4 Kühler Brunnen for generations. When they held the keys they would give up their Christian names and be called only Mutter. Personal names were for the family, not the work. But this was not the handing over of employment to Thaddeus. It was a temporary convenience because Mutter's health had dipped for a few days.

Thaddeus found his way to the featureless warehouse. Its huge locked gates stared down at his unimportance. A smaller human-size door was set into the blank thick wood.

Thaddeus looked at the keys and made the selection. Once inside, he adjusted to the gloom. Carefully locked the stooping door behind him. Nothing stirred in the long interior. Mutter had given him specific instructions. Their employers were fierce. The last time Mutter messed something up, it was Thaddeus who paid the price. Thaddeus was abducted, his hands surgically removed, crossed over, and then reattached.

Thaddeus had little memory of the ferocious event, which always seemed to him distant and without any trace of pain. He had also forgotten the time before it happened, when he was like everybody else. The weirdness of his hands and the way he had learned to use them held no horror. Their early clumsiness had provoked different levels of attitude and questioning, and these seemed to be balanced against the frustration of his manual dexterity. His emotional world was tightly held by the resistant but flexible web of his family. He was never expected to leave the house; his parents knew of the cruelty of the world. He was not expected to seek work; he became protected by his father's guilt and the substantial gritty love that grew from it. Thaddeus had become special and now trusted. Thus, it was he who had been given the keys, not his younger sister, Meta, as this job, like much else, was patriarchal. The task today was simple: Deliver his father's message and do not deviate. He had promised to tell nobody and on pain of death not to let another soul into the warehouse.

He walked through the cavernous building. There were four floors connected by broad wooden staircases. Each floor was lined with tall dark wooden shelving stacked with numbered boxes. Other smaller rooms occupied corners or irregular niches throughout the warehouse. Or at least that is what he imagined. He only really examined the ground floor and looked up the stairs into an echoing draft of glimpsed similar spaces. He was not here to explore. He was working under his father's strict instructions. He must enter the building, lock himself in, and walk to the central teller's desk. There he must kneel and speak the words they had so carefully rehearsed.

He knew that he would not meet anybody and that nobody would come to listen to the message. Quietness had settled everywhere like dust; perhaps that was why there was no dust. The quiet had displaced it permanently, he thought. It was not truly silent. The muffled sounds of the outside world were allowed in to nibble at its edges and hush at its secluded movement. He knew that the building would hear it, would swallow his voice and his father's message, and would in some way pass it on to their masters. Eventually he found the teller's desk. A simple basic structure of a lectern and counter fused to a long handrail that excluded a corner of the shelving and a small empty room that must have once been an office. It had been the building's centre, when it was used to ship vast quantities of materials. Its workforce rushing between the teller's commands and the gates of hectic commerce. Now stillness gave the unoccupied building a cathedral-like grandeur that far outweighed any sense of absence.

Thaddeus put one hand on the rail and knelt under the authority of the lectern. It was like a lonely play of communion. He cleared his throat to make the first sound to announce his intention of cracking the quiet.

"I have come today in the stead of my father, Sigmund Mutter, who has been taken ill of a sudden fever these last three days. He sends his apologies and asks that I might be given some of his tasks while he is sick."

He paused for a moment, shocked by hearing his own voice rise amplified through the layered, listening architecture.

"I do not have the strength of my father and my hands are only capable of some things, but I am willing and able to help in any way that I can."

There was a click from behind the lectern; it was caught on the resonance of his last word. It was small and metallic and came from behind the empty room. *Latch.* The sound spoke to him, and Thaddeus stood and moved towards its reply. This was not expected, his father had said nothing about a response. His heart was in his mouth, which hung open uncontrollably as he tiptoed around the lectern. From this vantage point he saw brightness behind the room, a brightness that made the windows gleam around their edges. Daylight was reaching into the far wall of the building. He crept behind the boxlike office and saw a gleaming door of panelled glass set into the dark interior. It was in a way that can come only from living things. The lenses of growth and vitality distorting the soft brutality of sunlight into a dappled question that can be answered only by proximity. And so he knew it to be a garden; this most unexpected thing drew him towards its glass door. He looked through its clean panes and put his hand on the silver door handle. He looked back into the warehouse and saw nothing move. Everything inside seemed cast in permanence, in an eerie but reassuring stillness. He again sent his thoughts out towards the emptiness, to radar, this time unconsciously, its hollow for an echo of life. His own hand answered and applied pressure to the handle, which turned downwards. The door opened and a wave of warmth, colour, and perfume engulfed him. High walls on all sides enclosed and hid the garden from the outside world. He looked up and around and slowly walked into its interior. He thought he understood its size and proportion until he realised that there was a sharp turn in the flanking wall.

The garden was L-shaped, with one of its sections being three times the length of the other. He was standing in the short arm, amazed by its strangeness and its vitality. Trees and tall scented bushes lined its main pathway. Yew hedges gave it structure and blocked the eye from understanding its true form. He walked past magnolias and into a woven trellis arcade of wrought iron, its pathway threaded with passionflowers and jasmine. It was roofed over in glass. Dizzying reflections could be seen stippling the angled surfaces. At some distance he could hear the high voice of their instigator: a delicate fountain. As he walked forward and turned out of the partial enclosure he gazed up at the huge cliff of red brick that sealed the far end of the garden.

There were no windows in its gigantic surface and its actual scale was becoming illusory. But there was nothing mysterious about this, he knew what it was. The back wall of the cold-storage house. The biggest secular building in all of Essenwald, indifferently rivalling the cathedral in its bulk and height. It was in the next adjacent street to the deserted warehouse that he had just passed through, and its energy was in total contrast. The business side of the building buzzed and jittered with activity. Workers and clients scurried through its multiple floors, stacking and moving all manner of goods in its endless frozen corridors. The whole building throbbed with mechanical pumps and freezing tubes, its white icy arteries steaming with pulsating coolant. In contrast, hot smoke billowed from the tall chimney of its boiler house where trees were fed into the furnace, its heart, to provide the power for its cold. Its size loomed over everything. But here on its blank side it provided a monumental screen of secrecy, quiet, and enclosure.

There was no wall to the west of the garden, just a screen of trees. The sun was beginning to slant its light through them into the lengthening shadows. There was intensity to the colours, a voracity that was different from the blur of midday. Now they gloated with light, not reflecting it but saturated in it, bastions to the first wave of receding day. The shadows too had a deeper hue, holding the ground and the negative spaces between the plants with a rich depth. The brighter insects were giving way to their more dappled kindred, which fluttered between camouflage and gleam. Heavier scents punctuated the air, forcing a sense of swollen tranquillity to occupy the warping atmosphere of the garden. The far cliff of brick glowed rose to cinder, magnificent in the lateness of the afternoon. Then, without warning, Thaddeus saw another in the garden with him. Standing motionless beside the fountain, which had come into view at his last turn. Panic snatched at him. Had he accidentally let another in? Had he broken the cardinal rule?

He froze, not knowing what to say or how to remove this stranger. He stared hard at the figure, which was no longer there. He looked around again; the other had gone. Thaddeus cautiously walked towards the glitter of the dancing fountain, holding his hands out and up before his face like a boxer's fists or a crucifix. The figure was there again on the other side of the fountain. It shimmered blue like the core of the transmuting shadows. As if the very essence of their colour had been drained to form this miasma. It sharpened to give the impression of a figure dressed in a long coat or gown of blue, its shape and features fragmented by the brilliant giggling water.

"Who . . ." said Thaddeus, and realised that he did not know or dare ask the rest of the question.

The figure moved slightly so that the sun was behind it. Thaddeus could see only a man-size silhouette behind the shimmering water. It looked tall and thin and unnaturally still. Was it a man at all? he pondered. Maybe only a statue and a trick of light. Then it moved again and fear entered the equation. It was not the movement of a solid form. Not of a man moving from one foot to another. It was a drift, a blur like smoke, or a swarm of distant birds or worrisome insects, coming apart and reforming again in the same place. Thaddeus grabbed at a known explanation, optical illusions of water and light being the most obvious. But his solar plexus told him that was a wasted excuse. What stood on the other side of the fountain had no simple name and was certainly not a phenomena made of misunderstanding. So Thaddeus gave in. He stopped thinking and resigned himself to terror, knowing he had not accidentally let this being into the warehouse and garden. It was not the miasma that so carefully watched him through the water that was the trespasser here.

He was rooted to the spot. He watched the blue figure move around towards him. He saw it move only out of the corner of his sight. When he looked directly at it, it remained stationary and stared back. So he now closed his eyes and waited. Another sound was making itself heard above the splashing water. A slight machine whirring like the insides of automata. He had heard that clockwork once when he was a child and was visiting the home of one of the city "burghers": a Christmas treat for the poorer workers and their families. This was a faster, more insistent, and smoother version. The presence was close and Thaddeus opened his eyes, sticky with dread, and looked into the grinning face of the being made of gas and thousands of cogwheels.

The blue was not a coat but a swirling lozenge of thick flowing gas or smoke. It seemed to wind its flowing layers of flesh-deep vapour around an inner spindle, which was the restless motor of the creature. A complication of wheels, ratchets, and gears grew outwards and up towards its face, which seemed to be made entirely of active ticking details of machinery. The blue mist was thinnest here, wrapping and folding over the twitching interior like a fluid lubricant skin. There was a familiarity about the smiling face, he had seen something like it before. It was obviously human, but tilted or coloured by another animal. A cricket, he remembered suddenly, a cartoon cricket from his infant books. A cricket that walked and dressed like a man. The terror, which had shaped Thaddeus's holding, turned into a letting go. The smiling thing had replaced horror with attraction. The eyes of the being were clear glass, which occasionally blushed blue, as if filling with the coloured smoke and gaining emphasis and expression. Its jaws opened, showing teeth also of glass or crystal. A rotation began behind them and thinner strands of blue looped and tugged inside the mouth. The slender, talented machines of its hands came up to its gaping mouth. They whirred at a different pitch. Thaddeus gulped as the metallic and ivory fingers probed inside the jaws, while the creature's eyes blinked and fluttered in a coquettish and theatrical manner. It watched him while it pinched at a ribbon deep in its mouth and gradually pulled it out like white ticker tape. Tweezing it forward like a reluctant tongue, making it taut beyond its gaping jaws. It turned its head to preen the moment into Thaddeus's vision. Nodding to indicate that Thaddeus should look at the extended tape. He tried to read the letters that were written on the ribbon. The creature nodded differently for approval. The language on the strip was unknown to him. He squinted at the meaningless scratches and felt stupid.

The sun was rubbing a great blush from the massive brick cliff behind him and it distracted him from the impossible task of reading the scribbles that were being shaken in front of him. A light gurgling from behind the scroll prompted him to respond. Thaddeus drew his eyes back from the glowing brick mass, aware of the command. Vacantly he looked again at the agitated text and mumbled, "I don't understand, this is not my language."

The blue being shuddered a wave of different contours that changed its height, weight, and what might have been its personality for a moment and dug into its mouth again, pulling a new script out.

The words looked a little different, but he still could not read them.

"It's still not my language," Thaddeus said, feeling inadequacy, irritation, and confusion blearing his purpose.

He was about to speak again when a strong breeze from the end of the day gusted through the garden. The creature was unprepared and shuddered apart in the draught. Every part of it dissolved and fluttered into a blue haze. It quickly restrained itself and braced against the wind, reforming the gears, the glass, the ivory, and all the mechanical parts.

Thaddeus glared in disbelief. This being was not a machine powered and sleeved in gas. It was a vapour dreaming a machine.

There were no hard sensible cogs, only ghost versions, mist clinging together to imitate precision. What could drive such an intense mimicry? What purposeful intelligence made this ghost want to be a mechanism? Then the young man shivered, a horror of strangeness shrivelled him. He was in conversation with an abnormality beyond understanding. The creature busied itself fishing for another message. Thaddeus wrenched his gaze from the contorting face and looked down the creature's body. There were no feet, just a spiralling out of the ever-active blue. It hovered above the ground, gently bobbing in the fluctuations of wind.

Another scroll was being displayed, the head nodding frantically like a woodpecker to gain his attention. This time he could read it. It said: *Bid your father well, our sympathies we give. His work is ours and five more moons he has to dwell and hereby live.*

The creature grinned again and tore the message free from the back of its mouth. Handing it to Thaddeus, pinched between its slim fingers, a gesture that almost read as disdain or disgust. Like the way his mother carried dead mice out of the house, at arm's length. By the tips of their tails. This gesture and the meaning of the message collided in a gasp and a chuckle that choked the young man into flapping his distorted hands in front of his coughing face. Warding off the offending gift.

The colour had drained from the great wall and the garden began to feel chilly. The shadows had deepened and removed the gaiety from the fountain. The blue messenger darkened and went to join them, moving away from the water, becoming fragmented by the solidity of the closing light that clung to the plants and architecture. Thaddeus stared at the coil of what should have been paper on the tidy gravel path, where the creature had dropped it. He had no intention of picking it up. He certainly was not going to take it back home, back to his father.

By the time he had framed the question and looked up to follow and ask the messenger, it had totally gone. Disappeared into the maze of the garden or the stillness of the warehouse. It would be much darker in there. The thought of this and his passage through it hastened his departure. He stumbled back the way he came, turning the corner of the right angle at some speed. Expecting to meet or bump into the blue entity or some other impossible being. He gained the glass door in the flush of twilight and stepped into the waiting gloom of the warehouse. Its atmosphere had changed. What before had seemed benign had now clenched into a lofty indifference. It stood cold and resentful to his presence. He took a deep breath and quickly walked through its echoing length. There was an overpowering sense of being watched. He ran to the gates and the promise of the outside world. It was now so dark inside that he could not find the human-size door in the thick oak of the gates. His odd hands flapped and banged over the surface, feeling for its contours or its latch, broken-winged gulls in panic. He kept looking over his shoulder and straining to hear if anything was moving in the cavernous space. He sensed approach, sensed momentum unwinding from the glacial shelves. One thumb caught the spring bolt and it moved, his other hand joined in the finding and pulled at the brass lever until it slunk back and the door rattled open into the street. He fell through it, scrabbling and twisting his long heavy body to be free from whatever was rushing inside. He sat panting and bruised, one trouser leg torn and rolled up over his bleeding knee. He stared at the door and knew that he had to go back to it and lock it shut. It took him fifteen minutes to summon the courage and the will. He held the keys in his shaking hand. The other gingerly pushed the hanging door back into its frame. Just as it started to close he thought he heard something. Something like clockwork, but distant, vast, and bigger than the city and the entire Vorrh. It was a vibration more than a noise. The hollow trembling of controlled unwinding, saturated energy, powerful enough to turn this mild gritty world inside out. Kneeling hard on the pavement with his strong knee, he leant his teetering weight against the little door and locked it shut. He put the keys deep in his pocket, painfully stood up, and began to limp home. He was a different man walking in different streets in a world that he no longer understood or knew, in a universe that was watching humanity with a baleful smirk. Against this rang the singsong words of the paper message. The irritating rhyme jilted and skipped sweetly in his head. Every few yards he faltered and looked back to make sure that nothing was behind him.

Frau Mutter was chewing the corner of her apron when Thaddeus returned.

"Well, well what did they say?"

She mouthed the damp cloth even deeper while her son gathered himself to explain.

"They say it's all right, Ma, that Papa is in no trouble and he will get better soon."

"Get better, how do they know?"

Quickly Thaddeus tried to swerve from his stupid inclusion.

"I told them his symptoms and they understood."

"Um . . ." she said. "What do they know? They ain't no doctors."

"We don't know what they are."

She pouted her lower lip, nodding in approval, and shrugged her shoulders in bewildered apprehension. The matter was over. Thaddeus had no more to say and nobody to say it to.

On his way home he had worked on the meaning of the ticker-tape message. Was it a sentence of death or, more innocently, one of changing, of moving on? He tried to work out exactly what five moons meant in months and days, assuming that each moon meant a month. But it was slippery, as was the instigator of the rhyming proclamation in the garden. Nobody should ever know this in advance, especially the son of the fated one, whatever the fate.

CHAPTER FIVE

*F*or a colonial city to exist and thrive thousands of miles from its homeland and on a completely different continent takes two essential things: an unquestionable sense of rightness, being demonstrated through its constant display of blind superiority, and an unlimited supply of a raw material of great value. Essenwald had both.

The city had been built on the edge of the Vorrh so it could feed on the trees and process their raw magnificence into planked dimensions and functions—boil the sap, bark, and essence out of their crude growth into tinctures of medicine and sheaths of rubber. Every brick that was brought here was laid for that purpose and that purpose alone. The German township with German streets and families would eat the forest forever. It had driven a train track in a straight line into its heart. It would have driven through and out the other side if the Vorrh had not fought back.

The elite families that formed the Timber Guild owned the city from roots to rooftops. Old established German rules of conduct and commerce made it efficient and prosperous and watertight against all the forces of corruption and paganism that to them throbbed in every lumen of sunlight and every grain of sand on the godforsaken continent of Africa.

No one could have foreseen that the forest had a malign

influence at its very core. Some said it was an unknown toxicology of plant and oxygen. Others said it was a disturbance in its magnetic resonance. A few said it was haunted and that its evil nature was responsible. In fact, nobody knew why prolonged exposure to the trees caused distressing symptoms of amnesia and mental disintegration. No matter what or who they tried, all was in vain. Nobody could work for more than two days in the Vorrh without contamination.

It was only when the Limboia were discovered that things began to work. The Limboia were hollow humans. A pack them. From where? No one cared. Just as long as they could work. They were capable of doing weeklong shifts in the forest. They were already so damaged that trees could do little more. So when they all disappeared, the sawmills fell quiet, the pulp mills went out, and the train tracks began to rust. Disastrous attempts to force immigrant labour, criminals, the unstable and insane to cut the trees and restart the flow of raw material had all failed. There was nobody left to pay or threaten and the industry's machines gathered rust and cobwebs.

The anxious remnants of the Timber Guild had gathered again to discuss their dwindling businesses and lack of wood harvested from the groaning forest. The meeting had been called by Anton Fleischer, one of the younger members of the old families. He had a plan. Fleischer's proposal was very simple and left the eight attendants of the meeting in stunned silence. Krespka, the eldest, was the first to speak.

"And how in God's name do you propose to find them and bring 'em back?"

Fleischer quaked slightly under the choked ferocity of the question. But he held his ground and kept his certitude.

"The Limboia must still be in the Vorrh. We send a search party in to find them and persuade them to return."

"As simple as that." Krespka coughed, his phlegm signalling rising anger.

The spiteful moment was softened by another voice.

"If we did find them, how would we persuade them to return and work for us again?" asked Quentin Talbot, a calm sallow man who looked and behaved like a shadow. His quiet levels of supposed shyness were silk gloves over the steel claws of one of the most ruthless businessmen the city had ever known. His question had been anticipated by Fleischer, who answered him with an equally calm and calculated response. A response that had no fact or calculated methodology, just a stern arrogance of fulfilment.

"The Limboia have never been medically studied, all we know is that their joint ailment is the lynchpin to the continuity of all commerce in Essenwald. I have read everything about them and spoken to all who had dealings with them. But my studies are not over yet. In two more weeks I will be *the* authority on their miserable existence."

"You have done all this by yourself?" asked Talbot.

"With the help of my dear friend Urs. We have a substantial track record of working together, working as one you might say."

"Indeed," said Talbot, who had heard the whispers about the young men's oneness.

"I believe the key to finding them and getting them back to work lies in their relationship with the late Dr. Hoffman and the overseer called Maclish. Under their supervision the efficiency of the workforce doubled."

"But Hoffman is dead, as you say, and Maclish vanished with the Limboia in the forest."

"He didn't vanish with them, he died."

"And how do you know this?"

"There were witnesses."

"I have never heard of this, there is no such report!" Talbot was mildly irritated by the young man's nerve.

"There is no report. But the engineer of the train, Oswald Macombo, and his fireman saw it happen. Maclish was slain. But the Limboia remained alive."

Talbot's annoyance had gleamed into hope.

"Excellent, then you have our permission to turn over any stone you wish."

Now that Fleischer had permission to extend his investigations inside the known world of Essenwald, he decided to also deepen his knowledge on the more allusive mythic history of the Vorrh. When he was asking about stories and legends of the Vorrh, one name kept coming up, a priest called Lutchen, who had written an academic paper on the mythic structure and minor tribes of the Vorrh region. Not a single copy of the learned work existed in Essenwald, but Lutchen presided at the Chapel of the Desert Fathers, which happened to be in the poorest part of Essenwald.

The interior was small and airless and remarkably dark. Fleischer stumbled against one of the cramped pews and cursed its hardness. When his eyes grew accustomed to the gloom he searched for a window somewhere in the wooden walls. He had tried to prop the door open to see where he was going, but it must have been hung or sprung to close automatically, making the interior seem darker each time it shut. After circumnavigating the chapel three times he eventually found his bearings and stood by a small wooden altar. Above it squints of cracked light were trying to squeeze into the dark from a shuttered window. He found a dangling rope, which connected to the window, and started to pull. A gated wooden shutter reluctantly opened, exposing a glaring stained-glass window. A thick viridian light poured over him and the altar. It shone down from a fragmented forest of green glass. A great tree stood at its centre, beneath which sheltered a tribe of disconnected men and other creatures. At first he thought it was a picture of the Limboia themselves. Haunted and lost, sheltering under the lofty branches. Then he realised the absent expressions and upturned eyes depicted saintly vision and holy otherworldliness. He stepped away from the altar and out of the sticky glare to look more closely at the composition. Some of the characters had speech bubbles of text on clear glass emanating from their mouths. He could not read them. The composite of distance and grime hid the archaic texts in obscurity. Those who did not converse stood with one hand above their heads as if showing that they were once taller or holding it to shield the top of their heads from the blistering sun. The other figures, who stood farther back in the undergrowth, seemed barely human at all. The forlorn half-naked man who seemed to be leaning against the trunk of the tree was Adam. Alone. Eve had been not allowed in the picture, she had been chased out of the composition by an angry male God and his posse of failed angels.

Adam looked straight down at the altar with an expression that was indescribable. One of his hands was closed around the offending apple, but with the index finger pointing to his chest, pointing at his heart. The other hand pointed away, directing the viewer's gaze outside the central focus of the vertical tree. Back in the darker foliage a flame had been painted. A flame emanating from a sword held aloft. The sword-bearer could not be seen in the present illumination of the window. A corner of the building or some other outside structure must have obscured the sunlight. Fleischer recalled enough of his Bible to know that this was one of the heavenly hosts sent down to guard and protect the tree of knowledge, which they had clearly failed to do. He took another step back to see the window in even more detail.

"Remarkable, isn't it?"

He spun round to find who had crept in under his awareness.

"It was made by the brothers Valdemar, who came here to make the great glass in the cathedral. I am Father Lutchen. This is my chapel."

Fleischer straightened himself and shook the cast of the window out of his mind. He was about to introduce himself to the priest when Lutchen said, "You are Anton Heinrich Fleischer. Son of Domenic and Hildegard. Grandson of Peter and Gudrun Fleischer and Wilfred and Madeline Brandt from Aachen."

It sounded like an accusation in this tight hutch of prophets. Even his identity was known by this man whom he had not yet met, who had been observing him without a word.

"True. I am," he said, and was pleased with the forcefulness of his tone. Succinct and formal. Clear and unafraid.

They turned in unison back to the window.

The Valdemar brothers were legendary. Their work, whether made of glass, wood, or steel, was marvelled at and greatly discussed all over Europe. This window had been commissioned with the intent to show paradise at its height, glowing with all God's creatures, brimming with balanced, congenial life. Radiant before the fall. A clarion of Christianity and culture. Pilgrims and scholars would make epic journeys to kneel before its power, dazzled by the savage light outside that would be tamed and channelled into and through an artwork that demanded respect. It alone was supposed to establish Essenwald forever.

However, during the Valdemars' research the brothers came to be fascinated by the Vorrh: Its extensive variation of vegetation. Its singular and erratic climate. Its damaging effects on the minds of men and, of course, its mythology. They wanted to go in. To gain access to the Vorrh. All tried to dissuade them, but they would not budge and work ground to a halt. Four days and four days only had been agreed. They returned three days later, safe but elsewhere. After that the brothers started to change the design. More fanciful creatures were added to the already over-crowded scene. Much of the optimistic lightness of the picture was becoming gloomily deformed. Its perfection and shudder-ing depth of field rivalled only by the vivid life that shone in the mysterious denizens that haunted and stared out of its entan-gled tale.

Lutchen led Fleischer around to the other side of the chapel, where a bleached discarded pew sat in the shade in the far corner of the garden. Fleischer was surprised by the old man's nimble-ness when he saw his age in the wrinkling daylight.

"Father, I have come to ask you about the Vorrh. I was told that the window you so proudly display here was a result of the Valdemar brothers going into it. I intend to do the same to find the Limboia."

"You know of its dangers, of course?" the priest said.

"Yes, Father, I know that prolonged exposure to the inte-rior produces states of amnesia and, some say, total dementia. I intend to make a series of quick raids into the forest, spending as little time as possible searching for the Limboia. No more than, say, three or four hours each day."

The old man sighed and said, "Did you know the effects of exposure are accumulative?"

Fleischer sat bolt upright. "But that cannot be, that's impossible."

"There are many things in the Vorrh that are far from pos-sible, but it does not stop them existing. Anyway, you will not find the lost ones like that, they will ignore and hide from your random incursions."

The young man stood up, angry and irritated by the old priest's pessimism. He had expected help, not this.

"Also your interventions will upset some of the other dwellers there."

"Who," the disappointed young man said, with a sneer and a curl of the lip, which demonstrated that a good part of his adolescence had not yet dispersed or been burnt off by experience.

"Pardon me for saying so, but you are not in the right frame of mind to discuss such matters. I think it best we meet when you really need me. Perhaps after you have learnt more, you will have other questions for me. That would be a wise thing to do before you go anywhere near the Vorrh." Lutchen also stood up, ready to terminate their brief meeting.

"Perhaps I have not explained myself adequately. I am sorry if I seem unprepared."

The priest moved off, slowly enough to indicate that he should be followed. They walked back along the side of the chapel towards its porch.

"I am concerned for your well-being, and the protection of the forest and its inhabitants," Lutchen said as they slowly turned the corner and stopped outside the door.

"I intend to be very careful."

"Do you know the Tulp family?"

Fleischer looked puzzled at the priest's sudden change of subject.

"Yes, I know Deacon Tulp, of course."

"And his daughter Ghertrude?"

Before Fleischer could answer, Lutchen curved his question into an answer.

"She knows a reclusive young man who recently passed through the forest unharmed, he might be somebody you should meet."

"Surely that can't be true. Normal people cannot pass through it unscathed."

"I did not say he was normal. There are more than the Limboia and us in this world."

Fleischer realised he was losing with this slippery old man.

"Thank you, Father. Do you know this man's name?"

"Yes! 'God listens.' 'His hand against every man, and every man's hand against him.'"

Fleischer's face looked like a cup of absent flint.

"You need far more facts before my fictions will mean anything to you. His name is Ishmael. Please close the window shutters before you leave," Lutchen said in an amiable way, then nodded again and walked away.

The puzzled Fleischer watched the old man go, scratched his head, and then turned back into the church. The vivid green light at the other end was now diluted and hung to one side of the altar like a slumped curtain. The forest of stained glass had darkened, suggesting a much greater depth to the composition than before. The modest window was performing astonishing illusions.

The tree of knowledge had quietened in the middle of the picture and now was little more than a great branching shadow. Truly this was a remarkable work, as the old man had suggested. As Fleischer walked forward he saw something new in the window. Just above the portion that held the flaming sword he saw a movement in the darkness, a flicker passing through clear glass. Not the speech banderols he had seen before but something tighter, squinting light into the gloom.

Eyes. As he walked closer they seemed to wink and change shape. A clever contrivance of lead and glass, he thought. Giving the impression that the sword-bearing host was now watching from its seclusion deep in the trees. It and the others had been waiting for the sun to shift. By the time he reached the altar and found the rope he had seen a dozen pairs hidden in the narrow glass. With shaky hands, he tugged on the trembling rope and the small complaining shutter clanked over the cunningly crafted eyes that splintered above. Fleischer then realised that he had been given a sign, a gift, or a warning. He left the chapel and walked home; each step dismissed a fragment of the old priest's knowledge but kept the flavour of his bias. The only thing that tightened into a fact was the existence of a man named Ishmael who knew more than anybody else about the Vorrh. Now his most immediate mission was to find him.

CHAPTER SIX

GERMANY, 1924

The first recorded specimens to be shipped home from the Vorrh were from during the foundation years of Essenwald. But there were stories of others being found by explorers centuries earlier and shipped back to Europe. There were even tribal stories of some being alive and mating with village ancestors. No one knew quite what they were. But they had been given a name, which translated into "Of Before" or "the Previous" and finally settled as "the Erstwhile." Some said they were undead, angels, spirits embodied in flesh. All that was known was they were as ancient as the forest itself.

The ones that had recently been sent to the fatherland from Essenwald were in perfect shape. Every detail of their folded crumpled bodies was intact. From the whiskers on their chins to the horny nails of their toes. Occasionally one would be found minus a significant part of their anatomy, and it was accepted as stolen by displacement and earth movement over hundreds of years. They looked the same as the previous samples—jet-black twisted shards of people locked in their perpetual moment of death. But on closer examination the leaves, vines, feathers, and scales that so encrusted them could not be removed. In the other bodies they were easily unwound or cut away with the rest of the detritus from their interment. Here the plant and animal matter had grown in, become part of the skin and the very fabric of the creature. These bodies like all the others had been flown back to the fatherland, where they received the expert attention of the newly formed Department of Paleolithic Anatomy at the University of Heidelberg.

Only when the decision was made to deeply dissect the second of the new batches did they discover that the stubborn other substances were integral. But it was the consistency and the constitution of the bone that sent the probers into a state of total confusion.

Then again, all this was nothing compared to the awakenings.

V.Ess.43/x was the first. As the dissectors leaned in to cut further, V.Ess.43/x clenched what everyone thought was dead tissue around the scalpel, sending the operator out of the room in a flood of tears. Three days later it opened its stiff hand like a rose of Jericho. Months later it was sitting up and moving its head to follow conversation. When the second one woke, they were all moved to a private location, and a great secrecy tented their existence.

It became clearer and clearer that they had never been humans, they had never been or come from that twisted pathway that leads from the ape to man. They were simply something quite different. So different that they were outside of all known mammalian varieties of tissue.

The Rupert the First Retirement Home was nestled in the upper arm of the eastern district of Ziegelhausen, an inverted appendix of Heidelberg pinched between the mass of the Odenwald forest and held by the curve of the river Neckar. Its three scrupulously clean floors had been previously dedicated to shelter the elderly academics who had long since retired from their senior positions at the university. The little band of widowers and confirmed bachelors charmed and snarled, whimpered, laughed, and complained their days away until their rooms got smaller in direct proportion to their hold on and understanding of the present world. They gently fell into the vividly expanding brightness of their past. Memories blossomed there and illuminated the path to the smallest room of all. Some of the private bedrooms were on the upper floor, below the eaves of the pointed red-tile roof. The second floor was divided into dormitories and dayrooms. The ground floor was for dining, recreation, and reception. The kitchen and other utility rooms also bustled there. Outside was an overly manicured garden that sat enclosed in the shelter of the L-shaped building and caught all the sun of the long afternoons.

This is where they put them, high in the attic. They exchanged the inspection tables for beds and chairs. And almost grudgingly gave them pyjamas and dressing gowns, which hung about their black sticklike bodies and made them look like a couple of lost, out-of-work scarecrows. They had their own staff and nurses who never mixed with the other inmates of the home. There were too many rumours fornicating in the gossip bowl of the university. Up here in the attic of the suburbs all hearsay could be blamed on bewildered old age. They were not expected to survive long, and their quarters and care had been put together as a hasty, temporary measure.

It was when they tried to drink the stale water that sulked in jugs by the side of each bed that the alarms bells went off. These long-dead atrophies were seeking sustenance, which of course meant they had at least the animal instinct or reaction of survival.

They had made a mess of it. V.Ess.44/x was not able to grip and manipulate the heavy glass vessel, and the weight of it spilling had pulled V.Ess.44/x out of its bed and onto the wet floor. Here it attempted to suck at the sodden square of carpet that sat by the side of each bed. But its mouth was still ridged and unused to movement and the tufts of the well-seasoned wool stuck to its face and clogged its gaping maw. To make matters worse the spilling seemed to have awakened the other to the presence of water and its need for it. They also seemed to be aware of each other for the first time. V.Ess.43/x slithered off its bed and scratched its way across the pine-scented floor towards the broken glass, the soggy carpet, and its thrashing comrade.

The noise brought Frau Gluck into the corner room. The sight that met her was beyond her wildest experience, even though she had witnessed many of the outcomes of prolonged trench warfare and seen the horrors of those who insisted on living through their appalling injuries. This was different. The scrabbling slow-motion tangle of dried black flesh in the fight over a puddle of water, decorated with dragged bedsheets and a spongy carpet, just made her laugh.

The shifts in routine and the new and elusive staff did not go unnoticed by everyone. The incident with the hysterical nurse raised the eyebrow of at least one of the home's more resilient residents. It gave Hector Ruben Schumann, an emeritus professor of theology, a new problem to solve. He was good at solving problems and even better at inventing them. His cantankerous scholarship had made him a celebrity in academic circles. His lectures and publications on the relationships between rabbinical law and the Lutheran Church were caustic, accurate, and spiteful. Basically because there were no relationships. H. R. Schumann was a stalwart about the influence of Jewish thinking in High German culture, and in 1924 this was still an expectable eccentricity. He enjoyed being a thorn in most people's sides, including many of the city's rabbis, who were happier with a much lower profile than the one he insisted they should have. He had forced himself into a reclusive corner. So after the death of his beloved Rachel, who had provided all of his worldly comforts, he became intolerably alone. He was incapable of boiling an egg or ironing a shirt, the devastating oppression of his empty house filling with absence and task. The blotting-paper duties of domestic life and the iron loneliness were more than he could bear. He moved into the Rupert the First Retirement Home two years later, after an almost successful attempt at being a self-contained bachelor again in a small room between the university and his present abode.

When the first stroke happened, it hit him like an axe. It carved into his wisdom and his vanity and spun him to stare into the mirror, frightened for the first time by what he saw. He had stood just over five feet. Lean and tight. His bright pointed face was highlighted by a clipped goatee and neat moustache. His clothing was immaculate, prim, and expensive. His mind flickered through his body, expressive, extravagant, and at intimate ease. H. R. Schumann had been the centre of attention for thirty years. Women loved his boisterous impishness. Most men outside his subject, and all were, admired his confidence and charisma without feeling threatened by its relentlessness. He always saw this interest as being a response to his brilliance. Others saw it as being a reaction to his size.

These days, the mirror held a twisted face. A distortion that could not be taken seriously. The left side hung limp with the weight of its injury, the eyelid sagged over its watery orb. A lop-sided, reversed snarl made it difficult to shave, so that now irregular tufts of whiskers sprung out from the clefts and folds of the new wrinkles. He also drooled. The gap of blood in his brain had yanked a wire downward through his body and displaced the entire left side. It bent his now-weak, tingling arm inwards, up, and across his chest, like a folded and flattened wing making his left hand useless. It corkscrewed his once dapper gait into a pitiful hopping shuffle.

This deplorable mockery of his previous self had slurred his place in the world and misshaped his speech into wet mumbles. Making those slow ridiculous noises was the final straw. He would not let his perfect mind be seen dressed in the limp rags and tatters of those sounds. He hid in his room for the first six months until his speech was willfully retrieved. He practised all day, every day until the porridged gurgles finally sharpened and cleared. Eventually, when he considered it good enough, he emerged. There was still a slight wet lisp, but the speed of thought and voice had reconnected in an expectably dubbed time. Even his walk and his arm tried to behave after a few months. Back on the ground floor he began to hold court again and started to seek something worthy to investigate and eventually de-wing in his final years.

Schumann had heard the alteration being made to the attic when he was on the second floor. Sometimes the sounds of construction interrupted his exercises and the low moans of those who had previously been quartered above. After the work was finished, there was only silence. Occasionally the lift would rattle and its clattering upper gates would be opened, but nothing more. The total stillness began to drain down into his consciousness.

All human abodes are full of the million tiny clamours of life. The continual composite whisper of movement, heat, breathing, digestion, and the endless readjustments between them and everything else. But above there was nothing; it was more than an absence of noise, it was an opposite. It permeated his ceiling and, he feared, his skull. While he was straining to refeed and ignite the suboptimal cells that so cloaked him, it would creep in between his concentrations and their results.

He sometimes thought that the very penumbra of his healing mind was under threat from this white milky silence. He saw it as an enemy that he could visualise, and he knew where it lived.

He made an oath that if he ever got his body working again, he would seek it out and discover its meaning.

By the time the noisy incident with the fat nurse broke the spell of discretion, he was already determined to find out what was going on. He was a terrier of a man and his illness had only loosened his teeth and slowed his body. His mind was still a ratter. Once his alertness was locked on its subject, nothing would dissuade him, and now he had the taste of the goings-on from the attic between his strengthening jaws.

He waited again for the superintendent to begin his weekly rounds.

"Herr Capek, have you read Dr. Messinger's recent article on new methods of nurture for invalids and the infirmed? It's most radical."

It was well known in clinical circles that Capek and Messinger hated each other and were serious rivals in the higher echelons of geriatric care in the good city of Heidelberg.

"You should read it, it's very thought-provoking."

"Really," said Capek, not letting his heavy voice breach from its puddle of irritant-driven disinterest.

"With the new improvements on the upper floors you must be considering a change in the home's care policies yourself. I was wondering if there was a relationship with the new developments here and Messinger's suggestions."

Capek's lurching momentum was gated by Hector's ferocious fragility, and his question stung as the big man wobbled to a halt.

"It's just that some of the residents and I were concerned about the implications of such changes. After all, our financial support and the continual patronage of the university are an essential part of this home, both in its past and in any future development. If Messinger's reforms were being instigated, then we—"

And here Capek had had enough.

"Messinger's ridiculous ideas will never be instigated in this institution. I have no intention of developing one of his insipid care units here. The man's an idiot, he thinks that he can isolate the aging process as if it is some sort of virus, he thinks that diet and therapy will hold back the inevitable."

His actions and the loudness of his voice attracted the attention of everybody present and they watched as the towering man flailed and shouted over the diminutive figure of the old academic, who was now sitting on the corner of his bed, looking almost half his size and secretly enjoying every moment of the tableau that he had invented. He was wearing his Jewish, mournful, downtrodden expression and it loudly broadcast his timidity under such oppression. He looked like he dare not ask the obvious question. But he did.

"Then what is the newly furnished unit upstairs?"

Capek suddenly had his volume turned off. He flailed and flapped, but only puffs and hisses came from where the strident, angry declarations had sheltered before.

"I think you should tell us what's going on," said Hector in a voice so quiet that only Capek could hear it. Then in a softer tone he said, "It would be very wise for you to involve me in your plans."

After a few minutes, Capek led them both into the varnished interior of the lift.

By the time they reached the upper floor Capek had regained something of his composure and a vapour of his dignity. When the lift jolted to a standstill in the attic he opened the cage door a fraction and disengaged the possibility of being recalled to descend. He looked down at Hector, who had adopted an innocent air of bemused expectation, as if he had been invited back to Capek's home for tea. The superintendent recognised the danger that this impish Nibelung might cause. He knew of his connections and his influence in the home. And he had just declared that he had opened a communication with the wretched Messinger. This business must be handled with care. He held the brass handle of the metal trellis door of the cage and calmly began his address: "Professor Schumann, this is a delicate business up here." He slightly rattled the cage door. "I have been entrusted by the university to undertake a strange and difficult task. It was my intention to consult you in the matter, but your stroke got in the way and I had to proceed without you."

The old man knew he was lying and used it to dig in and strengthen his foothold.

"Then tell me now," he said, concealing his contempt in urgency.

"Yes of course, but you must pledge me your oath of secrecy. This is now a state matter and under the direct jurisdiction of the Department of Internal Affairs."

Hector gave his pledge and Capek rattled the metal gate open into the silent corridor. They walked through its newly decorated length and as they approached the ward another smell swooned over the green paint: cinnamon, cinnamon mixed with a tang of the sea.

The door was wedged open and they both walked in to look at the two sleeping patients, propped up in their beds. Schumann's first reaction was that they were dummies or scarecrows, but as his scrutiny focused he recognised their gaunt and vacant humanity. Burn victims, he thought next, weirdly dressed in baggy, over-size pyjamas. He eventually tore his eyes away and looked at Capek, who had changed his expression from worried concern to repugnance.

"Who—what are they?" whispered Schumann.

"That is indeed the question," said Capek out of the corner of his mouth, his eyes never leaving the beds.

"May I go closer?"

Capek did not answer but extended his hand in a be-my-guest gesture.

The old man quietly walked towards them as if in fear of waking or startling them. On closer inspection they looked like wrinkled sculptures, carved or modelled out of some hard ebony or squid-ink china. They also smelt like that.

The closest one slowly opened its eyes and turned its head fractionally to look at Hector. The experience was unpleasant. It was as if an itching had been pushed inside him. Not a full-bodied irritation that demands a joyous scratch but the kind of nauseous tingling that often accompanies the healing of a wound. Without any prior thought Hector said, "Good afternoon, my name is Professor Schumann."

This opened the eyes of the other one, who also turned to watch him. The sensation in his head doubled and creamed, and for a moment he felt faint and feared that he would pass out. But the sensation quickly passed as his useless arm unbent. It fell limply to his side and filled with new energy. His mind spoke to it, the causeways opened, and the numb fingers flexed. Pain bit hard into the joints and he yelped with surprise.

"My arm . . . Capek, look at my arm."

He forgot the sensation in his head, he forgot the gazing statues, he forgot Capek, and he remembered only inside that pocket of scarred empty cells that had just flushed with hot sweet blood.

The eyes of the statues closed. The visitors had been dismissed and walked backwards away from the beds and out of the ward. Capek seemed to slowly awake from some reverie and joined him in the corridor. They took the lift and descended to the ground floor, where they left each other after saying, "Tomorrow." "Yes, tomorrow."

———

Professor Schumann awoke differently, stronger and hungry.

Capek, who had been sitting at the end of his bed, suddenly jumped up.

"Oh, thank God," he said, and started taking Schumann's pulse.

"Why are you doing this? I feel better today than I have for years. I don't know what happened yesterday, but I feel very far from unwell."

Capek looked at Hector. He leaned across towards him and spoke in a softer tone. "Professor, that was three days ago."

Capek explained that after his meeting with the occupants of the attic rooms he had simply gone to sleep for seventy-two hours. They had tried to wake him, but it was impossible. They feared a coma, but he did not show the symptoms of that death-like inertia, he was simply sleeping.

"Professor, are you feeling well enough for a meeting later today? Perhaps to view them again?"

Schumann practically jumped out of the bed.

"Yes, but only after a walk. I need to stretch my legs and lungs in some good fresh air."

Capek cautiously agreed, and Hector washed and dressed and rushed down to the breakfast room, where he ignored all the eyes. He grabbed a few things from the serving table and shovelled them into his satchel, gulped a cup of tepid coffee, and walked out into the crisp air. His feet cracked the stiff frozen grass as he strolled to the end of a long path, where he caught a tram. It carried him into the heart of the city and a little beyond. He stepped off at the highest intersection of the tram's route and the Philosophenweg. His leg felt strong, his arm was working, and he pulsed with a new vigour. He briskly set foot on the famous path and breathed in the dazzling air. The view across the city was magnificent. It gleamed below him like an intricate model, jewelry made in miniature. He had always loved the

Philosopher's Walk: its winding height, its otherworldliness, its lush vegetation, and indeed its history. He had often come here while he worked at the university. Up here he could step out of the everyday and imagine all those who had walked and discussed here before. Eichendorff, Hölderlin, and Goethe had trod this path, and the thought of it made him dizzy. He felt twenty or more years younger today, and he knew why. He had always been a didactic, objective thinker. One had to be if one studied theology outside the church or the synagogue. He was a rationalist who had spent his adult life wrestling with the testaments of divine intervention.

Miracles and manifestations had been his bread and butter. Humanities, enslavement to celestial forces his daily business. Belief had always evaded him. He knew the danger of faith and had seen its consequences writ large in the blood of history. All these were big ideas as he strolled high on this beautiful ledge over the city. The same big ideas he had pondered here before, except that now they had been challenged. Doubt in the form of healing had started to dissolve the rigid braces of opinion that he had insisted should hold all things in their sensible place. It could be argued that his dead arm might have regained some function at any time and that coincidence was responsible for its happening under the eyes of those living mummies in the attic room. But he knew what had happened. He knew it with a certainty that made all his sensible explanations candles to the sun. He knew that in some way those strange creatures had touched inside his brain and corrected the damaged tissue. Blown it awake to smoulder again, from ashes that all had thought were dead.

On the next turn he faced towards Ziegelhausen. He stopped and leant on the wooden balustrade that ran along the outer edge of the walk. He looked across and found the home snuggling between the roads, trees, and patches of leftover snow. From his satchel he took the binoculars and focused them on its distance.

Smoke rose from its chimneys, straight and high in the windless air. The home bobbed with his breathing, so he braced his elbows harder against the cold rail. The space between the lenses filled with that disconnected silence that glows around known objects when seen from afar. He adjusted the eyepiece to bring the space in the cold air into tighter detail. At this time of day, in this season, the home sat in the shadow of the low mountain, so that the sun was partially obscured by it while still rising. Half of the red-tile roof was in bright light, the other in dark shade. The dark shade was white. The melting rays had not yet touched the frost of the night. The shadow profile of the mountain was stealthy, being pushed away by the warming sun. He could actually see the movement and imagined it shaving the roof, ice crystal by ice crystal. He knew they were lying directly under this transaction. Sleeping, drowning, or swimming in their own version of nothing. He knew that soon he would be sitting next to them waiting for their eyes to open, and by the time they did this, every particle of ice on the roof would have been removed and replaced by a particle of sun. He put the glasses back in his bag and walked into the downward curve of the path.

He stood outside Capek's office, his cheeks still glowing from the fresh air and exercise. He could hear a conversation behind the muffling door and tried to listen before finally knocking.

"Come," said Capek, and Schumann timidly entered the office. The man Capek had been talking to was very thin and short. He wore thick metal-framed spectacles and had a pronounced Bavarian accent. He was introduced as Herr Himmelstrup. He clicked his heels when he spitefully shook the professor's hand.

"Herr Himmelstrup is from the newly founded Department of Internal Affairs. I had to tell him about your involvement with our guests."

Hector knew that Capek was far too arrogant to tell this

ministerial pen-pusher that he had been forced to involve Hector. That this aged academic had run rings around him and blackmailed him into submission.

"Yes, as I was saying, I thought that the professor's experience in these matters was invaluable to our purpose. And I have been proved right."

Schumann gave Capek a quizzical glance.

"There has been further development since our last meeting with them."

"Pray tell," said Schumann curtly.

This did not go unnoticed by Himmelstrup, whose small body movements and lack of facial expression were operatic in their reaction to Hector's rudeness. The old man instantly knew that this newcomer despised him and considered him to be both inferior and valueless to their "purpose."

"Late last night one of them spoke," said Capek, and handed a small scrap of paper to him.

Hector unfolded it and read the words. It said: *Wilhelm Block.*

"This is all?"

Capek nodded at the old man's question. "One of the night nurses wrote it down, just that name. Nothing more."

"Does the name mean anything to you?" asked Himmelstrup.

"No, nothing at all."

"There is nobody here called that," Capek feebly butted in.

"No one of your acquaintance? The name sounds Jewish to me."

Schumann glared at Himmelstrup and ferociously ignored his last comment, then parried, "No. Nobody I know. It sounds Schwäbisch to me."

There was a grating silence in the room for a long time. Capek broke it by rubbing his hands together and saying, "Shall we go and see our friends upstairs?"

Hector nodded his agreement but could not resist clicking his heels as he left the room. A chain of impassive but very sharp daggers went after him from the unblinking spectacles of the officer from the Department of Internal Affairs.

The three unspeaking men entered the dormitory and the unique smell of its unique inhabitants, whose eyes were closed. The three visitors drew up chairs to sit and watch the two sleepers. They did this for an hour, during the last quarter of which Himmelstrup kept looking at his watch. Eventually he stood up and made a slight bow before leaving. He did not click his heels. Capek jumped up and followed him to the door. He returned a few minutes later, lifted his chair, and put it next to Schumann's.

He whispered, "He's a difficult man, but we need him. We don't want to lose these." He nodded towards the beds. "Himmelstrup could move them on, maybe even to Berlin."

Hector knew what he meant and gave him an approving look.

"He brought this, I can't make head nor tail of it, tell me what you think." Capek passed him a white battered envelope. "I have other duties downstairs. Are you staying?"

"Yes, for a short while."

Hector was pleased to be rid of the fools. He sat quietly thinking about the bright roof outside, free of frost. He looked at the sleepers and they were as still as statues. There was something reassuring about their presence; the mysteriously calming sensation of enigma. After a few moments he noticed the envelope in his hand and opened it after reading the postmark, which was from Essenwald. The African home of the sleepers.

THE TIMBER GUILD OF ESSENWALD
12TH JUNE 1924

Dear Herr Himmelstrup,

My senior colleague Quentin Talbot suggested that I contact you so that we might keep a dialogue open about

our finds in the Vorrh forest and your analysis of their
significance and meaning. The two latter specimens we
sent you were found during fellings. Since their discovery
I have undertaken an investigation into the myths that
surround the forest. I hope some of this will be informative
to you, but it is difficult for me to gauge that value from
this distance.

In the course of my studies I have come across
a series of stories, almost a legend, concerning the
mummified bodies that were shipped to you in Germany.
I don't know how to say this without sounding like
the primitives that surround me, but I will attempt to
try: There is a deep belief that this land is sacred and
may be the physical geographic location of the biblical
Eden. It is also believed that those later finds were not
the bodies of human beings at all. It is believed that the
angels God placed here to supervise Adam and guard
the tree of knowledge were left here after the expulsion.
Their duties of protecting had failed and God turned
his back on them. It is said that they were forgotten and
isolated. It continues that they deteriorated in the core
of the great forest, where they devolved. Locally these
forgotten ones are called many different names. The
closest translation I can offer is the Before Ones or, more
succinctly, the Erstwhile.

I know this sounds like nonsense, but in these lands
the longer you stay, the more strangeness makes sense. The
mythic and the pragmatic go hand in hand. For example,
the labour force that is essential for the city's commerce
and our continual harvesting of wood to be sent back to the
fatherland relies on a group of people who would be useless
elsewhere, they being so deeply locked in a condition of

automatic slavery to forces that exist in the Vorrh. Our day-to-day usage of these workers is dependent on a control system that has more to do with magic than with management.

I intend to continue with my studies and will keep you informed about anything that concerns these extraordinary finds and other conditions here. I would also appreciate being kept informed about your anatomical findings.

Your humble servant,
ANTON FLEISCHER

Schumann held the paper in his hands. He read it twice more and then just stared at it. He did not know what to think. He folded the paper, sat back, and looked up. They were awake and staring at him. Their eyes focused as his did and again he felt the uncanny itching inside his mind, and this time that was the difference. Before, it had been his brain that had been rubbed alive. Now it was the ghost product of that mechanism. His mind was tingling and the paper fell slowly to the floor.

When he came to, he was back in his bedroom with a nurse watching him.

"Wh-what happened?" he said.

"You fainted, blacked out, up there." Her eyes and eyebrows swivelled and bobbed. She was obviously not one of the special staff but might have heard the rumours.

"They brought you down about twenty minutes ago. White as a sheet, you were." She peered at him. "You still look like you have just seen a ghost."

He did not know if her observation had any meaning or consequence, so he ignored it.

"I will fetch you some sugary tea or maybe a little glühwein." She grinned.

"Just coffee, please," he said, and she nodded and left.

When he awoke again, Capek was sitting in a chair by the side of his bed and was just about to speak. "Yes, I know I passed out again, and you brought me back here. Thank you." And then with a fierce twinkle in his wide-awake eyes Schumann added, "We must stop making a habit of this."

Capek saw the humour and agreed. Hector put on a dressing gown and they walked to Capek's study.

"May I see the letter again?"

"I am afraid not, it went back with Himmelstrup."

"Did they see it?"

"Only when it was in your hands and at no other time."

"And nothing else occurred while I slept?" Hector was stroking his beard and pronounced the word "slept" in a tone of disbelief.

"Nothing, only the parcel."

"Parcel?"

"Yes, a parcel came for them, but it had nothing in it."

Hector stood up. "May I see it?"

"Certainly, if it has not been thrown away."

"Thrown away," said Hector in harsher disbelief.

It was still in their room and Capek brought it out into the corridor and put it in Hector's hands. A cardboard box half the size of a shoe box, wrapped in brown paper. The address read:

The Guests from Africa
Rupert the First Retirement Home
Heidelberg, Germany

It had a London postmark. Hector's eyebrows were trying to escape his head as he turned the empty box over in his hands. A small shred of leaf fell from the lid.

"And it came just like this?"

Capek nodded. "There were a few more leaves but nothing else."

"Nothing?"

"It was completely empty"—Capek paused—"except for the ants."

"Ants."

"They must have been on the leaves. When we opened the box there were lots of dead ants."

"In what room did this occur?"

"Upstairs in their room, one of our attendants took the parcel straight up there from the post room. I only found out about it later."

"Most commendable," said Hector sarcastically. "And where are they now?"

"What?" said Capek.

"The ants, man, the ants."

They crept into the room that smelt of seashells and cinnamon and quietly looked around the floor. There was enough sunlight there without them having to pull the blinds completely open and perhaps wake the occupants. There was no trace, anywhere. Hector summoned his courage and went over to the far bed. The black gnarled thing lay motionless in the crisp white sheets. Hector drew closer and dreaded that the eyes would open any second and again peer into his soul.

Nothing was there. Capek tiptoed to stand behind him. Hector very slowly pulled the top sheet back from the rigid form and there inside the starched shadows ran a line of hectic black ants.

Both men flinched back from the movement as if it had come from the Erstwhile.

They stood, slightly out of breath, back in the corridor.

"But they were dead," said the baffled Capek.

Hector looked at him from beneath his now-static eyebrows.

"Or perhaps only sleeping," he said.

CHAPTER SEVEN

*T*hat vast bog was a bad place. Its desolate heart cared nothing for humans. The black peat wilderness was the Vorrh, or at least a manifestation of it as if it had rotted to nothing.

It should never have been here, some said, it was in the wrong part of the world. It was a freak, an anomaly. The roasting sun sealed its surface most of the year, but the change in the weather and the influence of the distant opened its wounds for a month each year. Nobody ever crossed it. There was no need. Only Sidrus lived out there on its twisted liquorish distance. It had in fact been created to curse Sidrus, who lived in its dank flatness.

There were many rumours about him, most of them malign or fantastic. If anyone dared enter the bog, they gave his make-shift wooden hut on the edge of the cuttings a wide berth. But he was the memory of the place and knew all there was to know about the strange finds that occasionally came to its oozing surface. At one point Sidrus was the guardian of the Vorrh, but he had fallen from grace, punished for killing the Englishman Williams, a man who was to be the first to cross the great forest in its entirety and Sidrus had stopped him. He thought he was doing his duty, but the world and some of its more potent Gods seemed to disagree. But Sidrus did not know exactly where this abominable curse had come from, who or what had marooned him in this dismal exile. It could have been a protection curse scented to the Englishman. Or it could have been a potent malediction from the Vorrh itself. Such a thought was too appalling to think on, so he accepted his plight and would wear it in spite against all those who crossed his path to the end of his days.

Sidrus was a disgrace to the long line of Sidrusians who had evolved their hieratic faith over the centuries. They kept the same name as their innocent founder, who had dragged the singed rabbi and the smoking sacred scrolls of the Sefer haYashar from the great conflagration in Jerusalem. This noble act performed by the famed centurion had started a quest for the true knowledge outside of the guarded tabernacle of authorised thought. In the case of the Sidrusians, it had declined and became sullied with the Tubal-Cain, the testaments of Enoch, and the Lilithian blasphemies. Until it finally settled on the cold stony ground of bigotry and hallucination.

The Sidrusians were famed for dwelling a long way from Samaria. They would cross the street to slit the throat of a fallen man, placing their badge of benediction in the wound and pressing the last breath from the lungs to make a confession and seal the soul to their cruellest vision of God. Their fanaticism was often useful to minor tyrants. The African strain of this incestuous pack had adapted well. Their Roman blood seeking manipulative levels in all fields of administration, military, or solitary power. The strangest thing is that their heightened levels of hallucinogenic perception sometimes actually worked, until now.

While some cut peat from the bog, Sidrus dug for something else: remains of the Erstwhile. He knew some were down there, hidden in the sulking depth. He knew it because he had found one and now kept it locked in with him, in his lopsided fossilized home. The wind whistled outside as he made the last test on the flattened soggy head that sat on a table before him.

"It's human," he said disappointedly.

"Well, almost human. But with a powerful bias that I don't understand," said the Erstwhile.

The wind came down the chimney into the bleached wooden shed and ruffled the flames of the tightly gathered fire, sending a hush of smoke into the room. Something coughed and creaked in the shadows.

"It's all right, Old Bones, I don't think it's an Erstwhile. Just the worn-out head of a mortal that lost its way and its body out there."

The burnt wind that gusted into the irregular room seemed to have gathered itself in the shadows and knotted together to make a voice.

"What will . . . you do . . . with it?" it asked.

"Tomorrow I will seek for the rest of its remains, but I don't hold out much hope of finding them. If that is so, then this is yours. There is not enough here for the scholars."

A fluttering sigh came from the shadows. It turned into a voice again near its end.

"If you give it to me . . . I will read it . . . and tell you more."

Sidrus's face slid into an agitated smear that on a normal face might have been a beaming smile. He had no respect for the Erstwhile. He saw them as failures and cowards. Rejected by God to scratch out an existence cursed by an aimless immortality. But some of them did possess powers and understandings that were far beyond those of humans. He might be able the harness those to show him a way back to the trees, back to health and a sainted pilgrimage of vengeance.

Sidrus peeled back the stringy wet cloth from the stringy wet flesh and put the head on a broad white enamel plate in the centre of his table. He sat back and waited.

The shadows shuffled and changed shape. His old greatcoat slid towards the table and seated itself before the plate. Inside it was the third bog find from the marshes. The one he recognised as something other than human and decided to keep. No one would ever dare enter his home. No one would ever expect that some of these things were not entirely dead.

He called it Char because it was, at the beginning, like a burnt figure. But after two months one of its hands and its jaw had grown new flesh. He also liked calling it Char because he sounded like he was calling a dog and that was the way he treated it. In the beginning it had been only curiosity and he intended to keep it until he became bored. Then it started talking. Telling him wonderful things about what he had only guessed were true before. This was his reward finally for years of service. He was getting the knowledge that was owed to him.

Char sat at the table, the long horny fingers of his dark hand moving on the enamel plate. His nails scratching for touch.

"Go on, take it, tell me what you feel."

The fingers dug into the squishy head. Mud ink ruptured inside it and ran out of its nostril and mouth. The fingers retreated and both hands held and turned it in quick rotations, much in the way of a spider wrapping its prey or a beetle scurrying a ball of dung. The speed of this transaction was markedly different from all his other movements, which were deliberate, sluggish, and vague. Sidrus chortled at the difference.

The flap of the head opened up and the brain moved in its loosened casing. Char aimed his new pink fingers inside and plugged into its tanned leathery case. They were so bright that they gave the impression of illuminating the collapsed interior. His incongruous pink jaw started chattering. At first without sound, like a gourmet enjoying the scent of a meal before tasting it.

"This is young one, half and half," Char croaked.

Sidrus sat back, waiting for the little gems of wisdom to be dictated.

"This one can mend your mind and body."

Sidrus thought he had misheard.

"What," he demanded.

"This one can heal you."

"How?"

Char looked up; his pale eyes had a golden core as if suddenly gilded with an idea.

"You must eat it," he said.

Char had turned the tables and Sidrus suddenly wanted more from him than he had from any man, let alone any thing. The disease that ate his face and other sensitive parts of his body had been purposefully inflicted on him by Nebsuel. He wanted to meet that man again. He had lots of time to think and imagine how he would punish him. And there was another, a youth who had witnessed and aided in his humiliation and attack. A youth with a mangled and sewn face. Nebsuel had called him Ishmael. He would find him too and unpick Nebsuel's handiwork stitch by stitch. But his face and his crippled body prevented him from taking this revenge. Out there he would have no power, no position to barter from. He had done well securing his living and leverage over those who needed the peat. But with a new face and the illness in abeyance all could be possible. He looked into the golden gleam in the black top half of the face and asked a question of the pink lower jaw.

"How do you know this, how can I trust you?"

"Because I can feel it, like I felt all the others and told you the truths of them. Did I not tell you where to look and what to tell? Did I not teach you the difference and the test? Have I not regrown myself from the scraps you brought of me? And you already trust me more than any other living thing."

Sidrus wanted to argue and put this grinning bag of black bones back into its place. But he knew Char was right.

"But why this one?" he said, pointing at the flattened Erstwhile head.

"Because it is very different, unlike all the rest. It has power."

"And I can gain it?"

"Yes. If you eat every scrap, even the hair, bristles, and teeth." Again the gold in the eyes deepened. It was almost as if Char were enjoying himself.

Sidrus stood up and fetched a dark bottle and a horn cup. He started drinking and then flared.

"If you are lying to me I will tear you apart."

"And I would not be able to stop you, master," said the new jaw on the ancient body.

"Shall I cook it a little?" said Sidrus, already fearing the answer.

"No, it would destroy all its properties."

Sidrus finished the bottle.

"May I wash it?" he asked.

There was a very long pause.

"You may, but do not lose any of its fibre or what is left of its fat and brain. Every pennyweight of it is valuable to you."

Sidrus picked up the plate and swayed to the slate sink, where he flooded cold water over it. He continued until the black muddy stream turned clear. Then he picked it up and brought it back to the table.

"You will need tools and a bowl," said Char.

"*What tools?*" bellowed Sidrus, enraged at the creature's pedagogic tone.

"I don't know what they are called. Something to break, something to cut, something to grime."

"Grind," corrected Sidrus.

"Yes, grind, that is right," said Char, "and a bowl to hold it all."

Sidrus went to get the tools, a bowl, and another bottle, he would not be able to devour this repast sober.

Char had to move away from the table, firstly because of the violence that was occurring there and secondly so that he did not get splashed.

Sidrus had started by wrenching the jaw off after cutting through some of the muscles of the face. He dug out the withered eyes and extracted all the teeth with a set of rusty pliers; many broke in the process. He scooped out all that he could from the brain pan and put it together with the other bits of yanked flesh, sinew, and the tongue. Finally he had taken a lump hammer to the skull and smashed it to pieces; that was the easy bit.

He drank and cursed continually, especially when Char pointed at the lost bits that had flown off the table during the wild percussion. Sidrus did not seem to appreciate the care and attention that such directions offered. When it was done, he dragged a large stone mortar to the table and sloped the fragments into its vacant expression. Every tiny morsel was added and he started to work the heavy pestle against its last resistance. He stopped after an hour when the crunching noise gave way to a slushy gurgle. He was sweating and his face looked even worse than before: A filigree of red capillaries writhed beneath the glowing whiteness of his skin, which now seemed to have lost all its internal supports. It was as if his own skull had been broken under the limp bladder of his head.

He emptied the mortar into a bowl and set it on the grisly table. He brought his bottle and spoon and stared into the bowl. He had given up using the horn beaker after the second bottle. He gave Char a spiteful vicious look and madly spooned the splintered gruel into his mouth. Char had one more note of advice before he was forced to flee the table again. All he had said was "If you regurgitate any then you must eat that as well."

He crawled into his bunk, wretched and debased. Full of contamination. Char hid in the shadows and the glee of knowing that it was really only the brains that would heal Sidrus, all else of the head was waste. A waste that he had forced Sidrus to devour.

Sidrus's night was dreamless but full of cantankerous masses and irregular forms. Sullen stomach poltergeists that distanced and declined full images, preferring gloating out-of-focus weights to roll uncontrollably in his long night head.

He awoke convinced he had been duped, until something in a remote corner of his grubby mind tilted. It was not a word or a meaning but an ambiance that had twisted towards healing. He got up and looked in the tiny scrap of broken mirror that he allowed himself.

The same bloated squalor of a wrecked hideous face looked back. But there was a turn in its expectations as if somebody else were wearing it for him.

The next day it increased enough for him to check every part of his rancid body with a hand mirror. There was no change, except his ability to look. He even examined his rotted genitals without shame and sadness. Not much of their exterior form was left, but he had the impression there was more bulk than the last time he dared look. There was a shred of optimism now where only the fear of further decay had hung before.

He made his morning devotions with a new zeal. He sat hunched over his shrine in the corner of the house for a full hour. Afterwards he questioned himself as to whether his new sense of well-being was a delusion or not. Just wishful thinking conjured up from a stomach full of human grit. He still felt nauseous at the thought.

"*Char,*" he shouted, "come here." The overcoated figure shuffled out of the shadows and stood before him as if waiting to be beaten. It had happened before.

"How long will it take before I feel something is happening, before I feel I am getting healed?"

"It has already started, master."

"How do you know?"

"Because you look and sound different."

Sidrus could have hugged the bag of bones but instead just slapped him heavily on the shoulder. "Yes, I do. I do feel better. What will happen next?" He turned to ask Char and seemed surprised and annoyed to see him prostrate on the earthen floor.

"Get up, man, I am talking to you."

Sidrus poured himself a healthy cup of wine; it was early in the day to drink, but this was an exceptional day. Char was up and leaning against the wall.

"Well, answer," barked Sidrus.

"It is different in all men. You have taken a large draft of a different kind of manna. From your present condition I would say that in four days you should see a physical difference."

"Wonderful."

"There is one thing." And here the glimmer of gold light appeared again, hidden at the back of Char's hurt eyes. "To get the maximum effect you must keep the manna in."

"What are you talking about?"

"You must not expel the manna as waste."

Sidrus's mercurial temper changed. "What the fuck are you talking about?"

"You must not pass the manna out."

"What, not shit?"

"Yes, master."

"For how long?"

"For as long as possible. The longer it stays in, the more benefit you shall receive."

There were two very difficult days during which Sidrus raged and groaned and held his extended hard abdomen with great care. Straining his internal muscles closed. He finally went to bed, finding the prone position gave him more control. Meanwhile he had noticed a slight change to his face. Many of the continually open sores had closed. New skin was forming there. It was a miracle. He dared not sleep, lest his treacherous bowels disobey and relax in the night, letting the precious healing manna escape. On the fourth day he harshly whispered to Char, who was sitting close by. He dared not raise his voice in case the reverberations cause a dislodging. A bouncing pebble instigating an avalanche. "I don't know how much longer I can keep it in. What should I do?"

There was a long impatient moment of silence.

"You could use a stopper, master."

Sidrus glared at the meek skeleton in a rage that he must control. "Find me one."

Char poked and rustled about the house for an hour, his slowness seeming more pronounced and amplified than ever. Sidrus spat suggestions and commands until, convinced that he was being ignored, bellowed, "For fuck sake, hurry up, man, I don't know—"

He stopped midsentence because something had moved, a leaking had taken place.

"Quick," he whispered and suddenly Char was there holding out a soiled irregular ball of natural sponge the size of a small fist. The difficult thing about skeletons is that they grin all the time. Even when they have a new fleshy jaw. Sidrus knew that Char would not dare to grin now. But his bony countenance looked like that anyway and it infuriated him even more.

"Give it here and begone."

The command was obeyed. Sidrus wrestled beneath the quaking sheets, trying to insert the quivering springy plug. The sheets flapped and the wood of the bunk creaked and joined in with another sound, so slight that it could have been imaginary, a thin tinny sound from the corner of the room like the shadows laughing.

CHAPTER EIGHT

*I*t took a great deal of resolve for Father Timothy to contemplate seeing Carmella again. The manifestation in the chapel had unhinged his confidence while strengthening his faith, and this paradox had produced a condition of numb lethargy. He had always been a devout and conscientious Christian, who conducted his beliefs with dignity and purpose. He had never doubted the existence of God. But there had never been any real experience of forces other than the mundane acting on his life, and all his faith had been coaxed out of those. Now he had witnessed. Been victim to a vivid and muscular phenomenon that could only be of supernatural origin.

Surely it was greater than many reported in the Scriptures. And addressed entirely unto him.

He had been told to protect a child, a child he had never met. The voices said that it had been buried. Was it dead? They said it was older than he, and he had no idea what this meant. He knew he had to talk to Carmella again and ask her what she knew.

He prayed in his little room for an hour, prayed for resolve, courage, and understanding. Then he opened the door and stepped into the furnace of the day. He knew that she would be home because nobody could work when the sun was high; most slept until the heat began to wear out.

Carmella's house was separate from all the others that

made up the poverty-blasted hamlet in the desiccated fields. He knocked at the frail door, and the animals in the courtyard on the other side became silent. When the old woman opened the door, she had changed. She was smiling; he had never seen this before and was taken aback. She ushered him through the courtyard, guiding his path between the animal droppings and into her modest home.

"She is waiting," she said, and touched his arm and nodded to the room ahead. An overpowering smell of mothballs and age removed the scent of the animals. At the foot of the old lady's ancient bed was a makeshift crib. Carmella went to it and lifted out a long bundle of lace.

"They said you were coming," she said as she folded the cloth back to reveal the child in her arms. He had never seen a pie-bald human before, which he thought explained the unpleasant sensation that was beginning to overcome him. The child twisted in Carmella's arms, straining to push itself erect. It did not have a fluid motion but moved between jerks to positions of stasis, edging towards sitting up to face the nervous priest. It was obviously very strong and much older than he expected. The old woman was treating it like a newborn, but it looked as if it were ready to walk and engage with the world. The hard squirming motion suddenly froze, not in an adjusted softening of posture but more like a machine coming to rest. Or somebody stiffening for a long photographic exposure. It clearly knew he was here and was straining towards him. Then it opened its eyes.

"Modesta, this is Father Timothy," Carmella said with something like joy in her voice. Father Timothy said nothing, he heard nothing, he was nothing. The pale eyes were not the eyes of a child, they were barely human and the expression they radiated did not have a name.

"Would you care to hold her," said Carmella, lifting the alert bundle. His blood was running cold, and when he saw the woman's movement towards him he stepped back. An unconscious part of him had converted the repulsion to animation and he automatically walked backwards out of the room. As he reached the door the child turned, corkscrewing back into the folds of lace, and he was released. Outside in the reassuring stink of the animals his senses returned and he stumbled and slid to the outer door, where he stood dumbfounded until Carmella joined him.

"You will get used to her little ways. She surprised and troubled me at the beginning, but now we understand each other. She is very special."

Timothy looked at her blankly and finally stammered, "Where did you get that thing?"

She ignored his rudeness. What did a celibate boy know of babies and motherhood?

"She was sleeping in the broken house on the ridge. She called me and I brought her back before the storm. She was so tiny then. But she has flourished and grown wondrous strong in my care."

Timothy gawped and spluttered, "How old is it? Who does it belong to?"

"It was days and now it's years and it's ours. But you know that."

"Years?"

"Yes, she is growing so fast, she is so impatient."

"We must find her parents."

"They have gone; we have that job now."

He was about to explain to this mad old crone that all this was impossible and she could not just take a child, if indeed that's what it was, when a sound came from the bedroom. A gurgle that turned into a syllable that stretched into a word: "Father," she said. *Father.*

———

Back in the sanity of his own home Timothy stopped panting and tried to find a prayer that would calm him. But questions strangled all the answers. Why was his God allowing all this to happen? Was he being tested? This could be the most significant thing in his life and he dare not hide from it. It was only fear, he told himself, not instinct that so filled him with dread. It was the child's eyes that affected him so. No baby should have eyes like that. There was not the slightest trace of innocence in them, and when she turned her open stare onto him his soul shrivelled. She looked through him with a level of unchallengeable knowing that no human being should possess. He never wanted that experience again. But he had no choice, he had been told to protect her. Later, when he had stopped trembling, he knew he needed the company of normal human beings and he also needed knowledge of what was really taking place around him. To soothe his anxieties he went to visit some of the people in his village who also worked the land and fished on the beaches near the high ledge. They too had grown up in and around those barren fields. He asked them about the deserted house on the brink of the cliff. The answers he got did little to restore his tranquillity. They all seemed to tell versions of the same story, of a pair of strangers who lived in total isolation. He a white man named Williams from distant lands and she a mysterious black girl named Irrinipeste, rumoured to have come from the Vorrh.

They had avoided contact with everyone, which explained why her partially buried murdered body was not found in the garden for weeks. Some said without any sign of decay or decomposition. No trace of the man was found and it was assumed by many that he had taken her life in a savage and abominable manner. He had certainly taken parts of her body away. Cannibalism had been suggested. There was also a tale about freak weather conditions when she was buried again, rain and winds that must have undone her grave because her remains would not stay covered. Timothy stopped the details there, unable to face the conclusion that was slithering towards him. But they answered him anyway. They said that some of the older men had gone up there to collect what was left and threw it into the sea. His last question was to be the easiest, but its answer was not. Did they have children?

"No."

"No child was ever seen. But one was heard crying in the hollow caves beneath their fallen house months after they had departed."

Timothy did not sleep that night.

The next day he decided to confront this place. He waited until the heat subsided; between eleven and three the parched lands were God's anvil. In the late afternoon he stood within the smudged confines of the overgrown garden of Williams and Irrinipeste's broken home. Below the sea crashed against the resolute cliffs and hollow caves, colliding the scent of ozone and dusty soil mixed with wild thyme and invigorating the warm breeze. This was a place of savage beauty and it made him grip the small silver crucifix tight in his left hand. He had also brought a flask of holy water.

An hour later, he had looked at everything and touched stones and stains, weeds and animal bones. There was no trace of a shallow grave. Every trace of Williams and Irrinipeste was gone. He declared the place neutral. In fact it was calm up there in the cooling open air; its atmosphere seemed benign and even pleasant. Whatever had happened was long since gone. He found it impossible to believe in crime and that abnormal child occurring here. Perhaps he was letting his imagination distort things. Perhaps that mad old woman had contaminated his good sense with her rambling insanity in her stinking home. Perhaps everything had been a delusion, brought on by too much sun and hard work. He decided to walk back through the fields where Carmella had heard the voices. Feeling brave enough to confront the origin of all this fantasy. The sun was low, sending slanting shadows amid the stones and plants. Swallows flew low, darting close to his path, their chirps optimistically catching the rose-coloured light. The day was settling well and quiet. It was becoming difficult to find the dread that he had felt before, something had changed. Everything was gently subsiding into normality.

That night after the service and a light supper he went to bed content, mildly chastising himself for so much fear. So much overreaction about Modesta. His small clean room was calm and he blew out the candle to let the last blue of twilight saturate the walls and the thin white sheet that covered him. Contentment flowed and he made a new prayer to it. He invented a blessing that he might use on other disturbed folk. He thanked God for this peace. It was almost dark when he saw the illuminations in his bed. He had pulled the sheet up to his chin and was looking down along its length. Two small blurs of light appeared under the sheet, inside his bed. Fireflies, glowworms of another species of phosphorescent bug had crept in. Something he had brought in from the fields, he guessed. He was more curious than irritated at their invasion, so very slowly he lifted the sheet enough to push his head beneath it and peered down at the imagined pests. In the dimness the lights moved together, between his legs, up to his knees, and stared directly at him. Modesta's disembodied eyes. Burning out of focus but locked onto his.

The screaming woke his neighbours and some of the people he had been questioning that day.

Timothy was out of his depth. There was no one to turn to. He had said nothing to anybody about what had happened. Then he remembered Father Lutchen. He had met him at the seminary after he arrived on this flyblown continent. The old priest had come to explain the ways of the natives and the customs and legends of the province. He had explained much of the natural and supernatural history and introduced ideas and possibilities that all the novice priests had never heard of. The week spent in his company had been expansive and profound and Timothy had gained a deep respect and admiration for the man. The thing he remembered the most about all the tales and legends was that the priest spoke of them with no sign towards quotation. No sneering distance to their contrast to Christian practice and belief. He simply spoke of them as quiet fact. When some of the more vehement members of the seminary sneered or repudiated his teaching, he ignored them and continued unflinchingly. Timothy knew that Lutchen had retired and lived in Essenwald. He hoped it was enough to send a communication through the frail church postal network that tottered through the jungle pathways once a month.

He never really expected to get answers to the weird array of questions that he had asked. He did not know if Lutchen still lived or was able and capable of understanding his plight. But he was the only one. On a fierce, airless afternoon the reply came.

Dear Timothy,

Yes, indeed I remember you from all those years ago in the seminary. I was impressed by your earnestness and the intelligent curiosity of your questions. And I am touched that you turn to me for understanding of your unusual predicament. Unusual only in a European context I fear.

Such events and phenomena are more than commonplace on this continent. Firstly, let me congratulate you on your steadfast faith and the unshakable rightness you bring to these matters. I hope that this letter will strengthen those qualities and give insight into what you are experiencing.

The visions you have witnessed and the strange life of

this infant girl do seem to be interwoven, but I think it best to separate them here to try and understand their purpose and origin.

The most pressing and anxious being the latter. As you say, there is serious doubt in the divinity of the voices and physical incidents you have witnessed. There are countless cases of demonic utterance masquerading as angelic manifestation. It is a constant deceit of the Devil to trick the innocent by pretending to be the voice of God. You must apply extraordinary vigilance in this matter and trust nothing you are told.

The extraordinary matter of the child growing older with such rapidity might have a medical foundation. Growth rates in all humans and animals are generally a constant, but in some cases there are abnormalities of acceleration that speed up the bodily development. The difference in your case seems to be that she is also maturing abnormally in her intelligence and cognitive understanding. This is very rare, I think. The fact that you have been asked to protect the child and escort her to the Vorrh is the most unusual and specific element in what you have told me. Most forces in and near the Vorrh are about protection and exclusion. Its adverse effect of prolonged exposure is legendary and understood as fact by every tribe within a hundred miles of its daunting vastness. The nomadic peoples who travel these lands and are famed for their expediency of directness give it an extremely wide berth. The source of your disembodied voices is unclear, but their message is not, which means this strange child must have some future purpose or supposed destiny. Which culminates somewhere in the forest.

Thinking on this matter long and hard, I feel it necessary to tell you something of another species of

*creature that lives in the Vorrh. The exact origin and
biology of them is unknown and all the circumstantial
and mythic knowledge claims them to be the deformed
and degenerate remnant of the celestial beings that were
placed on earth to protect the Garden of Eden. These are
not fallen angels but lost ones, physical creatures created
to interact in a physical world. To have communication
and consequence with plants, animals, and ultimately
humans. But Adam's sin unbound them and they failed
in the purpose they were created for. God never punished
or expelled them; they were forgotten and cast aside.
Thousands of years later, what's left of them still roams
the Vorrh without resolution or meaning. In the common
tongue they are called the Erstwhile, and some of them are
finding their way out of the forest's enormous boundaries.*

*I know this because I have seen and felt them and been
forced to be party to putting some of them out of their
misery. I tell you this in the strictest of confidences as a
means to explain the need to avoid their contamination
and not to let any of ours affect them and the sacred
centre of that terrible place. It is known that there is a
disconnection in time in their action and that this is often
experienced in a delay and separation of their visual being.
I have witnessed this personally so know of its truth. This
splitting off of their visibility seems much greater on the
perimeter of the Vorrh or indeed outside of its influence
entirely. It occurs to me that something of the kind may be
happening with their sound, with their voices if they have
any. It has long been known that there is a honeycomb
of passages and subterranean causeways beneath the
depopulated lands; it might be that some of these reach
to the Vorrh and become conduits of escape or at least an
audible exit. That is why I am speculating that your voices*

may have something to do with them. That it is neither the
Lord God nor Satan himself who whispers and shouts your
instructions. That it is something else: the Erstwhile who
speak for nobody. And their lost meaning for some reason
seems to have become focused on the demented child.

I hope my words do not alarm you. But I think
you must agree whatever they are cannot be as bad or
pernicious as the desires of the Devil himself. Take great
care, my son, and keep me informed, especially if you
decide to leave with the child and travel in this direction. If
there is anything else I can do to help, then please ask. You
are in my prayers.

May God's blessing be upon you, and the Lord keep you safe,
REV. GERVASIUS LUTCHEN

CHAPTER NINE

*A*nton Fleischer and Urs Tolgart sat at a circular mahogany table. The two friends had been close since their schooling back in Munich. Both had relatives in Essenwald, relatives who did not fit at home. So in their late teens they began to dream and plan of adventures and wealth in Africa. They also longed for freedom from the stifling morals and opinions of their immediate families. Fleischer had a calculated wisdom that was fed by a blind ambition. Tolgart was cautious and methodic, with the compassionless determination that makes for an excellent scientist. They made a perfect couple to work together, and their friendship was locked tight with fierce loyalty and a powerful mutual attraction. Fleischer had followed up Lutchen's clue about Ishmael, "a friend" of Ghertrude Tulp, and after tailing one of her servants and drinking in the same shabby beer hall, he finally heard the name and the fact that "He is now fucking the other one." The "other one" being Cyrena Lohr.

Anton wanted to act quickly, but Quentin Talbot suggested caution. This had to do with the Lohrs now, who were practically royalty in Essenwald.

Talbot had been crucial in their investigations, handing over all the records the Timber Guild had on Hoffman and Maclish. Fleischer did not want to lose or besmirch Talbot's valuable aid and knew when he brought the Limboia back it would be Talbot who would elevate him and Urs into the higher ranks of the Timber Guild and beyond. On this matter with Cyrena Lohr, Talbot was very clear: Respect and caution. Do not encroach on this family's domain. Keep your questions slight and deferential. There was no leeway in this advice, it was not a suggestion, it was a demand. It was known that Talbot was great friends with the Lohrs and that he was the family's business hand in Africa. Cyrena was the only member of the family living here, though it was her brother back in Berlin who always had the final say. But even Fleischer's canniness did not detect that Talbot had a great admiration that bordered on a secret love for the once blind splendour of Cyrena Lohr.

Fleischer made the appropriate solicitations and Cyrena agreed to see him without any idea of what his business was about. He had kept the nature of his enquiry to a minimal question about minor internal guild affairs.

Cyrena was waiting for him in one of her grand reception rooms. It had been a long time since anybody had consulted her on guild commerce, especially such a junior member. She felt some slight exhilaration at the prospect. The butler Guixpax showed the young gentleman to Cyrena and they exchanged pleasant greetings before seating themselves for business. Guixpax was sent off to fetch wine for them both.

"What may I and my family do to help you in guild matters, Herr Fleischer?"

"Er . . . it's a minor subsidiary matter, Mistress Lohr . . . er, it concerns . . . er, the disappearance of members of our staff."

There was an uneasy silence in the room.

"Really."

"Yes, ma'am. I am—"

He was interrupted by wine arriving and being poured from a silver-necked decanter. Guixpax left and his sharp steps timed the space to the continuation of the question. Fleischer darted quick looks at Cyrena, which received no recognition.

"We are seeking information about the business of Dr. Hoffman before he disappeared. There are notes in his diary that mention your name."

Cyrena put her glass down and it sounded icily in the large room.

"And how exactly do you come to be in possession of Hoffman's diary?"

Fleischer was on his toes and heard the tone in her voice when she said the doctor's name.

"The diary and some other parts of his estate were impounded when he disappeared. The Timber Guild have them in their possession and I am working for them trying to clarify certain matters."

"Very well," she said, and avoided the arrogant smile that flickered on Fleischer's lips.

"We have found an entry in his diary concerning yourself and a search for another in the Vorrh."

Cyrena plummeted inside and compensated by soaring above.

"Ah, you mean the little task that we asked Hoffman to perform?" She was on her feet and seeking her own diary or some other record of the event. "It is all here in my journal, we asked him to find a friend who had gone missing in the forest. Now, where is it . . ." She scurried about the room, looking perplexed and concerned. She turned quickly, her sharp mind racing. "Oh, you don't think the good doctor got lost seeking our friend?"

"No, Mistress Lohr, your business was some time before he vanished."

She stopped suddenly.

"Then why are you asking me about it?" There was a snap in her tone. A splinter of annoyance from above.

"We are checking all his known contacts before he disappeared."

"Checking," she said with the practiced sneer that is relished by the genteel.

Fleischer fell silent and she had him.

"Are you suggesting some connection with my family's business and Hoffman's mysterious disappearance?"

"No, ma'am."

"Very well, Herr Fleischer. I suggest any further enquiry of this nature should be conducted between Quentin Talbot and my brother in the fatherland. I cannot think what you expected of me." The angry and insulted woman left the room, sending Guixpax back to show the defeated intruder to the door.

Fleischer was collecting his hat in the corridor when a disfigured man came in from the garden. They saw each other and knew that an introduction was necessary. Ignoring each other would have caused insult and suspicion. Fleischer assumed that the wounds about the other man's face had come from his engagement in the Great War. A war he had missed by a few fortunate years. He had met others with similar disfigurements when he had been sent back to the fatherland on family business. He had great respect for such veterans.

"Good morning, sir," said Anton, thrusting his hand towards the approaching figure. He had looked before doing this to make sure that the man had all his limbs; he had made that mistake once before. The stranger shook his hand firmly. "I am Anton Fleischer, a member of the Timber Guild."

"Pleased to meet you. Ishmael Williams, a member of the family."

Anton looked at the wounds in the stiff smiling face again. Their introduction was over, there was nothing else to say.

Fleischer left the Lohr mansion in a daze. He walked down its front steps in slow motion. He turned into the next street without knowing he was there. It was only when he stepped into the path of a motor vehicle that screeched its horn at him that he fully awoke. He had just met the only living man who had been in the Vorrh for a sustained time without mental damage. The man who had decided to explore it single-handedly. And apart from facial wounds, which he had received prior to his expedition, he seemed normal and sane. Indeed, a man whom he could work with, if he could ever get past Cyrena Lohr again. He walked on, excited and confused. It had all happened so quickly. One minute a rumour, the next a reality. And yes, there was something else. Something about his name.

It was Urs who told him of a tribe called the Sea People that lived on the fringes of the forest and on the coast of the estuary. They were coastal fishermen with a complex and religious structure and an aptitude for surgio-magical innovation. Their stories told of a stranger being washed ashore on one of their beaches. Of them bringing him back to health and discovering that he had godlike powers. This made the Sea People great in the eyes of others and their enemies. The shipwrecked man had also been called Williams and was so greatly prized that their witch doctors fought one another over who could enhance him the most, adding to and modifying his anatomy. Several years later he fled with a young woman named Irrinipeste. After he disappeared, the Sea People did not worry. They knew one day he would return.

It was obvious this young man, this Ishmael Williams, was clearly not that man and had nothing to do with such barbarities. But that was no matter to Fleischer now. What was important was he had found the man he needed to find and he ran back to the house that he shared with Urs.

"Urs, I have found him!" Anton burst through the door, speaking before even seeing his friend. *"Urs, Urs, the man in the Vorrh!"*

Urs was in the kitchen eating a sandwich and standing by the sink. A kettle boiled on the stove behind him. He made a few surprised and responsive sounds through the bread and cheese. Anton could not wait for a more defined reaction.

"He lives in the Lohr house, he is the one who passed through the forest unharmed. I thought he was only a legend and now I have met him, shaken his hand. He can find the Limboia."

CHAPTER TEN

GERMANY, 1924

A week later Hector Schumann was back in front of them. The ants had been removed. He felt calm, relieved, and disappointed in their presence, because there was no sensation at all.

They watched him but seemed unfocused and drowsy.

Capek came to join them and they barely noticed he was there. Later in his office he said, "They seem more interested in you than anybody else. Did they speak again? Is that why you passed out?"

"No, no, nothing like that."

"Perhaps we better let the doctor give you an examination."

"*No*, that won't be necessary, I am perfectly all right. I had been walking and I had no breakfast or lunch. That's all," he lied.

"If you think best. Only I want you in tip-top health."

Hector groaned discouragingly at Capek.

"I have had another communication from Herr Himmelstrup's office."

Hector looked at him to reveal the restraint of his indifference.

"Have you ever wished to travel to England?" he quietly asked.

"England?"

"Yes. London, to be precise."

A chime of bells pealed in a distant tower. London had been a dream for Hector that had never been achieved. Packed away in a far corner, covered with a dust sheet and forgotten. He knew it was irrational, but we all have them, irrational places that call to us and demand we visit. Even if it's only in continual fantasy. English had been his second subject and he had read every line of Henry Mayhew, every sentence of Dickens. He had dreamt in English, he had glided on the golden Thames. He had floated through the courtyards and palaces, the hovels and the markets. He had heard the bard in the city's great theatres. He had been so many times in his imagination that the map there had become tattered and almost worn out. In reality a life in the wrong subject, feeble finances, a wife who detested the notion of travel, and a world war had blocked his journey across that dribble of sea that severed him from his dream. And now?

"What are you talking about?" he asked Capek, trying to hold back the hope that was leaping like a puppy about his waking expectations and snapping at his elapsed dreams.

"One of Himmelstrup's people in England has found word of another of them, somewhere in London."

Hector wet his lips.

"His superior wants someone who knows about ours to go and see it. Someone who speaks English and can be trusted. Someone who can make an adequate report. Himmelstrup has volunteered you." Capek looked gloomily at his shoes and did not see the old man before him bubble inside with joy and suppress an escaped giggle that could have easily turned into a roar.

Hector tried not to let his excitement keep him awake, but it was difficult. All the images that he thought he had forgotten came flooding back. And he tossed and turned that night anticipating their reality. By three a.m. he was getting cross with himself. "You old fool, you are behaving like a nine-year-old, get a grip, calm down, it still may not happen. It never did before." He was using disappointment as a conjurer of sleep and strangely it began to work.

He was in a boat. Standing on the high deck looking at the approaching shore. His bad arm had grotesquely extended, so that it hung over the side. His fingers trailing in the fast water three decks below. It was a blissful sensation. The rapid and heavy knocking capsized him from the boat, and he rose up in bed, slightly disoriented. He rubbed his eyes and beard and stumbled towards the door, dragging his dressing gown behind him.

"All right, all right, I am coming."

He opened the door to find Capek shifting his weight from foot to foot.

"Quick, one of them has gone. We must find him. You must help."

"What, who, who has gone?"

"One of them has gone."

"Who?"

"*Hinz und Kunz.* Upstairs." He pointed and shuffled off.

For a moment Hector was even more confused hearing them called by such a derisive term.

The professor knew that *Hinz und Kunz* was a term used for the common man, or rather a pair of them, that dated back to the eleventh century and was still in street parlance. He thought about asking why these two very uncommon specimens were labelled so; instead he just said, "You mean the Erstwhile?," using and savouring the name for the first time.

"The who?" said Capek, sounding irritated.

"The man in your letter said they were called the Erstwhile in Africa."

Capek had no idea what he was talking about and stared at

him with twitching eyeballs. After a moment he gave up trying to think and barked, "Get dressed, man, we have got to find him. Meet me upstairs."

Some part of Schumann was already rehearsing this incident as the coup de grâce to his London quest. Another part relished the drama and he dressed quickly. He was Sherlock Holmes and the game was afoot. On the upper floor Capek played more than an adequate Dr. Watson. Pacing up and down in front of the two beds. Jabbering and anxious. He did not even notice that the remaining Hinz was following his repetitions back and forth, like a spectator watching a tennis match. This gave the procedure an eerie comic atmosphere. The empty bed was peeled back and shouting escape.

"We have searched every inch of this floor. He must have gone below."

Schumann nodded.

"He must not be seen, he is to be concealed at all times. If we lose him the consequences will be severe."

He guessed that this reaction came from the superintendent's fear of Himmelstrup and his newly appointed office. These were strange and rumbling times. The mass gatherings of thought were uneasy and simplistic and they made Schumann apprehensive. He had noticed the discreet badge that Himmelstrup had worn on his lapel; he had been seeing it more and more recently and knew that it represented a new political devotion. And if Himmelstrup was an example, then his future in this country was looking bleak.

"Where could he have gone," fretted Capek.

"Have you asked Hinz?" said Schumann. "He has spoken before."

Capek looked at him as if he were insane. A fury growing under his panic.

Hector walked quietly to Hinz and softly spoke to him, hoping that this use of a colloquial name would not make things worse.

"Where do you think your friend might have gone?" he asked delicately.

The black figure moved slightly in the bed and then with great deliberation took the top sheet, which was tucked in around his waist, and pulled it up over its head, while sliding down flat to hide beneath it.

Capek watched, shook his head, and started to divide the group of the people in the know. Sending them to different floors. "Hector, leave him and go with Munks and search the ground floor."

"No," said Schumann, "I will search the grounds." He had understood what he had been told and now he wanted to act on it.

"Very well, Munks, go with him and search the grounds."

Outside it was getting colder and their breath curled white clouds in the icy air. The lights from the home picked up the plumes and dramatised them in the darkening garden.

Hector pointed to the front of the house and Munks started to search there. Looking behind trees and up in their branches.

"He won't be there," shouted Hector, sending a wave of vapour towards the baffled male nurse. "He will be close to the ground, look for footprints in the frost."

Now he really felt like Holmes, saying these things and giving commands straight out of the stories. He circled the garden towards the back of the house. He had gone only a few metres when he saw the tracks leading from the back door into the tiny orchard of apple trees. He followed them into the darkest corner of the garden, near a pile of raked leaves.

He kicked them aside and found where the earth had been clawed and dragged.

"Munks," he called. "Munks, he is here."

Munks came running and almost tripped over the garden fork. He swore and picked it up.

"There." Schumann pointed.

"Yes, Professor," said the panting nurse, and dug the fork into the ground.

"No, not with that, you will kill him."

Schumann pushed Munks back and started digging with his hands. He felt Kunz move under his labours, felt him try to burrow deeper.

"Help me, man," he shouted.

The two of them were on their knees, scraping and clawing the damp freezing earth aside. They grabbed at the pyjamas and started to pull the frail figure out of his shallow grave. He flapped and shrugged like a petulant child trying to escape from the will of overzealous parents. Once free from the soil, he gave up struggling and hung limp in their restraining grasp. Hector quickly looked for wounds. There were none, so he brushed him down and picked the leaves and sticks off his pyjamas. They assisted him towards the back door of the home. Hector leaned him against the wall and ordered the nurse to go ahead and make sure the way was clear.

When given the signal, he pushed him through the door and darted for the lift. Munks had wrapped one of the waterproof coats that hung behind the door over his head, just in case they bumped into a curious wandering inmate.

On the upper floor they met the other searchers, who stopped in their tracks at such a sight. The diminutive grinning Jewish professor, in his dressing gown and wet carpet slippers, propping up the tall gloomy black scarecrow in saggy dirt-stained pyjamas. Wet leaves sticking out from his ears and nose and the other places that Hector could not reach.

Hinz slowly shuffled himself to the edge of his bed and bent upwards; he stood taller than anyone present had imagined. He crossed the room like a marionette in molasses. His arms were extended before him, resembling a sleepwalker. He stopped before the ill-matched pair and lowered his arms to grab one of Schumann's trembling hands. Nobody else moved; the room froze. He bent his neck to stare down at the mesmerized Schumann. Gradually raising the trapped hand and placing it over his crusty heart. Kunz was ignored and just stood limp, lost, and dejected. Hinz started to speak, his strangled exhalation of air racked into an emaciated voice. It was directed solely at Hector.

"Lamb's breath," he said.

Capek was beaming.

"Himmelstrup is very pleased with you, or rather pleased with us for controlling a potential disaster. The London venture has been approved and you may leave next week. His office will book your passage. Because of your age and health I have persuaded them to send you first-class."

Hector bowed slightly in thanks and began to preen his beard.

"I will of course carry out my duties with diligence and care so that they repay every pfennig invested in me and this venture."

He was almost believable. He cared nothing for the wretched Himmelstrup and his bureaucratic hierarchies. He intended to spend as much of their money as he could. His days were numbered and he would wring every moment of pleasure and delight out of this unexpected windfall. He did, however, have a genuine interest in his task and intended to bring this mystery to a satisfactory conclusion.

The week passed quickly. He visited the Erstwhile twice more before he departed. No more words were exchanged, but he did experience a haunting sense of bonding with Hinz. He thought that sometimes he detected a faint smile on the burnt lips of the old statue but shrugged it off as wishful thinking.

The most extraordinary feature of his last visit was physiological. One of the upper-floor doctors drew his attention to the skin of Hinz's neck. At first he thought that its colour change was just an effect of light. But on closer examination it was revealed to be a completely new outcrop of healthy skin. Its pinkness looked like a garish collar or a plinth between the darkness and age of the body and the head. The doctor told him that there was also a small patch of regenerated skin on Kunz's back and that it was progressing. He joked that they might have grown two new humans by his return. The idea of this gave him goose bumps as he left the ward. Halfway to the lift he had a recollection, an intense déjà vu. He turned back to the glass double doors as the doctor turned the key in the recently fitted lock. Schumann raised his hand as if to stop the action. But the doctor did not see it. He completed his task and walked away. The moment faded and Hector lowered his hand. After a pause of trying to taste the invisible, he returned to the lift and the beginning of a journey that he had longed for all of his adult life.

Schumann savoured every moment of his journey to London, especially in first class. It was his second day in his adequate hotel on the Strand, and he waited in its Waterloo Bar, ready to take instructions from Himmelstrup's agent in London, Mr. Compton. The one who had sent the original news about another finding being kept somewhere here. It was 12:47 and Hector decided to finish his Gibson before the lackey arrived and cast a disapproving eye on his prelunch cocktail. He was just biting into the tiny gin-saturated onion when a raincoated oaf entered the bar. There could be no doubt it was he. Hector stood up and walked towards the man, who was shaking himself like a wet dog. An hour later he left; Hector had all the information he needed, a new chequebook, and unlimited time to investigate and report. All of this carried great portent, but was insignificant compared to the pressing and immediate business of his delayed lunch. His time had been planned with great care and there was just enough allocated for an unhurried meal and a snooze before the opera and a light, late dinner. Tomorrow his investigations began in earnest. And he was more than ready to meet the British Erstwhile, patient 126 as he was called, and his keepers across the river in St. George's Fields.

He wanted to squeeze every bit of pleasure out of this exhausting trip. So before his adventure and the meeting of patient 126 he indulged in the privacy of his hotel room. Spending an hour floating in the large white bath and even longer grooming himself, getting ready for the day and the people he would impress. This was luxury after the hard-timed regimen of the home. He meticulously combed, arranged, and recombed his hair into a latticework that covered almost all of his pink bald head. He dressed in his favourite suit with a taut new shirt to complete the effect. Before leaving his hotel he had breakfast delivered to his bedroom. He could not stand the enforced politeness of the communal breakfast room. The grating china smiles, the buttery stiffness of eating in public. The dining room in the home was bad enough, but a brittle British breakfast was beyond endurance. He sat by his window overlooking the Strand and enjoyed the rightness of the moment. He had brought the slim red leather-bound book with him for exactly this time. He sat at the cramped table with his coffee, eggs, bread, marmalade, and Wordsworth. The English, he thought, were masters of words. Some almost equal to Schiller. He pitied their talentless music and their crude and overblown art. Ah! But the words. It was Wordsworth's epic miniature that had so stirred him as a young man. His invocation of London from Westminster Bridge. The modernism of its simple, almost stark lines thrilled him. The grandeur of the vision they held was fresh, gleaming, and believable. When he first read it, it transported him to that majestic place. To the gleaming mythical city. And now under the weirdest of circumstances, after a hideous war with this country and in the last years of his being, he was actually here. He wanted to use the poem as a key to his understanding of this city. He read it again from the same prized book of his youth. And the thrill still seized him. He wanted to read it on the bridge but knew that to be the act of a buffoon. So he memorised it again to speak under his breath while standing over the fast-churning water of the immortal Thames.

It was raining and a heavy darkness saturated the air. He hailed a taxi from the steps of his hotel and quickly darted into its acrid interior, which stank of tobacco and disinfectant.

"Where to, guv?" said the cabbie.

"I would like to go to the south side of Westminster Bridge, please."

The driver wrinkled at his accent and grunted consent.

"Surry side," he said and pulled out into the stream of traffic.

"Pardon me?" said Hector.

"Why what avya done?"

"Excuse me, done?"

There was no answer, just a cough of cigarette smoke from the grinning driver. Hector sat back to enjoy the ride and the view. He had the excitement of a child as he stared out the steamy window into the traffic and statues of Trafalgar Square.

"Where you from?"

Hector leant forward to try to understand what the driver was saying. It seemed to be English, but unlike any he had ever heard before. He understood "from" and knew it to be an uncomfortable question.

"I am sorry but I find it difficult to understand what you are saying."

"Pure London, mate, pure cockney, where you from?"

"I have never heard cockney before."

"Never lived." The driver coughed. "But where you from?"

"Switzerland," lied Hector as they rattled past the bone-white stone cenotaph that dominated the centre of Whitehall.

The bridge and indeed all of London was very unbathed in the bright, glittering, and smokeless air of the poem. A driving wind came off the Thames in random gusts. Its energy prevented the fog that skulked in the clouds and the stone from consuming all. Undaunted, he held the radiant words in his mind and let them illuminate the view before him. He found a suitable view and ignored the dashing pedestrians and the noise of the traffic that thundered across the bridge. He closed his eyes and let the words unfold. It had been 122 years since they had been written and hardly anything was the same as that day on the third of September 1802. The enormous power of the industrial revolution had flung up buildings to denote importance and grandeur. The new palace of Westminster totally blocked and commanded the view to the left of the bridge. To the right was a mass of grandiose offices flanked by warehouses. The view across the steeples of London had been truncated and obscured. Still, the words told the real story, and the rain, pomp, and confusion would never dim their clarity. His oblation of presence had been achieved. He turned into the reality of the wind and made his way along the embankment path towards the depths of Lambeth. The sun in sympathy barged the swollen rain clouds aside and lightened and dried his way ahead.

Lambeth was almost entirely grey. The potent charm of London must have run out somewhere near its centre, because it had never touched here. He had walked along the embankment from Westminster Bridge. His leg was strong and he had felt vigour about his quest for the first time that morning.

The Surry side was dominated by St. Thomas' Hospital and Lambeth Palace. They provided a barrier and a screen; behind them the seething mass of Victorian slums had been built over, but their presence still jammed both the broad and the narrow streets of one of London's poorest boroughs. It had been six years since the end of the Great War, and England still shivered from its consequences. Its expenditure had absorbed the wealth and the confidence of the industrial empire. It was now shrivelled and hollowed of its male youth. There were more ghosts than people huddled in this dingy realm. The same was true of Germany, of course, but it was not worn the same way. Berlin in defeat still leant on the surrounding majesty of the rest of Europe. On this stony island the distant and meaningless war had isolated them from everything and perhaps even themselves. Their youth and future lay strewn and wasted on another continent. These were Schumann's thoughts as he turned off the palace road and headed into the brick mass seeking the fourth great building of the day. The vast white hospital that lay in St. George's Fields. The one that Londoners still called Bedlam.

CHAPTER ELEVEN

*G*hertrude and her child slept without dream or movement for many hours. While Luluwa and Seth recharged, Aklia kept watch. Her glands and receptacles swelled and squeezed. Her slender float tanks tilted to understand. The cream that flowed through her delineated body was overworking in its bubbling knowledge. A certain auricle sipped, nurtured, and pipetted the tastes and tinctures of such extreme abnormalities. She was puzzled and attracted by the birth. Even more by the aftereffects. She watched every twitch and adjustment, which shelved an infinity of questions. She wanted to understand more physically. She came very close to the sleeping mother and child. She gently touched them, feeling their pliant warm softness. Human beings were composed of different levels of firmness. Their entire bodies were held in different levels of suspension. There was none of the uniform hardness of the bodies of the Kin. She knew all this but wanted to feel it again. She touched the newborn and was astonished at its lack of tension. It was so soft that she thought that she could push her hard relentless finger through it without ever encountering any kind of internal structure. Her beautiful tender dagger of a finger stroked and teased, leaving little dimples of flesh that puffed back into perfect curves. She brought her hand up to touch the space between the child's dreaming automatically pouting lips and the mother's weight of breast. She touched the engorged nipple and instantly milk pulsed onto her Bakelite finger. She was shocked at the speed of response. She withdrew her hand and examined the globs of pearly extraction. They looked so like the essence of mind and life that flowed through her. The core of all the Kin: the cream of existence.

She now looked at the thinner, less substantial fluid on her finger. She knew it must be different. But this was not her area of expertise. She brought the white droplet inside her mouth, but the extract had found a way inside. Sulphur, salt, and bitterness. Is this what human infants fed on? She rushed from the bed to the sink and flooded her hard mouth with water. This was an unnatural act, but one she was told she might have to do, living in such close proximity to humans. It worked in flushing the acrid stuff away from her taste cleft, but there was a blister on her lips, like somebody had taken a hot poker to her face and reamed the resilient hardness of the perfect plastic. She touched and felt its inward lesion. She did not want the rest of them to know that she had been so stupid. It was her job to protect and care for the mother and child, not to probe and question them. She took a small nail file from the human's bathroom bag and re-curved her misshapen lip.

The days slid by, each folding the last into the next. A milky haze of warmth and reassurance. Life rewritten by life. The love of and for the child was beyond Ghertrude's wildest expectations. Her purpose in the world had been established and all else was fading into insignificant trivia. The Kin had brought her food and drink, all prepared in the same room where she slept and attended her child, whose waking eyes never left hers.

One morning Luluwa said, "We think it is time you moved upstairs and occupied one of the bedrooms. It is time you told the world of the great event."

Ghertrude's first reaction was a shrugging inward retreat. A gripping onto this territory of miracle. Wanting to stay and let nothing change forever. But after a while she reluctantly saw the sense of what they were saying.

"We will take you up there and settle you in. We will attend and visit at night and when nobody else is there. We will stay close. At your beck and call."

"But we will be alone up there," said Ghertrude in a flush of childhood anxiety, one that the child sensed, digging in deeper to its mother's body.

"You must get a human maid for the days."

"But where?"

"You must ask your friend to help. Shall we send for her?"

"Yes, Cyrena, yes, please."

And so it was done, everything was ferried up to a suite on the second floor. The Kin sprinted up and down carrying everything at a vast speed. Their nimble footfall barely touching the stairs in their gazelle-like athleticism. The bedroom was made perfect and the family installed. There were even flowers in a glass vase. One of them must have crept into the garden in the dead of night to pick them from their sleep.

>——→

A letter arrived for Cyrena the same evening.

My dearest friend, please come. I have a beautiful daughter. We are both very well and I long for you to meet her and be close by me again.

Please come now and come alone, this is a time for women.

Your loving friend,
GHERTRUDE

Cyrena stood for a moment with the letter in her hand. She still struggled with certain letters. She had learned to read and write in the way of sighted people, but secretly missed the dictation and the careful readings of previous correspondence by her secretary and maids. The intimate silence of the folded paper held no joy for her. She read it again, this time mouthing every word. Then she dropped it to the floor and rushed to collect her hat, coat, and gloves while wildly ringing for the chauffeur. She ran up into the library where Ishmael was reading. "I am going to see Ghertrude. I will be back later."

"Very well," he answered with amusement at her flurry.

Ishmael remained in the library, which was becoming his den. He could continue his education there. He was surprised how many volumes dealt with the origin and taxonomy of fable species and mythical beings. It would be ironic if the key to his existence was hidden here somewhere in the tens of thousands of pages. The library was also an excellent place for hiding things, because nobody else ever really used it and the servants were too lazy to clean above their reach in the shelves.

While the car was being made ready Cyrena found Guixpax and asked him to quickly select and cut her some flowers from the garden. "The very best," she said.

He wandered off towards the back door, secateurs in hand, softly tutting under his breath.

Guixpax seemed abnormally slow this evening. She waited in the hall, walking up and down and fidgeting with her silk gloves.

Finally the flowers and her gleaming lilac Phaeton limousine arrived and she sped across the city.

The front door of Ghertrude's house had a new lock. One that operated remotely from the inside. Cyrena had over-rung the bell, imagining the sullen Mutter far off in the house and his reaction being even slower than her sluggish retainers. When the latch clicked and the door swung inwards a few inches, she jumped in amazement. This ghostly use of mechanics was beyond her expectation. She gingerly entered and pushed the door closed behind her. "Ghertrude," she called out.

"Yes, Cyrena, up here, come up."

Cyrena forgot the creepy door and ascended the stairs two at a time, dropping one of her gloves in the process. They met on the upper landing and hugged with great force. They then stood back holding hands to look at each other. Ghertrude was radiant. Tired and softer at the edges, but radiant at her now-gentle core.

"Come and meet her," she said. And they walked hand in hand into the nursery, which now adjoined her new bedroom and parlour.

Ghertrude lifted her daughter from the cot. The child sleepily turned in her arms. Cyrena was surprised and weirdly hurt by two contrasting perceptions colliding. Seeing her friend holding her baby was the oddest of pictures and yet it was breathtakingly natural. Cyrena simultaneously felt a great love for them both and a bitter disappointment in her own loneliness. Ghertrude did not see any of this, for she was far too busy with the dynamic little life that needed her so violently.

"Would you like to hold her," she said without ever once taking her eyes off the waking bundle. Then without waiting for an answer from her stunned friend she stepped across the space between them and placed the child against Cyrena's breast. Her arms were there automatically, holding the small weight of stretching existence. The heat from the bundle penetrated her and the determination of the flexing, pumping movements made her fearful. Fearful at the containment of such force and fearful of the gigantic, implacable demand it made to be nurtured. Cyrena's eyes fluttered to her friend's in a moment of panic.

"It's all right, sit down with her," Ghertrude said gently.

The child was now fully awake. Cyrena sat in the armchair next to the cot and tried nervously to smile at the bundle. The child looked into her face and saw another. The blobs of out-of-focus features were wrong. The scent very different and there was no softness in the touch or the gravity of this body that held her. The child stared harder and Cyrena stared back, searching the tiny squashed face for traces of Ishmael's likeness and bearing. The mother felt the cry before it was launched and moved imperceptibly towards it.

Cyrena, who had never held a child before, did not see it coming until the face screwed up, opened, and bellowed at her. She nearly dropped it but Ghertrude was there. The weight already transferred to her arms. The sound subsiding.

"She just wants her mother," she said.

Cyrena felt relieved and lost. Her arms still frozen in the hollow brace of holding.

"Just a moment, please excuse me. We may still talk but I must attend to her needs."

Ghertrude moved behind a small Chinese screen and seated herself to suckle the child.

For a moment just nuzzling and sucking sounds came from behind the screen. The imp of the perverse awoke and Cyrena's mind leapt to early in the day, when Ishmael had been sucking and fondling her breast. She had remembered then the first time he had done it. During the carnival, with his whiskery long mask and his unquenchable appetite. Probably the same night that Ghertrude was fertilized by him or another masked reveler.

This morning he was harder and nipped rather than sucked at her longing. She had used the other memory to soften and excite the difference.

"How have you both been?" asked Ghertrude, her voice curiously distant behind the stretched silk. For a moment Cyrena thought it was a direct question about her erotic comparisons; then she understood its polite indifference.

"Oh, well, very well," she answered vacantly while removing her remembered nipple from his twice-remembered mouth.

"How is Ishmael?"

"He seems happy and content, he reads much and has just started showing an interest in the garden." She did not really want to talk or think about him, in such close proximity to the child. She knew this was emotive fear botching her sharp mind. How could a baby understand anything? But it was a strong instinct and felt like it was based on protecting. Of whom and against whom was a more worrying and unresolved question. So she changed direction and snatched the reins of the conversation.

"Have you been contacted by Anton Fleischer from the guild?"

"No," said Ghertrude in a disinterested manner.

"He came to see me. He is asking about Hoffman."

There was no change of sound to announce it, but Cyrena knew her friend had just stiffened into attention behind the screen.

"I sent him away."

The quiet had turned to silence.

"He is trying to find the Limboia, to get the city back on its feet."

There was a slight rustling and a tiny murmur from the child.

"He only came to see me because I was in his diary or journal or something. I think the matter is over with now."

Ghertrude came slowly from behind the screen, the infant held very tightly against her. She was sickly pale and had lost the blush that had so marked her at the beginning of their meeting.

"Do you think my name was in that book? Will he come and question me?"

Cyrena saw the anguish that had ruined her friend's joy and she felt a stabbing guilt at her motivations in bringing it up at all.

"He did not mention you, my dear. I only asked in case he had made separate enquiries. I am sure if it was, then you would have heard from him by now."

"But the business with that horrid thing." Their eyes met and for a moment Loverboy—the dwarfish, yellow-skinned member of the anthropophagi, who ate human flesh, that had been mistaken for Ishmael and captured by Hoffman and Maclish—was in the room with them again. Ghertrude hugged the child even closer.

"Hoffman was a snob. I think he was only attached by name to that little transaction," Cyrena said bitterly but with hope for her friend's humour. "May we have tea?" Cyrena suddenly chirped.

"Eh, well, yes . . . I can make it."

Cyrena looked confused.

"I am without servants at the moment. Mutter is sick and I need to employ a maid."

"Oh my dear, how can you possibly cope alone?"

"You know I am not alone."

"Oh, them?" she said. "I was talking about human company, not machines."

Ghertrude nodded while avoiding Cyrena's eyes.

After the relapse they both agreed that she needed a companion, a human maid to live above the other goings-on of the house. Someone she could trust and who could help her look after herself and the child.

"The problem is that you need somebody who won't probe, who won't ask questions. There are too many things for a stranger to become interested in about this house and our history with it."

Ghertrude agreed and bit her lip.

Suddenly her friend surprisingly smiled.

"Didn't you once tell me that Mutter had a daughter?"

The busy women wrote the message together, making sure that Mutter and his family could not say no. They praised his reliability, his loyalty, and above all his discretion. She wanted to flatter him and overemphasise her need of his help. Cyrena said that she could not possibly overstate that need. Ghertrude thought that the biggest problem might be his eldest son. It was always the eldest son who was expected to succeed his father. Asking his sister to join their household might put noses out of joint. So they left things unsaid and just hinted at their business together; all else could be manipulated when they spoke. They hoped to visit them the next day and would bring the child with them; after all, it was because of the child that they wanted to see them.

They were very pleased with the letter and sent it by Cyrena's driver, who was given instructions to wait for an answer.

He parked outside the address that was written on the letter. It was not a part of town that he frequently visited and he had no intention of leaving the automobile unattended in such an area. He also had no intention of entering the modest house. He would rather wait in his elegant limousine than enter the squalor of such a home. He knocked at the door and waited. A tall youth answered. He told him he would wait for an answer and handed over the envelope. The youth had deformed and repellent hands, which he assumed were the product of some ghastly, inbred mutation. He stepped away from the transaction briskly, wiping his hand savagely on his dark blue livery when the door had closed.

➤──→

Thaddeus took the letter inside.

"Mother," he called, and sat down at the table, staring at the envelope that he held taut between his long fingers. The family gathered around.

"It's from Mistress Tulp," he said. "I think we should call Father down."

Meta, the adolescent daughter, was dispatched upstairs to shoehorn Mutter out of his sickbed and bring him to the table. She had a way with her father that nobody really understood. In the slenderness of her twelve years, she had compacted the understanding and quiet certitude of most people twice her age. She also sometimes caught things before they were thrown. The family gathered at the table again and waited for the master of the house, whose wheezing was already slinking down the creaking wooden stairs. He sat wearing a thick plaid dressing gown over his flannel nightshirt, over his dense woollen under-wear. He was hot, he said, so a mug of water was placed next to him. Mutter snuffled and looked disapprovingly at the un-distilled liquid. He then pointed at the stone jar that held his mealtime beer. Thaddeus cleared his throat and tore open the envelope. He read it carefully in an even, regular voice.

Dear Sigmund,

I do hope that you are feeling much better. I would not have disturbed your convalescence, but this is a matter of some urgency. I have been feeling so lonely recently with just the baby and me rattling about in this old house without you. So I have decided to come and talk to you about all of our futures together. You have been of invaluable service to Kühler Brunnen, and of course to me personally. With another generation to think of, we must do the right thing. I have always greatly trusted your loyalty, honesty, and above all your discretion. Especially in certain matters that will be nameless here.

So may we call tomorrow morning and make our plans together? I will bring the little one with me so that you can see how well she is growing.

Your most appreciative mistress,

G

Bernd, the youngest of the Mutter brood, giggled. Meta said, "Oh." Mutter wheezed and slid his watery eyes towards his wife. A pink turning to purple flush was creeping up her throat into her jowls. Her eyes were burning like black coals. If it were possible for steam to hiss out of human ears, then it would have been hers. The children looked at their shoes and Mutter said, "My dear, I think Mistress Tulp wants to say—"

Frau Mutter exploded in tears and mucus, more than Mutter had bubbling in his cigar-saturated lungs.

"You horrible swine. You vile seducer. You filthy liar, you are my husband. I have had all these . . ." And here she flapped her hands around at her children, sending tears and snot to the sanctified heads and faces of her blessed brood. "I knew that carnival mite was yours, I knew all along and you lied to me." She sobbed into her apron, which she lifted to her wallowing eyes.

"Mother, you are wrong," pleaded Meta.

When their house was generously given to them at the same time as Ghertrude's pregnancy was announced, Frau Mutter had fallen into the panicked belief that the young mistress's mite who was conceived during carnival may be the progeny of her aging husband. A belief without foundation, but one that brought a great joy to Mutter's heart and groin, and momentary misery to his enduring wife. Nothing more had been said about the matter after Mutter had convinced her that the idea was absurd, even though his pride did allow him a small secret rude glow of fantasised possibility. It had all been forgotten, and now this.

They were now both screaming at each other. Bernd was bawling too. Meta was trying to lift him out of the war zone when the tablecloth became caught in the buckle of his flailing sandal. Everything slid towards the edge. Mutter's flagon of beer was upturned and spilt into Thaddeus's lap, sending him out of his seat like a jack-in-the-box to bang his head on the crossbeam. Mutter bellowed at the outrage, creating even louder shrieks from his furious wife. The cat, who had been sleeping nearby, bolted for its flap in the main door and exited the house like a bullet. Outside, the chauffeur was sitting in the lilac Hudson Phaeton making calculations in his tiny dignified notebook with a tiny silver pencil. The uproar from the house blundered against the highly polished exterior and gleaming windows of the car with great surprise. He stopped writing and lifted his eyes towards the bellowing door. Exactly what one would expect, he thought, and then continued with his computation.

Thaddeus was now trying to calm his raging parents.

"I am sure it's all a big mistake. Mistress Ghertrude is a kind lady," he said.

"Too kind," sobbed his mother.

The spilt beer had made its way into the soggy rear of the bread, and the sugar cubes were crunching on the floor under the shuffling and stamping feet.

"She has always been good to us," his father said and coughed.

"Too good to you, you filthy swine!" his mother squawked.

"Stop it, stop it," squealed Meta, holding Bernd in her red arms, his thumb corking suddenly his heaving wet face.

"That is enough. Enough!" shouted Thaddeus. "Enough of this. Miss Lohr's servant is outside waiting, he will hear every word of this. Think of the shame."

The noise slumped instantly.

"We must all be quiet now and calm down."

Everybody was sternly looking in different directions.

"Of course we must invite the ladies to visit us and not let them hear a word of this."

Thaddeus moved towards the door.

"I will tell him that the ladies will be welcome here anytime. I will tell him that we will all be here tomorrow at ten."

Nobody spoke; they just slowly trundled back to their grumpy seats while Thaddeus went outside.

He nervously stepped up to the gleaming car and knocked on the window. The chauffeur, who had been lost in a reverie about great wealth, flinched at the congenitally maimed hands pawing at his window. He wound down three inches of the protective glass and said, "Yes." It sounded like the steam that should have hissed from Frau Mutter's ears.

"Please tell the good ladies that they are welcome in our home at any time and that we will be expecting them tomorrow at ten o'clock. Thank you, sir."

The glass wound up and the ignition started. The long lilac car heaved and rocked out of the lumpy potholed road. It would take ten minutes at top speed for him to reach the garage. Ten minutes before he could hose down and disinfect the window.

CHAPTER TWELVE

$\mathcal{A}$ week later Sidrus was divided in two by his body and his mood, which were equally split. His top section with all the new growth about his face and hands filled him with overwhelming joy. He looked better than ever, but his insides were screaming.

He had never had a normal face. He had been born in the phase of the water moon and it had left its limp and irregular signature for all to see. There was never any question of him breeding. His father had made it clear that the determination of their line and the carrying of its zeal for the true spiritual doctrine must rest with his brother, who was born fair and strong. Sidrus's path was that of the securer. He who will hold the ground firm in ancient and new knowledge. He who will feed its growing wisdom to his brother and his offspring. That was the way it was. That was the way it had always been.

But this new face had grown out of that old dead moon. Grown beyond his wildest expectations. The skin had fully healed and the tissues beneath it had flexed taut, giving him a different and more defined look. His hands too had become stronger and without the pain of continual peeling. Even the stumps looked as if they were trying to sprout new fingers. How much further could this go? He was becoming something, someone else. The sun shone bright above his waist. Below, it was dark and had a weight of constant pain. A cannonball of misery sat in his extended gut. It groaned, flinched, and ached all the time. Its monstrous gravity held him to the same few paces of earth. He dared not go out; the strain of carrying it kept him tethered to the same patch of discomfort. His mood swings were violent and oppressive. He lashed out at Char, who brought him sugar water, which was his only means of sustenance. He taunted, abused, and cursed the old creature in between asking his advice and thanking him for his cure. His mangled knot of contradiction also squeezed out new questions to worry the long, painful days.

"So you got better when I found you those scraps of the other kind? Not human scraps like this." He pointed at his tender swelling. "So these others, you and the rest, how long have you been out there?"

"It is difficult for me to answer you. I need more sustenance to be able to explain."

"What, more scraps of that scrawny bark or hide or whatever it is that you are made of?"

"Yes, but I also need some passages from inside humans. To occupy them, to learn to be able to explain."

"I don't like the sound of that. If I thought you were sniffing around me, stealing anything from inside me, then I would kick you out and stomp you back into the marsh."

"Do not be concerned, there is nothing of you that I could use. I am grateful for your shelter and the 'scraps.'"

"Why then do you want the insides of humans?"

"To find a likeness, a proximity that I can stretch and make an impression of. If I learn the shape of their inner speech, then I can copy it into becoming."

"So you don't want to eat them?"

"Not in a physical sense."

"When I get better I will fetch you more and you can tell me more."

"Yes, of course, master, but I too hope to get better so that I can enter the world again."

"What?" jeered Sidrus. "You ain't going anywhere until I say."

There was a heavy silence from Char's corner of the room.

"You are mine, I found you, dug you up, got you breathing again. I could have shipped you off like the rest to be cut open back in Germany. But no, I took you in, and now you serve me."

"They are not dead," said Char.

"Who?"

"The others, the ones that were sent away."

"Oh yes they are. Cut to bits, floating in jars all labelled up."

"No, they live and walk."

"How do you know this?" snarled Sidrus.

"Because we can all sense movement and speech in our others. It is only when we are underground that things close down. Some of us walk and talk in the world as clearly as you."

"Nonsense! You are the most active mummy I have ever seen, all the rest are broken shards and rotted leather."

"No, master, some are more fluent than you."

"Don't fucking argue with me!" screamed Sidrus. "You know nothing, you are nothing."

The conversation had died, murdered while he groaned and held his rotting bowels with his strong new hands. The fire smouldered and spat, and the wind roamed outside the door.

"Anyway, you don't know what you are, or why you're here, do you?"

No sound came from the corner.

"Answer me when I talk to you, or by God I will make—" Sidrus started sitting up in his creaking bunk.

"I do not, but you will," said the slight but firm voice. "You have already known my kind, but forgotten them."

"What shit are you talking now?" growled Sidrus.

"Soon you will leave this place and walk back into the land and memories of your previous self, and then you will know me and my kind."

"Shit, more shit," said Sidrus, pulling himself out of the bunk. "Only my sacred God knows my path, not some withered old corpse with shit for brains. My path is written in the palm of the Almighty and his blessed manifestations on this earth. When he hears my prayers and wants me to continue his work, he will give me a sign."

The efforts of his shouting had brought about another spasm that doubled him up.

"I think it has come," said Char in an earnest whisper.

"What?" whined Sidrus.

"The time."

"What fucking time?!" screeched Sidrus, who was trying not to fall to his knees.

"The time to remove the plug."

Sidrus shot a long squinting glance into the shadow.

"You mean I can at last?"

"Yes, its job is done."

Sidrus scrabbled to the door and rushed outside into the adjoining squatting hutch.

The wind flapped the door and the fire smoked against each suction. There were sounds of straining coming from the hutch and then a silence. Char's eyes flickered in the dark. Then a yelp of pain was followed by a sound that is difficult to describe, it being like a hefty trunk falling down a long and echoing stair, and the flapping of a sail in a torrid storm. Then there was silence. Sometime later Sidrus dragged himself back into his bed. The entire colour had gone from his face, and he looked drawn and haggard. He crawled into his bunk as if in a daze. He eventually found himself and remembered Char and twisted his head in his direction.

"There was nothing there," he said, "just gas. Gas and stink."

The change in the next weeks was remarkable. Even some gristle had grown under where his nose should have been. He had examined his genitals, expecting nothing. But even there showed signs of new development. He felt strong and walked about outside in the raging open air and bright skies without his mask and gloves, the wind buffeting his face and purpose. He had even sought out new scrapes for Char, so ebullient was his soul. The first three were inappropriate, being human or animal. With the fourth and the fifth he was more fortunate, they being a shin and an unidentified chunk of something of Char's kind. He presented them to his servant, who after saying his usual mutterings over them, scoffed every particle enthusiastically. The mood in the ramshackle house had changed. Sidrus admitted his great debt to Char and listened to the old stick, who himself seemed firmer and more "there." He told more about his notion of the future, even though it sounded blasphemous and against Sidrus's hallowed God.

In the fifth week he decided to go. It was time to seek revenge on those who injured him. Ishmael would pay. Nebsuel would pay! To leave the cramped undertaking of the bog. To journey south for destiny and hope. He had it in his mind to leave Char in charge of the house, just in case his plans proved false. He might be able to work it, because he too had grown some new flesh and looked almost human, in a scarecrow kind of way. He had left him his wooden mask and gloves to hide under.

Sidrus packed a great rucksack full of his future hopes and past facts. He set it by the door with his heavy bog-wood staff and opened a new flask of wine. Char never drank, but today he would toast their farewell and the success of his departure. The old one had given up the greatcoat and now wore Sidrus's cast-off working clothes.

"Look at you, a prince among almost men." Sidrus cackled.

Char made a waving gesture that neither of them understood.

"One for the road," barked Sidrus, pouring two beakers of wine.

Char shook his head. "Not for me."

"Just this once."

"No."

"I say yes, just this once." He grabbed the beaker and thrust it into Char's hand.

Sidrus stepped back and held his drink high, grinning energetically and without warmth.

"To all other places." He quaffed the wine and beamed at Char, who turned his cup upside down, spilling the contents onto the floor.

"I cannot do this."

"Why?" screamed Sidrus, his new face a new purple with rage.

"Because I cannot drink it and your roads are your own."

"You fucking corpse," screamed Sidrus, "drink," and filled his beaker again and forced it towards the retreating figure, who had locked his good pink hand over his mouth. They tussled until Sidrus's superior strength prevailed, slipping and forcing the bag of bones to the earthen floor, his great weight pinning him down and the wine splashing into the earth.

"You will drink for me," he said.

"I dare not for you. I will tell the truth."

Sidrus leant back, giving Char space to breathe. There was a congealed quiet where new thinking was taking place. Sidrus filled the cup and put his hand behind his servant's head. He lifted him forward like a child or a sick friend, his eyes locked on the dim glimmer beyond Char's sight. No words were spoken. He jammed the ceramic lip of the cup hard against his jaw, cracking one of his original teeth. He slowly pulled his head backwards, pouring the ruby fluid down his throat. Char coughed and spluttered and fell backwards and away. Sidrus sat back and observed.

"Say it, then," he screamed with all his defeated might.

Char curled himself into a sitting position and wiped the wine and grit from his mouth.

"You will return whence you came. You have the strength of two now. You should have helped me to go, but you chose to keep me for this. Very well, I shall tell you that what you do next will cast you from your God forever and split you asunder. If you had just left, none of this would have happened. Now it is too late. I have sorrow for you."

Sidrus stood up, speechless, a white fuming heat burning inside him.

"How dare you say these blasphemous things to me." He retreated across the room, unable to believe the squalor of what had been said to him. "You have sorrow for me?"

Char scrambled to his feet and followed him, extending his arms to gently hold the shoulders of the shivering man. He then smiled and a great golden light beamed from behind his eyes.

"It is done," he said.

Sidrus violently shrugged himself free, stepped back three paces, and snatched at his staff by the door. He swung it through the room, making a great arc that crashed into Char's chest. Char fell backwards, arms flapping, until he hit the floor. Sidrus stood over him snarling, his staff raised like a spear or a pile driver.

"I am the first of my kind, the first to transform, and no human has ever done this," wheezed Char as the iron-hard end of the bog-wood staff was brought crashing down into his face. Again and again Sidrus stabbed at him, finally wrenching away his new jaw with a triumphant shout. To make sure his deed was complete, Sidrus broke into Char's rib cage with the staff and twisted it until all was ruined. He left the body on the floor and walked out of his house, chortling about the stories that the locals would tell when they found the mess. The blood flowed after he left. More would flow soon.

CHAPTER THIRTEEN

LONDON, 1924

*I*t was the most impressive hospital Hector had ever seen. Its long paleness stretched across the horizon of the fenced enclosure he had just entered by the main gate. The path led straight towards the grand steps that fronted its entrance. It was three storeys high and crowned by a dome at its centre. The arms extended out from there on both sides, affording a welcoming sense of order and commitment without oppressive grandeur. This was further heightened by its ivy-covered walls and park-like grounds. As he walked the path around the planted oval flower bed, a violent flapping could be heard behind the walled garden to his left. It was still windy and the trees shook in the punctuated sun that had blown away all of the previous damp. The flapping sound was increasing and he was chilled by it. It kicked at his life for no apparent reason. There was no explanation for its intensity or the unnecessary shudder of dread that it produced in him. He walked quickly now, wanting to be far from its malign energy. He hurried to gain the top steps. Once there, he stopped and looked back over the wall to find the solution to the spectres that had so dismayed him on the path. Uniformed staff were hanging out bedsheets; the humiliating simplicity of their pragmatic task made him feel stupid. Perhaps he was tired, reading the wrong literature, or had been secretly disturbed by the speed and strangeness of recent circumstances. Whatever it was that had made him convert common domestic necessity into psychic apparition was truly unwelcome. He adjusted his attire and made his way into the entrance, where he told a heavily moustached porter in a wooden box his name and business.

He was taken to a hard but generous wooden bench, where he sat and waited with three other visitors. He was early. Many people passed before him while he waited. He tried to distinguish which were patients, visitors, and staff. There was a growing excitement in him that was producing a slight sense of nausea and a contradictory wish to leave now before he became more deeply involved in this strange and unnatural business. The idea of scurrying back into concealed retirement seemed, for a moment, to be blissful. He shrugged it off. This was a quest, one that only he had been chosen for. This would make his name and give him a place in history far beyond the comprehension of Himmelstrup and his ilk. There might even be a book in it. He was enjoying the glee of an imaginary fame, so late in life, so well deserved after all those years of toil with dim students and even dimmer colleagues, when he became aware of a beaming man standing over him.

"Professor Shoe-man," said the lean, tall, sandy-haired man who smiled so affectionately over him.

"Yes, Schumann," corrected Hector.

The tall thin Englishman never stopped beaming. He put his hand out to shake and Hector pulled himself up from the seat. On closer inspection of him, he guessed the doctor to be in his early forties, but it was difficult to say. His smooth, long face and boyish innocent charm suggested youth. But his confidence and the way he stood leant towards maturity.

"I have come to see patient 126."

"Yes, that is right," said the doctor, as if he were talking about something else. "Welcome, Professor Shoe-man, everybody is very pleased that you have come so far to see us. Please come with me so that I may show you the treasures of the Bethlem Royal Hospital. My name is Nicholas." He beamed again and waited for the old man to start walking.

They passed through the high double doors into one of the main corridors. Nicholas went to the keeper's room and spoke to the three attendants inside. One of them came outside and looked up and down at the diminutive visitor. He then nodded to Nicholas, saying something that Hector could not hear. Both men laughed and looked back at Hector. He did not like their manner; his guide seemed like one of the new breed of overconfident medical men that had so irritated him the last few years. The other was obviously a lout, employed to keep control rather than to administer care. His smirking ways were a thin veneer over a thuggish authority.

Nicholas again joined him and they continued into the rifled perspective of the central male gallery. It appeared to be more than a hundred metres long, with an intersection two-thirds along its length. The ceiling was wood panelled and slightly vaulted. Its divisions drawing the perspective into an even tighter delineation. Hector had the giddying sensation of looking down the wrong end of a telescope. The corridor bustled with ornament and activity, having nothing to do with some of the new notions of austere cleanliness that were sweeping German institutions. Framed pictures and potted plants filled all the spaces between the tall arched doorways that led into the sleeping rooms on the left-hand side. Cabinets of geological curiosities and stuffed birds heckled the corridor's velocity. Dozens of patients and staff hustled to and fro, or stood in groups talking.

"This way, Professor," Nicholas said. "This gallery is called Albert, after the prince regent, who was also a German."

Hector did not care for this detail.

The right-hand side of the endless gallery was punctuated by many tall windows that looked out over the gardens. As Nicholas rushed ahead of him, the light from each window illuminated his cheerfulness and speed. He stopped in the brightness of one and gestured at Hector with both hands to hurry. Very much in the manner of an exasperated father being slowed by dawdling infants. In this light he looked overly washed and unnaturally clean. His hair was thick, wavy, and solid and flopped across his proud, high forehead. A glint of envy skewered Hector. His hair had never been like that, and the few limp strands he had left had to be woven over his balding pate every morning, arranged in a sullen attempt at vitality. This was not vanity, he assured himself, just a way of sustaining what had always been natural before. This "Nicholas" person was groomed from head to toe in the comfortable good looks of a matinee idol. So much handsomeness worried Hector. He had only ever seen it in dangerous or uncertain men. He remembered two from his student days in old Heidelberg. One had been a weak scholar but a rampant duelist, with highly neurotic tastes. The other had been a fanatical Lutheran whose perfect features shone even through a brimstone complexion that was caused by an ignored allergy to soap. Both were anti-Semites.

Nicholas moved out of the direct sunlight into the next bar of shadow between the evenly spaced windows, and engaged in conversation with a singular hectic-looking individual. Again he gestured to Hector to come to his side, and the old man was beginning to quietly snarl.

"Professor Shoe-man, this is Mr. Louis Wain. He will talk to you for one minute about cats."

The expression on Schumann's face was beyond description. "Cats?" he hissed.

The word instantly ignited Mr. Wain as if he had not heard it said by Nicholas a second before. He lunged at Schumann's arm, grasping it urgently.

"Yes! Let me show you, Professor, they are in my room and Nicholas has only given me one minute on the subject." He propelled the struggling visitor across the hall, through one of the tall doorways, into a generously proportioned bedroom.

"But I don't like cats," Hector whined.

"Neither do I," said Wain.

They stopped dead in front of a wall festooned with paintings. Some hung in frames and others were propped up or had fallen over. They were all of cats. They varied greatly, as if painted by many different artists. Some were sedate and innocuous. Some were sickeningly sweet group portraits of sentimentalised felines. Others were insane violent monsters that looked like they and the artist's vision had been electrocuted. Tufts of acid colour gouged at the viewer's sight. Spikes of fur and whiskers spat out of the canvases. Hector had never seen such crude daubs before, but could not take his gaze off of the spiralling split eyes of the ferocious creatures. They pounced and scratched savagely at his suddenly timid sensibility. Their arched bodies virulently painted in gashes of opposing, clashing colour. Finally he wrenched his stare away from them to seek assurance from his guide, but Nicholas only grinned back. Wain, all this time, was jabbering about his cats, saying their names and explaining their personalities. Schumann did not hear a single word; his nausea had returned and was mixing poisonously with his confusion.

A violent shrill whistle screeched out about Hector, making the professor cringe and shrivel into his clothing like a scalded tortoise.

"Time is up!" said Nicholas, his voice distorted by the military whistle he still held in his mouth. Wain had stopped talking and subsided into morose indifference. Nicholas moved towards the door.

"Shall we go on, Professor?"

Thirty minutes and three more inmates later Nicholas announced, "This might be of more interest to you," and pushed open a large set of double doors. Schumann was getting tired of this interminable hospital and the endless jolliness of his tiresome guide. The room they now stood in was full of high-backed solid chairs. Some with small wheels or castors. In each resided an elderly and decaying inmate. At last, he thought. He must be in here, now I shall meet and hopefully have some quiet time alone to attempt communication.

He quickly scanned the immediate residents. Looking for another wizened black scarecrow.

Then Nicholas started to introduce him to each lost soul in turn. He gave none of their case histories, just a name and sometimes their previous profession. Hector looked around the room and was horrified to see its length and how many old scraps of folks were propped up there, and none of them looked like patient 126. All looked at Nicholas, and it occurred to Hector that they were all waiting to receive their introduction from this foolish young man who was wasting his precious time.

"This is Ronald Crow, Professor Shoe-man. Say hello, Ronald . . . Ronald is seventy-one years old and use to be a ship's carpenter in the days of the wooden fleet . . . Say hello, Ronald. Tell us about the ships. Tell us about the carpentry. You have one minute on the subject, starting from now."

The effigy in the chair stared gormlessly out at his visitors. There was nothing there behind the squinting eyes. This man was younger than Hector, and it made his blood run cold. Why was he being shown these tragic wrecks of humanity? Why did Nicholas think that he would find them so interesting? A true anger began to rise. He looked again down the jagged displacement of the geriatrics in the square room and dug his heels in as his tour guide glided toward the next chair.

"This is John. He will tell us about animal husbandry."

"I have had enough, enough of this endless excursion. Please take me directly to the patient I have come all this way for."

He did not mean to be rude, but his exasperation had twisted the words bitterly in his need to say them. Nicholas looked at him blankly, his smile twitching out for a moment.

"You do know why I am here and who it is that I mean to see?"

Nicholas still looked perplexed, and Hector was appalled that he had wasted all this time with a menial who had no understanding of what he was doing here or who he had come to see.

"For God's sake, why don't you understand? I only want to see patient 126. Why didn't your supervisors instruct you to take me straight to him instead of parading me through all this?" Schumann waved his hands about him.

"But I thought you wanted to know where I lived."

This was the final straw.

"Why in God's name did you think I would be interested in where you lived?" the old man spat out.

"Because I am patient 126," Nicholas answered humbly, his smile teetering on his face.

➤ *Part Two*

Part Two

CHAPTER FOURTEEN

The walk across the stony fields felt hotter than normal. Carmella's house seemed blinding as Father Timothy approached; it had been nearly two months since he had been there and met the child and had the appalling vision in his bed. His bishop had recalled him for inspection and a concentrated time of retreat. He had told only Father Lutchen about the events. The old priest made it possible for him to understand what was happening and how special it was. He now knew it was just for him and grew to believe that the eyes in the bed were not a terrible haunting as he first believed but a sign that needed greater clarification. He had grown in the short time and his meditation and correspondence had given him a more stoic way of controlling his anxieties. The expectant wooden door opened and she stood there, radiating black in her worn formal clothing. He stiffened his joints as his bones started to become putty.

"Come in, Father. We have been expecting you. She is inside."

The door opened to an internal breeze of camphor, candle wax, and cooking. At its centre stood the child, who had grown far beyond his expectations. She now appeared to be a girl of four or five years, and the uncanny acceleration was not just physical; it was obvious just by her stance and posture that she now possessed a deeper level of experience and attitude. All his speech bunched up and bleached in his mouth.

"Modesta, say hello to Father Timothy."

The child looked directly at him with the same eyes that had terrified him; then he understood, because they had changed, that they now reflected his longing. The milkiness inside them was a concentrate of his being with all its doubts and hopes. The same kind of transmuting unification that occurs between new lovers had happened with them. She spoke, but he heard nothing; no sound passed between them. She lifted her small left hand and rotated it above her head as if smoothing down loose hair. She then untied the cord that was holding her simple cloth gown closed. She moved her arms and it slid to her feet; she stood naked before him, arms outstretched, palms upwards in a pose of giving.

"My grandfather was Eadweard, the collector of light, and my grandmother was Abunga of the dark Vorrh. This is their map of the future."

Patches of white and blue-black pigment made an irregular map all over her body and face.

"This is the countenance of the world after the Vorrh is gone. No Rumour will ever be heard again."

Then she smiled, lowered her eyes, and walked towards him, taking his cold damp hand in hers.

Suddenly he was standing in the middle of the forest where Adam had stood. He was not alone. The multitude that stood around him was not entirely human. But they were all whispering together, unaware of his proximity. Some were like long-vacant men. Others had wings of lichen and bark, twigs and soggy leaves articulating into faces. Others were animal-like and should have been disgusting, but he felt nothing about their vile features and what they were doing to each other. He turned away from their strangeness and looked high into the canopy of trees, where a viridian light sat like a vast heavy weight. Then the entire forest swivelled and divided horizontally into bars of shadow. Its depth swallowed inward in two dimensions. He and the forest had become a picture, no heavier than that, a glass picture. He was in a window of stained glass and the illumination in the trees shuddered and slid down to squeeze between the slats that were outside the window's contours. The forest was dark now and the multitude had stopped whispering to one another. They all looked out through the shutters, where far off on a low horizon two tiny crescent moons began to rise, the spectacle lenses of somebody who had been sitting in the dark shadows outside waiting for the shutters to open, and when they did, the small figure was Father Lutchen.

He came to hours later and found himself on the floor of Carmella's bedroom, the blanket from her ancient bed covering his legs and feet. The smell of candles was strong and the room swayed with the breeze in their flicker. The room next door was brighter and he could hear the sounds of spoons on china. The aroma of cooking instantly made him ravenous. He sat up and listened to the old woman talking to the child as they ate.

He stood and made his way through to the kitchen and slumped into a chair at the table. A place had been set for him. Carmella got up and served him a rich chicken stew. After minutes of silence the old woman said, "We must baptise the child."

Timothy said nothing until he had devoured the satin of broth from his bowl.

The first christening of Modesta was an incident that he and all those present would never forget. There had been six baptised that day. She was to be the seventh. All had gone smoothly, with the exception of the other parents' frozen distance towards Carmella and her child. Modesta was called to the front with her mother and the man who had been given the job of being her sponsor: Alphonse Turquet, the only black man Carmella knew. He was some kind of musician, who had studied in France as a young man. He had a calm but elsewhere manner about him. Father Timothy was pleased to meet such an educated and gentle soul to assist in this most complex inclusion to their small society. In his letter to Father Lutchen, Timothy praised his stability when things became abnormal.

Dear Father Lutchen,

I hope you are enjoying good health and that your retirement is still gratifying.

Thank you for your continuing support and your wisdom and patience considering my stream of questions and descriptions of disturbing events. However, I do have another, and in many ways its directness might throw some light on the matter. It occurred during the baptism of the strange child Modesta (who now appears to be a child of five years of age). I was to have baptised eight children that day and all had gone well until she, the seventh, approached the font. I began the opening remarks and prayers and was about to cup the water, when it flinched away. There is no other way to accurately describe the unnatural movement of the water away from my hand, it simply withdrew quickly as if in alarm. No matter what I did to catch it, it refused to be ladled or cupped, even a sponge did not work. When some of the congregation started to giggle, I let this happen. I think if it had not been for the kind stability of her sponsor, I might have lapsed back into the condition that I suffered after the last terrible phenomenon. Sometimes I believe that our Lord gave a benefaction of emotion to some of the darker races.

The only way I can read this latest event is through the negativity that you so generously warned me against.

*Surely the retreat of holy water from the christening of a
child must be seen as symbolic of that child's impurity and
possible evil. Please enlighten me again with your wisdom
and candour.*

> *Your most humble servant,*
> REV. TIMOTHY LEHMANN

Father Lutchen's letter of response was far too enigmatic for
the bewildered Timothy, but it did offer practical aid and continuing engagement with his plight.

Dear Timothy,

*I am sorry to hear that you are still beset by worrying
incidents that seem to be centered around your "mysterious
child" and that you view these signs as ungodliness on her
part. I cannot wholly agree with your fears because I have
witnessed many much more violent infestations of evil
possession and some forms of attendant maledictions that
have a more precise relationship with dark forces. Again
I warn you about over-reading these dramatic but not
malign anathemas, for the sake of your sanity and good
health. You say that her remarkable growth is continuing.
Yet there are multitudes of statements and eyewitness
accounts from every country in the world and in every
century in time of similar aberrations around female
children, far more alarming than your splashed water. I
think that this latest manifestation and the voices before
might all be part of her increased psychic aging and that it
might all wear itself out in a few months' time. However, I
do have a solution to your next christening of Modesta, a
literal one, forgive my jest!*

You have told me continually that she and the voices

have claimed allegiance to and origin of the Vorrh, so what
I suggest is that I send you some water from there for the
baptism. You must tell her this and it might increase the
normality of her reaction. But genuinely I, like others,
do believe that water particles may be capable of holding
memory, which I think I have mentioned before when
I sent you information about the Vorrh. I have never
understood why this has not been scientifically investigated
and a proper examination conducted on fluids taken
from that great forest. It is known that a huge network of
underground conduits runs the astonishing distance from
the centre of the forest all the way to Essenwald. Some say
that one such artery started from within the roots of the
tree of knowledge itself and that the reservoir there had
never seen the light of day. Some say that in the very wet
years the cistern was enormous. This is one of those times
and the meniscus at the bottom of the lightless wells in
the basements of many houses bulge and quiver with life.
Forgive me, I digress. I will consecrate the water myself
if you promise that you will not bless it again. Call it the
foibles of an old man, but I think such things are unwise.
Send me your agreement and the water will arrive.

May God's blessing be upon you, and the Lord keep you safe,

REV. GERVASIUS LUTCHEN

CHAPTER FIFTEEN

Cyrena was thinking about learning to drive again as Ghertrude and the newborn glided through the clarity of a tropical morning, three hours before the sun overcooked the day. Her taciturn chauffeur was annoying her again. His lack of communication and air of disinterest were feeling like insolence, and she was bored with the sight of his stiff liveried back, the hairs of his neck jauntily playing over his collar.

"What do you think about Isabel?" asked Ghertrude, cradling the baby. One of its tiny pink hands grasped her finger.

"Who?" said Cyrena, scraping her attention away from the chauffeur.

"The name Isabel."

"Well, it's a strong name, I suppose." Cyrena had not quite grasped the meaning or significance of the question and Ghertrude heard it in her voice.

"It's for the little one. I am thinking about names for her."

"Ah yes, of course. Isabel is a fine name. What others have you?"

"My grandmother's name was Ermentraud, which sounds good but it's very German and I want something more international, more modern."

"Mmm . . ."

"What do you think of Leonor?"

"Is it to do with lions?"

"I suppose so, it is from Poe, the name of his lost wife in 'The Raven.'"

"Lost?" asked Cyrena confused.

"Deceased, her presence haunts the writer, his house, and the poem."

"That's a bit gloomy for a newborn, isn't it?"

"What about Ligeia?"

"That's beautiful, is it Hungarian?"

"I don't know, it's also from Poe."

"Not another dead wife, I hope?"

"Actually yes," said Ghertrude in a snippy tone, which cauterised the subject.

There was quietness as they turned into Mutter's district.

"I have always liked the name Annelisse," said Cyrena, her comment falling on stony ground like lemon pips.

■—→

The Mutters were assembled around the scrubbed table. Everything had been cleaned and washed, even Mutter. His monthly bath had been moved up. Its importance was insisted upon by his wife, who ignored his protests and snivellings about catching pneumonia and a certain early death. The sharp of hearing might have heard minute agates and flints of "good" and "serves ya right" flying under his complaints.

She had prepared the tub herself, spilling all kinds of cleansing agents and soaps into its murky heat. While she did this, she seethed and clucked about his foul and licentious behavior. This steamy tableau could be easily misunderstood from anybody outside the family. Her incantation and scalding tuts over the bubbling cauldron might suggest an altogether different and more wicked preparation was being compiled.

They all stood waiting, darting glances at the door. Thaddeus slid his weird hand over his sugar-watered, sleeked-down hair, and Meta pulled Bernd's finger out of his nostril with a soft pop. The lilac limousine glided up outside and sent a blush to their polished windows that matched Frau Mutter's own growing hue.

Thaddeus opened the door before Cyrena knocked. Her hand was in midair at the height of his neck.

"Good morning, madam," he said in his best voice. "Please come in." He bowed slightly and stood aside.

Cyrena smiled and warmly said, "Thank you."

She looked around at Ghertrude, who was gently rocking the unnamed infant, and then walked in. She noticed the youth's deformed hands instantly and wondered how it would affect the equation. She was determined to find a trustworthy human maid for Ghertrude and to prize her away from her reliance on those horrid machines in the basement.

Mutter stepped forward and took their hands in an overly polite welcome. Ghertrude asked after his health and he explained that he was much better. Frau Mutter was then introduced. She made a quarter curtsey that was hardly noticed because of her girth; it looked more like a bobbing shudder. She could barely take her eyes off the carnival mite and only did so to confirm the heartbreaking splendour of its mother. Mutter's daughter was standing to one side holding the hand of a perky infant. Cyrena positioned herself to get a good look at their target for the day. The girl was in her early adolescence. She was short and compact. Her figure, like her height, had already reached its maturity and would only widen with age. She had nut-brown hair tied and tucked into a bun above her remarkable face. This was her prime; her youth was brimming and, once seen, it was impossible to drag attention away from its vibrance. Even in close proximity to the classic and enduring elegance of the fine ladies. There are some forms of beauty that have nothing to do with proportion or symmetry. That do not take their perfection from balance and delicacy but simply beam out of the ordinary with overwhelming radiance. Such was the smiling face of Mutter's daughter as she was propelled forward by her proud father to meet the ladies.

"And this is my Meta."

She looked at them both with wide clear eyes, curtseyed, and became tongue-tied.

"Say hello, child," said Mutter.

She flushed and said, "Good morning, ladies."

She then held out one of her work-wrinkled hands.

Introductions were finalised with Thaddeus bowing rather than shaking their hands. They all sat around the wooden table and waited for the conversation to start. There was a tension inside the awkwardness. It was expectant and cumbersome and seemed to be rumbling under the house or at least the table. Ghertrude moved the baby from one arm to the other. Frau Mutter gawped to see more of its bonneted face. At the same time her hands softly clenched and unfolded. Ghertrude saw this and knew what it was. She had seen it in her own mother and in others. It was the uncontrollable maternal desire to touch and hold a baby, any baby. Mothers, and especially those who had three or more children, developed this need in their later life. They found it impossible when near an infant to stop their hands from demanding affectionate touch. It was exactly the opposite reaction that Cyrena had displayed when she was first offered the child to hold.

"Would you like to see her, Frau Mutter?"

The child was lifted up and its bonnet undone and taken away. Ghertrude held the mite towards the silent and staring Frau. The family bit their lips. The automatic hands reached out and the baby was clasped. Cyrena sensed the odd vibration in the air. The holding of breath by all the Mutters. It changed the moment that the old mother felt the wriggling weight and looked into the eyes of the happy child, who bore not the slightest resemblance to her husband or any other member of her family. In a fraction of a second she knew that her fears were totally unjustified and that her good and faithful husband had been telling the truth all along. The child gurgled, enjoying the heat and the scent of the Frau's sturdy and established motherhood.

"She is adorable," said Frau Mutter, and burst into tears. Instantly Meta was at her side, taking the child from her quaking mother, saying, "Thaddeus, please help."

The tall youth put his arms about his mother and guided her towards the back of the kitchen. The baby was laughing at Meta, who carefully returned her to Ghertrude, saying, "Please excuse Mother, she does love babies so."

Cyrena watched every movement and gesture and knew that this girl would be perfect.

Pots and kettles that clanked between small sobs announced that tea was being made at the back of the kitchen. They talked about the weather, Mutter's illness, Berndt's new teeth, and Thaddeus's liking for books until the trove of homemade cakes and rolls were brought to the table. While they were munching their way through the mountain of pastries, Cyrena caught Ghertrude's eye and gave a quick nod. Ghertrude, her mouth full of meringue, nodded back, giving permission to open the business of the day.

"Ghertrude and I greatly wanted to come and talk to all of you today about her new life in Kühler Brunnen." There was a slight cooling between the cakes as the whole family stopped chewing and listened. "Ghertrude needs help with the baby and running the house. So we wondered if young Miss Meta would be interested in the position of maid and nanny."

A bung of cream fell out of Mutter's mouth and Meta's eyes were like saucers. Frau Mutter was the only one to move, thrusting the end of her apron into her gulping face. Gradually every-body turned to look at the girl.

"Well, child, what do you think?" asked Mutter.

"Me, be a maid for Mistress Ghertrude and the little one? I . . . I would love it . . . really love it."

Before Frau Mutter started crying again, Cyrena said, "Excel-lent, then we have an agreement. All we have to do is discuss your wages and hours of employment. Can you start on Monday?"

She did not mean to rush the matter, but she could see that Ghertrude was restless and keen to get the baby home. She kept one eye on Thaddeus to see if he showed any signs of feeling usurped. Far from it; he showed genuine delight at his sister's appointment. Cyrena stood up and thanked them for their mag-nificent hospitality. Ghertrude took the baby over to Frau Mut-ter and waved its tired little hand at her, saying, "Goodbye."

She did the same to Meta, who grinned back and held the tiny hand between her thumb and forefinger and gently shook it goodbye.

"Bye bye, Annelisse, see you Monday," she said, and stepped back with her little brother. Nobody saw Ghertrude's change of expression and she only said the word "Goodbye" when they were in the car and driving out onto the more substantial road.

"Well, that all went very well, a most pleasing and successful out-come," said Cyrena while enjoying the passing view and looking forward to returning and seeing Ishmael again. Ghertrude's lack of response made her stare sharply at her friend. She did not understand the expression that troubled her face.

"What's wrong, my dear?"

"When did you tell Meta about your desire for *my* child to be called Annelisse?" The words were chiselled out and her eyes blazed.

"But I didn't, what makes you think I did?"

"Because she said, 'Bye bye, Annelisse.'"

Cyrena imitated a fish for a moment. A very elegant, sensuous fish.

"But . . . but I said nothing about it, I hardly spoke to her at all."

"Then how did she know?"

"I haven't the faintest idea."

Ghertrude's face went through a series of appearances until it rested between surly child and perplexed.

"You do believe me, don't you?" asked Cyrena.

"Yes, but how could she . . . Do you think she might have heard us talking before we got out of the car?"

"It's the only sensible explanation," said Cyrena, and they stopped talking, put on their sunglasses, and watched the blinding light give way to their direction home.

That weekend Ghertrude settled on the name Rowena and had no intention of talking about the origins of her choice.

Meta Mutter arrived at nine o'clock on a bright Monday morning. Her father was already there working in the stables. All signs of his recent illness relinquished to the ritual of being there when his "little Meta" took up her new post. He had let her in from the street and now stood back and watched as she approached the main door. She walked between timidity and determination, each step sounding on the hard stone from the metal crescents on her heels. Ghertrude let her in with a radiant smile.

By the afternoon she had seen almost every room in the house. Everything was explained and she had asked sensible and intelligent questions about her duties and requirements. She made notes in a floppy exercise book that looked like it had been bought for the purpose. Ghertrude was most impressed that she could read and found her presence appealing and her manner gentle and easy.

She left at five. Mutter was waiting inside the gate. He almost bowed to Ghertrude when she said goodbye at the door and Meta skipped down the steps towards him. Once on the street he questioned her about the day and beamed at her triumph. They continued home together hand in hand.

Everything worked perfectly. Rowena had a great liking for her new friend. Meta embraced her tasks with relish and massive growing confidence. She had established a glowing and entertaining bond with the child and an admiring respect for Ghertrude. It almost verged upon friendship, if such things had not been taboo. The class and educational barriers were conventionally erected on both sides of the frail chasm. No circumstances could shift or erode them, especially here, in the back of the beyond. It bound consistency and showed the indigenous hoards the might of their foreign establishment. Even with Mutter, after all this time. Even with their shared secret, that he had murdered for her. That he had halted the threats and abuse of Dr. Hoffman in dispatching his life and body to oblivion. That unspoken fact stewed between them continually. In such cuisines those divisions are not confines. They become necessary contrasts that hold the flavour together and deepen the taste of memory.

Ghertrude felt a growing equilibrium, very different from the old days, when her world was filled only with her. A new root had grown and in its winding search it had gripped a part of life that she had never experienced before. Her love for the child was overwhelming and gave her a new depth of purpose; the world now grasped her in a more substantial fashion. Held fast to its shifting and the rolling lurch of its futures. She and Rowena would exist in a normal, stable life and put all the traumas and weirdness of her past behind them.

She was making lunch for them all in the newly constructed kitchenette on the second floor. Sometimes Meta did this between her other duties, but today she sat with the gurgling child while the soup was being made. Ghertrude enjoyed cooking; she liked the helm of the stove and the authority of balance that good food demanded. One day soon she would employ a cook and house-keeper, but for now the occupation pleased her.

Meta's trustworthy, good-natured presence was felt throughout the house. Even the Kin commented on it. Ghertrude still paid regular visits to the cellars and talked with them and received medical examinations from Luluwa. They asked to see Rowena and it seemed only natural after their part in the birth. When Meta wasn't there she invited them upstairs. She had even become used to their strange insect-like gait, which made itself most pro-nounced when they climbed the carpeted stairway, three steps at a time. They stood in a tight line around the cot, motionless and observing. Their shiny brown bodies gleaming in unaccustomed sunlight.

When Meta came home she sensed them. Felt a slight tingling like an hour after an electric shock. She stood in the hall, her key in her hand, and waited, listening and smelling the house. Ghertrude had heard her arrive and wondered why she was so quieted. She came to the landing and called down between the cascades of banisters, "Meta, is that you?"

"Yes, ma'am."

"Is something wrong?" Ghertrude was now descending to look more closely at the troubled girl.

"No, ma'am . . . but is there somebody else here?"

Her large eyes were tenderly suspicious and she still appeared to be listening for something. Some part of her opening all the doors, checking all the interiors.

"Nobody's here, just us," Ghertrude lied, and the listening part of Meta heard it.

That afternoon Ghertrude went to the stables to talk to Mutter. They had never talked about what had been locked in the basement. Now it was imperative.

"Sigmund, what does Meta know about the basement?"

He had been grooming one of the horses, which stood twitching between them. Ghertrude aimlessly stroked its flank as Mutter stopped brushing and retrieved the cigar stub from his unshaven face.

"Nothing, miss."

"I ask because I think she knows, or has heard something down there."

"Not her business," he growled, "to go poking about outside her duties. I will talk to the child."

"No, Sigmund, I don't want that. Your daughter is a good girl and I don't want her upset, I just wanted to know what she knew."

"Nothing," he said, almost nicely.

Ghertrude nodded and left. He watched her walk away as he continued brushing. The stub coming to life in his puffing mouth. The smoke joining the steam from the horse. His eyes on her back.

CHAPTER SIXTEEN

*T*he shock made Schumann suddenly feel very old, and he stared up at the smooth man with an expression that was not out of place with all those others around him, lost and confused in the echoing vastness of the hospital. His face had fallen into its previous apathy. His jaw hung open and he almost drooled.

"But ... but that's impossible," he barely said. "You are young and completely human ... This is a mistake ... a ... a misunderstanding."

"I am patient 126. I am now called Nicholas Parson, and you have come to see me. I have been expecting you." He again looked eager and ready to please.

Schumann found the nearest empty chair and sat down heavily.

"Shall we go straight to my room now?" asked Nicholas Parson.

Hector just nodded and Nicholas stepped behind him and adjusted a stiff rancorous brake so that he could propel the squeaking chair and its new occupant speedily through the long ward towards a small corridor with a bright green room at its end. On the door was stenciled 126.

"This is my room," said Nicholas.

It was simple and alarmingly bare. Apart from the institutional bed, a table with a wilting potted plant on it, and a chair, there was a two-drawer nightstand. On it sat a set of instruments that Schumann recognised after a while as being a crystal radio set. One wire of which laced across the room to exit through the partially opened window. Another looped to a set of headphones that hung on one of the posts of the narrow bed. Nicholas saw him looking at the wires.

"It's my cat's whisker, my radio. I can hear everything in there, with the whisker." He touched the long wound tube of coiled copper wire. "Would you like to try?"

Schumann was still sitting in the large chair, staring at the occupant of room 126.

"No, thank you," he said, and then in a more absent tone, "I thought you were a doctor."

"Oh, have I been challenged?" asked Nicholas. "Would you like me to talk about the radio or its voices or some other subject?"

"I would rather talk to you about your life."

There was a static pause; then Nicholas said, "Yes, of course. That is why you have come so far."

He sat on the edge of the bed and folded his long clean manicured fingers over his crossed knees.

"Just ask," he said.

"Do you know what or who you are?"

"Yes, I have become a man now, but before I was something else. It took a long time to change, I think."

"What was it that you were before?"

"I don't really know; I must have forgotten it."

"How did you become a man, Nicholas?"

And here there was a pause while he considered or tried to remember what the answer might be.

"Through other men, I think. I lived close by them and absorbed some of their humanity. I still do." His lips moved some more but without words, as if he were practising saying something. "It's easier with the old because they are giving up their future and present time."

He looked at Hector and his expression was subtly different.

"You are an old man, do you know what I mean?" He continued before he received a reply. "There is an enforced change of direction in old people. Like the tide changing in the Thames. The older they get, the less and less they can remember into the future, the less and less they can understand the present, and the more they are drawn back into the past. Back there memories become more vivid, more alive than anything else. If it is balanced perfectly they reach their birth and their death at the same time. Do you see what I mean?"

"I think so. Please continue," Hector said.

"Well, as the tide changes I begin to absorb the spaces left behind. I take the forgotten futures and presents. It's not stealing because they are of no further use to the old ones and it helps them go back further. It's a kindness to them, you see?"

Hector recognised the first real signs of delusion and it trapped him between anxiety and excitement. Now he was getting somewhere. How could this polished half-wit have anything to do with those back home, who had touched him so?

"Yes, I see, is this a natural process?"

"Very natural. Do you know what an enzyme is?"

Hector smiled with surprise. "Yes I do, they were discovered in my country."

For the first time Nicholas frowned and his hands changed shape on his knees.

"No, they are discovered in all countries in all men, not just yours."

"I did not mean that they only live in Germany. I meant that scientifically they were first discovered there by a doctor called Kühne."

Nicholas's mood had changed. He obviously did not understand what he was being told. He made a queer movement of his head, turning it backwards over his shoulder and moving his mouth in a few snapping actions, as if trying to bite the back of his collar. He gnashed there for a second or two, then returned, smiling, to look unblinkingly at Hector.

"The enzyme," he said in clear determined syllables, "the enzyme that I am talking about is a kindness enzyme given by God to all men."

And here he dramatically stopped so that his words might slowly sink gel-like into meaning. He pushed his wavy hair back with one hand and then slowly brought it to his face, where he removed the perspiration on his upper lip with his index finger.

"The kindness enzyme removes the horror of approaching death by accelerating the view and the tide that is turning backwards. My work in retrieving what is left on the foreshore is a natural one. I take nothing of value from them. They have all finished with those parts. They would just rot and vanish if not collected. Nobody has ever done it before because nobody ever needed to. I have used all these little remnants to build my humanity, and I have never hurt anybody in doing it." He was tranquil again, waiting for the next question.

Schumann had never seen such a combination of simplicity, righteousness, and arrogance. He was unfazed by it, until he realised that it was its binding agent that was so different. The gooey charm that held all of Nicholas's contradictions together had saturated into the very meaning of each. So that the hard kernels of consequence and implication had been dissolved like teeth in syrup. But there were hard gums driving his words and Hector had the ghastly image of Nicholas sitting with the older patients, chewing at the pale stringy parts of their being, while they winsomely rambled and drifted away, unaware of his purposeful gnashing. Moreover, he knew this apparition had come from the nervous tic or spasm he had seen a few moments ago and that it had no place in reality. He momentarily felt ashamed of himself for judging a poor patient thus. Nicholas had tried to answer his questions to the best of his abilities and he had no right to villainise him so.

Hector straightened himself for the next round of questions, which he would respond to with detached intelligence.

"Please, did you start collecting these fragments before you came here or is it a recent matter?"

This must have been a good question because Nicholas rubbed his hands excitedly and shimmied his body in anticipation of answering.

"We-ell, I must have been doing it longer than I remember. That's the problem, you see, I can't think back that far without it becoming uncertain." He rubbed his jaw to stimulate his explanation. "It's a bit like insomnia, I think you call it, when sleep evades you. Sometimes during those long nights, you sleep but dream you are awake. Sometimes you are awake in a condition where consciousness is barely noticeable. During these conditions, time is smudged and vague. Reality and dream are equal illusions. How can you make a clear and objective statement about it the next morning? Or in my case the next years." He was pleased with himself and sat back to see if Schumann was capable of understanding. He then pointed at Hector and laughed while saying, "I think I deserve extra points for that one."

"Yes . . . yes, you probably do." Hector was becoming confused. "Very well, can you tell me any impression of your previous life?"

"Oh! I think I have been on this island for at least two thousand years." His grin doubled. "That is why I am in here, you know," he said, and winked.

Hector ignored the change of tone and pushed on.

"How far back can you recall clearly?"

"Back before I came out of the river again, I had been in the mud, I think, farther upstream. It was just before a frost fair, when the Thames slows as it freezes. I think I must have become dislodged then and flowed down to the marshes at jolly old Lambeth, and been here ever since."

His flippant tone and the ease with which he told this nonsense was beginning to grate on the old man's patience. He suspected that he was wasting his time here and this was not one of the Erstwhile but a fully fledged lunatic. Perhaps Compton had been mistaken in his information. He needed some proof, something solid to hold on to in order to be convinced by this easy and infuriating man. He decided to ask the questions from a different direction.

"Can you cast your mind back to that time and tell me what happened, and when and how you came to be here?"

Nicholas made another flinching movement in his face and when it was over his countenance had changed. It had settled back in a different way.

"I came 'ere after me ol' man died, about two years after." His accent had dramatically changed. The softer toffee tuning had hoarsened; the sensitive nasality had fractured. Guttural brakes hit his words unpredictably. This was the same way the taxi driver had spoken. He was speaking in the cockney.

"You are speaking differently," exclaimed Hector, unable to contain his astonishment at such a theatrical change.

"I spoke like this then, weren't anuva way. We all spoke like this. Me ol' man did too. I learned it from 'im. I didn't 'ave no language when I came out the freezing water. I wandered about a bit. Then I found 'is garden and slept there. Covered meself up like, wiv leaves and earth. But he saw me after a while. Crept down to look at me. Nobody else did. Just 'im. The only one who saw me. So I stays there, don't I."

"I can't understand what you are saying, please speak as before."

"What."

"Please speak clearly like you were talking," said Hector, becoming confused and thinking in German.

"What, back there?"

"Yes."

"Then ask." The voice was getting ruder with each utterance.

"Ask what. What am I asking of?" Hector knew that his grammar was slipping, but he did not know why. He was losing his grip.

"Asking of me there," guffawed the madman, who was swaying with laughter.

"What, what asking?"

"There there!" shouted the thrashing figure as he rolled in uncontrollable laughter across the bed.

Then Hector had it. He knew what he meant and how to get him back.

"How long have you been in this room?" he called over the noise.

The effect was instantaneous. Nicholas sat bolt upright and wiped his tear-stained face, first with his hands and then with a towel that he snatched from beneath his dislodged pillow. He violently pushed his hair back into its proper contours and gradually regained his balance, his charm, and his smile.

Hector was a little breathless. He had heard about such things before but had never seen it. His colleagues in Heidelberg had been playing with some of Dr. Freud's techniques of hypnosis and trance therapy. Some of the philosophers had become interested in their apparent result. Beiger and Shultz had told him about one session that they had held with a fifty-year-old tradesman. During it, the hypnotised subject had been taken back to his childhood. They had regressed him to the age of six. While there, the subject spoke in a childish tongue, in an infant falsetto. When they returned him to normality he returned to his normal gruff baritone. Is this what he had just witnessed here? Had he in some way displaced reality so that Nicholas could return to another time when he spoke in a different way? Surely this was far too fanciful. Perhaps it was all an elaborate hoax and he was being played for a gullible patsy.

He stared at Nicholas again. He was composed but a little flushed.

"What voice will you speak in now, I wonder?" he said in a gentle taunt.

Nicholas frowned slightly. "What do you mean, Professor Shoe-man?"

Could this really be true? It was exactly the same tone as before. Absolutely no knowledge of what had gone on during his trance state. Schumann had to be certain. He would conduct another experiment. Deep down, below his hesitant doubt and his nauseous distaste, he was enjoying himself.

"Now, Nicholas," he said sternly, "I want you to tell me about your time under the Thames."

He leaned forward from the sucking stainproof covering of the large chair and watched the surprised man's reaction. Nicholas stooped forwards, extending his long neck towards the little professor. He started to move his mouth again in the same chewing motion as before. He looked as if he were mimicking, tasting or lightly sucking on Hector's last words. He then snapped his head backwards with such unexpected force that the old man jumped in his sticky seat. This time Nicholas's head did bite into the collar at the back of his shirt. The violent action yanked him upwards and forced him crashing back onto the complaining bed. His body arched and then softened. The bed groaned under the dead, unsupported weight. Air hissed out of the locked jaws and his anus. Air that became tinctured with the scent of seashells and cinnamon.

Schumann slid off the grey chair and walked to the bed. Nicholas, or what was only Nicholas in this building, was completely motionless. His skin had lost its glow and his eyes were without light. They looked like colourless photographs of eyes, cut out and inserted under his passive lids. His breathing seemed nonexistent and his pulse, which Hector was trying to find, was slight and fading.

"Nicholas, can you hear me? . . . Nicholas . . . Can you hear me, Nicholas?"

There was no response and a sibilant panic stirred against Schumann's confidence. He had put this being in a deathlike coma, without any idea of how to retrieve him. If he did not act quickly he would have a corpse on his hands. He had to use the present time to lever him back. A hook of now to dig into the suspended animation of then.

He stood away from the bed and demanded: "Nicholas, tell me, when did you first install your radio here?"

The teeth unclenched from the collar with a snap, and sound came out of the unmoving mouth. The voice had again changed. For a few moments while his life drained back, the voice was that of the radio. Thin, tinny, and ultimately distant. It made Schumann terrified and replaced his clandestine joy with shame.

"It was a present . . . given to me . . . three years ago."

The body quivered and made the voice shake into vibrato while his eyes brightened into almost-life. He started to sit up, looking around him, confused and tentative. Air was sucked hungrily into his hollowness before the next words escaped in the quiet but reassuring timbre of the man who was there before.

"I just remembered something from a long time ago, when I was with the others. Do you know what they used to call all you humans after old Adam?"

"No," said a bemused Hector.

"Rumours," said Nicholas, pleased with his memory. "Rumours because they ain't quite there yet, a bit like I am now in here." Then after a long quiet while he said, "That's why you been sent, to ask me to become more solid in this time, ain't it?"

Hector had no idea what to say. He needed to maintain this man's confidence and trust, but the changes in control and understanding were getting wilder and more unpredictable. Finally he settled for: "I have come to try and understand you."

"Why?" said Nicholas with a flat unsympathetic directness. There was no answer prepared for this. "Why come all the way from Germany?"

In the distasteful silence Hector asked himself the same question, and Nicholas heard it. He pointed a straight finger across the room at the old man and said, "Now you got it! You have come to question me into your life, the more you ask the more I answer and the score goes up. I hear what I say and it settles in the ol' brain box." He tapped his head with long straight fingers and it gave off an unsettling resonance of solidity; then he sat back and casually said, "Please ask more."

After some awkwardness they began again and talked for another twenty minutes, Schumann asking mundane, easy, and safe questions. Both men were exhausted and the old man hoped that Nicholas had enough energy to push him back to reception in the wheeled, straight-backed chair that he again occupied. He had a lot to think about and analyse. His last experiment had frightened him and given too much information about the authenticity of the young man's claims. Everything he had said before, even the spurious stuff, had now been given weight and validity by the near-death rigor mortis that Schumann had forced him to adopt. The guilt of it still ached in him, and it was not a sensation that he really understood or had any experience in.

He thought he ought to lighten the mood before leaving. The young man's attachment to and interest in his crystal radio set had helped to wind him back before, so now he could really ask a question about it before he departed. One that had no motive or need.

"Before I must go, please tell me about your fascinating radio, you obviously get a great deal of pleasure from it." The patronisation was well hidden by the old man's need.

"Would you like to try it?" The enthusiasm was back and gushing.

"Eh, well, yes, I would."

Nicholas sprang into action and unclipped the headphones from the bed and sprung them over the fastidious, carefully arranged hair of the cringing professor. He then hurried back to the nightstand and plugged in another pair and clamped them down over his own ears. He then clicked switches and carefully started to adjust a dial and a delicate wire inside a glass tube.

"It's the cat's whisker!" he called, just before a deafening blast of squawks and high-pitched whistles dissected Hector's tottering composure.

He shrieked like an old maid and fluttered his fingers about his bobbing head.

"Can you hear it?" said Nicholas with his back to the rattling chair, oblivious to the sounds of distress.

"Ah, get it off, get it off."

"There is a tide somewhere here, the one with the voices, it's the one that tells me things. It's where I got my name. It talks to me all the time. It explains things."

Hector had torn the insect-like headphones off and dislodged his strands of conceited hair, so that they now hung despondently in lank strands around his tight and rodent-like face, which twitched in annoyance.

"Here, listen, here it is." Without deviation or hesitation.

In his anger and tiredness Hector tugged on the wire of his headphones and shouted, "Nicholas."

The wire pulled out of the set and severed the communication. Nicholas spun around, the metal whistle in his mouth again as he raised his eyebrows, startled by the angry disarray of the little man. He was not alarmed by this behaviour, he had seen much worse over the last ninety-eight years he had been living in Bedlam. It was just unexpected; a very queer way to respond to the voices that he had trickled out of the ether for him. These were his favourite voices and he had only had them for the last three years. They came with the box of wires and the cat's whisker. He liked saying "the cat's whisker," it made him smile. He could probably talk about it for one minute without any deviation, hesitation, or repetition, if he wanted to. Each speech told him so much. He had tried to share them before, but it was not really the thing to do. It was best to keep your voices to yourselves. Most of the thousand patients had their own voices and they never shared them with anybody else.

Before the radio he had been called Tom, which came from a song or poem about the hospital itself: "Tom o' Bedlam's Song." But the radio names were better so he took one of the best ones. The one that was kind and clever. The one that knew all the answers and made all the others explain things to him. The one that caused the laughter and was very fair with the marks. That one was called Nicholas Parsons, which was a good name, so he took it and changed it a bit because he was singular, not like the other ones who were legion. So he became Parson, not Parsons. Which was also the word for a priest, so he was told. He could have told Professor Schumann all of this if he had asked. If he had kept the headphones on, heard the voices, and asked. But he didn't, and now it was too late.

Schumann asked to go back to reception. So Nicholas collected the wires and headphone while the old man patted and scratched his hair back into place. He then stood behind him and the chair, and started to push it out of his room and down the endless corridors full of endless voices. He was overly zealous at this task and Hector was apprehensive of the growing speed, shrivelling back into the heavy chair as it gained momentum. Nicholas made honking noises at the groups and individuals who blocked his way. When the velocity was at its greatest, he stood on the back of the chair, riding its weight. He swerved it from side to side, making unnecessary squalling curves in the straight corridors. As they approached reception, two nervous men, one in a white coat, pointed at them. Nicholas pushed the chair directly at them, and for a moment Hector thought he was going to ram them. At the last moment he halted the chair, jamming on the squealing brake, and nearly catapulted the cringing professor's light frame out of the chair and into the flinching men, who quaked and frowned. The charioteer beamed in delight.

"Professor Schumann?" said the man in the white coat. "I am Barratt, we have been expecting you, did you get lost?" He put out his hand to shake and Schumann used it to hoist himself out of the chair.

"I see you have met our Nicholas. How did you manage to find each other? I came to meet you as planned, but you must have already gone."

Schumann said nothing but glared at Barratt, using one of his shrivelling stares that had always proved so effective on his students.

"If you would please come this way."

He steered Hector with a clumsy curtsey towards the confusion of his office. Just before he entered, Hector looked back, but he had gone. So had the chair. Soundlessly, without any need to say farewell, he had disappeared back into the thronged perspective of the enormous hospital. Hector knew he was either collecting shards of discarded humanity from the geriatrics or listening to his voices that he was catching from the hurtling ether with his hooked whisker of soft metal.

He would not say this! It's just the Bethlem. "So, welcome to the Bethlem, Professor Schumann, I am so sorry about the confusion of your arrival."

Barratt was a plump, rugged man with a broken nose and a brash casual manner that gave him an air of genial disinterest. His white coat was grubby and frayed at the sleeves. Under it he wore an exhausted tweed suit, an almost white shirt, and a rugby-club tie.

"Well, what can we do for you?"

"Nothing really, it is already done. I have met the man I was asked to visit. All seems clear, I only have a few minor questions," said Schumann with a peevish taint.

"Fire away."

"I beg your pardon?"

"Fire away, ask your questions."

Schumann did not like this man and wanted the session to be over.

"How long has patient 126 been in this institution?"

"That's a good question. We think about fifteen years, but we can't be sure. Most of us have only been here for ten at the most and he was around when we all arrived. Some of the older patients have different ideas, but then they always do; some think he's been here forever," he said with a smirk.

"Surely you have records?"

"We did, but everything got messed up in the war. It was bloody chaos here and at the Vic for years. Must have been the same for you fellas."

Schumann ignored his last comment.

"Medical notes?"

"Same thing, a lot o' gaps and lost stuff, don't you see. I did have a bit of a poke-about when I knew you were coming, but couldn't find much." He lifted papers, books, and unopened letters from his slivering desk. Hector could see the rim of a plate buried deep in the sagging stacks of case files, X-rays, and journals.

"I had it here somewhere." He started to give up seriously looking and said, "Nicholas says he's been here for a hundred years."

"Yes, he told me. He also said that he thought he was two thousand years old and had spent some of that time buried under the Thames."

"Lightweight stuff, old chap, lightweight. We got some in here who claim to have been Methuselah's granddad and lived on the moon." He shuffled some more papers and found a biscuit, which brought genuine delight to his face. "No good, it's gawn walkabout. I am sure it will turn up. But there's not much there, really. He is one of our less interesting cases." He absentmindedly nibbled the biscuit. "I have to say that we were mightily surprised at your request to see him. It's a bloody long way to come to view such an insignificant specimen. We got some much juicier ones back there, fellas that would baffle even your old Sigmund."

Barratt's jocular gibbering was becoming offensive to Schumann.

"So what is it, then, is it a case of mistaken identity, a lost heir to a vast fortune, man in the iron mask, something like that? Certainly ain't clinical."

"Can you tell me what medication and treatment he is receiving?"

"That's easy—none."

Schumann looked at him with thinly disguised disgust. He didn't trust gentiles; they had always let him down. There was something intrinsically hollow and deceitful about them.

Like their misunderstood religion, he supposed. He imagined it had started when his mother began bringing them home. Not that he remembered anything from so long ago. But he knew it was the reason for their expulsion from the rest of his family. Ultimately it had made them strong together. The only thing that resounded in miserable tiny waves from that distant shore was the prayers. One of her Christian friends would pray out loud in the middle of the night. Pray for forgiveness from somewhere that sounded like it was beneath his cot.

"He's harmless and only mildly schizophrenic. We keep an eye on him, that's all. He just talks a lot, washes all day, and listens to his wireless. He is also very helpful with the other patients, especially the elderly ones. That's why he's got a room of his own."

It took Schumann until Barratt's middle sentence to be back in the untidy room again and listen to the meaning of his voice.

"You know he claims he helped with the war casualties, and that some of the oldens back him up. Did he tell you about his ol' man?"

"Yes, he did mention it," said Schumann, now fully focused again.

"Did he show you the pictures?"

"No."

"That's a shame, that's the most interesting part. He's got two little printed pictures that he musta tore out of a book sometime, guards them with his life, he does. Says one of them's his ol' man. We thought he meant his father at first, but no, it's better than that. He says it's the man who he lived with after he came out of the Thames. Which reminds me, are you going to Spike Island, the Vic?"

"The Vic? No, what do you mean?"

"Spike Island. The Royal Victoria at Netley."

Schumann looked puzzled. "I have only come to see 126."

"It's just that they have got a couple there. It's the rarest thing about Nicholas and his stories. We hear it all here, you know. The weirdest of delusions, the most fanciful and bizarre. The imagination turned inside out, raw and unpredictable. But I have only ever come across three like this."

"Like what?" Hector said with unnecessary impatience.

"Autointerers. People who actually want to bury themselves alive. I have never seen or read of another case and here, within eighty miles, are three."

Schumann's mind rushed back into the frosty garden and the sight of Kunz trying to snuggle himself into the cold earth, under the pile of leaves.

"Most manias are caused by the fear of such a nightmare, not an attraction. The Victorians had an obsession with it. Some ingenious entrepreneurs made a small fortune out of designing and selling coffins with bells and tubes attached, so if the prematurely buried awoke, they could ring or fire rockets or wave a flag from beneath and thus attract salvation. Edgar Allan Poe's morbid and thrilling stories are full of those accidentally or purposefully buried alive. Not even his fevered brain had ever conceived of self-burial." He suddenly heard himself talking too much. "I must apologise for rambling so, it's a bit of a hobby-horse of mine, the fanciful imagination."

Barratt waved his hand towards an overstuffed bookshelf that seemed full of artists' monographs, loose photographs of paintings, and thick well-used volumes on the history of art.

"But to conclude, Hedges at Netley has two war-trauma patients who have to be restrained from burying themselves in the grounds. You would have thought that after the trenches it would be the last thing in the world that would be desirable to them."

"And you say that Nich . . . that 126 does the same?"

"Yes, at least six times while I have been here. But it's

stopped now. Since he got his radio and his new name, he is a different man."

Schumann changed his tactic with Barratt now that he needed something.

"Do you think you might help me get an appointment to go to Netley to see these rarities?"

"Why of course, my dear chap. I will telephone Hedges this very afternoon."

Hector smiled and shook hands as they both walked towards the door. Then Barratt abruptly stopped, raised his index finger towards the ceiling, waggled it, and exclaimed, "I almost forgot."

He strode across the room and started rummaging in his bookcase. Pictures and pieces of paper fell out of the compressed and jumbled books. He finally seized on a volume and dragged it out, two or three other volumes falling out without his attention being diverted.

"Aha! This is what I wanted to show you. We were talking about Nicholas and his ol' man." He put the book on his desk, scattering and spilling everything in its path. He tore at the pages, thumbing through brightly coloured images and extravagant illuminated texts. He stopped on the portrait of the artist who was dressed in nineteenth-century costume that was rather dull. He had an artisan's face, a washed and scrubbed commoner. The only remarkable thing about this face was the luminous and bulbous eyes. This was not a handsome man; there was nothing refined or aristocratic about his features. If anything, the sitter looked a little dwarfish and simple.

"This is the same picture that Nicholas has hidden in his room, his prize possession with the exception of his radio. He says it's a picture of his ol' man. But in reality it is a print of Thomas Phillips's portrait of William Blake."

Hector looked more closely at the book on Barratt's cascading desk and a distant chime sounded, a fragment of memory from Heidelberg. Barratt lunged at the book again and broke the recollection's faint trace.

"He lived just down the road, you know, another Lambeth local."

Hector was only just understanding the implication when Barratt changed direction again.

"Here, here," he said, thumbing the pages and triumphantly opening the book hard against its spine, so that it sat flattened and defeated.

"This is his other picture. Delightful, isn't it!"

Hector looked at the small reproduction of a man crawling on all fours. His beard and hair wild and unkempt. His skin knotted with arteries and veins. Madness and terror locked in the wandering staring eyes.

"Blake painted it in 1805 and says it is Nebuchadnezzar, but that's not what Nicholas says."

Schumann tore his eyes away from the man-beast apparition and looked at the grinning doctor, waiting for the next revelation.

"He says it's him, a portrait that he dictated to Blake himself, how Nicholas looked centuries ago."

Hector glanced back to the picture and close to the face again. There was something there, a likeness under the savage identity. A similarity of bone and dimension.

"Have you read Blake, Professor?"

"Eh! No, I have not."

"Well, take a look, you might find it interesting. A genius and a visionary, some say. But I can't help thinking that it was a miracle he never ended up in here."

And with this he scooped up the fatigued book and pressed it into Schumann's hand as he guided him with kind firmness towards the door.

CHAPTER SEVENTEEN

Sidrus walked for three days and nights, stopping only to take short wary naps. The ground became firmer and lighter as he moved west. The bog was ceasing and an hour later he found metal bars surfacing through the undergrowth. Eventually they became parallel and clear. They were rail tracks drawing a line out of the marsh. He had not thought of Char once since he left his hut, but now some part of him or his destruction was beginning to make itself known. In the distance Sidrus could see a great outcrop of rock and he turned away from the tracks towards it. He stopped in a small gully and drank some water. It was comfortable there, dry and mossy. He undid his pack and made a resting place. He was quickly asleep, the tiredness of his muscles saturating his pale blood and the waiting places in his injured soul.

The Vorrh welcomed him back as only it can to those who must be sacrificed in its name. The essence of the ancient forest unwound its manipulative tongue and its exploitative fingers, which of course were invisible. The force that drives the bud and shapes the twig, the contour of the blind root and the inestimable pressure of density in the thickening trunk. The continual risings and fallings from the minutest white root hair to the sturdiest branch. The uncurling towards the sun and the semaphore of its countenance are all so much more than the mechanics of transpiration. The engine of photosynthesis. He was caught between a million breaths and a million adjustments of movement and pressure. Between the gigantic rustling canopy and the burrowing root mass below, equal in its compacted activity.

Sidrus knew that there were two parallel pulses in men and that the pulse of the soul lived inside the pulse of the body, and that neither could survive without the other. What he would never accept is that man is not alone in this. The idea that the forest had an invisible consciousness based on the exchange of nutrients rather than ideas was beyond his comprehension, even though at that very moment it was inside his brain-altering influence. The Vorrh was strong enough to change the weather, to warp the climate dramatically. Its collective energy influenced everything for hundreds of miles around. Imagine the strength at its core. Invisible and all-pervading. Minute atmospheres and adjusting causeways with a touch so subtle that no instrument could ever measure it. Millions of realignments without a single cell wall being punctured. It also wedded the electricity there and nudged the alkalis and acids. Tipping severe chemical balances with vibrations in water that were less than shadows.

The memory of an old guardian joined in, the man who had trained him. And told him that their task to protect the forest was a small detail compared to how the forest would protect itself if it ever came under real threat. All mammals' relationship with the mass was essentially about breathing. The trees processed the heavy air and worthless expirations, turning them to pure oxygen. This they did automatically, their very purpose on the planet, but that was untrue. This task was done in agreement. A commitment that was signed in sap before God even thought about humans. If humans ever dare to threaten the mass of the forest, then it would retaliate; slowly over years it would change the balance of transpiration. A 5 percent reduction in the purity of oxygen would stop all the breathers in their tracks, slow them to a standstill. Ten percent would annihilate them. There had been a great joy in the old man's words at the telling of this, and the velocity of that began to move back through his cursed time and the enforced separation from the forest. The sleeper started to rouse.

When he awoke, the forest surrounded him and his memories of it as a vast and vacant bogland were erased. Sticky white albino roots had ghosted their selves from the darkness inside their earth to the darkness inside this man. Memory and consciousness had been squeezed and tweaked on thousands of molecular levels. Some causeways pinched shut, some overexpanded, dried ones reopened, new ones were encouraged. His waters that bound, surrounded, and made everything were changed forever.

At last he was back in the forest. Previously entrance into its heart had been forbidden, even to him who had been one of its guardians. He had protected it all his life. Locking its boundaries against inquisitive men. He was now in its center for the first time; close to the tree of knowledge. Somehow he had earned the right to enter. Maybe the penalty of living in the peat bog had purchased him this right. It had all been about containment before, reinforcing the barrier. This often called for severe actions, because it was not just about keeping men out. Some things had to be kept in. Birds broke his chain of thought. Bright, loud, and audacious in the canopy above, crashing and squawking. Sending leaves and twigs fluttering down through the shafts of sunlight and living fragrant air. He had never felt so alive.

He gathered his kit, swung the pack on his back, and set foot on the path that had no known direction. But the head gruel he had digested knew that they were going back to the place where it had died, the place where Sidrus had tortured it. Sidrus had no idea that the head had once been the Englishman Williams and that his true curse had only just begun.

The sun cascaded down through the trees, and the scent of the earth rose to meet the scent of the leaves. Sidrus pushed forward, clearing the vines and tangled branches with his metre-long bush knife. He had never felt so alive, in his forest at last, stalking through the heart of it. He had not seen his face for days, something was happening to it, he could feel it tingling and aching. His hands had changed. None of the lost fingers had completely grown back, but the others had shed their knobbly, irregular, and bent appearance. They were strong and so was the rest of him. A flood of forgotten joy surged through him. He gulped deep on the gift of oxygen and powered his blood into every muscle that tensed and braced as he stretched himself tall and hard, as he bellowed out a laugh that shook the birds from the trees.

The broken chapel where Williams had died was on the edge of the Vorrh, and a road led around its boundary. He stood in the dust of the road, which had dunes dramatically making a six-foot hillock on one side. He was drawn towards it and felt its warm surface. A memory was hidden there, inside the mound. He covered his face with his right hand and the left hand clawed into the earth, dust, and loose weeds. It burrowed down. He did not know why. It was independent and blind. There were many things in his body that he did not understand. The new flesh was easy, but the old aches were like recollections cleated into the obstinate fibres of muscles, the grain of bone. His arm now gathered those into a drilling tool. He was not allowed to marvel at its strength and emphatic greed. The other hand forbade association, and that part of a normal mind that would question such actions was firmly switched off by the same rudimentary engine that previously drove his embedded dogma. He spent an hour groping in the depth until he touched something hard and cold. He gripped it and slowly pulled the massive heavy pistol out of its desiccated grave. It was Williams's beloved Gabbett-Fairfax Mars, a gun so deadly that it could stop a charging horse.

That night in the light of a small campfire by the side of the chapel, both hands worked together to clean the gun, taking it apart with a loving skill that miraculously had come from nowhere and had been waiting to prove itself. Both hands worked in precise unison to bring it and its grimy fat bullets back to gleaming blue-black life again. He oiled the gun with the last of the animal lard that he carried for cooking. So breakfast became a dry affair of shrunken fruits and brittle nuts. He chewed and stared at the road.

Somewhere along its ragged tributaries he had a house and tools, books and weapons. He suddenly longed for it and the surprising sensation erased the last recollection of the cursed bog. Then he suddenly remembered the shudder of Char's prophecy. And one half of him shivered while another began to turn over inside of him, sleeping peacefully for now, dreaming of a homecoming.

CHAPTER EIGHTEEN

Rowena was three months old when Ghertrude felt the need to flex her independence and demonstrate to herself that the bond between them would not be affected by time and distance. She wanted some time off and in true Ghertrude style needed a grander motivation. She wanted to show her new stability and superior womanhood to the world outside. Ghertrude decided to take her first excursion since Rowena was born. She was to meet Cyrena for a late tea at her home. It was to be a reunion of their former selves without children, spouse, or complications. They had got quite carried away with the idea. So much so that Cyrena, on second thoughts, had condemned tea and lavishly stated, "We will have champagne."

So it was planned that her car would collect and return the tipsy mother after "a delightful evening." Ishmael was to be dispatched to the garden or elsewhere and they would have the time to themselves.

It was a day of great celebration in Essenwald. One of the tribal kings was welcoming a distant chief and sealing the alliance with a marriage. They would linger in the city. Showing their magnificence to all. A procession of exotically clad warriors rode painted camels slowly through the bustling heat of midday. They rode in single file. The lumpy poise of the beasts transmitted upwards to their masters in wafts of unhurried, lopsided arrogance. Gold turbans and the polished long barrels of ancient rifles shone and bobbed around the jet-black skin. The lean eyes watching everything beneath them with the languid grace and fabled pity of panthers. Musicians followed behind with blaring bagpipes and great drums. The chief's sedan was carried in between, with he and the new bride glaring out at the rectangular ugliness of the European buildings from inside their dark silken cocoon that smelt of sandalwood and sweat.

By late afternoon the feast was being prepared. The smell of roasting meat sagged in the thick air. Singers had joined the musicians, and the warriors rode sedate and constant in a wide circle around the presence of their eminence. The chauffeur was being delayed by this pantomime. He could not squeeze the limousine through the circle of bodyguards without fear of injury. More to him than to the scarlet, white, and blue camels and their riders who floated above him and necklaced the streets and alleyways with their flowing vigilance. At one point he had edged too close, almost blocking the path of one of the riders. The camel stopped. The warrior peered down at him as if examining some minor vermin just before it was stamped on. The two-metre-long gun drifted like a stick in a lazy stream until it was notched still, pointing into the chauffeur's face. Its bore was impressive and hungry. There was a small click, like the sound of a tiny jaw opening, somewhere up near the warrior's tattooed and gold-bangled hand. The car was reversed without a word being shed, the driver looking for another route to 4 Kühler Brunnen.

Ghertrude was fluttery. The clear clean break from Rowena had become smudged and frayed by her ride's lateness. All had been prepared. Meta had been instructed over and over again. All emergencies had been catered for. Should the child fall ill or desperate for its mother, then Mutter was to be sent to Mistress Lohr's home. Ghertrude paced the living room with small twittering steps, occasionally pinching at the curtains, trying to pluck a sign of the lilac escape. She desperately wanted to go, to prove to herself that she could and that the world existed beyond the love and nappies of her greatest joy. But her body wanted to stay. It puffed and swelled in her going-out clothes.

Her neck and wrists itched in the restraint of the frilled lace. Her breasts leaked and ached. Where was that car? She felt tired and wanted nothing more than to curl up in her constant nest, snuggle into her daughter, and send the world away. But the old Ghertrude, the young one, fought back. She who had stood on the silver cobweb bridge above the city between the shuddering towers. She who had slain unnatural creatures. She who had rescued a child. She who had made love with such total abandon would not now be defeated by the kiln-like temperature of her maternal lodestone: sloth.

Meta fed the child from the little glass bottle that was always warm. She sang and hummed as she cradled her to sleep and very gently returned her to the cot. The muted music and gunfire sounded a thousand miles away from the comfortable security of the second floor. Meta had never been in a house so tall. She still marvelled at the views from the upper windows. It was dark now, with only an hour before her mistress's return. The stars were bright on the other side of the immaculate glass. Fireflies plunged and flared in the dark smoke of the trees.

She was thinking of her own future family when it happened. She had never thought that her scryings were unusual. They had always been there, and she could not tell the difference between them and all the other tides of thought that activated her mind. Her family was as familiar with them as she. It was only the drab ones that hurt her, but they were rare. When she understood things before they occurred, it was mostly good, a happy thing. The pearly ones were more abstract and the opposite of the drab. But this was something else. She walked to the centre of the room, closer to the cot. Unconscious defence steered her and made her muscles alert. She strained her senses to know what it was that was here in the house with her. There was a tingling in her toes and fingers and tiny bubbles of touch on her shoulders. Her eyes started to water and there was a metallic taste in her mouth, which was filling with saliva. Nothing like this had ever happened before; it was abnormal and began to scare her. Something was prowling the house. A something that felt malevolent and entirely inhuman.

The first glass hit Ghertrude in minutes. She had not drunk since before the birth and the cool giggling wine melted her fragile anxiety and told her that all was well. By the second, time had elongated and her balance was an echo. The evening was a great success. They laughed together, planning impossible futures and recalling improbable pasts.

The third glass was the peak of irresponsible and exhilarating pleasure. The slope from there ran down steadily over a precipice and then to the abyss where the worst fears live and stare upwards towards reality. Where babies lie in burning houses or choke on a morsel of joy. Ghertrude's first misgivings and sobering brakes were applied quite close to the summit, causing a flurry that loosely cascaded down the sides and sounded in the pit below. She looked at her wristwatch and then at Cyrena.

"Do you think she is all right?"

"Of course, my dear, she has Meta to look after her. If you had been needed, Mutter would have come."

The word "needed" stayed too long in the air. Cyrena tried to change the subject but the knot in Ghertrude's stomach hardened. More wine was discreetly poured into her glass.

She misguided the glass and it chinked hard against her teeth. She had been gathering horrors. Listing possible accidents, reasons why Mutter had not come to fetch her. She heard none of Cyrena's words, which had been buoyant and resounding. The clink stopped her and she looked at her dejected friend and was annoyed at her distraction. The evening was in decline and she could not rescue it. Ghertrude might as well have stayed at home if she could not control her overreactive fretting.

"Would you like me to get the car?" Cyrena said in a resigned and disappointed voice that had lost all character. Ghertrude was up and ready to go before her friend had finished the sentence.

It was below her. Meta felt its movement like a shadow or something under ice. She could not understand what it was. She thought of calling her father from the yard, but the idea of opening the door or shouting was fearful, as if it might draw attention to her or let something in.

Something was outside the door and Meta thought that it wanted the child. It had come from below, of this she was sure. From some part of the house that she had never seen. Rowena was in her arms, and she was back at the window. The farthest place from the door. She put one hand out behind her to steady herself against the glass, gripping the child even harder across her breast.

As they turned the corner Ghertrude bent sideways to look up at the second floor. She saw Meta holding the child by the window; she saw the palm of her hand, white and pressed flat against the glass, a far-off frail star compacted by eternity. A starfish compressed in a deep silent ocean. She looked up and twisted as the car braked and her blood ran cold. The vision was sure.

She was out of the car in seconds, leaving its wide door hanging open. She fumbled with her keys and swore at their ill-timed confusion. Once inside, she called Meta's name and thundered up the muffled carpeted stairs and threw herself across the landing and through the open door. Nobody was there. The empty lace-trimmed cot bellowed in the empty room.

Mutter heard her screaming as she ran through the house calling out their names. Even the chauffeur heard it as he sat motionless, his head bent towards the house. Mutter rushed across the courtyard towards the door, a small shower of sparks flinting from the cobblestones as he spat his cigar out on the way. Ghertrude had been in every room and found them all empty. She had now run to the top of the house and started again, flinging open cupboard and wardrobe doors, looking under beds, breathless and shouting. Mutter wheezed his way up towards her, almost colliding with her on the second floor.

"She's gone, she's gone," she wailed.

Mutter looked into her wet and ragged face.

"But Meta?" he said.

"Gone, both gone."

He turned quickly and paced down the corridor and through the open door of the nursery.

Ghertrude stopped dead in her panting tracks when she heard Mutter softly talking to someone. She laughed hysterically. He had found them! How had she missed them the first time? Her questions and her brain were yanked after her speeding body, which stopped rigid in the doorway as if she had hit a wall.

Mutter was inside gently talking to nobody.

"And how did it take her, and why did you not fight back?" He stopped to listen to the silent reply.

Ghertrude withered.

"But that is impossible, child, I saw nothing on the stairs and Mistress Ghertrude was already here."

A voice escaped from Ghertrude's glacial torpor. "What are you doing? Who are you speaking to?"

"Meta here is telling me what happened, miss. She says that a—"

"Are you mad? There is nobody here!"

Mutter tore his gaze away from Ghertrude's violent screaming face and looked back at Meta, who was shaking and crying at his side. He moved between the two women, blocking any possibility of attack from his hysterical mistress. In his kindest voice he said, "Mistress Ghertrude, you have had a terrible shock. Please come and be seated. I will contact the authorities and we will find the little one soon."

He held out his huge gnarled hands towards her, meaning to guide her into the room. She flinched from his approach. But stepped into the room and sat harshly on a chair.

"Leave now, child, and wait for me downstairs," said Mutter quietly.

"Who are you talking to? I demand to know what you are doing."

"Now, child."

Meta rushed from the room, avoiding the eyes of her angry weeping mistress.

"There's nobody here, they are both gone, what's wrong with you, man?"

It was said with the last gathered shreds of her control. She then wailed uncontrollably and Mutter left her slumped and sobbing on the creaking chair, next to the hollow cot. He found Meta outside the front door. He put his arm around her and sat her on the front step. He listened to her story again and nodded at the mystifying details. He then told her to go and fetch Mistress Lohr and to ask her to inform the police and Mistress Ghertrude's family. She was then to go home to her mother, he would see her there later, but now he must stay here to protect and help Ghertrude and look for the missing child. Meta left and the old man returned to his mistress, telling her what he had done and that she would be alone for only a few minutes. He did not tell her how he had sent the messages. He knew that something very wrong had occurred and that his poor innocent daughter was at the crux of it. He also told her that he was going to search every inch of the house and did he have her permission to start in the basement? She nodded silently, her face concealed in the wet folds of her sleeves.

On his way down he retrieved a length of the lead pipe that he had kept secreted in the hall stand, just in case he was called upon to deal with intruders.

It was immaculate in the basement. Clean and ordered. He went deeper into it than ever before. He found things he did not understand. The charging racks where the Kin "slept" had been remade, lengthened to accommodate their new height. He saw the workings of the change, the joining of the new and old materials. He understood their construction but not their purpose. He put his length of lead pipe down, so that he might feel the surface and the wires of the furnishings, hoping for the wisdom of the maker to pass through his hands. Nothing. He retrieved his trusty pipe and continued to search. The weight of the inert material gave him confidence. Not much would ever survive an encounter with him and a lead cudgel.

It had been a long time since he dispatched that wretch Hoffman, and some part of him missed it. Missed the power, the swallowing of absolute dominance standing over a wrecked and empty enemy. He changed the pipe from one hand to the other. Some part of him hoped to find an intruder or worse down here, so that he might enjoy the transmuting processes of breaking their skull. But nothing, there was nothing. He looked down the spiral stair to the mouth of the well. Its permanently open mouth being the core of the house.

The waters below connected the building to the city and the Vorrh itself. All the sounds in 4 Kühler Brunner seemed to drain here, as if the well were listening. Mutter's only concern was his potential prey and there was no sign of one here. He was alone with the plunging distance of its soundless depth. Nothing could be there; there was no place to hide. He did not need to go any farther. That is what he told himself as he ascended with his watched back crawling as he retreated from the lowest part of the house.

CHAPTER NINETEEN

*A*nton and Urs had come to watch the procession of violent-coloured noise. They sat outside Jonquil's crumbling bar and drank crushed mint and mango doused in dubious imported gin.

They had been pawing through Hoffman's journal again, and sitting here made an excellent contrast. They both knew that if Ishmael Williams joined them, then they had the key to the Vorrh and would be able to unlock the secret of the whereabouts of the Limboia and control them. If they had that, then their position and future eminence in the Timber Guild would be secured forever. They knew that Ishmael lived behind the locked domain of Cyrena Lohr and that they needed a way to confront him alone without the perfect gleaming protection of one of the most influential women in colonial Africa. They were in mid-sentence when the lilac Phaeton passed between buildings across the street. The cautious chauffeur was driving Mistress Lohr through the side streets to avoid the crowd and take her quickly to the other side of town. There was no other vehicle like this in the city and indeed on the rest of the continent. Anton's glass was frozen midway to his mouth as his eyes slid from the street to Urs's face.

"Did you see that?" he said.

"Yes, it was her."

"Do you think that—"

"Yes, your mysterious Herr Williams is at home alone."

Anton scattered coins on the rickety circular zinc table and they left, rushing in the opposite direction of the creeping car.

➤

Ishmael was taking a very unaccustomed walk outside. Normally he went out only after Cyrena had retired, and only when a powerful desire forced him to secretly visit the unspoken streets of the old town. Being out so early and so innocently left him feeling hollow and undriven.

Ishmael had left the house before Ghertrude arrived to have her little party with Cyrena. He had been out for three hours and was beginning to enjoy it. He had passed many people who hardly noticed his disfigurement. Some even gave him stern looks of approval. Probably believing that he was one of the many scarred and ruined young men who had survived the Great War in Europe.

He intended to do only a short circuit, read a little of the book that was stuffed into the pocket of his lightweight jacket, and return via the garden gate. But the noise of the raucous tribal celebration drew him towards it with magnetic insistence. The evening was steaming and sloughing into a thick restless night, which might just lead to other parts of town. He knew that back home the ladies would be giggling over their wine and salacious stories. Some, he thought, might even concern him. He often wondered if they discussed him during their frivolous times together. He wasn't anxious about it. His sexual prowess was beyond reproach and comparison. Perhaps they even admired him in his reflection between them. After all, he had tasted, learned from, and instructed both their bodies and their souls.

He moved through the crowded streets. The scents and temperatures chewing and saturating his day clothes. At last he understood what he had been missing, keeping himself locked up with Cyrena in that musty mansion. He smiled at the throng; this was like the carnival that he remembered so well. What excesses he had enjoyed there. He was intoxicated and touched the robes of the crowd as he passed through them unmasked. The musicians were flagging. Their pipes full of spit and their drums' skins soggy with sweat. Some of their less devout members fell into bars and smoking huts.

Ishmael followed them, savouring the wrongness again. He found a table outside. His face reflected warmly in its dull zinc surface. This was good, exactly what he needed. He called the waiter to remove the two half-finished glasses and bring him some champagne. He took the book from his pocket and settled in. The stories from the street flickered loudly a few paces from his seat. The words on the page would not adhere to his interest. They kept jumping lines and repeating. The street was much more interesting

He remembered that he had been warned about the carnival in this part of town. There was criminal grit stuck to all activities here. The excesses that all indulged in during those three days were in some way more extreme and darker here. This smelt true now, perhaps even more so in this wild celebration of the pagan kings. The wedding would be in the villages and a great deal of festivity had to take place in the entourage's staggering wake. Gold had been strewn in its advance. Palm wine had been opened and the European ownership of the city suspended. There was a great guffaw from the back of the bar. Two of the musicians had fallen off their chairs and were now sprawling and brawling on the tile floor.

Ishmael felt the quicksilver of violence erect in his veins. A flex of hunger rippling outside the polite confines of Cyrena's world. Then he smelt the woman who was approaching from across the street. Smelt her on his tongue because his nose had never been any good. He wanted to lick the air like a reptile. To catch the atoms of this devastating perfume and waft it back into his being for analysis and delight. She walked straight to his table, straight into his unflinching gaze. She looked Arabic or Persian. She was five and a half feet tall with a slender body. More like a boy's than the voluptuous body he was accustomed too. But her femininity scorched the air. The perfume came from her long thick black hair. Her eyes gleamed above a long blue veil. He knew that she must have been drawn by the bottle. The bottle that denoted wealth and frivolity and that he had demanded to be left and prominent on his table.

"Will you join me?" he asked.

She said nothing and waited for a chair to be brought. He poured the dizzy wine into the new glass.

"My name is Ishmael."

"I know," she said in a thick accent that matched her scent so perfectly that he did not notice it was the wrong answer.

"I am Sholeh," she said, unclipping her veil to drink. Her hand was tiny and slender. Its flawlessness matched only by its knowing strength. He was captivated, this was a courtesan of unsurpassed splendour. She locked eyes with him and removed the veil. He jolted at the sight and she smiled. The lower part of her face was a lacework of scar tissue. The corner of her beautiful mouth entrapped in its web. She leant forward and said one word: "Nebsuel."

➡

Mutter met Cyrena and the chauffeur at the gate of 4 Kühler Brunnen. He tried not to stare at the dapper man's accusing face. They hurried to the front door. The chauffeur returning to wait in the car. The old man tried to explain what had happened, what had gone wrong under his protection.

"She's in a very bad way, ma'am. In shock and unwell."

"I am not surprised. How could this have happened, Sigmund, how could you have let it?"

She left him in the hall and ran up the stairs. Mutter stared at his shoes, feeling ashamed and emasculated. He had been asking himself the same question, over and over again. How did the assailant get in? How did they escape with the child without him seeing anything? He had no answers and his stupidity confounded him. He was so desperate that he began questioning his own ruthless rules and inherited conditions of labour. Of course he knew that there had been others in the basement of the house, long before Mistress Tulp came. They had been down there with that one-eyed creature, but he had seen a glimpse of them only once, a shadowed flicker of one of their polished naked bodies. He had been told by his father that whatever occurred below the house was not and never would be his business. It simply did not exist and no matter what, he would never question or doubt its rightness. He supposed that Mistress Tulp had the same relationship and that it was his job to protect it and never intrude. All this he had explained to Meta and told her to think, see, and do the same. Surely those others had nothing to do with the disappearance of the child, that would be impossible.

Upstairs the story was being told again, Ghertrude held in the arms of her friend, jabbering.

"Gone, gone, they're gone. Someone has taken them away."

"We will find her, my dear, she will be saved."

Ghertrude hugged deeper.

"I have told your family and they are with the authorities now."

Ghertrude was silent and shaking.

"I told Meta to go home and that we would talk to her tomorrow."

Ghertrude shrunk and froze.

"Meta, you have found Meta?" she squalled.

They pulled apart and looked at each other in very different ways.

"I did not find Meta, she came to me. Her father sent her."

"He sent her, with Rowena?"

Cyrena could not understand her friend.

"No, my darling." And here she gripped her again. "We have not found the little one. Meta came straight to me after she left you here."

Ghertrude's eyes were mad. The pupils dilated and bottomless.

"She was not with me, she is gone, you are beginning to sound like Mutter, he was talking to her, talking to nobody, she is gone."

"No, my dear, this is the shock talking. She was here and now is home with her family."

"Family," said Ghertrude in a tone that made no sense. She then swooned a dead weight out of her friend's arms, falling boneless onto the ornate woven garden of the nursery's carpet.

Cyrena decided to stay with her friend through this terrible night. She wrote a note to Ishmael and sent it back with the dismissed chauffeur.

The great celebration had moved on to the villages. Wild dogs and hyenas had sniffed the singeing meat and moved in to scavenge. Fireflies stitched the night's swelter as a few dazed drunks waddled and fell in and out of the road. The chauffeur had to swerve once to avoid denting the car. He swore under his breath and accelerated towards the order and masculine tranquillity of his room over the garage.

➤—→

It was past midnight when Ishmael arrived home. He knew from the street corner that Cyrena was not home yet. The pattern of lights was wrong, set for evening, not this late. There would be more darkness if she had retired. He was glad she was away.

He was clad in the odour and embrace of Sholeh. Of the spell-binding woman who had also been carved into life by Nebsuel. He was reeling with the experience, also with the effects of the champagne and the cognac afterwards. He misplaced his dazed excitement into physical space, slipping on the step outside the garden gate and falling stupidly.

Strong arms from nowhere lifted him up.

"Herr Williams, may we help?"

It took him a few moments to remember his new name.

"Yes, yes, please, there was much celebration."

The two kindly young men helped him to the door.

"We have met before, Herr Williams, do you remember? My name is Anton Fleischer and this is my friend Urs. We met when I last came to visit Mistress Lohr."

"Yes, of course, yes, I know," said Ishmael without the faintest idea who they were. "Please come in," he said, inserting his key as if through an invisible funnel.

Once inside he sobered slightly and focused on the keen-eyed men who observed his every move. After the pleasantries ran out, he suddenly asked them, without knowing why, "Were you waiting for me?"

They looked at each other and the Anton one said, "Yes, we were."

The Urs one then took the baton and continued: "We have been searching for you for weeks, and we only recently discovered your name. Is it true that you have been into the interior of the Vorrh and returned uninjured?"

Ishmael nervously touched his eye; his hangover began to throb again. This was the last conversation he ever wanted today.

"Eh, well, yes, that is true, but I don't see why that is of interest."

The two young men quickly glanced at each other and then Urs continued: "Surely you have heard that the entire workforce of the Timber Guild has vanished in the Vorrh. Our 'interest' is to find them and bring them back."

It was obvious from Ishmael's twitching and general lack of attention that he had not heard or did not care. They tried to appeal to his sense of justice, his possible avarice, and even his loyalty to the Lohr family. It became apparent that all such tactics were useless and they were running out of gambits.

"Herr Williams, you are the only man alive who knows the Vorrh and you possess the ability to escape its mind-killing atmosphere. Please, can you share that secret with us?"

"I have no secret to impart or share. I survived the Vorrh because I am different from you."

Urs sensed that they were losing him.

"Then would you consider coming with us, being our guide and adviser in the forest?"

This was a sudden, blunt wild card.

"Why in God's name would I ever want to return to the Vorrh. There are things in there that wanted to eat me and nearly succeeded. Why would I want to leave all this?" He waved his arm flamboyantly about the room, which made him a little giddy.

Limply, Fleischer said he would offer him a position in the guild, on their return.

Ishmael smiled and said, "Gentlemen, I have other business." He then moved towards the door and they followed. On the front step they thanked him for his time and gave him their cards.

As he started to close the door, Urs said, "May I ask you one last thing?"

"If you must."

"Did you find what you were looking for in the Vorrh?"

Ishmael did not answer, but truthfully he wasn't sure if he had.

———

It was almost dawn when Cyrena returned. She was exhausted and pleased to be home, even though she was not staying, which she announced after kissing Ishmael on his recently sensitized cheek. She bathed and changed her clothes. Ishmael watched her in the water and selecting what to wear and pack, and she seemed a thousand miles away from him. She briefly touched his hand as she darted between rooms. She spoke about what had happened and what might happen next. Ishmael left mid-sentence and went downstairs to smoke. She eventually came down and bustled about, moving towards the door, where she accidentally caught his eye.

"I am sorry to rush off again, I just came home to change."

His eye did not change, it barely blinked.

"And of course to see you," she said unconvincingly.

"Of course," said Ishmael, with the detachment of a corpse.

"I am sorry, my dear, but I am so distracted by this horrible matter. Ghertrude is beside herself with grief, anxiety, and shock. I am trying to do all I can to help."

"Of course," he said again.

"You could come too, to help and keep me company."

She stopped and looked at him, waiting for a reply. He blew smoke towards the ceiling.

"Don't you care about any of this?" she said, her irritation with him beginning to show under the composure of her purpose.

"It's nothing really to do with me, I would just get in the way."

"Have you forgotten what Ghertrude has done for you?"

"No! Has she forgotten what I have done for her?" he said with smoke in his mouth, clouding the sneer. Cyrena turned, her eyes flaring, the strain of the last hours igniting against his sulking.

"That's incredibly selfish of you."

"It's the truth."

"What truth, what did you ever do for her?"

"I stopped her being a spoilt, frigid child. She knows that, it stays with her all the time."

"You selfish insensitive cur, why would she be thinking about you at all at a time like this."

"Cur, is it?" snarled Ishmael, getting to his feet. "That's what you think of me."

"Why don't you show some concern for somebody else?"

"Cur," he spat.

There was a moment of electric feline silence before she retreated.

"I did not mean it. It's just that this is all so horrible. I need you to show some care."

He refused to accept the rung to climb down, instead going higher in disdain.

"You don't need me, either of you. Why should I care now? How could a cur possibly feel anything?"

"Ishmael, we both care about you, that's not the problem."

"Yes it is," he shouted.

"Oh, for God's sake, grow up, I am talking about a stolen child, not your ridiculous ego or your insecurity." She almost bit her tongue. He turned a deathly pale. One eye staring from his head, the other becoming smoldering matt black and sunken.

She quickly tried again.

"Can't you see that this situation is grim and terrifying? Can't you see that it's not about you. I just want you to help me, to come and—"

"I can see everything, I have never been blind."

He should have left the room after that, but something held him there. Something that might have been spite or fear or even pity but was in fact premonition. He sat again and lit another cigarette and activated the thick buzzing air. Not looking at her defeated face, which seemed to have aged in seconds. It took a few minutes for her pride to retrieve her injury and limp with it around the circuit of hurt, gaining confidence as it approached the point of origin.

She collected her voice and said, "I am going back to Gertrude now, to be with her while they search for Rowena. If you want me, you know where I am."

She went to the door and rang the bell for her car. Ishmael glared from the doorway, his malicious triumph being stolen by her grace. She moved towards the front door and he followed automatically.

"I will see you tomorrow, I hope," she said quietly.

He tried to speak or nod but could not find a position or a motive to do it from. They were both about to depart. He with his watery hand holding the door and she with the glare of the lilac limousine gilding the edge of her dress. She softly confronted him again, and in what appeared to be kind words asked gently, "You do know, don't you, that Rowena might be your daughter?"

She left without looking back, swearing she smelled the scent of another on him.

Later that morning Ishmael's head was whirring while his body clung to the half-empty bed. He awoke blinking into some of the many impossibilities. Last night's fragments floated and bumped into one another without the wit to join. The memory of Sholeh was inside him, tucked behind his face. He had washed every surface trace of her away. But she was still there, as if naked and lewd by his side. He shook the image away, sat up, and grabbed at the facts, forcing their slippery chunks together.

She had been travelling with the wedding party. A solo singer of some renown. Nebsuel had told her that if she passed through Essenwald, then she must find Ishmael and give his greetings.

They had taken a room at the back of Jonquil's establishment. She allowed him to look closely at her face, even to touch it. No other except the old man had been permitted this. She examined his face, closer than Cyrena had ever dared. He put his fingers inside her mouth to feel the sutures and follow the ridges of folded scar tissue. She touched his live but unseeing eye. Squeezed gently around its constructed lid, finding his contours of sensibility and numbness. Her curved cheek was formed of a lacework of tiny scars. Nebsuel's finest needlework. He marvelled at its intricate crisscrossing and knew that the old man had perfected his technique. The fine skin stretched taut over a patchwork of fascia and muscle, which was anchored to sawn and jointed bone. She was careful that the pearly white daggers of her manicured fingernails did not hurt him as she pressed her fingers onto the eye. The pressure ran through him as though immediate tiny serpents had opened a cold and delicious gulf in his spine. Tears flowed from his other eye as he probed deeper into her mouth. The finger of his left hand had followed a ridge up past her constructed gum. The finger of his right hand had traced this movement from the outside. So now he had her face pinched at the same point between them. Her saliva ran free and his wrist was becoming soaked in it. They pulled their faces closer and kissed and sucked at each other without removing their grip or the ceaseless agitation, which had transformed from exploration to embrace. The rest of their bodies followed as if twisted on the spindle of their touch. Their triumph soared through their faces. The cluster of sense organs and remade pathways becoming one.

———

Later she had told him of her disfigurement from birth, of her journey to Nebsuel's leper isle, and of his kindness and the bond between them. Then she straightened and held his hand.

"I have something for you from Nebsuel and three things he told me to tell you, of which two are strange and fearful," she said, gathering his attention away from her body.

"The first is a warning. Nebsuel says that a great enemy that you all believed dead or disabled is returning with new strength. He is vengeful and will be seeking you. Second, there is a quest, which you must take. It will be in the Vorrh, and when you are there, open this." She gave him a small leather bag that felt as if it contained a heavy tube. "And finally, to sweeten the others, he said to tell you that I am a gift to you, to share pleasure and amplify the world."

Ishmael smiled mechanically at the last and gripped her perfect hands.

In his heart a cold black ink had flooded, and it now stained the lonely morning bed like blood or guilt. He pulled away from its consuming spilt shadow by focusing on the other parts of the night; the fight with Cyrena, the stolen child, and two young men who wanted him to take them into the Vorrh to look for the somnambulist workforce of the Limboia. Weirdly, in the cold light of day, this seemed the most unlikely disclosure of last night. Perhaps because it was the most real.

He got out of bed and drifted towards the kitchen, dismissing the maid and making the coffee himself. He sat and looked out over the garden. The violent plants straining towards the increasingly violent heat. His head pounded while he waited for the coffee to take effect. Could this expedition back into the forest be the quest that Nebsuel had foretold? Was there some great purpose and future meaning in such a venture? Could this be the straining towards his destiny that he so wanted to taste? It was certainly not the purpose that Anton and his friend had so stressed. The salvation of the business class through the reanimation of the timber industry. That held no interest for him. He cared nothing about this indifferent city or the wilderness that surrounded it. His world had been the comfort of Cyrena, her wealth and her home, and the vivid adventures that had led him there. The two youths had even tried to appeal to his loyalty and commitment, saying that the decline of the city would eventually affect Cyrena's family fortune. He would be dead or gone long before that happened. She had already made him a generous allowance for life. More than enough to keep him well and occasionally buy a few extra undisclosed personal pleasures.

He also topped up his stipend with little caches of cash and other things that he found lying about the house or abandoned in her purses and handbags. She had spent lavishly since he had given her sight. Her dressing table was a veritable beach of jewelry. Expensive and finally crafted gems washed ashore by her tides of whimsy and fad. She seemed to have no real idea of what she owned or where it was placed. He, a thief, or a passing acquaintance could take a random grab at her dresser and come away with enough to keep them comfortable for a lifetime. And if they lived like Nebsuel, maybe nine lifetimes.

CHAPTER TWENTY

*I*t had taken hours for Schumann to get to sleep, so many new ideas and strange experiences were darting through his mind, like a rat in a wheel, spinning away from rest and composure, and at the hub of the anxious turning was Compton, a spider in its web, always there, always watching and reporting back. All the wonders that Schumann beheld were soured by this spy and all the contamination in Germany that he represented. Hector did not know when he was finally asleep, the transition was out of his control somewhere in the middle of the night. He had been dreaming of one of the singers from the opera he had seen two evenings earlier. She had a long and beautiful neck, swan-like it was, and she moved her head exquisitely. But her face shimmered, indistinct as if in a heat haze or the overzealous footlights of the theatre. She was dancing closer to him as he stood by the side of the great river. Her face shifted and changed into his Rachel's. How he still missed and loved her.

It was not the elderly pain-filled face that he saw extinguish so unexpectedly, nor the face of calmness from all those years together; it was the face of the twenty-three-year-old beauty he had been instantly captivated by almost half a century ago. None of this seemed strange or alarming to him, it was natural, the way things were. Only his increasingly sluggish gravity caused concern. He tried to move towards her, his arms spread out, gulping for an embrace. But he could not move and nearly tumbled forward. His feet and lower legs were trapped in the thick, dense mud of the foreshore of the Thames. His arms waved helplessly and Rachel's glorious face shimmered again into the face of his mother. She saw him and danced towards his entrapment. She was coming to save him, to pull him out, and for a few moments he forgot all the bitter stickiness that held them together, even after her death. As she got closer she held her arms out towards him and he recognised that it was not a gesture of help but one of intimacy. A great hollowness was swallowed inside him; it sank to meet the mud and his weight and he settled deeper. She was almost touching him and she closed her eyes and opened her mouth, ready to kiss him and suck out his life. He tried to move his legs and they made terrible sucking noises in the mud. He had heard those before, heard them coming from his mother's bed when he was imprisoned in his cot at its foot. He had heard those mindless oafish men making that noise inside his mother from where he had been. She was now upon him, and the distant love and mid-ground hope he had earlier transformed into a fear of her proximity. Her mouth extended even more and her warm breath saturated his face. It smelt like an animal. A suffocating mixture of fur and grass, of wool and saliva. The breath of a monstrous goat, the breath of a sheep, the breath of a lamb. "Lamb of God that taketh away the sins of the world." The sucking and the pumping. The breath of a lamb, that's what he had said ... "lamb's breath" ... Hinz's cracked whisper, the whispering in his mother's bed. Lamb's breath. In the sucking banks of the Thames.

Lambeth.

He awoke with the word in his mouth, and it still tasted of cud and fleece. He almost tried to spit it out. He dragged and pulled at his legs, which were tangled in the tossed sheet of his bed.

"Lambeth," he said.

Hinz had said "lamb's breath" to him! But how had Hinz known, and why tell him? Hector finally stepped clear of the bed, turning to scowl at its audacity and loathsome innuendos. Then he remembered the only other utterance that had been reported. Written down by one of the nurses. The name on the scruffy piece of paper: Wilhelm Block. Then he knew everything. He understood that there was a connection, a communication between them. That the German Erstwhile wanted him here. Wanted him to contact Nicholas Parson in Lambeth and talk about his "ol' man": William Blake.

Hector steadied himself and slowly sat down in the creaking chair by the window. His mind changed gears into a wordless rush of shapeless thoughts that were trying to seek each other out, to grip and attach, but instead they slid past and over each other in a milky, luminous torpor. He focused on the rainy night outside. A sliver of moon had risen above the dark slatted rooftops and smoking chimneys. It looked like a rent in the darkness, a slit into another world of gleaming light, a world that should be more alien than this. But tonight the fidelity of Hector's warm little reality had waned to a shadow. He sat holding his once injured leg—his whole body seemed to be healing—and remembered the nothingness in his cot at the end of his mother's bed while she slept, alone.

Barratt was as good as his word. He had indeed contacted Hedges at Netley Hospital and arranged an appointment for the day after tomorrow. The good doctor had phoned the concierge of Schumann's hotel and left detailed instructions on how he would get there. In the cold light of day, and indeed it was cold this rainy morning in the Strand, Schumann overcame his night of impossible revelations. And over breakfast he even reconsidered his opinion about Barratt. He had underestimated this brash Englishman who had so willingly put him on a new scent in his intriguing pursuit of the unknown. He planned a quiet

and uneventful day. He would visit St. Paul's and possibly Westminster to pay tribute to the poets buried there.

The next day, the train from Waterloo to Southampton was
cramped and furious; huge numbers of travellers bustled and
shoved their way along the platform and through the carriages.
Thank God he was travelling first class and had a reserved seat
by the window. He had loved the journey, watching the English countryside glide and rumble by his rocking carriage. The
steam and smoke belted back from the engine and seemed to
flow under the train rather than above it, giving him the impression that he was being borne aloft towards his destination on a
cloud, rather than under one. On his arrival he waited for all the
other passengers to leave before he disembarked. The smoke was
still there in the station, flowing and eddying under the greasy
wheels in the hissing trench of the platform. He even stopped
to look at it, bending down closer to understand its movement.
A porter watched him suspiciously, also bending down to see
what the elderly gent had found. Schumann saw him and moved
on. This station also teemed with hundreds of people, suitcases,
and trolleys. It was all very confusing. He felt small and fragile
and buffeted by the deafening noise. There were long tunnels
leading out to the various waterfronts. The exotic names of distant destinations and the majestic names of the great ships that
sailed there hung above or beside each entrance. He read Rio
de Janeiro, Ceylon, Trinidad, New York, Tasmania, and Cathay.
The *Aquitania*, the *Laconia*, and the *Berengaria* of the Cunard
Line. And other great ships straining to leave for the orient and
Australia.

Bright, sharp light pumped up the aortic tunnels from the
docks outside into the station's dark heart-like interior. The light
was chopped and fanned by the passengers hurrying through

them. Their shadows and departures spiralling towards the blinding water.

Near the end of the dock was a small pitched hut. A wooden boat with twelve or more seats nodded under its canopy. Two men in peaked caps and odd uniforms stood near it and anxiously looked towards him. One of them waved. He walked closer.

"Spike Island," said the one with his foot on the land.

"Yes," said Hector, amazed at his skill of finding such a small vessel in this maze of departures and arrivals.

"You'll be the gent from Bedlam come to visit."

"Yes."

"It's 'im, Johnny, gent from Bedlam come to visit."

Johnny on the boat was lazily holding a rope.

"Come to visit it is," he said, and leant forward, pulling a lever that set the engine rumbling beneath his feet.

"Come aboard, sir," said Johnny.

"Aye, come aboard, sir," said the other one, who was called Hubert.

He held out his hand so that Hector might gain a secure hold while stepping down onto the polished wooden deck.

"Cast off," said Johnny.

"Aye, cast off," said Hubert.

The boat slid gracefully out of its moorings and turned its prow towards the wider water.

Some of the passengers on the steep gangplank turned their heads to watch him glide beneath them. He sat erect and smug, the only passenger on his very own ferry. Passing out of the liner's great sea shadow into the dazzling choppiness of the Southampton water.

"Normally takes fifteen minutes a journey," said Hubert.

"Aye, fifteen minutes," said Johnny.

"But maybe a bit longer today with the breeze against us."

"Aye, breeze against us."

Hector was aware that history was repeating itself and yet again he had been met by inmates. These two were either the naturally slow-witted members of the indigenous population or repatriated patients who had been given a sensible job to do. One that he prayed was well inside their joint capabilities.

The thought of his earlier meeting with Nicholas prompted a question that he meant to stop and think about. He remembered Nicholas's words about the tides of life. He had not questioned him about such an astonishing notion. He had had other things to ask. Now it came back, illustrating itself against the light of the estuary water. Nicholas's idea of "a kindness enzyme" had troubled him. There was something so simple about it, so outright that it might be true. "A kindness enzyme given by God," he had called it. A gift from the Almighty to quieten the horror of approaching death by increasing the vividness of distant memory. By making the past infinitely more real than the future and certainly more palatable than the present. He could believe in such a thing. He had seen the evidence, witnessed the empirical fact operate in his retirement home. He looked out across the fast-moving water towards the approaching headland. The thing that worried him about the sense of this madman's prophecy was its timing. Exactly when was this enzyme administered, at what age did the process begin; its acceleration was easy to understand, but what about its more fragile beginning? The first steps backwards would be unnoticed. They may have already occurred. He became determined to keep his eye on the future, straining forward, never looking back. Fighting against the extraction of his impending life. He became determined as the boat turned and the spray splashed against his trousers and shoes without him noticing.

"There she blows."

"There she blows."

The echoing boatmen brought him out of his reverie into the wet present. They had the sun behind them and were silhouetted against it. For a moment he exchanged this pair for Hinz and Kunz back in Germany. The comic image of the blackened bog creatures teetering about in a boat almost brought a smile to his tight lips and eradicated the weight of his previous thoughts. The sun shifted and they lost their darkness. Both were pointing ahead at something behind him, and he turned to look towards it. At first he could see nothing. It was too big to be seen. Too vast to be understood as a building, more easily comprehended as a distant cliff in the constant salt spray. He stood up and stepped farther back in the boat, wiping his face and eyes with a handkerchief. Then he understood that they had turned a bend and were now confronting the longest building he had ever seen. It had been a day for monstrosities. Monstrous crowds, monstrous ships, and now this. The rapidly approaching cliff was indeed the Royal Victoria Military Hospital at Netley, and it made the Bethlem look like a matchbox.

A long high pier that jutted out from the road leading to the hospital's grand entrance extended into a T junction nearly a quarter of a mile out into the water. It was deep water out there and the jetty was large enough to moor five or six ships at once, and indeed that is what it was made for. It had grown after the Boer Wars, been adapted for the numbers. The hospital ships would bring the wounded straight here, to this purpose-built hospital to house and mend the fallen of the first industrial wars.

"Big, ain't she?"

"Aye, big as forever."

Hector said nothing as he steadied himself in the swaying vessel, which now seemed even smaller than before.

"Fifty thousand of us came here."

"Aye, fifty thousand during the Great War."

Hector did not want to see if and how they might be looking at him. He kept his eyes on the bobbing building and the approaching pier and said nothing.

He began to feel a little queasy. The tall pier was waving above them as they slowed to run parallel with it. Then he saw the vertical ladder. It rose straight out of the sucking waves, ten metres or more, vertically to the boardwalk above. They came alongside it and tied up.

"After you, sir," said Hubert, waiting for Hector to move.

"Is this the only way?" he said, and pointed to the green slippery surface of the lower metal rungs that were festooned with seaweed.

"No one comes this way since they built the station."

"Not anymore."

"They said you wanted to come the old way."

Hector stared at them in incomprehension.

"There're no moorings 'ere for us little 'uns. We have to go back to S'thampton."

"No moorings, just the ladder."

He estimated the boat was rising and falling three rungs with each swell.

"You better go, sir, you got a bit a green about ya. You need get on the land."

"Better climb up to the land."

He could not be bothered to tell them that it was the vertiginous height that was turning him green and not the motion of boat, this being the driest thing for miles around.

The sun played joyfully on the water and he could hear people laughing and talking above. The boat's engines chugged under his fear and his nausea, and he lurched towards the ladder. He gripped it high with every ounce of strength. The boat ducked under his feet and he hung there for a moment, his weight dangling from his little white hands clenching the slimy metal. When the boat came up again and touched his feet, he jumped and pumped his feet at the rungs like somebody furiously pedalling an invisible bicycle, until they hit the rungs and he felt support. He pulled himself upwards slowly until he noticed the iron was no longer wet. He dared not look down or up or sideways. He dared not look at all. He closed his eyes and scurried up the dizzying height. He stopped when the rungs ran out and his hands felt a different contrivance before them. He felt sicker now than before. He knew he must open his eyes. The ladder started to tremble. Was it coming loose, the final horror? Then he realised it was Hubert, blissfully unaware of his terror and ascending the ladder behind him. His feet shook and he opened his eyes. He was standing with his knees at the same level as the sunlit boardwalk. People strolled about, unaware of his nightmarish plight. He thought about calling to them for help, if only he had a voice. All he had to do was to step up another three rungs, put his hand out to the guiding rail, and step off.

Everything trembled now: the ladder, his entire body, and his soul.

From just below Hubert called up, "You all right, sir, nearly there."

"Nearly there," came the diminutive echo from the waves far below.

Motion, like words, had dried up in him. Then from far off came salvation in the form of a picture.

He had once seen a series of black-and-white pictures made by an experimental photographer who had taken photographs of people moving in every action of normal and abnormal life. Frame by frame, each part of their bodies could be seen in the astonishing act of balancing and projecting through space, which most of us do every day of our lives and never notice.

The frozen heartsick Hector remembered one set of images of a man climbing a stair. Naked, poised, and unconsciously balletic. He closed his eyes again and engulfed the ghost, letting each frame be his interior. He, with the naked hero inside, climbed onto the solid sun and glazed wood of the pier above the gently crashing sea. There was an exchange of trembling. Ultimate. From fear to triumph.

Hubert was suddenly behind him.

"Sir, I have to take you to reception."

"Thank . . . you," wheezed Hector.

They walked the long and luxurious path to the entrance of the hospital. Hector felt every step of God's good earth firmly under his now-solid footfall, even though his knees still trembled.

Dr. Hedges was a big man who crowned the imposing stone steps with ease. He looked more like a pugilist than one of Freud's devotees. His hand completely engulfed Hector's rather dainty paw when they greeted. He held the door open and Hector bent under his arm into the eccentric hall. It was a museum, he thought. A great entrance hall full of the preserved and cast. It looked as if every creature that ever walked the planet was now stuffed and ornamentally hanging from the walls and corridors. This baroque manifestation even included humans. Interspersed between the glass-eyed animals were cases of human anatomical specimens. The place was festooned with the dead. Reptiles, monkeys, birds, and fish from every outpost of the empire. A fossilised natural history that Schumann walked through amazed, his jaw hanging open and his trouser legs dripping seawater behind him.

"Dr. Hedges, I am greatly surprised. What is this, a museum?"

"Yes, Professor. Some of my colleagues believe it to be beneficial to remove the first impression of clinical abruptness and replace it with a different sensation."

"You have certainly done that." Hector could not help himself. He found the gloomy menagerie of taxidermy and pickled organs grotesque, ridiculous, and vaguely unsettling. "But don't some of your patients get disturbed?"

Hedges frowned at the question. "I am sorry, Professor, I don't quite understand."

"Well, I would have thought that some of these things might alarm or upset unbalanced patients."

Hedges looked even more perplexed, so Hector elaborated: "In the Bethlem Royal Hospital they only have potted plants and a few fossils, and I did see one of the inmates talking to a fern."

Hedges stopped walking and laughed. "Oh! I see, you thought this was all an asylum like the Bethlem."

Now it was Hector's turn to frown.

"We are a military hospital. The asylum section where I work is just a small part of the Vic. My patients would hardly ever see the entrance hall. D block is actually a separate building." He started walking again and they were now outside the influence of the morbid museum. Hedges chuckled to himself and then saw Hector's face.

"I am sorry, please excuse me, it's just that the idea of the entire hospital being used to treat the unbalanced and insane is quite funny. There aren't enough lunatics in all of England to fill this place." He chuckled again, but Schumann didn't see anything amusing about his mistake.

They exited the side of the main hospital and entered another low building through a multiply locked door.

"Welcome to the infamous D block, Professor."

It occurred to Hector that all British medics had the same sense of humour; it must be part of their training. The walls were painted a cream colour and the corridors were surprisingly quiet. Hedges selected another key and opened the door into his office. He gave Hector a chair and then locked the door again.

"Now, Professor Schumann, what exactly do you know about our privates Dick and Harry?"

"Who?" said Hector peevishly.

"Our two mysterious patients who insist on burying themselves. You must already have some information about them."

"Only what Dr. Barratt told me, in that you have two inmates here who have some of the same behavioural symptoms as one of his patients at the Bethlem."

"Tom," said Hedges.

"Tom?" said Hector. "You mean patient 126, called Nicholas Parson."

"Tom. Tom, Dick, and Harry. They are placeholder names, used in English to group unknown people together," said Hedges.

"Ah! I see," said Hector. "In Germany we have the same: 'Hinz und Kunz.' The same, you see."

Hedges did not and his interest was obviously elsewhere.

"And why are you interested in Tom? Why come all the way from Germany to visit him?"

Schumann did not expect to be questioned so. He had not prepared answers for this inquisitive and irritating man. He stumbled for an answer and became aware that this doctor had a very different attitude towards him. An air of authority that he did not trust.

"I came to investigate him because we have two similar patients in Germany."

"Who is 'we'?" asked Hedges.

"Well, I represent the Department of Internal Affairs. And this is a medical question that concerns the institution where I abide."

"Why, Professor Schumann, you're not a medical man?"

For the first time somebody in England had pronounced his name perfectly.

"No, I am a philosophy scholar from the University of Heidelberg."

"Where?" said Hedges.

"I beg your pardon?" said Hector, who was becoming ruffled.

"I said 'where,' you have been retired now for seven years."

Hector was shocked and dismayed at this man's knowledge of him.

"And the institution where you 'abide' is the Rupert the First Retirement Home, is it not?"

Hector did not hear Hedges's cynical pronunciation of "abide," which indicated clearly that he had understood the old man's choice of the word to deflect the truth in a sentence that was almost a lie. He did, however, understand that this man who must know everything about him should not be lied to again.

"So my question is why should a government department send a retired academic all this way to interview three mental patients?"

Hector was trapped. He had been told in Germany to say nothing about the bog creatures. And even if he did, this man would not believe him. He needed a perfect lie and he needed to deliver it perfectly, and he had no chance of either.

"I have not come here to answer your questions. You have no right to investigate me like this."

"Oh but I do," said Hedges. "I told you, this is a military establishment. Apart from being a doctor I am an officer in His Majesty's armed forces. You will answer my questions. For your own sake and for whatever purpose you have come here. You will answer my questions or I will have you arrested within the hour."

"Arrested. Arrested for what?"

"Suspicion of espionage, for a start."

"Espionage?" Hector almost laughed the word out.

Hedges did not reply but slowly stood up, lifted his wooden chair, and brought it closer to the agitated professor so that he could look more clearly into his face.

"So, Professor, shall we start again?"

After an hour Hector had told him everything he knew at least twice and a few things he didn't once. Hedges stood and moved his chair farther away.

"Good," he said before picking up the telephone and ordering tea. "Now, do you have any questions for me?"

The shrivelled professor was again taken aback.

"Many," he said. "But first I need to know what you suspect me of."

"Now, nothing. I greatly suspect your employers, but I think you do too. Do you think that Himmelstrup thinks my two are German?"

"German, why would they be German?"

"Because they are not English or French. They arrived here from the trenches in the autumn of 1917. They were part of a batch of soldiers from different regiments, fighting only yards away from the enemy lines. There had been a huge bombardment and many of the wounded had been buried for days. The casualties in those last months were enormous. Most that came here either died or recovered and left; only a few were too badly injured to be returned to the front or to civilian life. The physically damaged went to the closed wards at Roehampton. The mentally damaged stayed here. You have to understand that the conditions of their wounds were so severe that many of those who had consciousness wanted their families to be told that they had perished on the front line. Some had no identities when they arrived. The shock had erased all their memories, we had to rely on other patients to recognise them. Dick and Harry were like that. Well, at least that's what we thought at the beginning."

"But they speak English?" said Hector.

"They don't speak at all, never a word in the nine years they have been here."

Hector was just about to ask if Hedges thought they were German when the door was banged hard. Hedges unlocked it to let the tea trolley be propelled into the room by a man with no ears. He jangled it hard across the floor to the doctor's desk against the window.

"Thank you, Roger," shouted Hedges.

Roger grunted, saluted like he was trying to catch a hectic fly, and started to leave the room. Midway he stopped and stared at Hector, head tilted to one side like a curious dog.

"Thank you, Roger!"

He made the spasmodic salute again and left the room, walking like a music-hall drunk.

"Don't mind Roger, he is one of those who never went home."

Hedges heaved a large bottle of Black & White whisky out of his desk and laced their tea without even asking if Hector approved. Hedges gave it to Hector with the prescribed biscuits.

"After this we will go and see them," said Hedges cheerily.

"And my interrogation is over?" said Hector, more to his cup than to the large man eating a biscuit.

"Yes, er, sorry I had to get a little rough with you back there, but I had to be sure."

"Sure of what?"

"That you were not sent here to give or collect information from them. Information that may be used against us, in future conflicts."

"You fear another war?"

"It's my job to be cautious and there have been some very strong rumblings coming out of your country recently. This Himmelstrup sounds like some of the jokers that we are watching closely."

Hector said nothing but accidentally slurped his tea.

"I need to clarify a few points, if you don't mind." The whisky had helped relax Hector back into his purpose and his curiosity.

Hedges was relaxed too, his feet up on the corner of his desk.

He poured more whisky than tea into the cup that was buried in his oversize hands.

"When these two patients arrived here, did they have no identification at all? No papers, clothing, or dog tags?"

Hedges gathered himself and almost sat up.

"No, nothing. They like many others were found naked, their clothes blown away in the blast. They received emergency treatment on the battlefield and then were sent back here posthaste. After their wounds were treated, it was obvious that there was still something seriously wrong. That's when they were sent to me."

"I understand, and then you treated them psychiatrically?"

"That's one word for it. Let me explain what it was like then. We had soldiers sent to us who were suffering from symptoms that none of us had ever seen before. There was nothing in the textbooks about it. We were under strict orders to get them patched up and shipped back to the front line in weeks." He stopped and poured himself another large slug of whisky. He fumbled in his pockets and found his cigarettes. After lighting one he continued. Hector noted that he had not been offered one, a common courtesy even if he would refuse, he being a cigar man.

"The symptoms were weird. All different but they had a common stem: cringing fear and debilitating shock. Traumas brought about by continual exposure to batteries of artillery, constant explosions. They had all manner of tics and shakes. We tried everything and hardly anything worked. Hypnosis and medication barely touched the sides and they were coming in by the dozens. Everything looked hopeless and the pressure from above was relentless. We patched up as many as we could and sent them back. We put the uniforms on the shaking wrecks and lined them up ready to go. Some killed themselves here rather than return."

There was a long pause.

"Anyway, it started to change when they arrived. I gave them their first once-over. Even then they were very odd. The clinical reports from across the yard were full of anomalies. Physiological abnormalities that were not caused by injury. We were under enormous pressure and such things became unimportant if a man could stand up, function basically, and take orders. They had been sent over here because of their stillness and lack of speech. I tried to get through, engage in any kind of communication, but nothing worked. After all manner of signing produced no results, we tried French and then even German. Nothing. They just stood and stared, we were locked out. Then the business with Corporal Gibbs started. He was brought here from Passchendaele, basically in good physical shape. Mentally he seemed fairly normal, slightly nervous about the eyes. But when anyone said the word 'bomb,' he automatically dived for cover, generally under his bed, where he went into fits of tremors. It took a great deal of persuasion to get him out. You could say the word anytime, anywhere and get exactly the same result. We were getting nowhere fast with him. One day I was showing a small party of generals around the wards. Explaining the symptoms and our treatment. The overall opinion of these types was that my patients were malingering, swinging the lead. Inventing these strange antics to avoid further battle. If a soldier had both arms and legs and was not blind, they saw no reason why he should not be fighting. Gibbs was going to be my test case, showing that such trauma was just as debilitating as amputation. We were standing around his bed chatting, giving the impression that this was a normal healthy man. Then I said 'bomb,' and to their horror he dived under his bed like a scolded cat. I was just about to prove my point when I was interrupted by a kerfuffle at the other end of the ward. One of my junior staff came running, saying that I must see this. I excused myself from the generals, irritated at the disturbance.

"The nurse pointed under the last two beds. Dick and Harry were skulking there, trembling like Gibbs. I was furious. 'They're taking the piss, get 'em out,' I said to the nurse and returned to the officers, who were watching what was happening. They were not impressed and paid little interest to anything else I said that day. Gibbs and the comedy duo were eventually coaxed out from under their beds . . . Are you still with me?" he asked Schumann, who certainly was.

"Yes, Doctor, please continue."

"Anyway, after the brass had left, I intended to tear a strip off those two clowns and went to find them. The nurse had them sitting on a bed opposite Gibbs. He had also emptied the ward in preparation for my tirade. I still had the temper about me when I confronted them. 'What the fuck do you mean by playing such a bloody stupid trick?' I said. 'This man is genuinely sick and you think it's sport to copy his afflictions?' They sat looking blankly forward, ignoring my raging. I became aware that the nurse standing to my side was trying to attract my attention. I am ashamed to say this made me even more enraged. 'What, man, what?' 'Sir, may I show you something?' 'What,' I blazed. He stepped timidly forward and said, 'Bomb.' Dick and Harry threw themselves to the floor and scurried under the bed. Gibbs absently lowered himself down to the floor and casually crawled under the bed next to the others. He looked like a man who had been asked to perform a silly task that he did not understand. For once I was speechless. Just staring at the bed with the three men under it. I looked at the nurse. 'This is the third time I have tried this and each time Corporal Gibbs performs the act with more reluctance,' he says. Of course by then my anger had gone and been replaced by a very different emotion."

He drank from the teacup again.

"Over the next weeks, months, and years, our patients began to quickly respond to our treatment. Sometimes in days we relieved them of their traumatic agues and terrifying visions. Hundreds of men came through here and almost all left 'cleansed.'" The last word he spoke between clenched teeth. "Gibbs was sent back to France within days of the dramatic event."

"And Dick and Harry?" Hector used their placeholder names for the first time.

Hedges looked up with eyes that were weary, distant, and scared.

"You better come and see for yourself," he said, pulling himself out of his chair.

His interrogator's air had changed remarkably, Schumann suspected because he now thought him safe and usable for his own needs. But there was something else, an undetermined aura of defeat about the man. Hector tried to lighten the atmosphere between them.

"Do you have many other patients in this section?"

"Not here, not in this corridor. They have spooked them and all my staff. You will see. It's their feeding time soon. Roger will be here with their food, he is the only one who does not mind them."

As they walked deeper into the building, the quietness that he had noticed before deepened. It was as if all the sound had been absorbed elsewhere. Even their own footfall seemed muted. It produced a kind of thick humming inside his head. He rubbed at his ears with the balls of his fists. At first he thought it might have been the whisky and for reassurance looked at the doctor towering above him.

"You have noticed it then?" said Hedges, whose voice seemed far away.

"The quietness, yes, it seems unusual."

"It's more than that."

Hedges pointed down the featureless corridor to the room at its end. "That's where they are and that's where the acoustics changed. It's the epicentre of this distortion. Directly outside that door a brass band could play and you would never hear it."

Hector was straining his ears to understand what his companion was saying, even though he was only a few feet away. He shouted back, "What's causing it?"

Hedges shrugged and said, "I think it's them."

They continued to approach the door. The last few metres were constructed of fatigue, as if the very air had thickened. Hedges shouted, "It will be all right once we are inside."

His words seemed percussive and distant and unpleasantly jarring in the ringing dense silence. He fumbled through his bunch of keys again, finding the appropriate one and unlocking the door, which swung inwards. Once inside he quickly closed it behind them and normality came back with a breeze of light sound. They were in a long room that looked like a furniture store. There were more than a dozen simple wooden chairs, like the ones in Hedges's office. A standard military issue, Hector supposed. They were randomly placed about the room, some had fallen on their back. There was a table with the remnants of two place settings and two metal-frame beds. Beyond there was a door open to the outside. Both visitors scanned the room for signs of life, to see if Dick and Harry might be in there somewhere, but unless they were hiding under the beds they must have been outside. Hector was reminded of visiting a zoo. Perhaps it was because Hedges had used the phrase "feeding time," but it was more like the sensation of peering into an exotic creature's cage and trying to make out its form and where it may be hiding inside its structured environment. Or if it was there at all.

"They must be in their airing yard," said Hedges, and for the first time Hector heard a fracture of uncertainty in his overconfident voice.

"Why do they have so many chairs?" he asked as they approached the door to the outside.

"They have been practising sitting."

An answer without connotation or comfort.

The impression of a zoo was getting stronger. There was a certain odour of cage. There was also a tincture of the Heidelberg rooms, a trace of seashore and cinnamon. Hedges had begun walking on the balls of his feet as if for stealth or to not disturb something. They both cautiously peered around the frame of the door into the enclosed yard. Seen from the outside this would have made a very comic picture. The bullish muscular head of the doctor hovering almost two feet higher that the small pointed goatlike face of the professor, both wearing the same expression of serious concern. Dick and Harry were totally unaware of them, showing no knowledge of or interest in their presence. They were too busy examining cracks. Schumann had no idea what to expect this time. Black hesitant scarecrows or fully formed eager young men.

"Hello, chaps," said Hedges in a jolly voice tinged with dread.

Dick had been lying in a straight line at the intersection between the back brick wall and the tarmac ground. He had been picking at the seam between them with his fingernails. He stopped and looked towards the door. So did Harry, who was examining the mortar between the brickwork of the side wall of the enclosure.

"I have brought a visitor to see you all the way from Germany."

Dick started to get up and Harry moved towards them. Hector's blood flushed cold. He had never seen men move like this before. He flinched backwards, bumping into the mass of Hedges, who whispered emotionally, "Now do you understand?"

Dick was standing; he had unwound his thin body from horizontal to vertical in a series of shaking tics, as if shunts of short but high-voltage galvanic energy had been wired through his twisted body. Harry too moved his few paces in terrible distortion, like a man walking on ice, negotiating the slippery fall with every inch. His arms seemed to move independently, jabbing at the flailing space around them. They both made their way towards their visitors in violently spasmodic tremors that were hypnotic to watch. They both shook and quaked in every inch of their out-of-focus bodies.

Hector put his hand over his mouth, he thought to stifle a groan but it was a giggle. He was laughing at the staggering cripples. Horrified, he clamped his other hand over his mouth and shot an impossible glance at Hedges.

"It's all right, we have all done it. We call it the Chaplin effect. It always happens when you first see them."

Instantly Hector understood his atrocious behaviour. It had been a spontaneous effect associated with a well-known thing. Dick and Harry walked like Charlie Chaplin's shuffling tramp, or was it the other way round? Indeed, all the early stars of American slapstick films could be identified in the movements of these two lost souls. It was as if the same effect of the mistiming of the camera and projector shutters had been mimicked by trauma in real time and three-dimensional space. Their frames of life continually over-cranked and out of synch. As they got closer Hector's giggles curdled. Their faces were blurred. The incessant ferocity of their tics and trembles, quivers and agitations made their features smudge. Their countenance totally uncertain. Hector felt a creeping horror, an uncontrollable loathing at their increasing proximity. It bit at his humanity and compassion. Brushing aside all thought of contact. He simply wanted to run, to be away from these terrifying wrecks of human beings, and then he remembered they weren't.

The visitors stepped back out of the doorway so Dick and Harry could enter. Their convulsions agitated them past the rigid men. At close range their individual features could not be distinguished. They could have been twins or opposites, it was impossible to tell, the tremors kept them continually out of focus. Every muscle of their visible body worked independently, jarred into ferocious spasms.

They staggered into the middle of the room and for one awful moment Hector thought they might start "practising sitting" and he feared for the ability to control his reaction at the sight. Instead they juddered at the table and tried to hold themselves there.

"This is Professor Schumann from Heidelberg in Germany. Last week he visited Tom in London."

At "Tom" there was a slight change in them, as if a gear of attention had been shifted.

"He tells me he has two of your kind in Germany."

This was totally unexpected. He had no idea that Hedges was going to quote him so. Hector was just about to say something to clarify his position when he noticed that the shivers were moving in unison. At first he thought it might just be a random phase shift. An accidental alignment of their spasms. Then it became more pronounced and then absolutely identical. He looked at Hedges and whispered, "How is this possible?"

"I don't know, I have never seen it before."

Dick and Harry were now moving very fast, like one body divided into two. They turned and lifted their left arms over each other's heads. The visitors were petrified by the event. Then their left hands started to move in staccato circles, as if describing jagged halos hovering above.

They twisted their gibbering faces and looked into Schumann's eyes. Hedges tried to do or say something but could do neither. Suddenly they stopped. Frozen. Motionless. And the room began to quiver. Their action had been shunted, transfused into every cell of every material in the room. Everything now moved like them while they remained motionless at its centre. The eye of its storm. Hector instinctively made for the door because he could feel his body trembling apart. Hedges broke out of his daze and rushed after him. They fell and slid on their buckling legs. They crawled, propelled by panic to within inches of the door while Hedges tried to control the metal flutter of keys in his jerky, undirected hands. Behind them they could hear things tearing apart, hear the grain in the wooden chairs chitter and splinter. Hear a tearing whimper, as if the torque of every atom was corkscrewed asunder. Hedges dropped the keys and Hector could taste blood in his mouth. The door was crying and warping in its frame. Hedges lurched back and then ran at it, his shoulder and head becoming a mindless battering ram. The thunderous collision cracked the door in two and dislocated the shouting man's arm. But he was out and so was Hector. Out into the soundless soup, which seemed to seal the portal like an air lock, the bubble of it smearing over the rattling room. They scrabbled through the corridors and collided with Roger, who was bringing food to Dick and Harry. He was nearly flattened by Hedges, who seized him up by one hand while his trolley went tumbling and spilling in the other direction.

"Open the door," he bellowed, pointing to his office with his other hand. Roger blinked red lashless eyes at him.

"Open the fucking door." He threw the shrivelled invalid down the corridor until he ended up kneeling and sobbing, trying to fit the key into the indifferent lock while Hedges roared, "Open it, open it, open it!" over his scared and bruised head.

Once inside, Hedges collapsed across his desk. Hector and Roger sat on the floor watching the great hulk of the doctor breathing painfully in unconscious dream. Hector crept across the floor on all fours to where the whisky bottle had rolled.

Nothing in his entire life had been like this day. And if he survived it, he considered his previously generous engagement fee now well earned. He uncapped the bottle and took a long hard swig. He sat back while the malted fire applauded in a peat eruption of well-being. He waved the bottle at Roger, who shook his head and hands and beamed a vast toothy smile at him from out of somewhere in his tear-stained face.

The orderlies arrived some time later and they were all taken off to the main hospital. Hedges on a stretcher, Roger and Hector limping behind, supported by strong arms.

At the end of twisting corridor things might have calmed down. The room might have relaxed back into its normal docile state and Dick and Harry might be sitting at the table waiting for their meal, which lay strewn across the floor outside. The discarded trolley standing over the broken plates and slowly cooling food like a large stupid metal dog, facing the wrong way. But nobody knew, and nobody cared to find out.

Roger was sent back to his dormitory after Hedges had found him and apologised for his offensive behaviour, blaming it on the severity of the phenomena in Dick and Harry's room. Roger sheepishly grinned and left. Hedges wandered about the wards, his arm in a sling and his head bandaged, until he found Schumann sitting in a cubicle of wheeled screens, making notes in a small pocket book.

"Professor, are you all right?"

"Yes, fine, thank you, just a few bumps and scratches. How are your arm and your head?"

"I'll live." He groaned and sat down next to Hector. "I don't really know what to say. Nothing like this has ever happened before; it's beyond my comprehension. I am so sorry that it occurred during your visit."

"But don't you think I instigated it?" asked Hector with great sincerity.

"I don't know what to think, it's beyond me."

"Now I understand why you kept them here."

"What else could I do? There was nowhere for them to go, and after what they have done for all the rest, I felt an obligation. We received great commendations for what we did here. Sometimes I fear we did nothing with our therapy. It was them that cleansed those men, and all we did was to send them back to their certain deaths."

"You really believe that, don't you? You believe that they have absorbed every wretched symptom and nightmare of your previous patients."

Hedges nodded his bandaged head in acquiescence, suddenly looking very small, and said quietly, "Good God, can you imagine how horrifying that would be, to live with that every day?"

"Yes, for a human being," said Hector quietly.

Back at his hotel in the Strand, Hector started to make his report in his head. How would he tell a dummkopf like Himmelstrup of the wonders and terrors that he had witnessed? How would he demonstrate the use of his mounting expenses? He scratched his woven head and a few strands fell backwards in relief. He pushed his papers and notebooks across the table and retrieved the letter that had been left for him in reception. He was relieved to see it had been hand-delivered and did not bear fatherland stamps.

Dear Professor Schumann,

I hope this catches you before your return home. I have just spoken to Duncan Hedges and he told me of your ordeal at the Royal Victoria. I do hope you are rested and recovered after such a traumatic encounter.

At the same time that you were at Spike Island, 126 (Nicholas Parson, or Tom, as I understand Hedges calls him) became very fretful and his condition started to deteriorate rapidly. I know that you must have had enough of all this by now, but these unusual events do seem to be linked to your enquiries in some inexplicable manner.

Nicholas was asking for you, saying that he must talk with you again and that you must not go. He became quite agitated and said that you must not go home.

I would not trouble you with these details if the situation had not become grave.

Shortly after this outburst, he went missing. I greatly fear that he might have buried himself again, and you know the size of our grounds, and even worse if he got outside them. We might never find him.

So if you do have both the time and the inclination before you return, please come and visit us again.

Yours most sincerely,
MELVIN BARRATT

Far from being put out or agitated at the request, Hector found that he had a muffled longing to see Nicholas Parson again and that this letter gave him the perfect reason. He had a pang of guilt about using it to prolong his trip, but he did now have some solid proof in his hand. Proof that he could demonstrate to the powers that sponsored him.

"Horrid," he thought to himself. Most horrid that Nicholas might be underground again. He did not worry in the same way that Barratt did, about his patient dying of asphyxiation. He was instead appalled by the idea of the interminable hibernation and all the forgetting of so much that the "young man" had achieved. It seemed an infinitely worse demise than the simple act of dying. He would go tomorrow after he postponed his passage home.

Hector settled in for the night. He remembered his last associated dreams and decided that he could do without one of those. He could also do without Compton and Himmelstrup nattering and sharpening their beaks on his attempts and rest. He asked room service for two very large gins, without ice. He planned to mix it with some of the hissing asthmatic hot water from his bathroom tap. Such a concoction would keep any dream at bay, and rampant nightmares would be extinguished by his breath, sent back to graze elsewhere.

CHAPTER TWENTY-ONE

*M*odesta was taken back to the church. She appeared to be in her early teens now. Already almost a young woman.

She held the hands of Timothy and Carmella and trusted their strangeness. Like the wells in Essenwald, a swelling was rising in her, a certainty where her womb should have been slowly growing. But that void was destined for something else. Now its little cavity hummed with pleasure. She knew the ceremony she was being taken to was the true generation of her life, and that the previous one had been no more than a sham rehearsal. The Vorrh would enter her now.

Timothy was very white and his skin was chilled and clammy. He held the flask of Vorrh water tight in one hand and held the other out towards her, his dense anthracite Bible squeezed under the wet pit of his arm. Carmella was more circumspect with her emotions and more resolute about the day. Now the child would receive the true water. As it had been foretold. She would guide this young priest towards his duty and away from wasteful speculation. His Jesus had no business here. The Jews never believed that the Nazarene was the Messiah, just another minor rabbi with delusions. Nothing compared to the prophets and saints of the old covenant. The water her child would now receive flowed long before half-mad wilderness visionaries dragged their struggling followers under their proclaimed streams of salvation. The blessing she would receive today was being administered centuries before a single word of the Septuagint was scrawled. They were in Timothy's church because it was a righteous place and it kept him engaged and driven.

Carmella had learned much under the constant tutelage of voices of the field and her home. They were everywhere now and she heard them day and night. She would sit among her goats or her tenacious crops grimly holding on to the parched soil. She would sit and listen while Modesta wandered the fields and the distant sea roared grey green, vast and high on her horizon. They had told her about the broken house, explained that it was not a site of infamy and crime but one of love and wonder. They had whispered about the sacred Irrinipeste who had lived there under the protection of the white man who had come from the corner of the earth. How she had been born in great Vorrh. And how the seed of her making had been taken from another white man, who made boxes to catch light and trap people in stillness forever. Carmella now understood why the child was a piebald and sometimes froze in a strange way between different points of motion. She also tried to understand all they had said about vanishings and arrivals and the angelic messenger that would one day come for them. To her great solace they had said that her god was also theirs and that the other gods had been allowed to help her because it was Africa.

When they gathered inside and reached the font, which of course was a model of a surrogate for a sacred well, the little priest dubiously poured the water from the flask into the receptacle inside the stone pedestal. He said his inappropriate words, daubed the teenager, and looked relieved that the roof was not ripped off and that his altar was not blown asunder. When they left the dense stone shade of the chapel, the light outside was blinding, the heat from the rough path of pale yellow gravel passing through the thin leather of their shoes. Modesta held her mother's hand as they walked home. Timothy stayed in the portal. As they reached a lumpy rise in the track, Modesta stopped and turned to look back, and Timothy saw something on her small brow where the water had been anointed. The exact spot where it had been splashed now shimmered bright blue. The same colour and intensity as the sky behind her. For a moment it looked like she had a hole in her head and he was seeing straight through it. He was shocked and horrified, and then she smiled, nodded at Carmella, and they walked away.

Timothy hoped and prayed that now the child was blessed, things might calm down. There had been no violent reaction to Lutchen's blessed water, so perhaps the old priest had been right all along. Modesta was not the spawn of the Devil—just some poltergeist-haunted orphan with an overactive thyroid. He tried to convince himself of this during the four days that he stayed away from the strange pair, busying himself with other matters of his neglected and now doubtful flock.

The voices had suddenly stopped speaking to Carmella, stopped the moment the water touched the child's head. At first she thought it was only a pause, a gap in the intimacy of their speech. Then she saw that Modesta was talking all the time, talking under her breath to herself. The old woman tried to hear what she was saying, but as soon as she got close or cocked her ears, the child stopped.

The first night without the voices was terrible for Carmella. She could not rest and was caught in a vise of expectation. Her mind and senses stretched, reaching out into the dark spaces, listening into every corner of her room, straining to hear in the cobwebs of her ceiling and the splintered gaps in her wooden floor. Then she heard them. Less than a shadow. Faint as the breath of birds but not in her room. The sound was coming from next door in the little room she had made for Modesta. They were talking in there. Talking to the girl. At first the old woman's response was relief that they had returned; then it chilled to disbelief, which curdled to envious outrage. These were her voices, they were what made her special, lifted her up from all others and the dirt of her dwelling. She now had wisdom and wanted more. It was unfair that the child had stolen them and kept them for herself. She entered Modesta's bedroom quickly and unannounced, expecting to feel the same vibration in the air. The same thrum of silence that the voices were always wrapped in. But it was not there. Instead there was a suction. A pulsing swallowing that moved towards the sleeping child. The words of the voices were riding on this and Carmella shivered at its oppositeness.

It was as if the girl were eating the words in her sleep. Chewing them out of the silent air into sound and then devouring them for herself alone. Carmella suddenly became aware that Modesta had never heard the voices before. Because she had never responded to them, even when they were speaking in the same room. They had only ever been for her. And now this. The girl had stolen and inverted them and changed their language, because the old woman could not understand a single word that was being spoken in this tiny room. The next morning she confronted Modesta, who stopped mumbling to herself and said nothing, her baleful eyes resolutely examining her breakfast. It was time for the lessons to begin. Timothy received a message from Carmella via one of his parishioners, who had been passing between the villages, that they were awaiting him. This was unheard of; the mad old woman spoke to nobody unless she was forced. To send a communication via another was beyond everything that he had come to understand about their relationship. And what did the message mean? Communion classes had been offered before and totally ignored. What demands were being asked of him now? Did they want him to teach her how to become a good Christian and a normal human being?

He found a picture book of stories from the Bible and a simplified common prayer. That would do to begin with. He put them in a small satchel and began his trudge across the fields. They were both waiting for him in the courtyard, surrounded by Carmella's fragrant livestock.

"I received your message and am here for the first lesson, which I do believe we should have had before."

He swung the satchel off his shoulder and walked forward into the glare of the child.

"Not here. In the chapel," she said and before he could protest she stepped up and took his hand and began their hot journey. To his displeasure and surprise the chapel was open, its old door unlocked. She pulled him inside and waited for his eyes to adjust. Some of the wood-and-string chairs had been moved, pushed back to make an open area of floor. The sandstone was glowing yellow with slatted sun and dust. A row of bottles, cups, and jars was in the middle of the waiting space, a bundle of twigs and a knife nearby.

"The first lesson is making the ink," she said. The words seeming to be chosen to become loud from a mass of others that stayed almost silent but agitated in her mouth.

"Lesson?" asked Timothy. "Whose lesson?"

"Your first lesson in writing."

"No." He almost laughed. "There is some mistake. I am here to teach you."

"What would you teach, little priest?"

He was about to tell her. Then she stared at him and he knew he was wrong.

"The first lesson is making the ink."

➤ *Part Three*

I am a robot, in a robot factory making other robots endlessly in the dark.

JAMES LEE BYARS

*I*shmael agreed to go back into the Vorrh. He had told Fleischer he could be ready in three days. He visited Sholeh again and told her of his decision, wanting approval, advice, and support, none of which he would get from Cyrena.

Sholeh listened carefully while his anger mounted his fears, and his hunger for destiny bled his comfort. Then she moved over him, clamping her perfect hand on his mouth and slithering her other hand into his waistband. His teeth hissed under her touch and his thick spiralled shaft swelled in her grip.

Nebsuel had told Sholeh that Ishmael was not of this time. That his lineage and empire had existed only in the old world. That he was a freak and a blessing. A being fallen out of time. Nebsuel had told her that he did not want to operate, to change the cyclops into a more acceptable creature. He had been given no choice. Sholeh had found this difficult to believe; she had seen the old sorcerer's cunning and wisdom, and it was difficult to believe that anybody could have made him act against his will. But she could not question him, because she would not dare and because he had two fingers in her mouth as he was speaking. He was massaging the sutures in her palate and gums, feeling for any errors in his handiwork, before he operated again.

"Ishmael forced me to make him look 'normal.' Not to correct an accident of birth, like you, my child, but to turn him into a different creature." He stopped when she winced, checking to see if it was pain at his touch or what he had just said. When he knew it was the former he continued. "He even brought a live eye for the counterfeit. A living eye that refused any form of decay and survived without sustenance. I wish I could have kept it and watched it, but he insisted on it being grafted onto his perfect face."

He took his hand out of her mouth and looked pleased. "He took the eye from one of the anthropophagi. It was a human eye. I later found out that an overseer from the slave house in Essenwald had gone missing in the Vorrh and that his body had never been discovered. There was a witness who claimed that it was taken by one of those creatures. It was near the place where Ishmael stumbled into a nest of them. How he survived that, I will never know."

"Why did you do it," she finally said.

"Because he threatened me with that bow. It was an unnatural thing with a vitality that nauseated me; literally its presence made me ill. It wasn't evil, but its strength was disgusting and in total opposition to everything in my home and my heart. Its magnetism even attracted an assassin here to slay a man inside this very threshold." He spat violently and muttered a blessing.

"So between the threat of the bow and the intrigue of the continually living eye, I acquiesced, and converted a myth into a man so he could wander into the common world. Where he is now and where you will go to see how he fares and comfort him as is necessary. You said you wanted to meet 'strange folk'—well, he is certainly one of those."

Now she was with the creature out of time and his strangeness excited her and it certainly excited him. The passion that flared between them was now channelled in her hands and she desperately wanted it inside her. Wanted to again feel this unique motion coil and entwine in her cunt. She stripped in seconds and mounted him, employing some caution against desire so that she might not be hurt by his initial and astonishing insertion.

For Ishmael, no woman had ever been like this. All who came before wilted into insignificance. Their hearts and bodies becoming pale impressions framed in weak embracings. There was a clasping fire in Sholeh and it seemed to match his own. It was not just magnitude or technique; it was a unique unquenchable radiance spoken in hunger. Totally different from other flames, as if gathered from another planet, another magma core. They rocked and plunged for hours, eventually falling into a sumptuous tiredness. A heavy-lidded and syrupy sleep that ignored all resistance. Their bodies entwined in fatigue, fallen in action. The now-hidden eager nucleus still continued to move. As if autonomous. Neither wanted the world time to break the power of this meeting. So when the cathedral clock chimed they both groaned silently as the room cracked and they began their slow disengagement of leaving. They dressed without words until both were part of elsewhere.

Fleischer and Urs waited at the station. They had recruited a band of nine others to go with them into the Vorrh. Six were police and the other three were passing mercenaries seeking employment. Oswald Macombo was an Ashanti from the Gold Coast, and he had never seen a horse until he arrived in Essenwald in the wake of the Possession wars. He had been called Hoss because of his size and the sleekness of his complexion. He was the engineer and train driver and his given name greatly suited his profession. He had been bribed to return, and brought his brother-in-law as the new fireman. It was Hoss who had been driving the train on that fateful day when the overseer Maclish disappeared and the Limboia vanished into the forest. He swore never to return, but he had to admit that it was good to hear the throb and hiss of the engine. Its absence in the northeast corner of the city had been felt like a drought. Bladelike wedges had been bolted onto the cattle irons to clear the fallen trees and overgrowth that were expected to block the track on the inner section, close to the lumber station where the forest was at its thickest. Chains, hooks, and saws had also been loaded to tackle the imagined obstacles.

A shrill blast of high-pressure steam announced the train's readiness. It also fanfared Ishmael's arrival on the platform. He unslung his rucksack to shake hands with his new comrades. It looked more like a hunting or safari party than a scouting mission to find the Limboia. Each man was equipped with a rifle and a sidearm. One had a Hotchkiss machine gun balanced across his shoulders.

"Are we expecting trouble?" asked Ishmael.

"Better to be safe and prepared. The Limboia have been in there for a long time. God knows what condition they are in," said Anton.

"And then there are other beasts," said Urs.

"Enough for a machine gun?"

The men all laughed.

"It's the forest itself you should fear," said Ishmael.

"Just in case . . ." Anton rummaged about in a green canvas kit bag and brought out a Webley revolver in its thick military holster. He offered it to Ishmael with a grin.

Ishmael swung his rucksack around, showing a highly polished black leather holster attached to its side.

"Just in case," he said.

"What is it?" said Urs.

Ishmael sprung the catch on the expensive container. He put the bag down and with the same movement withdrew the long elegant body of the semiautomatic pistol.

"It's a Steyr Mannlicher," said Ishmael.

"My God, how did you get one of those out here?" said Anton.

"Cyrena Lohr had it imported for me. A birthday present."

Before either of the men could comment or change their expressions from admiration into contempt, Ishmael pulled the slide back and cocked the pistol. The oiled steel sounded like reptile perfection. He knew what the men were thinking and decided to edit those thoughts here and now. He turned and stretched out his arm, pointing the gun down the platform towards the train and the band of men standing next to the coaches. Before anybody could violently object he swung the barrel up towards the tin roof of the station house. A family of yellow-tailed monkeys gambolled there under the shade of a low-hanging branch. The Mannlicher barked eight times and whipped the air, sending Anton and Urs leaping aside from their new companion. Brass cartridge cases tinkled on the boardwalk and blood-splattered fur slid down the galvanized roof, the animals' shrill voices locked still on their screeching tongues. Ishmael lowered the pistol. Its sleek breech was extended, locked open with the last shot. It looked like it had been gutted. A curl of lazy blue smoke arose from its empty interior. The shots were made over twenty metres. Made with an accuracy and conviction that stilled all questions and doubts. Such was the advantage of a marksman who had one perfectly trained eye and a gun that matched it.

The train growled out of the station. The fireman shovelled furiously and the engineer was allowing the power of the steam, steel, and fire to overcome his fears. His hand again on the reassurance of the hot, oiled throttle. Without its normal load of flatbed trucks, the train moved with new certainty. The first workforce carriage with SLAVES painted on its sides carried the armed men. The other five were empty and expectant of returning full. The upholstered mahogany carriage next to the guard's van carried Ishmael, Anton, and Urs. Their joint velocity rattled forward with a growing excitement. The Vorrh awaited, sucking at their approach.

The sleep overcame them quickly. Its irresistible weight increasing with the magnitude of trees. All except the engineer Hoss and his fireman were snoring and nodding with the motion of the carriages clacking over the iron rails. The two men at the front of the train worked furiously and watched the forever perspective of the rail for obstacles.

It was at dawn when Hoss saw some sort of group walk across the tracks. Bleary-eyed he did not even notice the first one being crunched under the engine's wheels. It was the third or the fourth that made an impression on his senses. He looked forward and saw their gathering. Hoss barked a command at his fireman and pushed the throttle back and strangled the steam escaping from the boiler. He grabbed at the brake and heaved it along its notched ratchet. The fireman fell backwards onto the coal, swearing and dropping his shovel. The wheels screamed against the rusted iron track. The engine tried to shake loose the carriage and Hoss diverted the angry steam to escape vents under the boiler. The scream trebled and the couplings punched and wrenched. The men in the carriages were thrown out of their sleep and into tangled fury. Some stood up as the train shuddered and jolted along the track.

Ishmael rolled and braced himself against the bunk. Anton and Urs were standing upright and vague like sleepwalkers; when the train violently stopped, Anton waved his arms about, trying to find something to grab on to, but was too late in his response and fell heavily against Urs, who absorbed the impact, sending him cannoning forward, to crack his head against the carriage door. It was a sickening sound. Neither man could reach him because they were holding on to their own anchored balance. Urs slid back onto the floor, his face covered in blood. He stopped moving minutes after the carriage was still.

The silence around the pulsing train was as tangible as ill-fitting wrapping paper.

The forest hushed and examined the intrusion and listened carefully to the small splintered sounds and groaning that came from the carriages as their occupants righted themselves.

Ishmael and Anton were examining Urs. Ishmael stood and watched as Anton knelt next to his friend and dabbed at his lacerated head. Urs remained unconscious. The wound was now stanched and no more blood flowed. Ishmael said, "I think he needs a doctor."

"We would have to go back, I think it might just be a nasty cut and he is dazed. Head wounds always bleed so much and look worse than they are. We need Wirth, he has some experience with first aid and field wounds. Would you mind fetching him here?"

Ishmael left the compartment and walked along the gravel track to the slave carriage.

"Mr. Wirth?" he called loudly.

There was a lot of slow moaning, then a sudden quick movement and a sharp response.

"Sergeant Wirth to you," the large white man said as he pushed through and jumped down to look at Ishmael, who shrank in his shadow. He was over six feet tall, broad and bull-chested. The four words he spoke were coloured purple by a thick Afrikaans. It was made darker by his brutalizing delivery; there was anger and dominance gating the words.

"We have a wounded man, would you please come and help?"

"Heinz," he barked into Ishmael's face without turning to look at the carriage, "get my medical bag, the one with the cross on it."

Heinz obeyed and brought the kit bag to the door. "Here," he said and hurled it down towards Wirth, who turned and caught it with one hand. His physicality, response, and reaction were impressive and Ishmael had received the full force. Wirth then glared back at the skinny freak who earlier had tried to impress him by firing a semiautomatic pistol at a target over his head.

"Why are you waiting, lead on."

He patched Urs's head, took his pulse, and looked carefully into his eyes.

"This man has a concussion, maybe a fracture."

"What can we do?" asked Anton.

"We? Nothing. He needs a hospital."

"Must he go back now? Could he stay on board for three more days until we are finished here? Concussions are not very serious, are they?"

Wirth left his patient and squared up to Anton.

"True, many men have concussions and get better in days. We don't know what is happening under his skull. There might be a hemorrhage, or worse. He needs an X-ray."

Anton looked anxious and disappointed. "Could it be fatal?" he asked.

"Yes, if he cones."

"Cones?" asked Anton cautiously.

Wirth narrowed his eyes and explained. "If there is an uncontrolled swelling, the brain is compressed. With nowhere to go, it takes the only route possible to expand." He looked into Fleischer's quivering eyes. "It comes down into the spine."

The carriage was silent. The distant heart of the waiting train seemed to be counting time, very far away.

"We must return now, immediately," said Anton in a very weak voice.

"There is another way," said Wirth.

Everybody turned to hear it. He waited and made Fleischer ask for it.

"We are one day from the lumber station, yes? The moment we arrive, we send the train back with only this carriage, the patient, and you. We use the other carriages as a base and go on to do our job. He leads." He pointed harshly at Ishmael.

Fleischer felt his world, his opportunity, fall away. He was to be sent back like a nursemaid, while Wirth and Ishmael stole the glory, or the whole thing would be postponed or called off. They had started the expedition very near the beginning of the rainy season. He would have to wait months to get another chance. He had no choice. Anyway, it might be only a few days. He could deposit Urs, refuel the train, and head back in; by then they might have completed the work, and he could regain command and return triumphant with the Limboia locked in their hutches. His new plans were interrupted by a voice at the back of the room.

"Why me?" said Ishmael, who did not like the idea of entering the wretched forest with only a band of bullies and thugs for company.

"Simple. You've been here before. You survived for more than two weeks in there, without any damage. It's true, is it not, man?" said Wirth.

"Yes, but I was not alone."

"You are not alone now."

Some of the other men laughed and the matter was sealed.

"Anyway, you look like you've seen a bit of action."

Different laughter and Ishmael said nothing.

"We don't have time to waste," said Wirth, taking command.

Some of the men got off the train to clear the tracks, expecting to find the dismembered bodies of the Limboia. What they actually found changed their minds, so after a quick exchange, the train rolled on, dragging torn lumps of anthropophagi under its wheels until they were shredded off.

The lumber station was overgrown and chaotic. The piles of cut and unmoved trees had slumped and rotted. The station house was covered in ivy and other tenacious creepers. The trees happily sharing their parasitic lacework with the shelters of men. There was no sign of human life, but hordes of monkeys and flights of birds fled with the train's arrival. They quickly got the manually powered turntable working and shunted all the carriages except the one with the wounded Urs onto a siding. Wirth gathered the expedition together and brought them to the edge of the jungle, where Ishmael was waiting.

"Now we can do some real work," he said.

Ishmael tuned into the conversation.

"Ready to receive your orders, *bwana*," Wirth said, grinning facetiously.

With a confidence that was unaccustomed to him, Ishmael began his instructions. First asking Wirth's advice on which men should stay behind with Fleischer and his wounded friend. They selected two of the policemen, because they had some basic knowledge of first aid, and ordered them to protect the two gentlemen and keep the train crew under control until they returned. They would leave a portion of medical supplies and rations with them. The rest of them would walk along the track until it divided, at which point the party would split and begin a more widespread search of the forest.

"How will we find our way back?" asked Wirth, courteous for the first time.

Ishmael produced a small sack and handed it to Wirth. "There is a compass and wristwatch for each man. Once we start to disperse we can move in circles using these in standard procedures." He looked at Wirth quizzically.

Wirth grinned and nodded. "We all know that mapping."

"Good, then we won't have to practise. I have also brought this," said Ishmael, and handed a larger sack to Wirth. It contained four cans of paint.

"Doing a bit of redecoration are we, in between the exploration?"

"The paint is fluorescent and we will mark the trees in our path, so on the return there'll be no mistakes, no one will get lost."

Wirth laughed out loud. "That's real clever, man, now I see why they brought you along."

Ishmael allowed himself to share Wirth's humour and the whole party joined in.

CHAPTER TWENTY-THREE

Sidrus watched. Their faces dissolved and shimmered in the hot metal tube of his telescope. They blurred and obscenely mated like pink Plasticine, being fluidly fused by the brightness of the sun. The heat in its brass barrel increasing during Sidrus's watching. He had been there when the train arrived. He had heard it from afar and sped to find a vantage point to see who was coming. He had climbed a tree and settled himself in the branches, his telescope trained on the bleached platform of the lumber station. He watched the men talking. He had followed the one giving the orders, watched him join the other. The leaders of this safari. There was something about the younger one with the scarred face. He could not be sure if it was him or not. His luck had never been this good. This was the first group of men he had seen since his transformation and his time in the Vorrh, and one of them looked like the wretch he had sworn to rip apart. The youth that Nebsuel had operated on. He who had witnessed his degradation and wicked infection. They would not be laughing for much longer. He was more alive than ever and the anticipation of his vengeance ached and fuelled his waking hours and the greased tempest of his dreams. Their memories would frizzle as he peeled off the thin pale covers of all their nerves. He saw the party split up, leaving the smaller number with the train at the lumber station. He climbed back down the tree and knew which he would massacre first. Their number and armaments meant nothing to his new growing power.

Before the whistle of the train drew him to this spot he had been travelling for weeks in his beloved forest without a single ill effect. He had gained strength and determination. His diet of fresh game, roots, and berries sustained his evolution into the growing disbelief of his own health and vigor. On the ninth day he stopped by a pool that flowed out from a rock. He was about to drink when he saw his reflection. He jumped back, startled, letting his horn beaker fall into the water. It took a long time for the ripples to subside. A time in which his whole reflection gradually came together, passing through all his previous ugliness with curved agitations of light. In the water mirror he looked like his brother, the one who was allowed to have offspring. All the sores were gone. The puffiness banished. The sun had cooked and stretched his pallor. He looked normal.

The next morning, while hacking the track before him, he felt a change of atmosphere . . . a tension in the air, and a part of him awoke to respond to it. An unfurling that was in no way disturbing. He stopped and looked around for signs of another. He stared through the screens of foliage that contained a million forms of life, seething and pushing their existence forward without a consideration for anything else. He admired nature, its relentless passion free of constraint or doubt. In many ways it ran close parallels to his own faith with its morality of righteous direction. And it was that which had now stopped him, looking around to find the cause of the eerie tugging. He stared through the trees and hanging vines. Before him was a low mound. A slumped form in a scarred enclosure. The trees here were different. They felt sentinelled and wary. He stepped cautiously forward, pushing between ancient trunks. The mound had been grown over by centuries of serpentine roots. Each writhing mass crawling over the other. So that now a lattice of live, dead, and fossilised tendrils described a tangled cage. The original shape of the mound had become a ghost, a negative of the thing that once stood there. Sidrus bent down to peer in through the woven cast. As his shiny new eyes wiggled deeper, he was overcome by a growing wonder. He circled the mass and found an entrance. There was a gully running into it on its farthest side. He sloughed off his pack and weapons belt and tried to crawl along the hollow into the interior. But he was too large. Whatever had occupied it was a leaner smaller creature of man. He decided at least he might look inside. It was the breadth of his shoulders that prevented him, not the size of his head. So he wormed down again, shuffling sideward.

He managed to get three-quarters of his head inside the space. It was a perfectly protected habitation. Incredibly shrunk from its original structure, which must have been rectangular. The smell inside was distinctly simian. The earth looked tired and unraked, as if it had not been disturbed for months or possibly years. Whatever had lived here was long since gone. He was enjoying musing over these mysteries, and the sunlight that waffled through the interlaced roots was gentle and divided from its glare. He let his muscles relax and turned his head to see more of this original dwelling. Near his face were traces of white hair, long and thin, looking more like it had been plucked from the beard of a biblical prophet than the arse of a scratching baboon. Even the birdsong was filtered by the roots. Perhaps something in the continually moving nutrients had sucked the immediacy out of their raucous calls, making them sound faint, gentle, and distant. He turned his head again so that his chin scraped the ground. It turned over a small sliver of bark, or was it leather?

Then he smelt it. Cinnamon and seashells. It did not bother with his frontal lobes, but leaped and bolted itself to the old brain, the reptile mind. Charging up the limbic system, like the hurtling rings of Saturn. He forced himself to lie still and to not become agitated. However wonderful this place was, he did not want to be stuck here. He focused on the scrap again and forcefully sniffed more deeply. Erstwhile. They had been here, but this dwelling had not been made by them; they were incapable of such things. Here they were the intruders. They had been living in holes in the ground and the hollows of trees and now here was direct proof that they had cuckooed somebody else's dwelling. They were breaking more and more sacred rules each year of each century.

Some had tried to mate with humans; some were thought to have escaped and even left the continent. Some had returned, which was the worst situation of all, because they would carry their contamination by humans to the very heart of the forest. Such beings must be stopped and destroyed. This was not work for normal men. A stern and ruthless resolution was needed to burn what had been God's own angels. Most men knew nothing of this.

In Essenwald only he and Lutchen had the knowledge and the courage for such an act. They had little in common and shared nothing but distaste for each other's spiritual views. But those were as niceties compared to the matter-of-fact wrongness of the Erstwhile moving in and out of the forest at will. A panic-stricken young priest had discovered two Erstwhile worrying the Chapel of the Desert Fathers. They had been drawn to it and the pictures that hung within. They were renegades. Reawoken ones who had slept too deeply, where they had knitted together wisps and dregs of dreams. Dreams of becoming angels again—or worse, men. He and Lutchen had trapped them and burnt them alive, raking the twitching remains to ashes. Then he remembered the wake. He had experienced it only once before that prolonged night. The very few Erstwhile that left the

Vorrh did so by shedding their visibility. They did this by temporal division. Somehow they separated their visual reference from their corporeal existence, stretched it backwards behind them. So that the Erstwhile in the chapel that night could touch and move things without being seen. A long, strung-out part of their visible form would arrive hours later and be totally indifferent to circumstances and the effect they would have on mere mortals. When the visible part arrived in the growing shock of the demise of conscious self it was called "a wake." The novice had been sent away. It was he and Lutchen who had to await the hideous vision. They were compulsory witnesses and eyelids or blindfolds would not keep them out. He shuddered in the peaceful hutch and saw a fragment of the tidal wave that previously charged through his head. He tried not to smell again and began edging himself back out of the hollow. He sat outside in the violent light, questioning what all this meant and how it fitted together. Erstwhile do not live in enclosures. The thing that dwelt here must have brought that scrap. But for what purpose?

This was not a good place for fires, so after he had constructed his bed he sat in the twilight, chewing on a rind of dried meat. As the sun vanished, the trees and the ground held their luminosity for a few seconds and it seemed to coalesce inside the nest of roots, and for a moment he saw its previous dimensions. It was as if the interior had never been seen before, and now that it had been disturbed it sent a vibration or a charge along his enquiring, into his sight, ramming through his optic nerve, straight into his gaping brain. He was overpowered by the knowledge of what this was and it sent him reeling. The tough meat stopped being chewed and sat stiff in his watery nonmoving mouth. The form that once occupied this place was manmade. It was the first form ever created by God's tool on earth: the human hand. It had once been Adam's house in paradise.

He prayed for the rest of the day, thanking his savage God for this earthshaking sign. The confirmation of his transformation, his revenge, and the rest of his implacable life.

He took his tinctures before he slept. Putting three drops of the rigidly framed chemicals into each eye. These were not for sleep but to fire up the demons under his need of sleeping, which he always saw as a waste of time. He knew that he would not be alone in his sleep, that the Vorrh watched him and took his pulse, smelt his breath and fingered the blood in his brain. There was no fighting it, so he gave up to its omnipresence, allowing himself to become porous to its need.

Others came to him that night. Not with the usual wrath and baiting. The blistering sleep that he found so useful was shuttered out and its reverse was sluiced in. A sluggish torpor of exotic fathomless space, that smelt of spice and the ocean. They came out of the forest, from under the fallen leaves and earth. Out of the sloth camouflage of the canopy. Their slowness moved at exactly the same pace as his drenched mind, so they were entirely invisible. They whispered inside his dream. The first human words they had manufactured in a very long time. They told him of an awakening in the forest. They were being given purpose again, but not from God. The forest itself was reviving them so that they might communicate with the ones that had left. The Erstwhile that had buried themselves in the world of the Rumour and who now were called men. A great threat was moving towards Africa, a war, one that would annihilate the Vorrh without a thought.

After many hours his body moved wormlike across the rough ground. Eyes shut, it slipped and wriggled back into the root enclosure. He slid into the enclosure with great ease, his wide shoulders now folded or shrunken. He was scratching the earthen floor inside with great purpose. They sat or lay around outside, watching him through the entwined roots, feeling the rousing that listened to them so carefully. It was finished, and a heavy cloud of dust blanketed their view of him inside. He crawled back out and into his sleep, which sealed the moment forever. Williams would soon be sloughing this creature and emerging.

The next day he continued south, charged and blissfully unaware that the Erstwhile had licked at the seam of the other inside him. Char's words were being spoken in the deaf, densely packed parts of his flesh that did not totally belong to him. Williams, the first Bowman, the former enemy, stirred in his torturer's body, and Sidrus's mind would never find him hiding there. Sidrus was locked on his future and the journey through this place of benediction. His left hand hurt this morning. It had from waking, when he found his fingernails were broken and covered in earth. He had cleaned it in some cool refreshing grasses that grew nearby, but the ache continued and confused him. He put it down to bad dreams and nervous scratching where he lay. He did not look inside the enclosure that he so greatly admired. He did not see the script written across the entire floor. He heard a train in the distance and he sheathed his machete and gathered speed.

The path led to the tree Sidrus had climbed to watch the train arrive. Now he had them. He watched Ishmael's party disappear into the other side of forest and then moved in closer to watch those who had been left behind.

Hours later the train workers were cutting wood for the engine when he heard Fleischer shouting; by the time he got to the carriage the expedition leader was silent and punching out the wooden slates of the compartment windows.

"Urs is dead," he said to one of the policemen who had been left with him. "Urs is dead and we aren't going anywhere."

As the darkness began to slide out of the trees, one of the policemen broached the subject of defence. Fleischer was too doomed in his own grief and disappointment to understand what the man was saying.

"We had better occupy one of the carriages or the lumber hut before nightfall. So as to be contained and shuttered. We should also decide on a perimeter and make a rota for guards."

"What do you expect to attack us? The Limboia? We could just shoot them all here and save us this bother and expense."

The soldier refused to hear Fleischer's insults and said, "There are worse than the Limboia out here. There are animals and things that eat people."

Fleischer had of course heard the stories. He like every other Essenwaldian had grown up on them. Now for the first time he and three other men and the corpse of the only human being he had ever cared about, ever loved, were at the centre of those tales for at least the next three days.

"We will use the hut," he announced. "It will be easier to defend."

All the men began to move quickly to get the two-room hut habitable and secure.

"We can light a fire. There is a small grate in here. The chimney is clear, I can see daylight."

Hoss heard his master say this and shook his head. "It will attract things, tell them that we are here."

"What things, animals are scared of fire and it will get cold at night."

"Not all things here are animals, some might like fire," said Hoss.

"Just do what you are told," Fleischer demanded. After they

were finished with the hut, Hoss went back to the train to compress its cinder tray and pile dampish wood into its firebox. He had already filled its belly with water from the water tank that collected the rain above the hut. He had no intention of letting the train run cold. He wanted at least enough power to move them out of the lumber station in a hurry if needed. He heard Fleischer shouting again and came to see what was happening now. He was screaming at the policemen, who stood resolutely unimpressed. He was demanding that they help him carry Urs's body from the train to the hut. They refused point-blank.

Hoss stepped in.

"We can lock it in the compartment tonight and bury him in the morning."

"I am not burying Urs Tolgart in this godforsaken place. I am taking him back with the others when they arrive."

"But you cannot bring him into the house."

Fleischer was losing ground and he knew he dare not lose face with a black workman in front of the two policeman whose loyalty and firepower he desperately needed. So he nailed the compartment shut and made arrangements to construct a coffin in the morning.

Their first night in the hut was comparatively quiet, with only one shot fired up into the ceiling to scare away whatever was scratching and hammering on the roof at three a.m. After that, nothing moved or spoke until the riot of the dawn chorus. They came out of the hut into brilliant sun-filled rain. It appeared that all was under control until they discovered that Urs's body was no longer there.

CHAPTER TWENTY-FOUR

*T*he Mutter home was severely disturbed by Rowena's abduction. It had been three days since she was taken and no trace of her had been found. There was no explanation for the mistress's behaviour and it produced a cloak of blame that swamped the bewildered family. Frau Mutter cursed and tutted at such goings-on, misdirecting her emotions that flailed between the horror of a stolen babe and the harsh and unkind things that had been said to her daughter by Mistress Ghertrude, whose morals and trustworthiness she still doubted. Sigmund had said that the stupid woman refused to acknowledge poor Meta. Saying that she was lost and looking through her as if she were not there. "Seen right through," he said.

Frau Mutter hoped it was just malice or madness, because she knew that there were worse reasons for such selective blindness. And that innocence could be sucked invisibly by malign forces. When she was a child, she had been dragged to a small mud hamlet on the far side of the Vorrh. Her father needed employment and took the first shoddy job that was offered. She had seen things there that were outside of all good Christian understanding. She had seen things that touched her in the night and licked at her during the day. Invisible people stood free, famished, and filthy.

She had seen people fall sick and die or become insane under the spells of juju and the contempt of gris-gris.

If her poor daughter or Mistress Ghertrude had been infected or cursed by that, then no manner of prayer would save them. The baby might have been taken for sacrifice or worse. The creatures of the Vorrh might be released and follow the scent of shame to their door. She rattled about her kitchen and sobbed into her apron, and swore at her husband for being a fool and exposing little Meta to such a disaster.

Upstairs in his cramped bedroom Thaddeus scratched another day out of his thoughts and off the thin paper calendar that hung on his wall. The five moons of his father's allotted time were waning. If the matter-of-fact prophecy from the blue thing in the garden was true, then it might be next month. It was impossible to be sure about which part of the moon was being counted, let alone the consequences of its arrival. He feared the worst. Thaddeus was horrified that in such a short time he might become the head of the family. He also shrank under the burden of knowledge. He could tell no one. The insistent rhyme of his father's sentence was wedged in his head. All the paper-scratching and crossing-out, all the red-ringed dates could not muffle or relax the words from the paper strip that were ringing in his ears.

Meta sat in the kitchen, forlorn and uncomprehending. What had happened? How had her care become so lost in that house of approaching horrors? The pressure that bloomed up from under the stairs had had no face. It had sucked her consciousness out and left her faint and shivering on that terrible night. When she came to, Rowena was gone and all was calm. After Ghertrude arrived and her father told her to leave, she stopped on the way out. Stopped to look in the hall mirror to be sure that she was not invisible. Since then, her guilt had been growing in the place where she could not be seen; another her was being composed of the loss and the responsibility she felt for Rowena. A doppelgänger that continually stood opposite and confirmed all her anxieties and grinned into her fleeting moments of composure.

➡→

After Mutter had reported back to Ghertrude that he had again searched the house and the basement and found nothing, she sat for a long time staring into space. She heard Mutter locking the gate on his way home. She cast her hearing into every corner of the house, waiting for a sound to dare betray a movement. Eventually she stood up and walked downstairs like a somnambulist. Her tears had dried to painful grit in her eyes. She went to the hall stand where the coats and cloaks were hung, untouched, waiting for the approaching rainy season. Beneath them, like so many skeletal legs, was a collection of prized or abandoned walking sticks, canes, umbrellas, shooting sticks, and other walking aids and appendages. She rummaged among them, pushing the coats violently aside. One dislodged and fell like a dead gunnera leaf at her feet. She ignored it and continued to search with her snatching hands until she touched the cold steel. She withdrew a metre-long crowbar. She grabbed the keys from their secluded peg to the side of the cellar door and let herself in and went down.

She was in the birthing room and all had been cleaned away as if nothing that matched her memory had ever occurred there. She found a box and sat and waited. Eventually Luluwa appeared, and kept her distance near the far door. Seth and Aklia waited inside its escape.

"What have you done with her?" asked Ghertrude, with a mouth that was disconnected from her wrath and everything else.

"Do you mean to break us with that?" said Luluwa in the

oscillating flutter that Ghertrude had learned to trust. Her thin and perfect brown arm extended to point at the crowbar.

"Did you take her?" answered Ghertrude.

"She is safe and well."

Ghertrude arose, a great agitation spilling into her blood and running fast, in unison with the adrenaline, gushing.

"Where is she?" Her voice was broken and sounded like theirs. "Where is she?" Ferocious words, knifed out in advance of attack.

They suddenly moved with a speed she had never seen before. They were around her, equidistant, mantis sprung, ready to snatch with sudden force.

"I have said it. She is safe and well."

"Did you take her?"

Ghertrude was fighting herself and seeking a crevice to attack from. She knew she would not win this time. Every move or inflection she could produce would be parried by a strength beyond her rage. Even her sense of justice seemed to be threatened now. She had only maternal velocity and hurt on her side, and she knew they were blunt and imprecise weapons in this arena. So while she sped through her gear changes of tactics, emotion wallowed out, unedited and vulnerable.

"But you helped me with her birth, you were always on my side."

Seth spoke: "We were always on the side of the child, the side of right."

The tears were rising behind her words. "But she is mine."

"She is ours."

"I am her mother."

"And those who made us are her father," said Luluwa.

"As they were Ishmael's, who you stole," said Aklia.

The weight of meaning and the weight of the crowbar became one. Ghertrude let her arms fall with a sigh of defeat.

"What are you talking about? Rowena was sired during the carnival by Ishmael or one of the revelers I met there."

"No, she was not," said Seth.

Ghertrude was turning in a sluggish dizzy circle to see their faces as they spoke.

"But . . . but . . ."

"Rowena was instigated in your own bed by us while you slept."

The giddiness was turning to nausea.

"No, this can't be true." They moved closer, and she dropped the iron and held her belly. "Can't be tr—"

"We inseminated you a week before the carnival, and sealed your womb to protect the little one from other intrusions."

Ghertrude fainted in a slurred S, as if her strings had been cut. They caught her before she touched the ground and lifted her gently.

It looked like a careful giant spider climbing the stairs, her body being its centre, their legs stretching out, moving in unison, bearing her up to her bed on the second floor. The bed they all knew so well.

Ghertrude lay, staring at the ceiling. She would never sleep in that bed again. She had moved to the floor. She would never sleep. She was on her back because the carpet was wet from her lying on her side. Her swollen breasts had leaked through her clothing. The milk saturating the hungry, dusty pattern of the abstract woven garden. She wanted to smash the Kin into pieces, to spill and splatter their fluid minds and save Rowena from their evil plans. But it could not happen that way. Ghertrude would be lost forever. She must understand more. All she really understood was that it was her fault: for seducing Ishmael so long ago, for becoming pregnant, for leaving her child unprotected. The pain was unbearable. She wanted to cry or scream, but the crawling hollow ache had plugged and sandpapered away all her expressions of self. Those indulgences had been banished forever. Suicide had always been a fiction. A thought that had only ever been a quote in her head. Something for the underclasses, those weak in mind or purpose. Poor people and cowards. Now it sat on her heart like a warm toad. Cherishing the place as a natural habitat.

When Aklia brought her food, she bit her lip and clenched her fists.

"Is she far from here?" she asked.

"No, she is close and safe. If things go well you might see her again."

"When?"

"Later."

Aklia moved towards the door.

"Which one of you did it?" asked Ghertrude.

"Did what?"

"Fucked me when I was sleeping."

The word sounded strange on her lips and so close to the floor. She had never said it before. She had overheard it many times and never imagined that she would say it, and with so much spite. Aklia did not understand.

"Which one of you things made me pregnant?"

"Oh, I see what you mean. We all did." She looked at Ghertrude, tilted her head, and touched the filed ridge on her mouth.

"We took it in turns, I think you say."

A final chill entered her bones through the damp patch in the carpet. The toad became heavier and restless.

"Because we love you," said Aklia.

The toad flinched.

"W-w-what?"

"Because we were asked to gather our fluids together, to have them converted for you."

"But you raped me."

The Bakelite considered the word.

"No, we did not take you by force. We stroked and encouraged you, like we did when you were a child."

The toad shrank to a frog.

"When I was a child? What do you mean?" Ghertrude sat up, her spine hurting.

"We have known you all of your life. You are not supposed to remember."

Ghertrude Tulp stood up and said, "I don't understand."

"Dearest one, why do you think you were so attracted to this house? What did your parents say about it? Why were they so understanding about you moving in 'alone'?"

A tadpole of guilt fell from her heart.

"My father," she said.

"Yes, and your grandfather. The Tulps have, like others in the guild, been our friends for decades. This city is founded on our coexistence."

All the triumph of Ghertrude's young life drained. Her ownership of Kühler Brunnen was diminished. When anger turns through all the degrees, when it changes direction, it often doubles in strength and purpose. She gave an involuntary smile to Aklia as her rage contorted towards her father.

"How did I forget you before? How did I forget so much?"

Aklia crossed the room, looked into her eyes, and held out a hand. Ghertrude accepted it and was reassured by the cool hardness. They walked out onto the landing hand in hand. It was quiet and meaningless there. They sat together on the stairs.

"Below us is an ancient well. It is directly connected to the Vorrh. The water is deep underground where no man can touch it. It has properties of absence," said Aklia with a pressure that felt like pride.

"You fed the water to me?"

"Fed, no. You must not drink it. That was the mistake we made with the others."

"What others?"

"The wrong ones."

"What wrong ones?"

"The Verloren. The ones you call the Limboia."

CHAPTER TWENTY-FIVE

Schumann was seated on the vast wooden bench. This time there would be no mistakes, the professor had demanded to be collected by Barratt, and only Barratt, from his unannounced arrival in reception. The scruffy doctor shook Hector's small hand with far too much vigour.

"May we start in the room of patient 126, please?"

"Yes, yes, of course, Professor, this way, please," stammered Barratt.

The long barrel of the upper corridor dived into the same impossible perspective as before. They hurried along its length, Hector sometimes slowing for breath and almost losing the hectic doctor. Various patients approached them, telling questions and asking answers. The Cat Man waved at them and Hector stopped.

"How are you, Mister . . . er—"

"Wain," interceded Barratt.

"Yes, Mr. Wain, how is the painting coming on?"

The Cat Man leaned forward until their noses were almost touching. He was the same size as Hector and equally dapper, or had been. He had an angular, sharply carved face with slanting, soft, and deeply melancholic eyes. Hector wondered if he too might be Jewish. The curve in his face ran vertically, arcing his forehead and chin away from his dipping nose. His finely trimmed moustache extended beyond the contours of his lean jaw. Hector wondered if he thought of it as whiskers.

"Very spiky," he said. "Do attend."

Barratt looked confused at their change of direction but made no complaint about going to see the new pictures. There were three very bright recent works propped up before Wain's bed, so that he might watch them before he slept.

"Umm," said Hector stroking his chin. "Spiky indeed."

The three portraits veered from almost normal to a jagged owl-eyed beast, whose pattern ruffled and surged in repeating geometric screams of energy. As if the cat's contours had become alive and split into linked and ever-repeating symmetrical inkblots of themselves. In another time they would be called fractal. The colours were wild and ferocious, radiating out in electric, acid shock waves.

"Fierce beings," said Hector.

"He has the eye," said Wain, speaking to the cat, then turning back to Hector. "You came before, came to attend with Nicholas."

"That's right. Have you seen him today?"

The Cat Man tugged at his whiskers. "Tricky question," he said, and picked up a piece of paper. "Come back later."

The bleak little room seemed twice as empty when Hector projected the beaming absent Nicholas into its narrow stillness. Everything was just the same. Abysmally institutional except for the radio and headphones.

"Where does he keep his picture, the one you told me about? Blake?"

They searched everywhere. There was no trace of it.

"Does this mean he took it with him?" asked Barratt.

"I have no idea, Doctor, he is your patient, but you told me it was his only prized possession."

Barratt looked put out. "Yes it was, that and the radio."

Barratt crossed the room and started looking under the crystal set to see if it might be there. He stopped and slowly put his head to the radio. Then to the earphones.

"It's on," he said, "it's still on."

"What is it?" said Hector, not really believing that this irritating toy could be of any consequence.

"I don't know," said Barratt. "It's a voice. I think it's in German." He held out the skeletal metal clip as though it were an unknown and suspicious new form of life. Hector took it and carefully put it to his ear, cautious of his previous experience. He then frowned and started to listen more carefully. The tinny voice inside was shouting from a long way off. Hector's face changed. Barratt saw it and did not understand. The old man's eyes no longer registered his presence. He was totally alone, falling inwards towards damnation. Barratt had seen such a thing only twice before. Seen it on the wards. It was realisation. Realisation stripped of all the protective coatings of illusion. Realisation that indeed the tragically inflicted man was mad. A lightning flash of sight, a hideous total reflection of himself. A glimpse of a horrifying future to torture him through the unchanging years ahead. Hector sat on the bed and dropped the headphones to the floor.

"Professor Schumann. Professor Schumann, what is it? May I help?"

Hector shook his head and understood one reason why the gentle Nicholas did not want him to go home.

"I need some fresh air, may we go outside?"

"Of course, sir, may I help?" Barratt gave Hector his arm and they walked into the corridor.

"You know, it is my fate to always leave that room so, last time in a wheelchair, and now this." He half smiled as they descended the back stair past the burly guard, who touched his cap as they passed. They were now in what had been the airing yard of the incurables. The one directly under Nicholas's window. The grass was unkempt and ragged. A few bed frames leant against the brick wall. Schumann took several deep breaths.

"What was it that you heard, Professor?"

Hector swallowed and eventually said, "It was from the fatherland. The ravings of a tyrant."

"Ah! I have read something of your new politics."

Hector gave him a look that sealed the doctor's next jocular sentence and waved his hand, signalling that he could say nothing.

"I am sorry, please . . . but."

"It's all right, Professor, forgive my inquisitiveness."

Hector straightened and said, "Enough of this, now we will find him." He took another deep breath and called with all his might. "Nicholas, I am still here."

The effort seemed to empty the little man and he sat down awkwardly on the rough patchy grass. Neither man spoke, and they enjoyed the moist cool air.

A small sound mewed from above. A slight chiseled face was at Nicholas's window.

"Meow," it said, "meow, meow, meow."

Barratt smiled, craning his neck up towards Wain. Schumann was watching the breeze rippling the short scraggy grass. He suddenly moved forward, staring intently down.

Barratt turned to watch the old man, who was on all fours, moving like a crab across the yard.

"Professor?"

"Come quickly, look at this."

The doctor trotted to stand over his guest, who he thought

might be becoming his patient. Then he saw it. The rippling pattern fingering through the grass. It moved as if it were the only thing there. "Meow, meow, meow," still echoed from above. The eyes stared out from the leaves; they were the leaves. Patterns of force rippled out from them.

"It's Wain's cat, the one in the painting," said Hector. "It looks like Wain's cat patterned in the grass. Follow it."

It may have only been a minute windstorm moving through the walled enclosure. It might have only been an accidental shudder that looked like the head of a demented beast, but both men believed it and followed it to the far corner of the garden. There it stopped and disappeared, and they started digging.

"Meow, meow, meow."

Four other stronger men had joined Barratt and Schumann in the yard. They had brought shovels and quickly found the sleeping man.

William Blake looked up from the shallow trench. The witness of angels. Poet, prophet, visionary, madman. Well, a picture of him did. Clasped in Nicholas's hands.

"Nicholas, Nicholas, come back, it is Hector. You wanted me to come and here I am, where are you?"

The picture of Blake moved in the stained hands, under the broken fingernails.

He was washed and clothed and allowed to walk back to his room. Hector stayed at his side throughout the process. Nicholas wanted it that way. Slowly they returned towards the green door together.

A bluish evening moved in, almost as if the quietened sun wanted to aid the approaching transaction, which Schumann felt in his bones might offer an answer or at least redefine the question. An un-fog-like mist came in from the Thames and mated with the vespertine light. The millions of bricks that defined, that contained the institution tried to absorb it, and some part of them did. To transubstantiate in the last rays of the sun setting on a world that would forget the depth of its yesterdays and strain only towards the limitations of its tomorrows. As they walked towards room 126, Schumann lightly mused that this time he might leave it on a stretcher. The first time was in a wheelchair, the second was with the support of Barratt. A stretcher would seem the next natural successor. Out of the whimsical speculation floated a truth that almost stopped him. The tall wavy-haired man in the dressing gown did stop. He looked down and showed concern through his beaming smile.

"Is something wrong, Professor?"

Schumann hesitated and then said, "No, Nicholas. Not wrong, but rather odd." He paused under Nicholas's suspended moment in the shade of his enquiry. "You really must call me Hector," he said.

"Hector, yes, I will."

Schumann patted his arranged hair and looked up at this strangest of all beings.

"It's just occurred to me that I am very well. Before I started this enquiry I was a sick old man getting over a stroke and believing that my life was slowly shutting down, and now? Now I have forgotten to think about my age, the aches and pains, the slowness. Over the last few weeks I have been too busy."

Nicholas beamed down, held Hector's arm, and as they started to walk again, said, "But that's good, Hector, the tide has changed."

Hector was just about to agree without really understanding when they turned the corner and almost bumped into Mr. Wain. He looked very serious, his sad eyes overly focused on Hector. He said nothing.

"Ah, Mr. Wain, I think we owe you a great thank-you for your help in finding our friend here."

Wain said nothing but trembled slightly. Then Hector saw his hands. They were bunched into tight white fists.

"Is something wrong?"

"You let him out," snapped Wain.

Nicholas let go of Hector's arm and moved across to stand at Wain's side. He towered over the concise man, who seemed knotted in barely controlled rage. Hector tried to placate the irate Cat Man.

"Do you mean that we found Nicholas? You know we had to. We had to get him out of the ground."

"You let him out."

"Yes, we had to."

"He is not yours."

Hector was perplexed and concerned about this man's furious retorts. He did not know what to say next. He looked at Nicholas, who, to his chagrin, was now looking down at him with the same stance of accusation, the same questioning disapproval.

"He's not yours, he's mine." Tears were in Wain's lost eyes and utter anguish was in his voice. What could he mean? Had he trespassed upon their friendship by wanting to save Nicholas? It certainly looked like this by the way they were standing together. How had this so quickly turned and why did Wain think that he owned Nicholas? A strange sensation was rising in Hector, an emotion that he had forgotten about years ago.

"Nicholas is my friend too, nobody owns him, Mr. Wain."

"I not talking about Nicholas," said Wain, his voice now hoarse and broken. "I am talking about Wilkie."

"Wilkie," said Hector. "Who is Wilkie?"

"The one you let out, the one that followed you into the yard."

All of Hector's previous waves of feeling were now confounded. They stayed still and stagnant, waiting for something sensible to bait them into action again. Nicholas shook his head and made tutting sounds towards Hector. But it was not bait enough. Bewilderment had swamped and flattened all.

"I don't understand," he said.

Nicholas stooped down and said, "He thinks that you let Wilkie out. That he escaped to follow you into the yard. He thinks you want him for yourself."

Hector snapped. "For God's sake, who is Wilkie?"

Wain took one step forward and pointed at Hector; at his nose. "The spiky one," he said.

Nicholas nodded again and both men stared at the accused.

The noises that eventually came out of Hector's mouth were a miscellany of nonverbal exclamations, intakes, and exhalations. Swallowing sounds, finally ending in an open and unexpected laugh.

"Are we talking about a cat?"

"My cat," said Wain, wiping tears from his eyes.

They all went into Wain's room, where Nicholas sat with his arm hugging the little man. For a moment Hector glimpsed a reflection of his previous flare of emotion. Again he was surprised at it. Jealousy or something like it had been obsolescent for years. He felt curiously exposed by it and hoped that nobody had noticed. The cats watched him. Smirking and growling at his predicament. The spiky one was nowhere to be seen.

Over the next few minutes Hector explained to Wain that he had no intention of taking his cat. And if it accidentally got out, then it had been a mistake and was never intentional. Wain did not allow himself to hear this explanation, which made Schumann lose his patience with the situation. The idea of a serious, heartfelt plea of innocence about an imaginary cat was beyond his normal tolerance. But these were not normal days.

They were quite different, and he preferred them. He had had a lifetime of normal days.

"It's getting late," said Nicholas, "they will be asking you to leave soon. We must go."

He very formally shook hands with Wain and waited for Hector to do the same. His hands were wet, not damp but wet, and Hector was convinced that he could smell the overpowering and distinctive smell of tomcats or at least their urine.

Hector was relieved to gain the bland sanctuary of Nicholas's room. He made himself comfortable in the only chair, while Nicholas sat on the bed. Occasionally Hector eyed the radio set with suspicion.

"Why did you bury yourself again, Nicholas?"

The tall man stretched out with his head cradled on his hands resting on the pillow.

"It was a deviation," he said.

"A deviation from what?"

"From what is written on the card."

Hector did not want his strange friend to start talking obscurities again. Did not want to get lost in his tangled references.

"Did you hear something on the radio?"

"I hear many things on and in it."

"Did you hear something that made you hide in the ground?"

"That's repetition," said Nicholas.

"Did you hear something about me?"

Nicholas sat up and made the same gesture of twisting his neck and snapping it back that Hector had witnessed once before. He then readjusted his pillow and sat more upright against it.

"Sometimes I just have to go back to get away from the time of Rumours. All the fast minutes become too much. All hurried and crowded together. It was easier when I was Tom. But I knew it was going to be this way, that's why I came."

"Where did you come from?" asked Schumann, knowing that he would not understand the answer.

"From under the Thames, I told you that before."

"No, Nicholas, I mean before that."

"Ah! I can't tell you that until you believe in me sleeping under the water."

"But that's impossible for me to believe."

"You sound just like my ol' man when he first found me. He had to be adjusted too."

"Go back, you say, like the tides changing." Hector held tight to what was left of his understanding. "You mean William Blake, he was your old man?"

"That it, guv, that's the feller." Nicholas was shifting voices again, playfully becoming cockney. "When I came out of the water his eyes nearly fell out, he just sat and gawped just like you now. Would you like to see it?"

"See?" said the confused Hector.

"I can let you for a bit, I can let you be there, be him if you're lucky." Nicholas sprang off the bed and stood behind his seated friend. "Do just what I say and nuffin else."

He took the professor's head in his hand and turned it quickly before Hector could complain.

"Close your eyes and keep them closed until I get into the underwater pose."

Hector did what he was told, because he had to. Something tugged at his eyes as he struggled to stay conscious, poised on the hard chair. He heard the bedsprings squeaking. Some serious activity was taking place in it and he refused to let those distant memories of his mother return now.

"I am ready, open your eyes when you hear the water."

Hector had enough sensible energy left to stop this nonsense before it went any further and was about to find the words when

Nicholas began making hissing and blowing noises pretending to be flowing water. "Ah! The Thames," Hector nearly said, but was stopped by the evolution of the sounds. They deepened and became massive and low. Real water. The sounds of a vast river. Hector opened his eyes and there it was before him. The broad expanse of the Thames at Lambeth, but without many of the buildings that now stood there. He was seated on scrubby turfs of grass that led down to a small shingle beach. Animal bones and oyster shells had been washed ashore there. He blinked and was back in the room. He closed his eyes tightly and saw the sheets of the bed moving. Someone was hiding beneath them and imitating the tides by moving back and forth. He opened his eyes again and was back on the foreshore staring at the water. He closed them again and saw Nicholas raise a hand above the billowing sheet, saw him push it upwards. He opened his eyes and saw the hand break the waves. There was somebody out there, somebody drowning. He looked around for help, but nobody else was there. He had to do something. He called out, "Swim, man, swim." He stood up and was shouting as the figure spluttered upright in the water.

Hector closed his eyes and saw Nicholas acting wildly on the creaking bed. He opened them and saw another Nicholas wade towards him, his arms outstretched like a pretend sleepwalker. He closed his eyes and saw the sheet on the floor of the bedroom, one end wrapped about the angel's feet as he staggered forward. The vision was bright and clean, but which was the vision? He did not want to block either of them out. He wanted to widen his sight and fight back any kind of blink. The effort was straining his eyes and the nervous blinking was totally disorientating and giddy.

The opposing flickering realities produced a juddering disconnected motion that looked like the frantic figures running inside a zoetrope. A tableau in a spinning wheel.

The mud-slithering man came towards him and embraced him desperately. Hector nearly fell off the chair while Blake steadied the wet man with his arms.

"You see, Hector, that's how it happened, that's how I met my ol' man."

Nicholas was grinning from ear to ear when he yanked Hector's head back into one world. He was laughing as he removed the knotted bedsheet from his ankles and returned to the bed, where he stretched out in mock exhaustion.

Hector said nothing because his voice was still searching for a connection to his brain, which was a surprisingly pleasant sensation. Apart from the slight sickness caused by his eyes being the shuttering gate between two worlds, the whole shocking event had given him a jolt of unattached joy, instead of fear or dread. It had all been so fast and so vivid that the wonder had not had time to be flooded and replaced by uncanny horror. He had been Blake or some kind of ghost or stand-in for him. His vision had been separated and sent back 133 years to meet the partially formed Nicholas. Surely it had been a dream or some form of hypnosis. He looked at his arms and clothing and felt a disappointment that they were dry and not cloyed in mud. He marvelled at his new capacity to experience the inexplicable so easily and wanted to taste more. To return to taste and see that time and that man again.

"Can I go there again?"

"Where?"

"To Lambeth with Blake, back then."

Nicholas turned over on the bed and said, "But that would be another deviation, you would become addicted."

"But I could understand so much more. I would have insight that nobody before ever—"

"Why are you here, Hector?" Nicholas interrupted in a voice that neither of them had heard before.

"Because you asked me to come."

"No, I don't mean that. Why are you in England?" This was a very different tone and one that it was uncomfortable to place. There was an edge of superiority in it, a conceit.

"I came here at the request of officers of my government to meet you."

"Yes, but why did you say yes to such a task?"

This was a question that he had continually asked himself, especially at the beginning of the venture. He did not expect to be questioned about it, especially by a creature he had just dug up and then shared an overwhelming out-of-body experience with. The strange thing was that he could not answer this elemental question, he could not think of a reason that made sense. All those motives and excuses he told himself were meaningless to anybody else. He was now without words, and the lies and delusions that form them. All he could think about saying was that he was there to be with him, and he knew it sounded weak and pathetic. He opened his hands and waved them as if to conduct all the things that he could not say. He looked for a response to his tongue-tied puppetry but got none, because Nicholas was asleep. Passed out after the vinegar sharpness of his last question. Hector watched the shallow breathing and wondered if it was possible for him to dream.

He sat there as it became dark. Various members of staff peered in, none of them asked him to leave. None of them said anything at all. He sat until only a yellow bar of illumination from the corridor and the weak rising stars over the airing yards entered the room. He sat and was spellbound about the peacefulness of the waiting. The only sounds were a very faint hiss from the radiator and the clock that sounded the quarter hours from some remote part of the hospital. Nicholas never stirred, never made any of those continual adjustments that sleepers make in their journey towards morning. Hector almost dozed in the quiet warmth. Eventually he decided that his vigil was worthless. Better to come back tomorrow when they were both less tired. He eased himself out of the chair and came to the side of the bed. He touched the radio. It was cold and did not have the vibration he had felt before. As he passed the window on his return he saw something move in the shadows below, by the wall. It was momentary and unusual. It seemed to flicker as if shimmering quickly to hide. His nose almost touched the glass, which he assumed was the logical source of the phenomenon. The thing he thought he saw in the airing yard looked like a tall curved tadpole or a diagram of a sperm. No! It was stranger than that, it was a pale comma, a living punctuation mark, the moment he grasped its identity it twisted out of his sight, leaving Hector to doubt if he had seen it at all.

Only a reflection, he said to himself as he crossed the room, stopping at the door to look at the sleeping Nicholas again. He seemed peaceful and unmoving. Hector left, closing the door quietly on another world.

He walked through the dark and quietening asylum. A male nurse met him and walked silently at his side down towards the entrance hall. Small light sounds of whimpers and sighs, sobs and breathing cobwebbed the air. Schumann looked at the nurse.

"It's always like this, sir, it's the time they remember their lives from before. It will be quiet by three a.m."

The great door was locked behind him and he took a deep reassuring breath. As he walked down the moonlit white steps into the sap-green darkness of the garden he became aware that he had forgotten something. Something important about Lambeth and the Thames. It had left a residue of sweet excitement in him, but he could not place its meaning or the contours of its image. The last taste of it had gone by the time he reached the gate to the road. He turned and looked back at the multiple windows of the hospital and imagined the sad and misplaced lives behind them. He thought of Nicholas and considered that his centuries of life might be true. He thought of all the years he had lived and slept. All the history that passed him by. He thought of the question that the angel had asked him and wondered if the comma he had seen hiding in the yard was in fact a question mark.

CHAPTER TWENTY-SIX

*F*ather Timothy was having trouble making a sugar ink. He had tried honey and rose water, but it became too sticky for the pen. He had used Demerara and rainwater, and it clogged the sentences. He was beginning to think that he might have to use a brush. He had discovered that preparation was everything. The rough sandstone floor was difficult to use. Its porous nature was good for absorbing the ink, but it also attracted dust, which was everywhere. Even after he had swept it twice, there was still a powdery yellow residue. He had had to get down on his hands and knees and use a sponge before he could polish it in preparation for the viscous words. The balance between keeping it clean and driving the messengers away was crucial. They were at home in the dust. It never stuck to them and their black legs glistened as they moved through all manner of obstacles. But the broom was violent to them, uncompromising in its attack. The first time he cleaned the floor he damaged many. Modesta saw his impatient brutishness and screamed. He hid in the makeshift vestry until she had repaired the damage, making a pile of the dead ones outside the chapel. The others would come and carry their injured black bodies away.

He was now afraid of her. There it is. Said. Out in the open. He was talking to the empty room and it listened, bemused and disinterested. Her insistence on teaching him how to write on the floor had seemed a mild inversion of their roles at the beginning, but three days into this pedantic and pointless labour he had been getting angry at her commands, which he did not understand why he was obeying. So he protested and let his temper spill. The moment it escaped she made a sign and spat at him. His venom trebled around her saliva and lashed his face like barbed wire. He fell back crying amid the jars of sugar water. He covered his face against further attack, and to his astonishment there was no blood. She grinned and beckoned him.

"Back to your lesson, you have a short time to learn this well."

He returned to his work and she ignored him until he had over-brushed the insects in the dust. After she had carried the mangled bodies outside she left and he felt safe enough to come out again. The floor and jars were as he left them and he picked up his broom again. Then he saw there was writing on the wall behind. A careful scrawl of charcoal on the yellow stone: *Don't hurt them or they will hurt you.*

Emphatic and to the point, more a warning than a threat, he hoped. He did not know she could write. Such a precocious child. Some would say abnormal. He put the broom down and picked up the polishing cloth. Twenty minutes later it was ready for the test. He collected his latest batch of ink and his new brush. He put one of the kneelers down and bent close to the ground. He wrote the letter "A" there with great solemnity. Then he used the kneeler as a cushion and sat back and waited. This concoction was sweet syrup mixed with a quarter-dram of the special water that Lutchen had sent from Essenwald. Nothing happened for a long while and he felt sleepy and lightly slumped against the wall, the yellow stone signing his sloth on the back of his threadbare cassock. He did not know how long he was "out," but when he looked at the invisible, sweet letter, he almost jumped. A perfect black "A" was formed there now. It had worked. He had found the right formula. He nearly danced, but heeded the recent warning and contained himself. He got down on all fours and crept across the floor like a cat stalking the "A." It was a tiny miracle. They did as predicted and relished the taste of his ink. They crowded into the brush mark, their feeding bodies compressed and busy. The girl had been right and he felt a pang of conscience about the damaged and dead ones that she had put outside, the ones he had crushed with the broom. The pang distilled into a molecule of guilt. All that he could squeeze out for an ant.

Soon an entire alphabet gleamed jet-black and twitching on the chapel floor and the girl was pleased—not with him, of course, that had become clearer and clearer. His position as her protector was now obsolete. The power that she could summon was vastly superior to anything he could muster. She was pleased with the feeding ants. It was midafternoon when Carmella joined them, by which time half the ants had gone, leaving an island of letters randomly broken on the dusty floor. Carmella had not spoken on any of her visits to the chapel to watch his labour. So he was surprised when she announced that it would soon be time to leave. The idea of which greatly excited him. He hoped they might quickly receive the sign he had been waiting for to leave his miserable village for once and for good. Surely that was what the ant writing was all about. Carmella then went on to say, "A seraphim will soon come to guide us, out towards the great forest."

She had obviously had another prophecy from the voices, because it was the only time she ever spoke with the authority of a biblical vocabulary.

"Seraphim?" he said.

"Our guide is to come from the highest rank of angels."

He smirked. He was standing by the small wooden pulpit in

the chapel when he heard a sound from above. He had not seen or heard Modesta climb its squeaking stairs. She was standing in its high enclosure.

"Come hither," she called to him, not a request but a demand. "Come and listen and become unblind, it is time to write again."

He shuffled closer and looked up at her. She lifted her hands in the same stop-motion as before and his stomach turned.

"All your life has been worthless until now, and now you must work to be born."

No one had ever spoken to him like this, let alone a girl. He wanted outrage, but found only truth. Anger, but found only fear.

"Well, little liar, now you have truth. What will you do?"

He almost felt like speaking, for the first time in years. He almost spoke to protect himself. A vanity of defence.

"Your tongue is as useless as your mouldering cordis. You have nothing of a man, so what you have to do is listen, write, and carry."

She stepped down out of the pulpit and crossed the room in a moment. She spoke again and each sound shaped itself in his brain, the words forming visually in a much larger space than he had ever perceived before. He saw the inside of his head increase with each word. Not crowded or bustling together like previous ideas but landscaped and floating in a cavernous hall waiting to be filled.

"Bring your ink but not the brushes, you won't be needing those. You will write in the caves beneath us. I will show you."

She held out her hand and he took it. They left the chapel and walked onto the stony road. She had put on a wide-brimmed hat not unlike his. They walked like opposite versions of the same thing through the sleepy village. Occasionally one of the pumpkins that sat warming on a first-floor wall would wink or adjust its viewpoint, the bald round heads of some of the villagers being indistinct from the swollen vegetables. Shutters twitched as they passed hand in hand. He was in a kind of daze. The satchel, which until now had never left his side or his sight, was still stuffed under a quiet stern pew, that forebode even the curiosity and hunger of mice. At the edge of the houses they took the winding path down into the wadi. Workers in the field lifted their gaze, saw the couple, and quickly looked back into the parched earth. Some crossed themselves. Juniper and figs gave way to cacti and thorns. They climbed out of the valley onto the cliff high above the great blue ocean. The stone here shone honey-gold and wheat-yellow against the muscular sky and water that braced against each other in brightness and hue. She took him out to the broken house and its overgrown garden where she had been buried. They pushed the desiccated beams aside in the shell of the second room.

She let go of his hand for the first time since the chapel, and he stumbled. As if missing his step in a dream, slipping on an imaginary change of plane. She scrabbled on the floor, pulling away all manner of broken shards, dead plants, and crusted earth. Beneath her hands was a pattern, an atrophied puddle of mud with tassels. She dragged hard on its rim, her small bunched fists looking like tense alabaster bespeckled with black granite. Her slender arms knotted, and as she pulled the trapdoor open, he watched the modest body under the thin smock tighten. He saw the budding of womanhood. There was a hollow sucking sound. Lungs that had not been used for a long time, desperate with their first breath. The wooden lid and sealed carpet fell back and she peered down into the resounding depth. She made a small squeal of delight, which dipped and spiralled and bounded back with the volume of the chasm between its obedient jaws. She held up her hand and he gripped it as she walked into the hole. The stairs here were immaculate. Not the rough-hewn slabs of the church but perfect symmetrical steps cut out of the living rock. No village craftsman had made these. Their proportion and elegance were from a very different time. The light came from below and glowed around the interior of the cave. As they stepped cautiously down, the sound of the perpetual sea arose to greet them. Midway, Timothy looked back up at the rectangle in the ceiling of the cathedral-like space. It seemed a long way off and the stairway that wound down gave little reassurance. For a moment, vertigo clutched at his guts and frosted his spine. The child felt it through his hand and tightened her grip. He winced back to her reality as the tiny vise with its hard nails compressed his concentration back into her service. They continued and turned onto another flight that passed through a low arch. This was no normal cave. They entered a stone chamber that was breathing. Rhythmic inhalations and exhalations filled its almost circular interior. A rectangular aperture was in the middle of the floor. It matched the aperture into the house high above.

The breathing was coming through the hole. A great water cave was below. As the sea drove in, its vast mass filling and displacing the space, the air was pushed in and sucked out of the narrow angular opening.

"This is where you write," she said. "You may sleep above until you are finished."

He was confused and disturbed by the simple command, and so replied with two simple questions.

"What do I write?"

"I will tell you that," she said.

"And what do I write with?"

She impishly grinned at him and realigned her grip on his hand so that she now held only one finger, which she shook vigorously, the knuckle clicking.

"With this, silly."

CHAPTER TWENTY-SEVEN

*I*shmael made his men spend the remaining daylight hours circling the known paths. The ones drawn on the faded map in the station house. They circled looking for tracks and signs and then returned to report. There was nothing, just a few exhausted traces of long-absent visitors and the fresh spoors of passing indifferent game. Everybody knew that they would not find the Limboia on their first haul. It was just a ritual exercise, limbering up for the deeper entrance at dawn tomorrow. Ishmael had his own tent. The one he was supposed to share with Anton and Urs. It was huge, with two separate chambers and an inclined entrance. He could stand up in it and spread his possessions around the folding furniture he had been given. Wirth's subordinates had erected it for him. This was their base camp and it would be guarded day and night.

He sat in the leaning stoop of his outer room with a glass of tepid gin and a cigar. The mixture of the tobacco and the pungent canvas made a reassuring enclosure. He was glad the other two had been left back with the train; this was a good space to have to oneself. He unfocused his eye, letting the cloth room flatten into a picture plane. This often happened when he relaxed. It first began in Nebsuel's house after the surgery. In convalescence he spent many hours pawing over the old wizard's collection of odd books. He greatly enjoyed looking at the prints of paintings.

Masterworks that fired his imagination and need. They entered his eye and his brain flat and clear, the way the rest of the world should have projected into it. He was certain that the confusion that all two-eyed humans had came from the division in their brain and bipolar complexity of their sight.

His thoughts drifted back to Sholeh, to the folds and firmness of her body. The curve of her back and the force of her hips. The clearness of her mind. The smoke rose in the still moist khaki air and he saw her scars arabesque with her fine long hair and wondered why he was in this forsaken forest rather than her bed. Outside, the reptiles and amphibians began to call to the stars as the shadows squeezed out from the trees and the overpowering darkness pulled the infinite through the intimate with ease.

He held the thin black silk scarf that she had given him. The one that she said Nebsuel had made from his own worms. Ishmael had it hidden deep in a pocket of his leather satchel. Away from the prying eyes of Cyrena. He never thought about her once. Such an intrusion would have irritated him. Then he remembered Nebsuel's gift and dug deep in the bag to retrieve the small leather pouch. He opened it with a blade and removed the brass tube, inside of which was a scroll. He took it to the brightest place in the fading light. The writing was tiny and cramped. At first he thought it was Persian or Phoenician; then he realised it was a tight old Saxon form of German. He drew the unrolled paper close to his face and read:

> *Ishmael, I write knowing that you have returned to the great Vorrh and that it was always your destiny to do so. We spoke much of its vastness, of the beings that dwell within, and of your longing to find your origins there. I more than anybody you have met or ever will meet understand your uniqueness, and you know how much I treasure it. I have*

already sent you warnings of the vicious hatred held against you by Sidrus. But this imminent danger is as nothing compared to the peril that awaits you if you increase your proximity to the Erstwhile. When we spoke of that desolate tribe before, I guarded knowledge of them to protect you and dissuade your curiosity. This was foolish because of course you will always confront your desires with fire. So now I say it clearly: Avoid every sign and presence of them. They are beginning to awaken. They who have been forsaken by God have been adopted by a greater, slower master. The forest itself. Over the centuries it has entered every vein, every follicle, and every pore of their rotting bodies, and now it runs through them like the endless chatter in humans. They are waking because the Vorrh feels a threat, far off and constant, a force that could wipe it away forever. It has known of this for centuries and now the actual time is approaching; it has been preparing, by changing its breathing, its denizens, and the Erstwhile. Some have already left, some are transforming, and all of them know of you. Your future in the forest cannot be spoken of and this is your last chance to develop your instinct and flee. Take the woman I sent you and go east to the lands of sea, where trees are nothing. Go to the great oceans, because water is the memory of the world and all the forests are its blind ambition.

It is two days since I penned the words above and I now know that I will see you again soon outside of that damned forest and that fleeing will never be your way. Go with courage, slyness, and passion, and survive to become unique again.

The first thin rain fell through the canopy, making a new sound in the Vorrh. At least new for that season. The team moved in a line. Machetes in hand. Ishmael and Wirth were the third and fourth in line and the only ones to travel abreast.

"So how did you receive the injuries?" asked Wirth.

Ishmael tilted his head, letting rain drip from the rim of his waterproof hat.

"In a conflict that I would rather forget," he lied, trying to seal off this oaf's intrusions.

"Was it in France?" Wirth asked.

Ishmael mumbled.

"I can't hear ya, man. Speak more clearly."

Wirth's southern African accent was grating in its confidence and infuriating in its narrow insistence. They moved through the forest cautiously.

A sudden rush and shrieking of animal life butted in. A flurry of creatures ran under the men's feet and sailed over their heads, sending leaves falling and grasses rattling. Creatures running from something scarier than men. Wirth stopped the line with one word: "Arm."

Everybody was stationary after they shouldered their firearms. Everybody listened and peered towards the trees from which the animals had run. Nothing moved except the last dislodged foliage, which floated down through their tension and the soft rain like a lazy fish. After a few moments, when the silence had slid back beneath the forest's noise, they continued, hacking their way forward and looking for tracks.

"What do you think it was?" asked Ishmael.

"Nothing, just animals, a leopard, maybe," said Wirth.

This was a better topic of conversation than the origin of his face, so Ishmael decided to keep it here. He wanted to find out more about this man.

"Have you travelled much in the bush, Sergeant Wirth?"

"I have spent some time in the Bruintjieshoogte and a little more in the Ituri in Zaire."

"Were you a hunter?"

"Some of the time."

Ishmael sensed there was an equal unease growing about his questions. Perhaps all stones about former lives were best left unturned here, he thought. "How far in do you think the Limboia might have gone?" he asked, shifting the subject.

"Christ knows where those weird bastards have gone."

"Will they have stayed together, do you think?"

Wirth wiped his face with the back of his hairy perspiring hand. "Fuck knows, man, did you ever see or work with them?"

"Not really," said Ishmael, hearing the feebleness in his voice.

"Weird bastards. Gave me the horrors. I knew Maclish, you know." He looked into Ishmael's face to see if he understood the name, then continued. "I first came through when he was recruiting for fellow overseers. Thought I'd give it a go for a while. It was good work, well paid. The only problem was being around them all day. They had a way of looking at you. You'd be standing there and they would ignore you. Look straight through. You got used to that. That wasn't the problem. Then all of a sudden you feel their eyes on you, turn around to find a bunch of them staring straight at you. Looking right inside. Made the flesh crawl. Some of 'em even grinning like fucking monkeys." He stopped to wipe his face again. "I had to take me whip or the butt of me gun to 'em. Knock their smirks and their eyes in another direction."

"Are they dangerous?"

"Fuck knows what they are. Only Maclish could control them."

"How did he do it?"

Wirth said nothing for a while and Ishmael wondered if he had heard the question.

"Drugs, I think," he suddenly said as if rehearsing the words. "Maclish and the doctor Hoffman often worked together. Thick as thieves they were, a secretive pair. I chucked up my job with them after the monster hunt they organised."

The pace ahead slowed as they entered a clearing. Wirth was canny enough to recognise need in his men.

"Okay, cigarette break!" he shouted.

They settled, some sitting on their packs and some on low, fallen logs. In seconds the air was tinted with reassuring tobacco smoke.

"Monster hunt?" said the excited Ishmael, fumbling with his cigar case and offering one to Wirth. They smoked for a while, waiting for the answer to come.

"We went into the Vorrh looking for a cyclops. Can you believe that?"

Ishmael said nothing.

"Some demented rich bitch paid them a shedload of money to go and find her lost boyfriend, who was some kind of one-eyed freak." Wirth chuckled and gobbed out ladles of cigar smoke. "Anyway we found one, we actually found this horrible fucking monster. Dragged it back screaming for the lady, we did. Man, the worst thing I've ever seen it was, yellow squat monster, no neck and a face and bollocks from your worst nightmare."

Wirth spat and looked at Ishmael to make sure the full force of the story was hitting home. It was.

"So we cart it back and hold it in a cell. It stank and shrieked all the fucking time. But this is the best bit. When lady muck and one of her toffee-nosed larney chums comes to pick up 'her friend' she goes nuts, they both do. I was just outside the room and heard all the screaming, crying, and shouting." Wirth started to chortle again. "Guess what . . . we got the wrong monster." He could barely compose himself. "Wrong fucking monster! Not her boyfriend but some other fucking horrible one-eyed freak."

Eventually he stopped, hissing and holding his side with the ache of mirth. He searched Ishmael's face for a trace of humour. Finding none, he groaned and relit his cigar, looking around at the others to see if they were ready to go.

"Did the woman find her friend?"

"What?"

"Did she find the 'freak' she was searching for?"

"Fuck knows. Who cares? That's not the point of the story."

"What is?"

"Forget it, if you don't get it, then you don't get it." Wirth stamped the cigar out and stood up, stretching his arms high over his head. "Okay, saddle up, let's go."

They all slumped their packs back on, took up their rifles, and pushed forward into the forest.

"Anyway, I chucked the job. We were promised a sweet bonus for that hunt and we never got it. Maclish and Hoffman kept it for themselves, I reckon. I reckon I earned it, smelling the stink of that yellow thing and putting up with all that bullshit."

The conversation was over and they trampled on unspeaking in the flickering humid light, until it started to fade.

While they were away Sidrus entered the camp. He easily slipped past the two remaining guards. He had watched them at dawn and ascertained which tent belonged to the man he hoped was his prey. He slit open its blind side and entered. He went through every possession and article of clothing. Purposely not replacing them in their original positions. He had the scent of this man and was convinced it was the same one. Then his hand touched the black silk of Sholeh's scarf. He sensed Nebsuel nearby. Knew his touch in the life of this rag. He thrust it into his pocket and pissed into the satchel where it had been so delicately hidden. He had him. He was as good as dead. His joy was so immense he thought he might bellow and alert the guards. So he stopped for a moment, grinned, and put on a comic gesture. Comedy had been rare in his previous life, so he savoured his pantomime even more. He tiptoed out of the tent, allowing himself the jest of playing the stage villain. Hands raised in an overly dramatic clawlike pose. He would have tweaked and curled his long black moustache if he had one.

CHAPTER TWENTY-EIGHT

*M*utter had been idly working in the stables when he saw the front door of 4 Kühler Brunnen open. He knew nobody was at home. His mistress had left to stay with Cyrena while her creepy man friend was playing safari in the Vorrh. His little Meta never came back here; there was no purpose and she now disliked the quiet in the house. The poor child just sat at home in gloomy recollection and uncertainty. So who opened the door? He understood the automatic latch that had been fitted, and he distrusted such contrivances. Perhaps it had gone wrong as he had continually predicted. Or it might be an intruder or the kidnapper returned to negotiate ransom. Or one of those who had scared his daughter. He would really like to get his hands on those.

He picked up the short-shafted axe from the woodpile and ploughed towards the door, a little bit of excitement in each approaching step. He would enjoy finding a villain or a thief inside. He would have the law on his side to sport in a bit of bruisery or bone breaking.

Mutter was one of those born without fear. He had never understood it. If something threatened or scared, it was always better to go and meet it. To walk into its domain quickly and choke its nerve before it had a chance to finish its sentence. It also helped having the genetically given physique of a rhinoceros. The only things that daunted him were authority and his wife, which were often the same thing. This had made him an excellent soldier, a good servant, and a man you always wanted in your tent, pissing out. He bounded up the front steps, his formidable weight carried on surprisingly agile feet. He spat his wet cigar stub out and entered the house.

"Who's here?" he bellowed. "Show yourselves or you'll be sorry."

He pushed the door closed and rattled the newfangled lock, which seemed to work fine.

Then he heard the Goedhart device play a single distinct ripple in the attic. He had not heard anything from there in years and he bounded up to catch the culprit.

The Goedhart device was a series of long piano wires set into the floor of the attic. Hanging above them and suspended by strings were a collection of heavy metal balls with a quill attached. When the pendulum was set in motion, the quill delicately plucked the strings, sending tingling unearthly vibrations playing under the eaves. He had heard the whole house shimmer under its eerie music. Even his old boiled boot of a heart had been affected by its plaintive rhythms. He was up the last flight on a wooden ladder that quaked and groaned under his weight. He squeezed through the narrow flap and was standing in the twilight-tinged room, axe in hand, seeking the fray.

The only movement was two languidly swinging pendulums at the far end of the tall pointed space, and dust and pollen motes gliding in silent beams of light.

"Who's here?" he barked, and his voice was felt by the piano strings that retuned it and sang it back. As its resonance faded away another voice could be heard in the sympathetic harmonies. He listened but it was very indistinct. He was making his way along the wall towards the skylight window that opened onto the cathedral square. He pulled the solid latch and pushed it open. A flurry of dozing pigeons exploded into the vertiginous air and bright heat flooded into the secret space. No intruder could hide now.

He barked again: "Come out or I'll skin ya."

Again his squawk was amplified and corrected, and this time he heard the residual voice with much greater clarity.

>——>

Meta had never heard the sounds that her father and brother had listened to. Not when she was in the house. But now she heard them in her body, speaking to her. The singsong voice of the strings said something different to those who listened for its after-voice. Mutter heard the importance of his son's journey. Thaddeus heard the directions of his pilgrimage. Meta heard Rowena calling to her. She left the house and walked towards the crying. It sounded like it was passing through water, but not the steaming rain that she was now walking through. It sounded underground, lonely, and imperative. The messages in the attic were slow and faint. Rowena's after-voice was fast and focused. Meta was soaked to the bone as she turned from one street into another, until she stood outside the gigantic warehouse where her brother had been only months ago. She put her ear to the small door in its vast double gate. It was an instinctive action. She knew that no wood or brick, no matter how thick, was between her and the calling. The door was locked, so she walked around the building. Her diminutive figure the only one moving outside in the rain. The warehouse was impregnable, high walls and locked gates on all sides. She stopped when she reached the refrigeration works, which was even bigger. A mountain of a building. She had never seen so many bricks. So many units piled immaculately towards the sky.

Extracted heat was vented from its rooftop, where it bred

with the weather in an unsettling way. It hurt her neck to stare so high for so long and the wonder wore out.

She walked back to the first gate and past it to the other side. The road narrowed and the walls became lower. Three-quarters of the way around there was a small house and a fenced wood. The gate was not locked. She ignored the house and entered the domestic forest. Meta was strongest here. Some of Mutter's fearless genes were in his daughter and she marched through the trees until they stopped at an ancient wall. Its surface was patterned in lichen, the delicate tracery covering every inch. She knew the warehouse was on the other side. She hitched her skirt up, tightened her belt, and examined the branches of the trees.

On the other side of the wall there was no lichen. Nothing of its kind grew there. Deeper in the shifting shadowed heart of the garden the fountain played. Meta dropped, catlike, from the overhanging branch to the ground and readjusted her dress. She ignored the organised beauty of the garden and followed the sound echoing in her blood towards a glass-panelled door into the warehouse. It was unlocked. She passed through it into a temporary office enclosure, which led into the vastness of the warehouse itself. The moment she entered its volume, Rowena's calling ceased and she felt the drop again. Not from the sturdy branch to the solid ground but inside. Her anticipation landing heavily onto her fear.

She listened for Rowena, movement, or voices. There was nothing, not even silence. She looked up through the stacked floors and wide stairs. She looked between the shelving and the numbered crates. The only other interior as large as this that she knew was the cathedral. But that was full of things: pictures and gold statues, chandeliers and incense.

Here there were only building and crates. She walked towards one of the staircases, passing an area framed by a wooden rail.

Something caught her eye in the umbrageous stillness. A dash of white. A crumpled piece of paper. She closed in on it and picked it up. It felt stiff and brittle with disuse. She looked around, then carefully unfolded it. She could not help the little sound she made. A kind of hiccup yelp escaped from her wide mouth and flew up between the stairs, balconies, and floors. Swallowed by the grateful emptiness.

The random faded words on the scrap of paper were about her family, her father. And the handwriting was that of her brother. She was utterly astonished. How could this be? Was the whole thing an elaborate trick? Then she remembered the stories of the crates. How her father had complained about the variations of size and weight. How one had hurt his back. It must have been this place that he frequently visited. Loading and unloading the cart, back and forth to Kühler Brunnen. A great wave of comfort swept through the cavernous building as she looked around again and saw her father everywhere. With fortified determination she opened some of her receivers that she had so purposefully closed before. She had locked them against the terrors of this place and the evil that had stolen Rowena. She closed her eyes and made the invitation inside the ventricles of her invisible organs of perception. There was no onslaught, just a gentle trickle of tellings.

She drifted towards the nearest stair and sat on its wide thick wood. There was something here with her. Something nearby and it wanted to help. She opened her eyes when she heard the whirring coming from above. A faint busy machine was moving up there. She turned and excitedly climbed the stairs, stopping on the landing of the first floor. It was higher. She climbed again. It was lighter on the third floor, a tall high metal-framed window flooding the stair and giving an unexpected view of this corner of the city. She saw where the river met the rail line and the low long timber mills that surrounded it.

She saw the station, where ant-size men lounged and drifted. She thought she saw steam or smoke rising from the siding. Or was it just another effect of the rain. Like that which was agitating the wooden floor from a skylight above. The rivulets of water that quickly ran across the glass had been amplified by the sun, casting thick pulsing snakes of shadow that squirmed and knotted across the floorboards. A filigree of emphasis tugged in her other sight, pulling her attention away from the projected serpents. There was movement in the shelves. An out-of-focus haze was shimmering in the distant stacks. Meta opened all her channels to perceive it. It was so like the good omens that often floated to her. No spite or malice tinged its vibration. It had none of the colourless hollow that came with the gripping dead. If anything, it seemed curious.

She closed down her senses and approached it with a hitherto unknown mixture of caution and excitement. The whirring sound of clockwork got louder. Whatever this was, it knew her father and maybe Thaddeus too. It might help find Rowena. Perhaps she was here, under its care. The haze had a bluish tinge that shifted and flowed with a greater insistence than the rain and sun of the window.

"Hello, I am Meta, daughter of Sigmund Mutter," she said in an almost confident voice.

A different series of mechanical gears seemed to be working from the other side of the shelves. It moved towards the end of the stack and turned the corner. It stuck its head around and peeped at her in a shy manner. She almost laughed. It had the face of the Little Mermaid, the one from her storybook when she was a child. The face gradually flushed pink, while it looked like the partially obscured part of its body remained blue. Just like the mermaid swimming in the book. The timid creature also had a bobbing motion that gave the impression of floating. The mermaid had always attracted and bothered

Meta. In shape and features it looked a lot like her. The wideness of the cheeks. The same far-apart, downward-slanting eyes, the same long straight nose crowned by a narrow brow and thick rich brown hair. It was what was behind the face that was different. The artist Dulac had made her full of sadness and it animated her every expression in an entirely different way than Meta's. Indeed it was only she who could see the likeness at all. The girl peeking around the shelves at her had another expression that was different again. The woefulness had given way to enquiry. Introspection to inquisitiveness. This being was very strange but not unknown, and Meta walked closer. The whirring became more intense. One of its delicate hands appeared and waved its long coy fingers at her. Meta raised her short, thick, work-reddened hand and waved back.

"What is your name?" Meta said.

The creature's eyes widened and she moved back a few inches as if taken by surprise, her hand slightly flexing. Meta smiled to have such an effect on a fabled and fantastic being.

"Do you live here?" Meta politely asked.

The mermaid raised one finger to her lips and then tapped and waved it there.

"Oh, you don't speak."

The mermaid nodded, without the expected sadness in her eyes. She then made another series of gestures, now with both hands. They were standing opposite each other and the eerie likeness was made stranger because the mermaid was constructed out of coalescing gas and some kind of unseen clockwork. She made the movement again and this time Meta thought she understood.

"Are you asking why I came here? What I want?"

The mermaid nodded.

"I am looking for a child, her name is Rowena."

There was no change of expression on the glowing face, but the sound of the gears shifted slightly.

"Is she here, have you seen or heard her?"

The creature shook its head, and as it did so, Meta thought she saw another face flicker inside the motion.

"I followed her calling to this building."

Again the little mermaid shook its head, more vigourously, and somebody else was definitely inside her face. Meta was becoming a little frustrated with the denials.

"You must have seen her. She is only a baby, a few months old. May I look around?" Before the creature reacted, she added, "I am sure my father would approve. If he were here he might even help."

This time the head was shaken with such force that it dislodged its cohesion, making a kind of jellied mass of the movement. The soulful face of the girl concertinaed, allowing other less attractive faces to peer through. With it there was a change of posture that made Meta start. The shy peeper had been replaced by the tension of something like a fierce dog. Meta stepped back.

"I am the child's nurse it's my responsib—"

And here she was cut short by a distinctly new head forming. She was more amazed than frightened. It was also from the book. The picture of the Merman King, an old bearded gentleman feeding two angry deep-sea fish. The kind you never eat or even see in the fish market. The girl's face was gone and the colour was changing. There was much whirring of heavier gears in the process. The face lengthened and started to bend towards the ancient worn features of the king, when suddenly it shrank, becoming tighter and unpleasant. Meta looked back the way she had come and was reassured to see the carpet of shadow snakes still writhing near the stairs. When she looked back the face was entirely fish. A bony wide-eyed thing all mouth and

voracity. She still could not fear it. None of her highly tuned
cavities were picking up malice or danger. Perhaps it was just
a game and soon the fish would turn back into the mermaid.
Then it thickened and became her father. Horror came from
somewhere she had never been before. She suddenly realized
why she was picking nothing up from it. It took on the shabby
dark appearance of his clothing, looking like swirling soot. The
face was bloated and cross. It had not touched her fine channels because it had no soul. None of the vibrations that all God's
creatures possessed, even the dead ones. Real fear engulfed her
and she turned and ran. She was just before the landing and
the stairs of escape when it hit. The fist of it punched and pum-
melled up into her skirt. Gas fingers went into her mouth and
nostrils and writhed inside her. She was hammered off her feet
and fell into the dashing shadow snakes, the light from the skylight flashing blindingly. It still had her father's shape and the
cruel illusion was so believable she could not help herself as it
probed and scurried inside her, seeking something that it did
not understand. Against all her sense the horror blurted out,
"No, Poppa, no, no."

It ceased her tongue and found under it the first enclave of
her other perception. It skewered into it, wrecking its invisible
lining. Now it had the taste and it plunged towards the same
scent everywhere inside her. The snorting head of her father
zebra-striped in the strobing light as it wallowed in the violence.
The black-boned night fish snapping inside its contours. It whistled through her brain, popping cysts and ventricles. The sound
of its impossible motors on hyperdrive, the teeth of their gears
screaming. It flipped her over and clawed towards her solar
plexus through her cervix and bowels. It found the core of her
psychic body and ripped it out from between her thrashing legs,
which seemed to be fighting off the snakes. It stood back gloating, black as sin and fat as paternity. The cogs had all reached a

similar frequency and it pitched back and forth sounding like mocking squealing laughter that even resembled Mutter's when he got nasty drunk.

The gas moved away back into the shadow and was gone. She crawled into an upright stance, teetering in the now-ugly light. She had just been gutted and her innocence and part of her soul torn out and stolen. Her normal body was intact, apart from some small bruises and splinters. She did not need to run. Nothing worse could happen to her now. So she slowly walked down the stairs towards the cramped door in the gate. Before she left she turned to look again within the still-waiting building. Gradually a noise arose, quietly at first, then growing outward and echoing above. The great emptiness choked on the sound of raw aggressive grating. It came from the diminutive figure by the door. Meta was grinding her teeth.

CHAPTER TWENTY-NINE

LONDON, 1925

*T*he next day Nicholas was back in his beaming chattering form. The sun was out and the hospital authorities decided it was a good enough reason to turn the community lunch into an alfresco affair. They had set up portable tables in the airing yard. There was a festive and bustling picnic nature to the day, totally opposite to last night's melancholic vision. Nicholas waved at him. He had been seated with his back to the very spot where Hector had seen his question mark.

A growing breeze was moving around the yard and the sunlit trees, causing them to sway in gentle agitation. There were ten at each table sitting on benches, five to a side. There were eight tables. Hector was pleased to see that Louis Wain was sitting at a different table. They did not speak, but he was aware that the Cat Man's cheerless baleful eyes watched him continually. There were bottles of weak beer and jugs of lemonade. The lunch itself consisted of plates of sandwiches. Everybody ate ferociously. The limp anemic flaps of bread were falling apart in the hasty fists, their unidentifiable contents falling onto the tablecloths. Hector nibbled at one of the delicacies and could not identify what he was eating. He peeled back the uneaten half and inspected it. A drab smear of something that may have once been fish stained the thin butter. Nicholas had a mouthful and was gobbling with pleasure.

"Good, good," he said.

"What is it?"

"Fish," said Nicholas, "fish without bones."

A large man with protruding eyes sat next to Hector, nodding his head in rapid agreement.

"It's fish paste!" he said with great enthusiasm, sending some of the said half-chewed paste flying out of his mouth in Hector's direction. He did not stop.

"They squash 'em flat, bones an' all. Squash 'em in a mangle thing, all flat, then scrape 'em into little pots, all neat and tight like, never goes off, lovely."

Schumann looked down at the thing in his hand.

"Don't ya wan' it?" said the large man.

"Eh! No, I think not."

A large pink hand engulfed the bread and paste and scooped it into his face.

Nicholas was watching with a difficult face—chewing a thought and the sandwich together.

"Last night did you go when I was sleeping?"

"Yes, Nicholas, I waited a while then left."

Nicholas chewed again. "Was I still visible then?"

Hector didn't understand. "Visible?" he said.

"We all have a lot of trouble with that, it's separated you see, only comes together in the final score, rest of the time it's a bit detached, needs nailing down."

Hector said nothing and just looked at Nicholas's chewing mouth.

"Did you see anything in the room or outside?" he said in what sounded like an absentminded tone.

The hairs on Schumann's neck prickled and a chill rose inside him. "What do you mean?"

Nicholas stopped chewing. "Did you see something? You did, didn't you?"

"What do you mean?"

"What do you mean?" replied Nicholas.

There was a lot of shouting, laughing, and chewing around the noisy interchange, but none of the boisterous sounds could touch the quietening listening air. Only the wind that now gusted the trees joined in the moment and became a herald of disquiet and inexplicable menace.

"Yes, I thought I saw something down here in this yard," he said.

Nicholas pointed over his shoulder. "Over there," he said.

"Yes."

"Good," said Nicholas.

"Was it your question, a sign of it?" asked Hector, realising that he was beginning to talk in the same obscurities as Nicholas.

Nicholas frowned and strained his eyes against the sun to look at Schumann more carefully.

"You saw a question, Hector, how can you do that?"

"You must have made it for me, a question mark drawn on the glass of the window so that it caught the light."

Nicholas's face stayed the same for a long time until it shook into hysterical laughter. He put one hand on his chest and guffawed. Falling about in his seat and infecting those around him, who joined in with the great mirth.

Hector sipped his warm beer and waited for the jollity to fade away. He knew something else waited behind the humour, waited behind his irritation and sudden unbearable loneliness. Nicholas finally let it go. And all those around him followed suit.

"Sorry, my friend Hector, what you said is such a funny idea. You get extra points for it. But it's absolute deviation from the subject."

A few giggles were still lubricating his earnestness. A small scrap of paste had stuck to his chin.

"The truth is that what you saw was real, it was over there." Again he pointed; this time he turned and stretched his arm out to indicate the back wall of the enclosed space. Some of the other patients at the table joined in.

"What you saw is what you look like to me." He grinned mightily at Schumann. "I don't see things like you. I have different eyes. I don't see all your body, face and hands, legs and arms and stuff. I know they are there, but I don't see them. Except for actors and people on the stage, like the great Madam Feinmann."

"Who?"

"Doesn't matter now," said Nicholas, lost in thought. "I was saying I don't see like you."

"What do you see?" said Hector in a shaky thin voice.

"Just the core, the real you. What you saw last night. Just the brain and spinal cord."

Hector could not speak.

"I only see that part of you all, and because I don't see the rest, it looks like it floats about in space. It's what you saw last night. That was the shy question mark you saw hiding in the garden."

Hector was clutching at straws, the tablecloth, and the wooden trellis beneath.

"Then how do you recognise us?"

Nicholas laughed again. "Because you are all different," he said with some surprise.

Schumann looked around him at the merriment among the crazed and broken lives, and for a second he saw it. Not the lost and overindulgent munching, shouting, and talking, but rows of floating white brains with pigtail spinal cords hanging down and shifting with movement. One was nodding in active approval of the conversation that its invisible body was having with the invisible body across the table. Hector twisted on his bench looking at all the tables. He spotted Wain nibbling a sandwich ratlike, clenched in both paws while intently watching him. He imagined only his brain straining and luminous with the effort. Imagined its folds sucking at the pink paste. He felt sick. The sandwich and the flat beer congealing with the smell of cats in his invisible stomach.

Nicholas continued his explanation in an almost careless manner.

"I can only understand your 'moods' by your voice and the little shifts of colour that you all have. It's the same for all of us." He paused for a moment. "I wanted you to see, to understand, that's why I showed you your reflection last night."

"My reflection?"

"Yes, Hector, I slept so you could see it. So you might understand."

"Yes," said Hector. To what or why he did not know.

"Now you don't have to go back and be burnt with all those innocent others."

This seemed to make Nicholas's day. He clapped his hands together in glee and very soon everybody except Wain was clapping their hands in a ramshackle applause. Nicholas excitedly pointed to Hector's neighbour, the man with the protruding eyes.

"Hector, this is Hymie. He has a large family in London, they will help you stay here for the next twenty years."

Dazed, incongruous, and partly believing, Schumann said, "I will be more than ninety then."

Nicholas stood up, clapped his hands again, and said, "Yes, you told me you were feeling better. Your tide has turned."

Hymie grabbed his hand and shook it enthusiastically, helping him to stand.

All the other picnickers stood up and applauded.

———

Hector had been following Nicholas the Erstwhile on his daily visits around the wards of the hospital and for the first time was taking some pleasure in the oddness of its cast.

"How many others are there like you?"

"None," said Nicholas, stopping sharply and glaring down at the ridiculousness of the question. "None. I am unique."

A sudden thin line of sweat glistened on his upper lip. This made the old man wary of his next question, so he sidestepped it. The truth was that Hector had been compiling a series of questions to ask, back in his hotel room in the Strand. He had learned them by heart even though he had brought the list with him. Just in case. They were a sequence of interlocking keys that he thought would reveal the many different stratifications of this strange creature. He now doubted that he would ever tell anybody in Germany exactly what he had found.

"Yes, of course I know that, but you said that I may ask you anything."

"True, but not the obvious."

"Are there many that came out of the forest that you told me about? Apart from those I have met?"

"And they are nothing like me."

"Of course not. I was just—"

"Asking the wrong question?" insisted Nicholas while turning his head away and looking around for a better conversation. Hector was becoming peeved with the rigidity of his arrogance.

"Let me put it another way."

Nicholas spat out a loud and discordant laugh. "That's what all you Rumour think about. Putting it in, in another way. Night and day. Putting it in and taking it out. It's better in here, of course, and better with the old ones, but out there it fills the air and blocks all rapture."

Nicholas was becoming upset and Schumann did not really understand why.

"You Rumour are worse than the animals. They don't plan the action of their carcass, you think of nothing else. Even my ol' man got obsessed before his wisdom."

"Why are you calling me a Rumour?"

"Because that's what you are! It's what you were always meant to be!"

He was shouting now and bunching his fists. The speed of his change of personality had been triggered by one question. All Hector's other questions shrivelled and fled to join the folded sheet of paper deep in the sanctuary of his overcoat pocket. Some of the other patients were also becoming excited and Hector inadvertently scanned the windows in the large dayroom for signs of a guard or nurse. Nicholas saw this and it made things worse.

"Are you wanting to go? Seeking escape? Running away?"

"No, Nicholas, I was just looking around because you have changed so and you make me nervous with what you are saying."

"I am saying the truth to the questions you wait to ask. The questions about the tree."

"Tree?"

"Yes, ask it."

Hector was totally lost. He had no idea what they were now talking about.

"You will never get the answer right. No Rumour can, except my ol' man. In the end he understood and made a great plural of it. But I had to tell him and now I will have to tell you. The answer is trees."

The expression on Hector's face in some way defused all the Erstwhile's anger and frustration. He bent double to look deep into the little man's eyes and then exploded in a great bellow of softening laughter. He clapped his hands on both of Hector's upper arms and lifted him as if he were made of paper. Bringing Hector's eyes parallel to his own. There was no outrage in this and Hector accepted his floating as a minor miracle. He was becoming accustomed to the abnormal and knew in every bone that this was meant with a species of kindness or detachment that no other human had ever experienced, except of course Nicholas's ol' man.

The Erstwhile heard that and said, "Ask about him, you have a taste of his sight, the tongue of it licks your need. But not here, let's do it in sight of the stone forest so as to remember him."

Nicholas swung a long straight arm that indicated they were to move some distance away from the small gathering of patients who had so loved their little stage show. They walked out into the central corridor, then up several flights of grand stairs and to the far northeast corner of the vast building. The Erstwhile opened a door that was not to a ward; it had a preserved elegance about it. He put his finger to his lips and waited for Hector to nod his understanding; then they went in. It was hung with paintings and panelled with books. Fine furniture graced its uncluttered domain. But its most dominant feature was a large window with a magnificent view towards the city. Nicholas dragged a chair across the room in what Hector thought was an unnecessarily disrespectful manner. He then sat the old man in it and waited for his total concentration to be beyond the glass.

"Now you are going to be my ol' man, don't worry I will do all the voices, but we got to face the right way, where he was in those times."

Hector nodded and hoped this was going to be like his last manifestation of William Blake. Then he turned his head again.

"But isn't Lambeth over there?"

He pointed away from the window towards a shelf of books.

"Sharp as an eraser you are. Lambeth is there, but the ol' man moved again, didn't he, that's what made it so easy, him living in Fountain Court and all." Nicholas was slipping into his South London voice again, the first voice he had ever learned. "At the end he lived down there."

Again he turned the professor's head, aiming his eyes through the glass, across the river and into the nest of streets that had been demolished sixty years ago. Triggering a trajectory out of his body, through the glass and over the water, while he sat motionless and heard every word. Nicholas continued to explain or at least attempt to. Much of it made no sense until Hector realised he was talking about Blake's art.

"We had been working on it for years, the plural me and the ol' man. But we always had the same problem: his need to broadcast and show. He made pictures for other people all the time, did it for money, he did, but he couldn't stop. Every time he made a relic or a nub, he had to pick at it or make a picture of it. It's important, you see, to leave it alone. To let a crust form and then more silt over that so it gets solid. 'Cos it ain't going to have no outcome on paper."

Hector heard little because he had finally slowed down in a cobbled street that ran up from the embankment. He slowed because he was watching two figures walking arm in arm away from him.

"Infernal picture making both with words and scribbled colour. He even invented a way to make more than one at a time. Always filling in, he was, always colouring and rhyming. 'Twas hard to make him swallow the meanings and save up for the big one."

His feet weren't touching the ground as he seemed to paddle forwards, which was just as well, because the cobbles were glistening and treacherous. The smaller of the two men kept losing his foothold on the wet incline. It was when the taller man took the weight of the other one that Hector knew it was Nicholas and his ol' man that he was following.

"I could not be in the internment of our plural, that was his job, that's why it was difficult, keeping the song inside him, stoppered up. The song made the halo, you see, and there was only one place to confine its countenance."

The pair were now weaving along a pavement that was compressed by a great weight of traffic, all of which they seemed oblivious to. Nicholas was speaking down to the artist while holding him up by his arm; there was no resistance, just a slight faltering as they stumbled onwards.

"It had to be rendered up in a place devoid of trees, without a splinter of wood. In a forest of stone. High above all the leaves and branches."

Hector drifted closer as they entered the shadow of the enormous building that dominated everything around it. He knew it was St. Paul's, London's greatest cathedral. He saw the Erstwhile steer Blake through the grand entrance and he tried to follow, but the light on the front steps was too solid, the shadows too distinctive. His blur had no purchase here and the reality of his projection diminished, so that he lost the sight and began to wind back across the Thames to the room in Bedlam.

"Only there above the city, in a curve of stone, can an impression of the poem be made."

Hector was back in the room and turning his dazed head into the Erstwhile's meaningless words.

"So I held his head close to the wall of whispers and he began to chant, the wondrous poem that rang a great halo in the dome and set its resonance in that curve. This was his great part in the plural, his final greatest work singing in the stone of the whispering gallery above and away from all those trees forever."

CHAPTER THIRTY

*I*shmael was exhausted on his return. They had walked all day and found not the slightest trace of the Limboia. How could so many men leave nothing of their presence behind? He entered his tent and shucked off his boots, rucksack, trousers, damp coat, and shirt. He fell into the camp bed and lay motionless, waiting for the much-anticipated sleep to remove all the strain and boorishness of his day in the forest.

One side of the tent glowed from the oil lamp that was mounted on a shaft outside. It burnt all night and illuminated his sleeping room with soft khaki shadows. The rain hissed against its metal hood. His heavy lids started to close as he fell headfirst down the flights of consciousness, jolting on each step into awaiting sleep. But a wire held him, did not let him fall all the way. Something was winding him back into the tent. He fought against it, but it was an insistent, imperative winch of instinct that demanded his attention at the surface. He opened his eyes. There was a different smell and sound in his domain. He looked for immediate danger before moving. Was there somebody else here? That's what the smell told him. The sound was a thin sucking, flapping noise. He looked towards his rucksack and the pistol, under his discarded clothes. It would take too long to dig it out, the machete was closer. The sound lessened and stopped for a moment. He slid off the bed and grabbed at the scabbard attached to his utility belt. The sucking arose again. The blade was out. Then he knew what it was. It was rising and falling with the wind outside in the trees. He allowed himself to listen more carefully and stalked the sound to the far side of the tent. The slit in the canvas was wet and breathing in time with the air outside. He examined it. This was no tear but a bold and vindictive cut. He looked back into the room. To the table and folding chair, to his wooden chest, his satchel. Everything was different, moved out of place. Not the ramshackle turnover of a passing thief nor the stealthy care of a cat burglar or spy but something else. This was a different kind of intruder and it made his blood chill. He went to the table and touched his things, reclaiming them by shifting each a few inches. Or by picking them up, unlocking their previous gravity of alien placement. He lifted his satchel and instantly felt the wet smell. He tore it open, ready to confront and strangle anything that might be living there. His papers, money, and other personal possessions fell onto the table. The engraved gold pocket watch from Cyrena was still there. He spun the now-offensive satchel like a wounded animal. Held by its throat, tearing open all its side pockets. When he reached the wettest one, he knew what was gone and why the bag was dripping. He dropped the limp leather to the floor and picked up the machete on his way to the bed. His exhaustion was impatiently waiting for him there and he gave himself up to it. He gave himself up to all things, knowing that he had no protection and no friends. His death had been the intruder that day and it had taken the only thing he really valued. It had pissed on his hopes and marked its territory inside his life. He hoped it would come back through the slit and take him now, struggle with him while he hacked at its merciless velocity. But in his sinking bed and fatigued heart he knew it would go for the girl first.

The rain increased overnight, falling fast and vertical while it waited for the winds to join its seasonal arrival. Pools of water surrounded the tents and motionless carriages. Water slid into every crevice and depression. Its percussion from the leaves and the canvas sounded like an ocean, and was louder than anything during the day. It was like a drum inside the carriages.

The hard varnished wood braced itself against the onslaught. But nobody woke to hear it; it had the opposite effect, the drumming fluid finding kinship with their heart pumping blood, squeezing through the dream cells of their tight night brains. It eased slightly by morning and a haze hung over the camp. The heat of the men had dented the immediate climate and their dwellings steamed with the effect.

The next morning, Ishmael insisted that two of the policemen stay and guard the camp while they were out scouting. Wirth agreed without any argument.

They had been out walking and cutting back a different curve in the forest when the shot rang out above the rattling leaves and the hissing rain. Everybody stopped and unslung their arms in a single motion. Wirth looked to where the shot had come from.

"Who fired?" he barked.

The last man in the line called out and Wirth rushed to his side.

"There was somebody there, following me . . . er, us! I have been feeling him for the last two hours. Then I turned and he was there, behind."

"Did you hit him?"

"Must have, he was so close."

"Did you speak to him?"

Kranz, who was one of the policemen, did not understand the question. He gawped at Wirth, moving his mouth as if trying to catch the meaning in his teeth. Wirth looked over Kranz's shoulder.

"Where's the body, man?"

Wirth walked back down the track, dodging and moving sideways in an unpredictable manner, his eyes darting into the undergrowth, his rifle swinging back and forth. Sometime in the last few moments the sergeant had attached a triangular sectioned bayonet, and its half-metre-long spike glimmered in the rain. Ishmael had heard about these from Nebsuel. The triangular stab wound could not naturally close and such injuries were nightmares for field surgeons. The triangular bayonet had been banned, outlawed for years.

Wirth stopped and bawled back. "Come here, man."

Kranz ran to his side. There was a heated discussion before they both returned.

"Gather round. Kranz here thinks he saw somebody tailing us and took a potshot at him. Well, whatever it was, it's gone now and there's not a trace of blood. So I am changing the marching rig and putting two at the back and front. One scouting, the other cutting. Any questions?"

There were none and they continued into the trees.

Just before twilight and their turning back, Kranz fell to his knees and put his hands over his ears. The line stopped and Wirth approached.

"What is it now, Kranz?"

"Did you hear it?" he said between chattering teeth.

"What the fuck are you talking about, man, I can't hear a damn thing except your blubbering." He kicked Kranz hard on the shin. "Get to your feet, man, I will have no more of this."

Kranz crawled upright and fell back in line.

"Grumann, keep an eye on him, let me know if he goes off again," he said to the man walking behind the shuddering Kranz.

By dark they were halfway back along the track that they had marked by splashing off-white water-resistant paint on the trees. The leader carried a flashlight that darted through the wood, sniffing for the marked trunks: the way home.

"What's wrong with Kranz?" asked Ishmael.

"Fuck knows, just gone off. It happens to some," said Wirth.

"Do you think he really saw somebody and that they are still out there?"

"I hope so. That's what we came for."

They were an hour away from camp when the rain stopped. The noise dropped to dripping and the singing frogs. Everybody was anticipating their dinner and an allowance of alcohol. They had traipsed back and forth for the last two days and found nothing. Two of the men were showing signs of forgetfulness and Wirth kept a keen eye on the rest. Kranz's outbursts had been the only exciting thing to happen since they arrived.

They entered a small clearing and Wirth was thinking about a cigarette break when they all heard it. Kranz screamed out, "There it is, there it is, do you hear it?"

"Quite, man," bellowed Wirth.

It sounded again and the sergeant moved closer to Ishmael.

"You ever heard the like before?"

"N-no, not here."

Nobody unslung their weapons this time. They just looked about and stood closer to one another. The sound that stained the darkness was the unmistakable penetrating wail of a baby crying.

"It might just be an animal, they sometimes copy people," said one of the searchers.

"That's no fucking animal, man, it's human, it must be them, they got a child." Wirth spoke with absolute certainty and a new zeal.

"How do you know?" said Ishmael, moving to his side and unbuttoning his holster.

"The Limboia have been taking them for years."

Ishmael had never heard of this. The folklore of the zombie workers was Fleischer's area of expertise, and for the first time he was missed.

"It means they are here," said Wirth.

"What shall we do?" said Ishmael.

One of the men overheard them.

"We can't leave a child here," he said.

"We are less than an hour from base. I suggest we send three back to get the others and more torches. We stay here and make a search," said Wirth.

The baby's cry rang out again from deep in the trees and the sky opened for heavier rain.

"Well, boss, what shall do?" said Wirth with his hands on his hips, confronting Ishmael.

Ishmael looked at the men, into the forever trees, the pouring canopy, and back at the sergeant.

"As you say."

Wirth called out three names and gave them their orders. They took one of the torches and moved towards the marked path.

"Follow the paint and lock light," barked Wirth.

And they were gone.

The child stopped.

"Cigarette break," Wirth announced.

Ishmael glared at him.

"We will wait here for the others."

The plaintive crying occurred three times over the next two hours.

Ishmael was constantly watching the marked track for the reinforcements and Wirth frequently consulted his watch. Then without any warning he stood up, stretched dramatically, and commanded, "Saddle up. Hand span and bayonets and lock light."

The men arose, separated, reloaded their rifles, and attached bayonets. They stood three metres apart and waited for the next command.

"Stay in sight and let's go."

They moved slowly towards where the cry was last heard. Wirth beckoned to Ishmael to join the phalanx as they entered the trees.

"What is 'light'?"

"Tracer bullets, I want to see what we might have to kill and where they are skulking," said Wirth.

"We have come here to bring the Limboia back alive to work, not to hunt them like game," said Ishmael, speaking more for Anton than for himself.

"If those bastards have stolen a child they deserve all they get. Don't worry, we will save you a few."

Wirth was in his element. Enjoying the mechanical precision of his new killing machine.

The first man strapped the torch onto his rifle and waved it from side to side in slow motion as he progressed and the others followed.

"Where the fuck are they?" said one of men.

"Hush now, we want to hear them, not them us," said Wirth.

The rain was getting heavier and the forest seemed to lean away from all this human action. The first wind started to pick up and rattle the darkness around the soaking intrusion. They pushed through the big waxy leaves, which spilled water in all directions.

Ten minutes in and they were in their stride, sending out

sensor rays to catch the slightest movement or sound in the lush undergrowth.

"There, there!" shrieked Kranz, pointing forward.

All the men stopped and raised their rifles.

"Wait," shouted Wirth.

Kranz fired. A vicious wasp of hard luminescence spat from his rifle, drawing a long beautiful line into the black core of the Vorrh. Seconds later it was returned.

There is a strange phenomenon about tracer rounds. Those seeing the incoming light witness a slowing down midway—a moment to appreciate its speeding linear beauty. It then seems to accelerate. That is what Kranz saw before a red-hot bullet split his sternum, shredding and burning his lungs with splintered bone and phosphorus. The searchers ducked, resting on one knee and sending a volley of hard light into the trees. Again it was returned and a constant exchange began. Ishmael got behind a tree, close to the ground, and watched in awe. The light was fading now, allowing the silver-white rods of perspective to illuminate the depth of the forest. The wet leaves above catching their rigid shimmer. The velocity that darted through the rain was contradicting all the verticals around it. It was spellbinding and lethal. Ishmael suddenly saw another forest, another battle superimposed over this one. Another hunt where men ran into darkness, sending dogs and spears darting like bullets into the vanishing point of flickering trees. It had been a painting reproduced in a book that Nebsuel had. The artist was called Uccello. Ishmael had looked at it for hours, with both his old and his new face.

He could not shake it off. It became more real in the comparison. The soggy bloodbath before him lit the magical reality of the picture in a dazzling paradox. A man staggered backwards towards him, his hair on fire and his brain exposed. He looked at Ishmael with the rotating eyes of a chameleon and tried to speak. The effort yanked part of his cortex loose into the flames in his hair where it spluttered. He fell and died within three feet and Ishmael reached out and retrieved his rifle. There was shouting now, echoing through the branches as the light got less, and then a great charging of Wirth's men into the fray. Ishmael ran after them, not wanting to remain with the dead where he might be picked off. They hurled themselves forward, screaming like demons. Smashing the foliage aside. The gunfire from the others had ceased as they crashed closer. The blurred silhouettes of two standing and one fallen man could be seen on the other side of a smaller wood where the trees were different. Slender, delicate leaves unlike the larger heavier ones they had just shredded in their attack. Wirth and four others ignored the narrow gap between the fleshy trees behind them and the poised symmetry ahead. They were at full pelt, smashing through the branches. Bayonets at jousting speed impatient to spear the foe. Then their battle cries stopped, changed octaves, and were interrupted by a violent thrashing. The grove of elegant, densely packed, inoffensive-looking trees had halted their onslaught. The low delicate branches looked like no kind of obstacle for such a minotaur force. But they had all stopped in the middle of the glade and now whimpered and struggled in its foliage. Ishmael slowed to a cautious walk, crossed the gap, and entered the spinney. He pushed a small branch aside to get a closer look ahead.

It bit him hard and deep and he instinctively withdrew his arm with great speed. It bit deeper, this time into the underside of his wrist. He twisted it and it tore into his fingers and beneath his elbow. The more he moved, the worse it got. He dropped the rifle, yelped, and grabbed at his machete, bringing the blade around to hack at the branch that held his arm. Eventually it came away, still attached to his clothes and his bleeding skin. It was too dark to see what manner of vicious predator had assailed him. The men up ahead in the trees were quieter now and were moving hardly at all. He tried to pull the branch off, but it still bit and held fast. He looked around. There were only two sources of light. One was coming from deep in the sinister trees, where a small pool spilt from the torch on a fallen rifle. The other was flickering back from where he had come, flickering disgustingly from the dead man's head like an ornate crown. He walked back to the horror and knelt by the body, avoiding the face. He held his arm and the branch out towards the burning head like an obscene salute or a grotesque barbecue. In the meek spitting light he carefully unpicked the plant and saw the enemy. Thorns. Long and daggerlike on every inch of the black stems and delicate steel-hard branches. They faced all directions in a regularly dispersed geometry of protection. He rotated the branch and unhooked it from his punctured arm. Even the smallest of stems were infested with needle-sharp, hair-thin spikes. As the stems got thicker and harder, so did the thorns. The biggest one on this small fragment was more than ten centimetres long, thick and solidly uncompromising at its base, tapering up an inflexible shaft to a hungry spiteful tip. One of God's little masterpieces, he thought as he looked back towards the delicate grove and wondered about the size of the thorns on the trunks. He kicked wet earth and leaves over the flame and it smouldered and choked out, tainting the air with sickening incense.

Ishmael walked back to the trees and called out. There was no direct answer, just a wash of indistinct moans. He sat and waited with them until dawn and then for the sun to be bright enough for him to be able to cut a path towards the friends and foes who were now very quiet and still.

It took him all morning to free the two living ones and move them over to the other bodies: the imagined enemy that they had exchanged fire with, who turned out to be the returning party from the base camp. One was alive. One stood dead, locked into an impossible rigor mortis. The others were shot to pieces.

Wirth still breathed, but he had lost a lot of blood through an impaled artery and his face had been multiply punctured. Both eyes had been pierced and were now swollen, black and blind. The other man could still stand and helped drag the sergeant away from the delicate spinney, where they left the dead ones hanging in the branches. They looked like jesters or Morris dancers frozen mid-gambol in a gentle mysterious Shakespearean wood. One of the men had even wound himself up into the relentless thicker thorns, so that now his feet did not touch the ground.

Ishmael found the portable medical bag and did the best he could to dress the wounds. His own hands had been punctured again while freeing the men and removing the plant from their entangled flesh. There was blood everywhere. When he ran out of bandages he tore up the shirts of the dead. Their stiff drying blood tightly wrapped over the fresh bleedings.

The warmth of the sunlight gave them confidence and they started to build a sledge stretcher for Wirth. Ishmael had given morphine to Wirth and Brucker, the other survivor from the dagger glade, and kept some back for himself. It was difficult to ascertain their injuries. The thorns had an oval cross section, which meant that the wound could quickly close, making it impossible to guess its depth. Brucker had more than forty such wounds and only a few scratches on his face. Miraculously they had missed his eyes completely. He was in pain and shock and the morphine helped both. Wirth's stabbed face and eyes were still swelling and Ishmael wondered if the wood of the tree was also poisonous. He did not know the name of the other man, who seemed to be completely unhurt.

"Can you help us load him onto the stretcher?"

The man looked straight through him.

"Can you help, please?"

"How did this happen? We followed the paint markings on the trees, it's impossible that we ended up on the other side of you."

Ishmael ignored the question because there was no answer. They loaded the dead weight of Wirth onto the tied-together stretcher.

"We must get back as quickly as possible," he said.

"What about the child?" said Brucker. Ishmael glanced at him quickly, a passing quill of anger between them.

"What child?" said Ishmael.

The sorry troops began moving back towards the white paint mark that was gradually being washed away by the constant rain. As he passed, the unnamed man touched it and stopped moving. The others paused and waited.

"We must go," snapped Ishmael.

The man was smelling his hand, which was stained white.

"Bird shit," he said.

"What?"

"It's not paint, it's bird shit, guano."

Ishmael joined him to look at the marked tree.

"It was a trap," the man said, "somebody changed the trail. Removed the original paint and replaced it with this." He smelt his hand again. "They led us around the forest in a circle. The marks ran out when we were directly opposite you and those fucking nightmare trees."

"If this is the work of the Limboia, then they have certainly changed," said the weak-voiced Brucker.

"Let's try and get back today, we don't want to spend another night out here," said Ishmael, and lifted one end of the stretcher. The unnamed man came to help and took the other strut.

"How will we find our way back?" he said.

Ishmael grinned through the horror and said, "We will follow the shit until it becomes paint and then look at the sun."

It was hard going: the stretcher got caught in the trees and vines continually. Brucker was still bleeding, his fatigue and the movement opening his weakly sealed wounds. Ishmael's hands were swollen and the thoughts of his emissary prowled ahead. Only the other man, who announced that he was called Saul, was not struggling. He seemed driven by a need to find some revenge for having been led into the ambush. Wirth had been tipped from the stretcher twice and the drugs had worn off. Their supply was finished except for the little that Ishmael kept back. The shit had indeed become paint again at the point in the track where the night diversion had taken place. This was a bad moment for Saul and he fumed. He had been taking most of the weight of dragging and carrying Wirth. He put him down with a jolt that made him howl in pain when he saw the place in daylight. He raved again, ignoring the others. Screaming into the jungle for "the scum to show themselves," white foam bubbling in the corners of his mouth. Ishmael feared that he had become insane. They were only an hour or two from the camp now and he needed his strength to get Wirth back.

"When we get back and patch these others up, you and I can take the Hotchkiss for a walk back here."

Saul stared at Ishmael, and for the first time he understood what "eyes like saucers" meant. After what seemed like a very long time Saul grinned and nodded.

"Hot kiss," he said, and picked up the wrong end of stretcher, marching forward down the track. Wirth slid out in a tangled foetal coil, gasping for breath between his screams.

"Stop stop," said Ishmael.

Saul was speeding ahead, unaware why his burden had become so light.

"Stop."

Brucker limped after Saul, who now stood stock-still, as he had been when Ishmael first found him. Eventually they loaded the now-silent Wirth back onto the stretcher.

Thirty minutes later Saul's request came true. They entered a small clearing that was full of the Limboia all looking in their direction, as if they had been there waiting for them. They froze for a second, blinking at the pack. One of the Limboia stepped forward, smiling and lifting something towards them. They reached for their guns. The smiler walked towards them, a bundle in his hands. To his horror, Ishmael's fingers were too swollen to fit inside the trigger guard of his rifle. He dropped it and fumbled for the Mannlicher. Brucker was working the bolt of his Enfield, and Saul was too amazed to do anything now that his moment had come. The smiler held up the bundle, which had once been some kind of elaborately embroidered bag. Through use it had become worn, frayed, and sun-bleached. As it turned, the body of the child could be seen nestling in the folds. Brucker took his eyes away from the aligned sights of his rifle. Ishmael stopped trying to cock the pistol, and Saul slowly lowered the stretcher to the ground.

"Fleyber gone," said the herald of the Limboia.

Ishmael crossed the few strides to confront the alien being, his gun useless in his hand. As he got closer, he could see and smell the child. It was dead and rotting.

"Fleyber gone, you give new one worn out," said the herald, and thrust the bundle at the approaching figure.

They now stood very close and Ishmael tried to read the vacant man's expression and not look at what he held. For the first time the creature took his eyes off the stinking bundle. They looked up languidly to taste the space around him and the intruders standing by. Then his head slumped down again as if exhausted from the weight it had felt from so much attention.

Suddenly the head and eyes of the herald of the Limboia lurched back up to stare directly into the face of Ishmael. Its mouth began to work without words. Dribble running down its chin as one hand was raised to its chest. The Mannlicher was twitching in Ishmael's hand. The herald began beating his chest violently. Each blow making him rock backwards and teeter. All the while the other hand balanced the noxious bundle as if it had some kind of independent life from the rest of the shaking body.

The herald was stepping backwards, his eyes never leaving Ishmael's face. He staggered into clear view of Ishmael's companions, no longer shielded by his presence.

"They killed it," Saul barked, and aimed his rifle.

"No!" shouted Ishmael.

The hasty shot missed the herald and passed through the child. It flew apart, its rotting flesh splashing in all directions. Ishmael shielded his face far too late and the herald fell to the ground, quickly imitated by the rest of the Limboia. The second shot killed one of the prone figures while it lay motionless.

"Kiss kiss," shouted Saul between the shots. Then he turned the rifle on Brucker, who was standing only a few feet away.

"Kiss kiss."

Brucker's rifle was still held in firing position. He had been watching the last shocking moments along its length. He spun it towards the foaming Saul as the bullet went through his chest, the jolt triggering his own round into Saul's left eye. Everybody heard it hit bone. He was still loaded with tracer, and the ignited bullet sped around the containing skull like an incendiary lead wasp, liquidizing everything inside. The same crown of flames that Ishmael had witnessed before danced from the cracks in his head.

"Kyyyth," Saul hissed, and toppled backwards into the shadows of the forest.

Nobody moved until the herald stood up and adopted the

same posture he had been in before the conflict. Except he covered his eyes with one hand as if protecting them from bright light or a sandstorm. Only then could he address Ishmael again.

"You give new one," he said as if nothing had happened. "New fleyber."

When his voice came back, Ishmael said, "You come back to work and I will get you anything you want."

"New fleyber?"

CHAPTER THIRTY-ONE

*T*he Lohr household felt as if it were made of glass. The tension between Cyrena and Ghertrude and their absent loved ones made everything brittle and transparently empty. Ghertrude had told her only friend everything the Kin had said about Rowena, Ishmael, herself, and the history and foundation of Essenwald. It redefined the friends' understanding of the world and veined the structure of reality, making stress lines or impending fractures in the crystal architecture of their lives. Long periods of silence cracked between the intense torque of frantic questions and the inertia of unknown answers. When they were not talking, each woman became locked in the isolation of her own depressive worrying.

Ghertrude could not bear being near the Kin. Her frustration, anger, and compulsive fascination asked spiteful and impossible things of them, and they replied only with understated enigmas that sounded greatly like the truth. She, like everybody else, had a fundamental belief that machines don't lie, devious gears and fallacious motors being an anathema, a contradiction. A mendacity engine was beyond contemplation. But when the mechanism so resembled humans, anything was possible.

Cyrena had always stayed clear of the details of her family's business. The respected wealth of the Lohrs was founded in the birth of Essenwald, even though there had been some faded aristocracy before. Ghertrude's chilling stories of unscrupulous pacts turned the key in her own cellar of doubts. This and her growing unease about Ishmael made a bilious cocktail of anxiety that chafed remorselessly at her long-established tranquillity. She had always enjoyed being the sole representative of a significant family. She let her brother drive the intricacies of the business from his remote gleaming office in Berlin. Nobody ever expected the blind sister to participate in the politics of fortune, even after her miraculous gift of sight. Her gratitude to Ishmael for being the conduit of the dramatic change had long since worn out. It was first replaced by love. Unconditional and from every fibre of her being. Her strength and beauty united to hold and need him, and she provided every comfort and amenity to make him happy. The confused and hurt young man gradually softened and yielded up his pain. There had been one year of calm euphoria together. Then they reached his other side. The unknown man beneath the fictional countenance. He had shown her so much of himself, given her access to everything so that she might heal the wounds that he avoided. Once they were sewn closed, he pretended they had never existed and found her ministrations irksome, her touch too revealing. Then he retreated even further. Cyrena hid her confusion and growing fear under her sense of duty and held tight. She encouraged and validated his increasingly strange sexual demands, even the painful and humiliating ones. It made him happy for a short while and kept him near. She had tried to convince herself that his curt indifference was just a temporary phase, exasperated by his boredom. But deep down she knew he was becoming emotionally detached. The complex rituals and elaborate brutality of their couplings only emphasised it. He fetishised her bruising, kissing the hurts with mock affection. Explaining that they were reaching new levels of sensual awareness. All the while, she was feeling less and less. His insistent demands and ferocious rummagings were nowhere near her heart.

The withdrawal of the city's power occurred at the same time. The gradual running down of industry and purpose. A sense of despair was contaminating everyone. Her personal fortune would not be directly affected. She had enough money elsewhere to see her through all her days in modest luxury. But her safe isolation from the drought outside made her position more difficult and morally uncomfortable. For the first time she considered moving. Maybe following the exodus south to the rich and stable lands of the veldt.

She had written to consult her brother, who did not approve and told her that this was a minor hiccup, a glitch in the expanding prospect of Essenwald. And that the presence of a Lohr was essential for all their futures. This was her destiny, her opportunity to finally put her shoulder to the family wheel.

She put the letter in a corner drawer of her bureau. Away from the persnickety curiosity of Ishmael. She had not told him of her possible plan or of the consultation with her brother. It was better not to bait his anger any more than necessary. She was going to conceal the envelope amid another shallow bundle of family papers that sat beneath one of her jewel boxes. She lifted the old box from the drawer and it slipped and fell open. She quietly swore at the expensive clatter of the contents hitting the floor. She did not need attention being brought to her little act of clandestine peacekeeping. She deftly scooped up the heirlooms—the brooches, emerald earrings, and strings of pearls—and lovingly placed them back in the intimate nest. It had been a long time since she had worn any of her treasured inheritance, much preferring the new and more flamboyant purchases of her sighted years. She touched them, remembering each without knowing of its visual excellence. Most had been her mother's, and her seeing fingers had known them since childhood. Jolts of vivid memory unexpectedly charged through her and without reason moved her to instant tears. Her touch had held those moments safely locked away, where sight could never pick the lock and overexpose them. It all came back. Helping her mother to dress, her small focused fingers selecting the necklace, working the clasp, feeling the radiance of her mother's perfect neck and shoulders warm the polished spears until they gleamed to her touch. She could still do it. Her hands still saw. She pushed aside the other things that expensively littered the bureau's top and separated the tangled streams of pearls. There were four single strands and two doubles. She laid them out, then closed her eyes and waited a moment. The previous touch that had caused such a flood of joy and memory had been accidental. Her eyes were off guard. This was different; she was now testing the power and endurance of her almost forgotten sensitivity. After a slow intake of breath her hands began to roam. They felt the first string and began to warm. Vienna. She was six. Her first opera. Figs and cream. The taffeta dress that felt purple. She moved to the next and another flood of wondrous happiness glided through her body. It was so powerful that she had to force her hand away. It was the weekend at her cousins when she became a woman.

She paused, took another deep breath, and anxiously touched the next. Nothing. Less than nothing, these pearls were dead, empty. She tried again and the sensation to her now-enlightened fingers felt shallow and grey. She almost opened her eyes. She moved on to the next.

"Thank God," she sighed to herself as another little wave of her past hit, and so it continued to the last, one of the double strands that she knew to be her grandmother's.

Again, nothing. The same sick hollow. Now she opened her eyes. Yes, it was the double strand and it looked like it was supposed to, as far as she could be sure. But it was wrong, seriously wrong. Nausea's disquiet was welling inside her in the very places that had just basked and flushed in such great warmth. On the afternoon of his departure, she went back to the fake pearls. She examined them with great care, then called for her car.

Tissa Chakrabarty was not an entirely honest man, but he was a polite one and knew his place. In fact he guarded his exact status with ruthless and dogmatic precision. He was the most respected jeweler in the city. The only man who could give a definite verdict on Cyrena's growing suspicions. When the lilac limousine stopped in a cloud of livid dust outside his premises and the fine lady walked into his tiny immaculate shop, he flew from his perch in the corner of the room, his magnifying lens popping from his beaming eye.

"Madam," he fawned, making sweeping movements towards his counter with its rows of locked cabinets. He waved at the door and the huge man who was sitting in its shadow.

"Wait in the street, look after the lady's automobile," he called to his watchman, who barged out the door to glare at the chauffeur.

"My security, madam, to keep out the riffraff."

He pulled out a seat and dusted it for her.

"What may I do for you, please, madam?"

Cyrena lifted the case out of her bag, opened it, and took out the tangled strings of pearls.

"I want you to tell me about these. I will reward you for your professional information."

Chakrabarty went to the other side of the counter, retrieved his eyeglass, and became very serious and formal. He untangled the strands and laid them out on a black velvet cloth. He pulled a thin metal chain behind him, which opened a vent in the ceiling. Bright light fell directly onto the counter.

He worked quietly, turning the necklaces with his pointed fingers. He occasionally made small sounds of appreciation. He stopped midway, suddenly aware of Cyrena again.

"May I offer you something to drink, madam?"

"No thank you."

He was caught off guard by her magnificent eyes.

"Please continue," she said.

"Yes, yes," he said, and dragged his eyes back to the other precious orbs. After another ten minutes he put the eyepiece down and said, "Magnificent. Some of the finest examples I have ever seen. Beyond price, it is my privilege to witness them."

"All of them?" asked Cyrena.

He choked slightly and said, "No. Two of them are unworthy, artificial substitutes."

"Why would somebody need such a thing?"

"As a ruse for thieves or something to wear while the real ones are locked in the bank."

There was an awkward silence between them. A mournful clock could be heard ticking somewhere in a back room.

Her eyes were sharper now; she stood up and came closer to him.

"In this city, who else would know the value and meaning of these gems?" she asked.

He said nothing, but thought quickly, seeking a believable answer.

"Do you know who I am, Mr. Chakrabarty?" She was now agitated and becoming more compressed, as if controlling a rage inside her elegant composure. He was shrinking and dreading the next question. "Have you recently purchased pearls of this quality?"

He was suddenly relieved and laughed. "Oh no, madam, such prices are beyond my meager finances."

She looked even deeper.

"Very well. Have you recently sold three strings of the worthless copies?"

He took a step back, his mouth dry and straining. "I am an honest trader, madam."

"Then answer my question."

He gulped and said, "Yes, to a gentleman of quality, a well-dressed man, an officer, I think."

"Officer?" she said.

"Yes, a soldier."

"How do you know that?"

"Because, madam, he bore the noble scars of battle."

"Where?"

Chakrabarty took his hand off the black velvet and pointed to his eyes. "On his face," he said in a voice that was worried by her expression.

Not another word was spoken. She slowly picked up her possessions, leaving the two fakes behind. She placed a large crisp note on the counter. Chakrabarty was about to protest, when she held a finger to her lips, picked up her bag, and left. He stood behind the counter, looking at the forsaken necklaces and wishing he had never seen them before.

When Cyrena returned home, she said nothing to Ghertrude. She fastidiously made an inventory of all her possessions and added the new injuries to the collective fissures growing in her home.

CHAPTER THIRTY-TWO

One hundred thirty-five men shuffled down the narrow track towards the logging station. Ishmael and the herald were at their head and Wirth was being carried towards the rear. It would have been a triumphant return to camp if there had been anybody there to see it. The monkeys were everywhere and unimpressed by the arrival of another bunch of bewildering subhumans. The other beasts of the forest, however, were more than grateful to the odd strangers for the fresh and bountiful supplies of meat that they had left in their wake.

Ishmael called out for Fleischer and the policemen. No one was in sight; birds flew in and out of the open windows of the logging station hut. The atmosphere was stiff and awkward and Ishmael pulled out his pistol; his fingers were less swollen now and he could touch the trigger. He cautiously circled the hut and then made for the train. The Limboia ignored him and walked straight into their slave carriages without a word, as if they had never been away. He climbed up onto the footplate and touched the engine. It was cold. Something was wrong. He kicked at the metal door of the firebox and something moved inside. He jumped back and then after a few minutes kicked the latch again and swung the door open, the muzzle of the Mann-licher pointing inside.

"No, master, don't shoot!"

It was Hoss.

It took some time to persuade him to come out. When he did he was shaking and his eyes were darting everywhere. He stuttered and fumbled for breath and words.

"Where's Fleischer?" asked Ishmael.

Hoss looked like he had never heard the name before and then suddenly jolted into sense.

"He must be gone with the others, all gone."

"Gone where?"

"Dunno, just gone. Disappeared, taken."

"Taken by who?"

"Dunno. The forest, I think. There is something, someone out there. That's why I hid here."

Ishmael decided further questioning was pointless.

"Fire up the train—now! I will send the Limboia to carry the wood."

"The Limboia are back?"

"Yes and ready to go home, now fire up!"

Ishmael had the wounded man loaded into another carriage and told the herald of the Limboia to find dry wood and take it to the engine. He then walked to the hut, constantly pointing the pistol before him. Inside there were cinders in the fireplace and signs of a meal having been made. All traces of food had been erased by the marauding animals. Only the gin, ammunition, and medical supplies remained intact. He opened a bottle, lifted one of the fallen chairs, and made himself comfortable. He had done it. He had found the workforce and he was the only sane one standing. He took a deep gulp of the gin and bellowed a resounding laugh.

He knew he was going to be a hero. Was this it? The destiny that he had so desperately wanted to find? It felt too easy, even with all the bloodshed. The return of the workforce would restart the industrial heart of the city and change his life forever.

His days of seclusion were over. He took another slug of gin and imagined the bells ringing out from the cathedral spire. Imagined the crowd cheering at his return with the army to start up the city again. If he could control the Limboia he would have power over everybody. But to begin he needed a child, one for them to play with. Where would he get one? The only one he knew of had been kidnapped at exactly the wrong time. The time when he could have put her to good use.

Hoss had stoked the boiler and greased the steam-hot muscles, making the thirsty pistons strain for action. It would take an hour before there would be enough power to move. The light rain had turned into rods of stinging water and the puddles began to hiss and grow. Ishmael grabbed the bottle and made one last circuit of the station for any trace of Fleischer and the other men. There was none, but he did find the Hotchkiss machine gun, turned upside down in a bush, without any sign that it had ever been fired. He shouldered the weapon and walked back to make a tour of the injured fighters and the strange cargo of hollow men.

Now that he was the only commanding officer, he had to look in on Wirth and see what condition he was in. Not that he cared. He had dragged him back only because he thought he might need his knowledge. But that was before the arrival of the Limboia and the entire reconditioning of the expedition. If he could patch him up and get him back alive, then he would be the witness to Ishmael's heroic adventure. It was also interesting practising some of the surgical skills that Nebsuel had taught him. It helped pass the waiting hours. But before that, he wanted to get a better look at his prize. He had never been so close to so many of the Limboia before.

He strolled between the soggy presence looking for the vacant face of the herald among all the other vacant faces. Often when he got close, some of the lost tribe would make a gesture. They would avert their eyes and point at their hearts.

Once, out of idle curiosity, he mimicked it back to one of them. The demented creature fell to floor, as they had all done in the clearing in the forest. He shuffled under the slave carriage and seemed to instantly fall asleep. Ishmael was baffled. Then out of the corner of his eye he noticed the herald watching from afar. He waved.

"Come here, man. Come here."

Reluctantly the herald waddled over, keeping his eyes on the ground and raising one hand to shield his face.

"What's wrong with him?" Ishmael pointed beneath the carriage. "Him under there."

The herald bent low, looked for a few seconds, and said, "Finished."

"What do you mean?" said Ishmael.

"Finished, used up."

"What?"

"Death."

Ishmael could not believe his ears, but his eyes told him that the prostrate figure had not moved a muscle since hiding. He looked back to herald.

"I only did this." He raised his index finger and the herald shrank and quivered, mumbling, "No, master, no . . ."

Ishmael stopped. What was happening? Had he become a God, that he could smite a man with one simple gesture? He must try this again, but not with this one. He was valuable, the only one who spoke.

"Stay here," he barked at the herald and walked quickly, splashing through the puddles to the other side of the second carriage. A place from where none of the previous incident could have been seen. He entered the carriage and pointed at the first seated figure.

"Come out."

It slowly rose and descended the metal steps onto the rail. Ishmael looked at the bedraggled figure of the half-naked zombie. It was difficult to believe that the entire city and his personal future depended on this tribe of mindless wrecks.

"Look at me," he commanded.

It lifted its pale vacant eyes up to his and Ishmael shuddered. Not in fear or disgust but in recognition. For a moment he saw himself reflected inside the opaque mirrored interior of this imageless man. The creature saw it too and smiled. The reflection was being swallowed, and worse, it was going towards someplace that was a natural habitat for it. Ishmael savagely pointed at his own heart and the eyes went out. The man fell backwards without a twitch of restraint. Fell as if he had been dead for hours. He splashed into a deep puddle by the side of the tracks. The toes of his work boots, one of his hands, and his face stuck out of the water, staring up into the downpour, still smiling. Ishmael wrenched his attention away from the ghastly apparition and returned to the herald, who had not moved from his assigned position.

"Come with me."

Ishmael took him to shelter in the third carriage in the boxed-in section where Wirth was sleeping.

"Sit," he said as if to a dog. "I want some answers from you." While he spoke he kept pointing at the herald. He kept his index finger locked into a point like a cocked gun waving before the herald's face. The eyes of which never left the direction of its aim.

After the first ten minutes Ishmael sat down and lit a cigar. It was difficult to understand what the herald was saying, and he knew he would say nothing without the threat. He had started with the simple questions. That had been difficult enough. But now the answers were making no sense at all.

"Tell me again, about fleyber."

"Fleyber given to us to bring out best, best work best make Orm for hollowing. Fleyber worn out, needs new one. You give fleyber, we work best."

"Before, you said 'master' gave you the fleyber. Do you mean Maclish, the boss with red hair?"

The herald thought for a long time, moving his mouth as if chewing each word dozens of times.

"He and other."

"What other?"

"Other that brings more fleyber for us tell Orm hollow master."

"Who is other?" Ishmael said, impatience rising in his voice.

"He's talking about Hoffman," said a croaking voice from the other side of the wooden chamber. Ishmael had entirely forgotten about the sleeping Wirth. He stood up and went over to the bunk bed. Wirth looked terrible but seemed lucid. The bandages over his eyes had blackened again and his other wounds had continued to seep and fester. There was an odour of death and decay about the man. Ishmael sucked heavily on his cigar.

"We are awaiting the train to fire up and get us back, it should be soon now."

Wirth tried to prop himself up, but did not have the strength. Ishmael got another blanket, made it into a ball, and put it behind Wirth's neck and shoulder, lifting him higher in the bunk.

"How many survived?"

"Who?"

"Us."

"Just you and me, all the others are dead."

"Jeez," said Wirth. "And these fuckers?"

"Over a hundred."

"Objective achieved, then, bwana."

"I am glad to see that you have retained your sense of humour, Sergeant Wirth."

"That's all I have retained, and I think I'm going to bloody well need it, if I survive this lot."

Ishmael saw that Wirth was in pain and each word cost him dearly.

"I am going to get you some more morphine," he said. "I will be right back. Are you all right being left alone with our friend here?"

"Not much choice. At least I don't have to look at the ugly fuck. Can you get me something to wash the morph down?"

"There is water by the side of your bed."

"I was talking about gin."

Ishmael agreed, smiled, and left the carriage.

"Hey, joker, why did you make the trap for us?"

The herald said nothing, ignoring the wounded man.

"Why did you paint the guano on the wrong path?"

Not a word.

"Better tell me or no more fleyber."

After a long while the herald spoke again. "Not self, another. Lone him."

"You telling me there was some other cunt out there with us?"

The herald nodded and shrugged. Wirth heard it through the bandages.

A few minutes went by, then Wirth said, "Tell me about the Orm, did it kill Maclish?"

"We make Orm for hollow. Other want hollow for master. We give and leave."

"Other, you mean Hoffman?"

"That one bring last fleyber. We take and go."

Wirth twisted in the bed and whimpered, biting in his breath before he spoke again.

"So that old fucker did for Maclish!" he wheezed. "What be this Orm and its hollow?"

"We come together to squeeze Orm out, Orm hungry worm, it eat out man, make him hollow. Nothing left inside."

"Is Orm here now?"

"Orm always near, we want."

"Is that what kept you alive for so long in the Vorrh?"

"Fleyber and Orm protect. Plenty grub."

"What the fuck did you eat in there?"

"Trees and self."

Wirth gurgled a laugh, which was worth the pain. "You ate the fucking trees?"

"With self."

Wirth shifted, tilting his mummified head in the direction of the voice. "Self?"

"Each," said the herald.

"Long-pig," chortled Wirth, sliding back into his hurt and mirth. "You fucking ate each fucking other."

The herald nodded enthusiastically, while making chewing noises directed towards Wirth.

"Jesus," he said. Then before the pain stopped him, he said, "So where is the last freyber?"

The herald looked oddly at Wirth. "You all shit it up with guns."

"What?"

"We show you old worn-out fleyber and you shit it up with guns."

Wirth was just about to attempt a shout when he suddenly realised what the goon was talking about.

"Jesus, you mean the fleyber was that dead rotting child you were carrying?"

"Fleyber," the herald said.

"Fuck me, you're telling me that Maclish and that old cunt doctor were paying you in dead babies?"

"Fleyber," said the herald.

When Ishmael returned with the bottle and pills, he was confronted by the bizarre tableau of the herald sitting stock-still grinning and Wirth chuckling in pain. He could not imagine a joke that they could share with such uncontrollable innocent joy.

They both heard it after the drugs and half the bottle of gin had been devoured. The whistle from the train.

"It's ready, we can go now," said Ishmael.

Wirth slipped into a deep dark sleep, which would embalm him until he was carried into the Timber Guild hospital two days later.

Ishmael had grown weary of questioning the vacant-eyed herald, tired of his obtuse answers. But one more thing had to be known.

"Tell me one more thing and then you can go."

For the first time a flicker of animation could be detected.

"Why do the Limboia die when I do this?"

It was a cruel moment that Ishmael greatly relished. The half-completed gesture over his heart galvanised the herald into the quickest answer of the day.

"You make hollow."

"What?"

"You fetch up Orm. Like self, but other way round."

"You mean I am doing what you do together to make the Orm?"

"Same but more."

"How can I do that?"

"Same but more."

"Why me?"

"Same."

The idea that he had anything in common with these zombies disgusted him. First it had been the anthropophagi and now the Limboia. This was not the lineage he had been seeking. Was he only ever going to be coupled with freaks and monsters? And whatever power he shared with this subhuman, it did not come from the same source.

"Same," the herald said.

And while the consequence of the simple word crept into Ishmael, the herald made another sign. He stood up, placed one hand over his heart, and rotated the other hand flatly above his head, as if polishing a halo that wasn't there. Ishmael stared in silence; he had seen this gesture before.

They had barely looked up when the engine gave the carriages a first jolt of movement, Hoss hanging on the string of the whistle. Ishmael gave his first orders to the Limboia to move Wirth into his own compartment. When they returned, Ishmael gave the word and the train left the lumber station to the monkeys and birds. A great bellow of steam hushed beneath the wheels and gradually the bulk of the carriages shunted forward, the engine nudging them onwards from its place at the back, its reverse gear engaged.

Fifteen minutes later, when the train was still crawling along, Ishmael bellowed for it to stop.

Hoss applied the screaming brakes and Ishmael jumped from the train, pointing back along the track towards something hanging in the trees.

"Help me get him down," he shouted to Hoss, who was staring at the luminescent white thing hanging in the dark wet dripping branches. It was the naked body of Anton Fleischer. With much difficulty and the aid of one of the Limboia who was forced to climb the tree, they lowered the body and discovered that it was still breathing. While the drama unfolded, Sidrus slipped into the slave carriage and squeezed in among the lost men. None of them noticed or cared. Fleischer was wrapped in blankets and placed next to Wirth, where he groaned and snored for five hours. The train started again and began to rattle along at a growing speed.

The 133 Limboia did not respond to the other creature who travelled with them. They did not want to have contact with this stranger who seemed to be made of two men; they had never come across a being like this before and feared its proximity. To Sidrus these ghosts meant nothing and so he stretched out among their cringing forms, determined on sleeping his way back into Essenwald.

Fleischer awoke at noon the following day to find Ishmael sitting and watching him in the shuddering carriage. After he had drunk some water and devoured some of the fruit and hardtack rations he was ready to speak.

"Was it the anthropophagi?" asked Ishmael.

Fleischer shook his head, with tears in his eyes.

"Who, then? What took the other men?"

He shook his head again.

"Who put you in that tree, you must know that?"

"A . . . a . . . shadow, it was like a shadow."

Ishmael realised that it was a waste of time trying to talk to this man while he was still in shock.

"You better pull yourself together. We will be back in the city in a few hours. There are clothes at the end of your bunk."

How the news spread it was impossible to say, but spread it did. It must have been the sound of the train's whistle or its smoke rising out of the forest that first gave the alarm. But how they knew that the Limboia had been found and that they were returning, nobody ever explained. The rumour spread fast and hard: The city could start again. Everybody would benefit. A great flock began to descend on the Timber Guild station. And those who slept there and loafed under its shelter found brooms and shovels and started clearing the place up. There would be new jobs available if the heart started again. Guixpax had told Cyrena the news and was astonished at her lack of response. The young master was either injured or a hero, or perhaps both. There had been rumours of distant gunfire and the entire city was churning with the news. Cyrena told Ghertrude and they agreed it would be shabby if the Lohr family were not represented at the arrival. So they decided to go together and the limousine was called. The rumour had, of course, hit the old town first and Sholeh had heard it half a day before the gentry. He would want her, but she knew better than to go to the station. She would be seen and they would be compromised. He had explained the situation and she knew they had to wait. She would prepare her cosy room for him and he would find great solace in her body. He would root himself again in her passion.

The sense of expectation was solid and unknown. Nobody knew what would be coming up the track. Deacon Tulp feared a total disaster. Talbot hoped for an unqualified success. Everybody else hoped for something in between. An enterprising trader had brought food and drink, and even in the rain a party started to brew. Some of the itinerants wandered about the track, hoping to be the first to see it arriving. One had his ear pressed against the iron rails, listening for the distant rumble.

Ishmael had ordered Hoss to stop the train on the far outskirts of the city. To come back and wake him and give him time to wash and dress. The engineer did not understand the order but executed it anyway. The engine huffed and gurgled in its braked position while Ishmael shaved those parts of his face that still grew hair. He dressed in his clean bush kit and re-bandaged his hands. They were much better. But he did not intend to present himself unfrayed. His wounds had always been valuable to him and today might be his biggest audience yet. He looked into the small hand mirror and adjusted his hat. He then went to the prone body of Wirth and felt for his heart. It still beat; his witness was intact. There was a small patch of congealing blood by his left ear. Ishmael put his fingers on it, breaking its blister meniscus. He returned to the mirror and, in very much the same way he had seen Cyrena apply lipstick, he smeared the sticky blood around his new eye and the most obvious tangle of scars. The effect was perfect. He washed his fingers again and left the carriage, walking to the engine, where he would find the most dramatic position to be seen from. He then gave the command to continue and the train shuddered into locomotion and Hoss sounded the whistle in a long harsh blast.

An hour after the station was packed, the engine's whistle was heard, followed by a stuttering burst of machine-gun fire, which inspired a great flurry of activity around the station. At the first glimpse of the smoking black dot, a frenzied turmoil broke out. People started to run down the track towards it. By the time its braking bulk screeched into the station and Hoss sounded the last deafening blast, it was covered in waving bodies.

Ghertrude and Cyrena sat stiffly in the Phaeton, waiting for someone to come to them.

"They got 'em all," someone shouted from the slave carriage. And a great roar began to rise up from the mob.

Ishmael looked immaculate. He had moved down the train until he was in the front open carriage, where he sat on an upturned box, the Hotchkiss across his knees. He stood and barked orders down to the crowd as the train stopped. Demanding that medics should attend the first carriage. There were "men to be taken to the hospital." He called for help marshalling the Limboia back to the slave house. He pretended not to see the lilac Phaeton parked at the entrance of the station. They could wait and watch his triumph. Ishmael stepped down onto the platform and walked back to the carriage where Wirth had been strapped to a stretcher. He slid open the door and waited for the medics. Then he saw Talbot and three other men of importance pushing their way through the crowd. He turned his back on them and stepped inside the compartment. Talbot's group had stopped short of the track while being told what was going on. Ishmael theatrically appeared at the carriage door, holding up a dishevelled and vacant-looking Fleischer, whom he helped down the steps like a sick child or a frail maiden aunt. Talbot rushed forward and took Fleischer's other hand and exchanged a look of shock and admiration with Ishmael.

The rain stopped and the hot sun escaped, hammering the steaming station house and platform. Ishmael stepped away from the thanks that were being bestowed on him into the thronging crowd, knowing that he was not going to see the girl tonight. He would milk this moment for all he could and spending the night in Cyrena's bed was part of it. At least she could have nothing but praise for him now and it might make her a bit more appreciative and responsive between the sheets.

Wirth's stretcher passed alongside on its way to an ambulance, and Ishmael barked, "Make haste and take great care, that man is a hero."

The word was out and spoken loudly enough for it to be snapped up by all around. Strangely it did not settle on the pungent filthy half corpse being sped through the multitude, but turned onto the immaculate wounded young man who had brought the

Limboia back and was now organising their arrival and the care of his friends.

Unfortunately for Ishmael there were no palm leaves growing near the station.

The Limboia were escorted off the carriages and marched back to the slave house by a crowd that did not know whether to slap them on their backs or beat them. The herald looked back towards Ishmael and the hero raised his arm above his head, pointing towards the sky, his index finger greatly extended. The herald looked away and the Limboia shuffled at double speed.

"Feed them," shouted the hero as they left the station. Talbot was behind him.

"We owe you a great gratitude, Mr. Williams. You must come and see me the moment you have recovered from your gruelling expedition."

Ishmael was ready to talk now, to get his anxious teeth into the future.

"But for now I think you have more pressing matters."

He beamed a radiant smile, put his arm around the hero's shoulder and kindly turned him to face the other end of the station, and the waiting lilac Phaeton.

"Someone's come to take you home."

In the agitated disorder, no one saw Sidrus sneak out the other side of the train. He changed clothes and shoes on the shadow side, and then walked around the back of the guard's van to join the happy throng. Someone thrust a mug of warm beer in his hand as others danced around the train and clapped for Hoss as he waved from the footplate. Sidrus watched as his prey got into the pink car. Saw the perfunctory kisses and laughed. It had not gone quite the way he wanted, but this was better. He had let his emotions get the better of him and could not wait in the forest. He had wanted blood, but never expected so much of it. He had expected Ishmael's party to run and head back for camp after the first shot. So that he might then pluck him out and carve him slowly in the depth of the Vorrh. But they had fought to the bitter end. The bat guano that he had found in a cave had worked perfectly, and he had sat back and watched the two strands of men rip each other apart with tracer rounds. The thorn wood was an extra. He had intervened only twice, when it looked like some of the better shots might take Ishmael out. He could not have that. He would never forgive himself for allowing such an easy death. The limousine pulled away and he slurped his welcome beer and thought about the pleasure that awaited him.

CHAPTER THIRTY-THREE

After the first hour Father Timothy's finger started to bleed. The sugar-water ink helped to stanch it every time he dipped it into the solution, but the pressure of writing on the hard stone was taking its toll. The pain became unbearable after he lost his nail. He was on his hands and knees and Modesta was perched above him and watched his every move from the last step of the stone stairs that led up to the door in the roof of the cave that opened out into the roofless shell of the broken house. She dictated the message in a ceaseless sermon that he wrote down word by word. Many of which he had never heard before and she had to spell for him. This irritated her but gave him more time to pause in between his scribing. The sun was slanting in from the rectangular hole above and a shimmering glow was rising from somewhere below, from one of the more open caves he assumed. The flat stone surface was shining in the patch that he had covered in wet partially invisible words. The first sentences were transparent, but as he wrote they were becoming more opaque because of the blood. She was overjoyed at this event and dictated with a relish he had never seen in her before. Her voice, like her body, had reached a new maturity, and its resonance danced in the ozone-pulsing air that the sea was breathing around them. The pain made him wince and he lifted his hand from the unfinished letter and held it towards her so that she might see the damage. He was hoping for sympathy or at least a rest. He got neither.

"Why have you stopped? The word is 'unpeeling' with two 'E's."

"I can't write any more; my finger is breaking."

She laughed and stood up, her hands on the distinctive new curve of her hips.

"You will write because that is why you are here, this is the purpose of your life."

The anger that was bubbling under his pain rose in his mouth like bile.

"How dare you, you abomination. How dare you treat me like this. I have protected you and you make me do this?"

"I treat you the way you are made and nothing else."

"I can do no more." He shuddered.

"You can and will do what you must, because that is why you live."

"For God's sake," he shouted at her.

"Exactly for God's sake," she said, grinning down at him.

"You wretched cunt," he screamed, with a rage he had never tasted before.

Her laughter was louder than his wrath and filled the cathedral-like vaulting of the caves.

"Exactly," she said, and tore open her simple dress, sending the little buttons cascading like newborn butterflies. She stood bright, proud, and defiant, holding the divided cloth in her outstretched arms like wings. He looked up at her and shrank under the smile of her womanhood.

He wrote the second "E" of "unpeeling" with tears in his eyes and a lump in his throat that felt like anthracite. Thus he continued, biting back the riot of emotions that churned inside him. She called out more sentences and he did not notice that she was climbing down to stand next to him. She picked up the jar with the now-brown ink and spat loudly into it, making him turn around, shuffling into her naked proximity. She stirred the water, sugar, blood, and phlegm with her delicate finger and looked down hard into his pathetic eyes.

"I . . . I . . . just want to . . ." he started to say.

She put her stained finger to her lips and hushed him, then pointed to his gawping face and quickly thrust the finger into his open mouth.

"This will make it better," she said. The effect was almost instant. The pain drained and a warmth flooded through him and centred in his loins.

"Now write," she said, this time in a softer voice. She watched him turn away, head down, not daring to look at her again. Over the next hours he continued to write, never once raising his eyes to her sonorous naked voice. To help his concentration and avert his eyes, he remembered Lutchen's last letter and repeated parts of it continually under his breath. The old priest had been wrong about Modesta, but his stern words helped now as a chant to dilute her overpowering presence and give Timothy a shallow space to hide in.

Dear Timothy,

My dear boy, I was so sorry to hear about your shocking ordeal. I think this child must be very different to my first surmise and that I might have given you the wrong advice about how to deal with her. It is important to guard yourself against such severe shock. The mind is a delicately balanced instrument that can become overwhelmed by such experiences.

However, the soul is a sturdier thing and I have no doubt that yours is stoic and profoundly aware of some of the jeopardy that it might befall. I am sure the christening will eventually calm things, once the essence of our Lord settles in the child's heart.

I have no doubt that whatever it is that vexes Modesta will be dissolved when she makes her pilgrimage to the Vorrh. There must be something in the curdled mix of her native and foreign blood that needs the great forest's influence. Your work with her now as she passes through innocence into maturity will be the groundwork to the salvation of her soul.

I will be here for her and for you when you arrive in Essenwald. Should there be any more difficulties, if it worsens or anything gets in the way of her passage here, then consult the Roman Ritual and Saint Benedict, and know that you can confront her with:

Sunt mala quae libas. Ipse venena bibas!

Salvation of her soul, salvation of her soul. What you offer me is evil.

Drink the poison yourself! Salvation of her soul. Drink the poison yourself.

CHAPTER THIRTY-FOUR

$\mathcal{E}$verybody was talking about him. Everywhere Sholeh went. The hero of the Vorrh, he who fought and survived a horrible battle. The saviour of the city. She was so proud.

She desperately wanted to see Ishmael, hear every incident from his own lips when they were not being used for more strenuous purposes. This was the day of his return. His first day back in the city and she longed for him. She could not sleep for the waiting. She listened all night for his foot on the stair. Imagined him creeping, shoes in hand, to her bedroom like he had before. Trying to not put his weight on the creaking boards. That Cyrena woman would keep him to herself. Smother him in her attentions. Sholeh had once been to look at her while he was away. Ishmael had mentioned her trips to the blind home. Every first Friday of the month she would pay them a visit and bring financial gifts. "Lady Bountiful," he had called her, and "blind leading the blind." They had both laughed at her folly.

The day had arrived for her next visit and Sholeh was already there, escorting the two beggars she had befriended by the old town gate. She had told them that they needed a little painless treatment to make their useless eyes less sore and help keep the flies away. She told them that if they went with her on that Friday she would give them more money for one hour than they could make in a day. Chalky and his sister agreed. The three of them were waiting near the side door of the clinic section of the blind home. She did not want to miss her opportunity, so timing was everything. She had bought them lemon ices in biscuit cones. A rare treat for professional beggars who gave all their spoils to their father. They were trying to eat it before the sun did. The sticky water already running down their hands. The coldness snatching at the inside of their throats.

The lilac car glided past them and Sholeh was galvanized into action. This was her business, her control, and had nothing to do with Ishmael. He would never know, never see what she was doing now. He sat in a bliss of ignorance on the other side of town.

"Right now," she said and grabbed at Chalky's sleeve, pushing him and his sister across the path to the small queue by the clinic door. So sudden was the propulsion that the delicious ice was jolted out of the sister's cone to instantly melt on stove-hot paving. The desolate girl did not know what had happened or where it had gone and woefully contented herself by sucking on the soggy biscuit.

Cyrena glided into the home after her chauffeur had parked the car directly outside. There were five people waiting before Sholeh and the sticky children. This had to be done right. She needed to be at the counter now.

"Don't touch them, they will become more infected," said Sholeh loudly to the bewildered girl. "And you must not touch anybody else, you know what happened yesterday. That poor woman, and she only wanted to help."

There was a shudder in the queue. Chalky was looking up at the lady.

"Do you mean the Touch, Fräulein?" he asked politely.

Nobody had said that word in two years. The horror of the

Touch, the Fang-dick-krank pestilence, had been excommunicated from memory. Banished from conversation and thought. Some of the people in the line looked back at the strangely scarred woman and the blind children, one with no eyes at all.

"Shush now, don't let these people hear."

"But we don't—"

A firm hand stifled Chalky, pretending to dab at his face with a wet handkerchief.

"Shush now, they will hear."

Hear they did, and quickly faded away. Sholeh sauntered to the front of the queue, maternally guiding her poor blind foundlings. She was at the treatment desk as Cyrena was being escorted around the ground floor, making her way towards the staircase. All eyes watched the grand lady who was about to pass. Sholeh saw the stainless-steel tray of instruments just behind Chalky's sister. Without anyone seeing, she flipped it over quickly and returned to her concerned stance before it crashed glassily to the polished floor. The girl jumped horribly and burst into tears. Chalky started to panic and prepared to run. Sholeh knelt before them, shushing their alarm. Cyrena instantly changed directions and approached the desperate scene.

"Poor child," she said. "It wasn't your fault, never mind, never mind."

Sholeh was shocked by her beauty. From Ishmael's tales she had imagined somebody much older, more desiccated, and without her spectacular eyes.

"Are you all right, my dear?" she asked of Sholeh, the perfect eyes reading every stitch and wrinkle of her scarred face.

"Yes, ma'am," said Sholeh, instantly hating her.

The kind hands moved over the children reassuringly, in the way that only the blind or previously blind can do. There was an instant reaction. As if a terror had been removed.

"Are they your children?" asked Cyrena, knowing they weren't.

Well, at least not by birth. Sholeh was dark-skinned but not the Congo ebony of the little ones.

"No, ma'am, I found them in the street and thought they needed treatment."

"Wonderful, very kind. We need more like you," said Cyrena, who then, in another voice and at a different speed, called her attendant over. "And yes, you are right, they do need treatment."

She said a few words to the attendant and then to the children.

"Are you hungry?"

They both nodded and for the first time Sholeh felt ashamed.

"This nice lady will take care of you."

"But we have to collect money for the family," said Chalky anxiously.

Cyrena stiffened, and then in an even kinder voice said, "Don't worry about that, I will give you money for your *family*."

The attendant, who also knew how to touch them, took them away and out of the clinic sector. Cyrena then turned her full attention on Sholeh.

"You are not part of their *family*?"

"No, ma'am." Sholeh feared for her safety if she had been. There was a look in Cyrena's commanding eyes that was chilling and endless. She feared this woman that she had heard so much about, and none of it now made sense. Stalking her had been a mistake and she wanted to get as far away as possible. Cyrena opened her bag and took out two notes. She put them into the young woman's hand.

"This is for you." As she said it, she looked again at Nebsuel's handiwork and Sholeh feared she would recognise the same signature there as in Ishmael's face, and that she would be found out and exposed to the magnificence of her vengeance. Instead Cyrena smiled a genuine and complex smile of great warmth.

"It's for you, for your kindness. I will take care of them now." She shook Sholeh's hand and said, "Goodbye, my dear."

Sholeh had been dismissed and her anger and hatred deepened as she walked away. Her previously unknown maternal pride veered up wrathfully at such treatment. She left the home drowning in the swirling tides of contempt, humiliation, and longing.

By dark she was determined to take him away from that conceited bitch. The thought of Ishmael being ravished by Cyrena's weird sexual whims revolted her. He had told her about the abnormal appetites that he was expected to fulfil and that he was looking for an opportunity to escape. Well, it had arrived. He was his own man in the world, with all of Essenwald at his feet. He just had to remove himself from the hungry clutches of that passionate woman. It was her obvious capacity for love that so scared Sholeh. He had never mentioned that part of her.

She needn't have worried. Cyrena's house was brittle.

→

Ishmael had seen it the moment he approached the car. Those eyes, capable of so much, could never lie, and the expression in them now was the opposite of the one he expected. The one he was owed. The joyous celebration of his genius was shut out the moment he entered and the car door closed. The sound of it muffled and rejected by the upholstered indifferent interior.

He could not believe Cyrena's coldness; it was impertinent and grossly unfair. Even Ghertrude had shown more warmth in the car on their return. This was not what he expected. He had been in great turmoil and discomfort for days. Near death, working hard for the city. The city that fed her and her family's coffers. He had returned triumphant and everybody celebrated his enormous success. But she treated him like a stranger.

The atmosphere in the car had grown steadily more glacial. By the time they reached the house, nobody was speaking. Ghertrude's attempts to lighten the mood had all fallen on stony ground. He was also aware of the chauffeur's supercilious eyes darting in the mirror.

The servants showed some pleasure at seeing him and hurriedly took his bags inside.

"Guixpax, I expect Ishmael would like a bath. Run one for him, please," said Cyrena, who then turned to her friends.

"I will be back in under an hour." She smiled slightly and left the entrance hall. Ghertrude was obviously embarrassed.

Ishmael was furious.

"What's wrong with her?" he snarled after she was gone.

Ghertrude ignored the question.

"I will be in the library when you are refreshed," she said.

He had been dismissed again. He snatched up his hat and stomped up the stairs to the bathroom. Ghertrude watched him go and sadly shook her head. He had not asked about Rowena once since his return.

He lay soaking in the enormous bath, fuming and rehearsing all manner of vicious verbal attacks. He boiled under the white lather of antiseptic soap that had been so meaningfully laid out for him. He fashioned spiteful looks and heartrending sermons about her injustice and insensitivity. His fingers and toes knotted and scratched at the enamel, as his rhetoric grew harder and more personal. "How dare she," he almost spat out loud. After all he had done for her. If he could dig the sight out of the blind bitch he would, make her beg for it back. On her fucking knees. He drank from the whisky that was perched at his elbow and kicked impotently at the water.

Cyrena was reassuring herself about all the inconsistencies she had found while making her itinerary. Checking for the hundredth time that they could not be mistakes: slips in book-keeping or precious things gone accidentally astray. While she objectively measured her life through the ligatures of her possessions, she gained a distant higher ground. A vantage point from which she could examine the previously unquestioned mechanism of her love for Ishmael and their existence together. She saw that much of what she thought was a committed continuum was in fact bolted together by circumstance. Their day-to-day equilibrium being not that at all but an asymmetrical contrivance entirely held together by her good faith. The missing items finally tilted the balance of her lopsided perspective, their ghosted heavy agitation picking the lock of illusion.

It was her grandmother's pearls that lived in her head more vehemently than they had ever existed in fact. Their immaculate absence gave her real pain and turned her lack of understanding and her disbelief into anger and contempt. She had been back to Chakrabarty. This time giving the shrivelled man an ultimatum. She wanted the pearls back at any price and he would help her find them. She had said that she "knew" he was not directly involved with the purloined treasure but that he could find out who was and save her the trouble of calling in the police. His reputation would remain unscathed if they were returned.

"But, madam," he had said just the once before she spelt out the full consequences of police and Timber Guild involvement.

Many other things had vanished too. Including a chequebook from a distant and unused savings account that she had tucked away and actually forgotten about. She had visited the bank and sealed off all such accounts when she found out how much money had evaporated.

It was a trivial amount in relation to her real assets. But a tiny fortune for somebody who had all their worldly expenses taken care of. She had made him a monthly allowance. What would, or could, he do with more? She would have happily given it to him, if he had asked. But no, he had chosen this despicable route and soiled everything they had ever had before. And now the pompous thief demanded adoration.

Dinner that night was a travesty. Indigestion silver-serviced. Appetite shredded by immaculate cutlery. None of them had met again during that day, until the gong sounded. Ghertrude had fretted over a book she could not read in the library. Cyrena quietly fumed and was secretly enjoying biding her time before she made the accusation. This was a new attribute to her already plentiful personality. She suspected that it was a direct genetic contribution from the Lohrs, and she liked being back in the ancestral fold. Ishmael had brooded and drunk himself to sleep. After a while the whisky and his substantial weariness joined forces and changed his bleary focus from vengeance to Sholeh. He knew he could not go there tonight, but he planned to be there tomorrow and maybe forever.

At the dining table his intoxication and hangover passed through each other and wanted to be more coherent than he. He gripped the polished mahogany and stared at the steaming soup before him. Ghertrude attempted to disturb the icy atmosphere.

"This must be the first good food you have had in a week," she said, not accepting Cyrena's dagger glare from the other end of the table. Ishmael took five spoonfuls and then heard her voice.

"Thasright," he said, trying to focus on her weightless face. He looked down the table to Cyrena and then quickly back into his bowl.

On a side table, Guixpax delicately arranged Guinea fowl and vegetables on large gold-rimmed plates that were perfectly warmed. He butlered them to the diners, then stood back to soundlessly hover.

"It's your favourite," said Ghertrude.

"Thasright, my faforit," said Ishmael, extending his arm and pointing at Guixpax. "Heknows vat." He suddenly saw his hand

and index finger. "Youwodent belivf the powa I ave." He waved it at Cyrena, who was precisely dissecting her food. "Youwodent belifff it."

He bought his finger back and tapped his chest as if trying to massage a miniature heart awake.

"You must be a very important man," said Cyrena in a colourless voice.

"Thasrigh," said Ishmael, lifting his finger again.

"You'd better eat your food before it gets cold," said Ghertrude, avoiding her friend's razored smile. Ishmael stared at the prim corpse on the immaculate plate. Eventually he forked a heavy daub of mashed potato almost into his mouth.

"Forit getscold." He chewed.

Guixpax poured white wine into long-stemmed glasses, and upstairs the clock ticked out the inevitable dissections of existence.

The silence in the dining room was chiselled only by the dental skating of steel on china. Ghertrude was thinking about Rowena, Cyrena was thinking about her grandmother, and Ishmael was having trouble with peas and bones. Suddenly the hacked carcass of his fowl flew off the plate with a stream of vegetables.

"Fk," he half snapped.

Guixpax glided forward, only to be stopped by Cyrena's raised hand.

Ishmael lurched from his chair, leaning across his plate and the table trying to retrieve the absconding bird. He could not quite reach it, his pinching fingertips easing the greasy rib cage inches away instead of restraining it. In his struggle Ishmael's coat toppled his glass, which broke and puddled towards Ghertrude.

Suddenly, and totally without warning, Cyrena let out a devastating peal of laughter. It crashed around the room and infectiously attacked the openmouthed Ghertrude, who after a few moments also burst into raucous guffaws that refused to be stifled by her starched napkin. Ishmael gave up on his quarry and slumped back into his seat, filching Ghertrude's half-filled glass in the process. He was greatly perplexed by these screeching women and turned for some support to Guixpax, who had vanished, discreetly sliding into the kitchen at the beginning of the hilarity.

The laughter was dying down and Ishmael decided to take control again. He sloped forward and solemnly raised his glass. The women watched from behind their napkins.

"Tuuda laidizz," he grandly said.

Their explosive roar of near hysteria nearly knocked him from his seat. Five minutes later, when all the sound had been used up and they no longer ached and clutched at their sides, they were able to stand up. Before leaving, Cyrena ferried a new open bottle of wine to his end of the table. Then the women linked arms and went upstairs. That night Ghertrude and Cyrena never left each other's side and Ishmael never left the table. The women shared a bed and drifted to sleep over an ocean of troubles on a surprising raft of exhausted giggles. He passed out and snored randomly, the scars of his face glued to the table with congealed Guinea fowl lard and stale wine.

Ishmael did not fully awake before two p.m. the next day. Sometime in the night he had slid from the table to the couch next door, relieving himself in the soup tureen that Guixpax hadn't had the opportunity of removing before the evening turned unruly and he made himself absent. The letter from Talbot arrived at eleven requesting Ishmael to come to his offices at nine the next morning. He sat with the alert letter in his limp hand. He had managed to get to the bathroom by three and now he sat on the toilet seat, leaning against the wall and watching the steaming water filling the bath. His animal brain was working and scheming ahead. He would see Sholeh tonight and luxuriate in her open and active body. He would pack a bag and put it by the side door. He would leave this miserable house after dinner with a change of clothes so he could go straight from her room to Talbot's in the morning, full of the zest and enthusiasm that a night with Sholeh would give him. He had not seen the other two. He knew they were in the house, he sometimes heard them giggling.

After his bath he dressed, carefully combing and recombing his long hair. He was becoming sober again and the mild throb of his headache was bearable now. To his great relief he had an erection when he next thought about her and what she would do to him. He was shaping up for his new life and nobody here would give a damn where he was or where he had been, everything was ahead now. This night, tomorrow, and forever would be his.

CHAPTER THIRTY-FIVE

*H*immelstrup was furious. He paced about his office swearing and blaming Capek, who was sitting meekly on a bentwood chair. He blamed him for the disaster of the London project.

"You said this idiot old man, this Jew, this Hector, was trustworthy. We have not heard from him in six months. He has completely vanished along with thousands of marks of my department's money."

Capek tried to answer but was shouted down.

"Compton and his men have combed all the parts of London he visited. They searched his hotel room and found nothing. His unpaid hotel room with our name attached to it. Compton has looked all over London, it's like trying to find a needle in a haystack. He even visited the lunatic asylum that he went to."

"Did he find anything?" asked Capek disinterestedly.

"What do you expect him to find, that he was talking to cretins and imbeciles?"

"But earlier you said they sent him somewhere else," piped up Capek.

"Yes . . . I did. The London asylum doctor sent him to another hospital, somewhere on the coast. He took two other men with him to question the staff."

"So?"

"So while he was interrogating the doctor, the man hit him

and then had him arrested. He is being questioned now. They think he is some kind of spy."

"But he is, isn't he?"

Between gritted teeth Himmelstrup spat out, "You are as stupid as that disgusting old Jew."

➤——→

It was worse than trying to find a needle in a haystack. Schumann was in Whitechapel, the most densely populated Jewish area of London. Compton would be seeking a particular straw, a singular strand of hay in that vast, interlocking, bristling, and defensive stack. Even worse for the bandaged and bruised Compton and his equally tattered and talentless posse, Hector was under the protection of Solomon "Solli" Diamond and his cohorts. There were many such interwoven mobs in the gritty maze of Whitechapel, Aldgate, and Stepney, but few had the reputation of Rabbi S. For he had sinned against all, his race, his religion, and his God. Hence the irony of the nickname, which he openly enjoyed. The only loyalty he kept sacrosanct was family. And those who his family admitted to their protection. Hector had been one of these. Solli's favourite uncle, Hymie, whom the rest of the family had sent to Bedlam, had called him, sent a note through the spiderweb. He had argued bitterly with his father and other uncles about Hymie. Very well, he was a little strange, he got enthusiastic about nothing, he devoured food like an animal, but he had a heart. He wouldn't hurt a fly. He had been so kind to him when he was nothing but a snot-nosed infant with his arse hanging out of his trousers.

"I will take care of him, he will be under my personal protection," he begged of the elders. But they would not have it. He needed help and was an embarrassment. Solli lost his case and his uncle. If it had been anybody else, then he would have settled it another way. He would have paid them a visit in the small hours. Coming in over the sloping tile roofs. Chewing away the rotten window frames. Whispering in their ears in the dark before clipping all or bits of their lives away. So Uncle Hymie had been sent away to live with stinking goys. Solli would never forgive the elders but was unable to rip their ears off their devout solemn faces.

He visited Hymie as much as he could. Until his heart fatigued. Even that scar-encrusted, crime-tempered heart, whose pitilessness had long since bleached all the warmth and colour away from the core of his feeling, could not endure seeing Uncle Hymie tethered so. Instead he sent money and gifts, and when Hymie and a few of the goys who helped and protected him wanted a party, he would pay for it. That was generally the reason that Hymie sent for him. But today was different, he wanted something else.

Rabbi Solli dragged his resisting bones across the Thames with his shiftless khevre of three hungry-looking men accompanying him, but their hollow spindliness was nothing compared to his. His twenty-three years in the slums of Whitechapel had robbed him of the sweet fat of kindness. He was lean and hard as spite. Quick, flinching gestures marked his readiness and burnt off the slightest trace of calm or the indulgent sugars of introspection. His icy flame was constant and purple-black and could become incandescent in seconds. All of his khevre knew this and bathed their own hands in its hissing coldness. His mood this day was swamped and unpredictable and they watched him as he became more unsettled, crossing over to the Surry side. They waited outside on the giant white steps while he plodded towards his uncle's room, almost dragging his ebony cane behind him like a rigid resistant tail. He hated everything about this place; the meshugoim-azil had the stink of the workhouse on it. He, of course, was too young to have seen an active one, but the old buildings were still there and the ancestral memory of them was buried deep. Its stink hummed in his bones. He bowled into his uncle's room, into a reception party waiting for him. He flinched and made ready when he saw them, smelling a trap, a compromise, or, worse, a hope.

"Come in, my boy, come in," said Hymie, waving with both hands. To his right stood the tall spooky figure of Nicholas. They had met before, and he had given the rabbi the ultimate creeps. But Uncle Hymie said he was good man and that he helped him every day.

"He's an angel," the old man had said loudly and with great passion. "My malokhim." So he was grudgingly accepted.

To Hymie's left was a little man, older than Hymie, he guessed, and curiously foreign and out of place.

"You know Nicholas," Hymie gestured, "and this, this is my new friend Hector, he is very special."

Solli looked again at the nervous stranger.

"Come closer," Hymie said.

Solli gathered a chair and pulled it close to his seated uncle and the stranger. Nicholas remained standing behind the grinning uncle.

"Solli, you're a good boy, like my own. I have something special, something important for you to do."

Solli nodded and took shifty looks at the others.

"Hector is a German."

"So are we, uncle."

"No, Hector is a new German. He arrived a few weeks ago."

Solli tightened automatically, glaring at Schumann.

"But he is one of us, more than one of us, he is many of us and we shall be on his lips."

Both Solli and Hector looked equally confused.

"He is Nun-Beit-Yod-Alef, do you understand?"

Neither of the confused men knew the meaning and dabbled about in their memory to find it. They both went back to the

Talmud at the same time, catching a glimpse in each other's eyes that welded a union, a possible friendship that neither of them wanted to recognise.

"Solli, you are a good boy and I have asked you for many things."

"No, uncle, you have asked me for nothing."

"You are kind, thank you. Very well, I ask you for everything now."

Solli focused, almost beyond his normal quickness, into the alertness of predatory animals.

"Guard this man with all you have. I want him in your care."

Nobody spoke and the tableau just exchanged small, quiet glances.

Nicholas stood above them all, beaming.

➤—→

Three days later Hector had a room in the stack. The tight core of Jewish East London had shrunk much over the last twenty years. Dispersal was the reward of success, and many of the fanatically hardworking community had prospered and moved on, their children being forced to take the scent of new ambitions and greener territories. Hymie's tribe were stickers, they were going nowhere. Their ambitions were to lock down, dig in, and own this the last piece of land where they had settled. Nothing was going to move them. Wealth or pogrom, war or peace would not make them budge. The room was on the top, the attic floor of a tenement block that, it was rumoured, had been the hiding place of the Whitechapel murderer. This was not an unusual thing: dozens of dwellings had claimed intimate knowledge of the most infamous unidentified killer ever. The true identity and whereabouts of old Leather Apron were secretly known and whispered in every pub and alleyway in the East End. And they were all wrong. If Jack the Ripper himself had used the first-floor rooms, then there was no trace of him now. Oddly, the apartment remained locked and untenanted, which added much to its reputation and the mysterious nature of the gloomy property. The ground floor was a small shop selling cat meat and string. Hector's immediate neighbour below him was a fearsome, perpetually vigilant harridan called Betty Fishburn. She had been there for only ten years but ruled the staircase as if she had built every mouldering step that led to and past her violently red-leaded doorstep. After a week she knew everything about the "professor" and it was clear that she had been given the job of being his formidable guard dog. She had many "sons," a few "daughters," and very many "girls" who called on her and stayed for irregular periods. All of them were in some way connected to the business of Mr. Fishburn (now deceased) and their occupation of the stairs was always brisk, whispered, and furtive. Hector kept himself to himself despite the strongest sensation of being watched and spied upon. Mrs. Fishburn wanted to tell him everything about her life and "goings-on," but he rarely had the time and scurried past her peering, listening door. She was in some way connected to Solomon Diamond, whose name she never spoke, but only ever called him "His Nibs." Hector was puzzled at first about how he was meant to survive here and how to use his time. Then the books started to arrive. Intriguing, then extraordinary, then remarkable books. They arrived with Solli and his henchmen, along with his food, coal, and alcohol. No money was ever exchanged and certainly no conversation about the books. They came from "Uncle Hymie and his pal," who, it had to be said, had astonishing taste and knowledge. It seemed that each volume referenced the one before and that each twisted byway that Hector decided to take would be met by the next book, being a signpost or an index to it. Thus weeks flowed into months and months tiptoed towards years.

———

On a quiet day, almost four months after Hector had arrived, there was a rapid knock on his mostly unvisited door. His Nibs had come to call.

"Solli, do come in," he warmly invited.

"Ain't got the time, we got to get to the Pavilion before eleven."

"Where?"

"Someone there to see ya."

Hector grabbed his topcoat, hat, and scarf and tried to keep up with His Nibs as he ferreted along the narrow wintry streets, his cane swishing aside imaginary obstacles in his fast, sharp walk. Puffs of smoke punctuated his velocity from the Burma cheroot that lived in the corner of his hectic mouth. Two other men strode with them. Solli never went anywhere alone.

He wheeled fast out of the dripping alley into the noise and confusion of Whitechapel High Street, with the scurrying Hector out of breath behind him. The air was brown passing through grey, and churned and ebbed against the hunchback shops that gaggled against the rushing tide of the overcast morning populace. They pushed through the bustle and noise, turning sharply into one of three tall but unremarkable doors of a remarkable building. Solli and crew disappeared while Hector slowed and stood back from the doors to look at the huge circular window above the entrance, the great eye of an unblinking cyclops staring across and over the chaos of pedestrians and the river of traffic that jostled and nudged along inside the constricting banks of paving. The head of one of Solli's henchmen appeared at the door. His scrutiny stabbing at the passing crowd until he saw Hector, staring upwards.

"Oi, come on, 'e's waitin'."

Hector quickly joined him, and they entered a long shadowy corridor punctuated by framed pictures of weird and wonderful people. Some had been coloured in tints and hues far beyond the normal pallor of mortals. Hector slowed, wanting to stop and look into the glassed outrageous faces.

"What is this place?" he asked, almost as if speaking to the picture itself. Solli rattled his cane, sounding his impatience and throating the distance to the doors at the end of the passage. Music could be heard polkaing in the room beyond.

"Come on, Professor, he's waiting," he said, touching the old man's sleeve. They pushed through the swinging doors into a swirling shuddering theatre overpowered by a rippling stage. The auditorium was unexpectedly large, with two vast looming balconies, the gilt of the empty seats bobbing with reflected light, as the brightness flashed and sparkled off the mass of moving figures romping across the stage. Hector's jaw dropped at the spectacle. Twenty or more dancers sang and gestured at one another with violently unnatural faces, their makeup melting in the arc lights. Their words were sharp and cunningly comic and snapped out in old-world Yiddish. He could understand the core German but became lost in the other twists and knots of vocabulary and expression. But the meaning of the acts, the drift of this most eccentric play was beyond his comprehension. The centre of which now seemed dominated by a dwarfish child dressed in a grotesque parody of an Egyptian or Far East potentate. His jaw could not drop any more, so he did. He plumped into one of the front seats, just behind the orchestra, which studiously ignored him. He sat and stared grinning at the stage.

"What is this?" he said with bewildered good humour, never taking his eyes from the loud sequined acting.

"Rehearsals," said Solli. "Last week it was Shakespeare, more your kinda thing."

The rabbi did not wait for an answer. He nodded to one of his men to watch Hector while he rapidly headed backstage.

The next song was about a forgotten mother left in the homeland, the crooner feeling and squeezing the life out of every word under the papier-mâché cactus that loomed beside him, casting its striking shadow across the stage floor. Hector loved it, it was ridiculous, it was Crummles and Company writ large and real. Dickens alive, well, and totally Jewish, sparkling in the colourless, secret mass of Whitechapel. He was lost in the wonder of it. And did not notice anybody else come and go as the acts poured onto and flooded off the stage.

"You look like you're enjoying yourself," said Solli from the seat behind him.

"Yes, it's wonderful."

"It's dead."

Hector turned in his seat. "What?"

"It's on its way out, it's dying here. Not enough of the old tribes anymore. This place used to be bursting at the seams. More than three thousand packed in 'ere once. They couldn't make so many acts. And now they're lucky if they can fill the front stalls." Solli laughed acridly. "Even the voice is going."

"Yiddish?" asked Hector.

"Yes. The bones of us, the ligaments that hold us together and keep us here."

Hector nodded.

"You speak it?" asked Solli.

"No, only Hebrew, Aramaic, and a little post-Achaemenid."

Solli made a snuffling shrugging movement; Hector was dismissed.

"You're wanted backstage," he said abruptly and was gone, clearing the end of the aisle. Before Hector could catch his breath. He reluctantly left his seat, accepting the young man's irritation, and made his way through the auditorium to the side entrance of the stage.

Backstage was even more chaotic. Groups of performers and frantic dressers collided and pushed between the narrow walkways. The hushed shouting backstage almost drowned out the current performing act. Thank God that on "the night" the audiences were even louder.

Hector was buffeted about, caught between a flight of tenors and a row of temple dancers, some of their body makeup rubbing off on his charcoal-grey topcoat. A few of the girls fluttered their ostrichlike eyelashes, smiled, and winked at "the old gent." Hector flattened his hair and smiled back through thirty years.

"Over here," said Solli, and forcibly steered Hector to catch up with another flock of tall willowy men who were exiting the stage. They were dressed as cowboys in wide gleaming white jackets with lots of long fringes dangling from their sleeves. Tall ten-gallon hats made them even larger. They were excited, flushed, and hectic and rippled past him, laughing and immense. Hector looked up at their perspiring faces and exaggerated makeup, turned away, then quickly looked back again. Under the thick white-and-pink greasepaint of the sixth singer he recognised the smiling countenance of Nicholas, the Erstwhile, a long way from the closed subdued corridors of Bedlam.

Solli shepherded both of them into a small dressing room next to the ever-active toilet with a determination that bordered on rudeness. Once inside, Nicholas took off his white Stetson and ruffled his immaculate hair.

"Bit of a surprise for you, Professor?" he said.

"I am flabbergasted, Nicholas," he replied quickly, adding, "by all of this, but even more amazed to find you acting in the middle of it."

"Singing, actually," beamed the angel, who seemed to be still glowing from the spotlight, his white costume dazzling the auburn air of the dim backstage.

"He's here to warn you and take you on a job," said Solli in clouds of heavy cigar smoke.

Hector looked disturbed and turned his attention to the most unlikely cowboy in the world.

"There have been some men, one in particular . . . what did you call him, Solomon?"

"Shtik drek," said Solli, flinching under his proper name.

"Shtik drek, quite so," said Nicholas. "He came to the Bethlem asking about you, when you had been there, who you spoke to, that kind of thing. He then came to see Hymie and me."

Hector took a quick glance at Solli.

"He is called Compton," continued Nicholas.

"What did you tell him?" said Hector, feeling the ground becoming unstable.

"I told him that we had talked for a long while about my ol' man and cats."

Hector's expression became limp.

"I told him that he should talk to Mr. Wain. Which he did for three hours."

Hector began to chortle behind his anxiety.

"He then went to talk to Hymie. He tried to threaten him into telling him where you were."

Hector sobered again and Solli became serious, dangerous, and shrewd.

"And what did Hymie tell him?" asked Hector.

"Oh, he told him to fuck off."

When they had stopped laughing, Nicholas was waiting to continue.

"There is one more thing. I don't know if it is good or bad. After he spoke to us he talked to the doctors and it was overheard that one of them told him to go to Netley and talk to a Dr. Hodges."

"Hedges," corrected Hector, before he started to giggle uncontrollably.

The other men stared at him.

"What's so funny?" said Solli unpleasantly.

It was difficult for Hector to get the words out. Finally he said, "Compton and Hedges," hissing on the "Hedges."

He looked at Solli's angry bewilderment.

"You would like Hedges, Solli, he's your kinda man. He will give Compton your kind of answers to his questions."

"Why did you want to see me?" The question came much later, after Nicholas had removed his makeup and was dressed in his normal daily clothes.

"We will talk about it on the boat," said Nicholas, who was weirdly distracted.

"Boat?" said Hector, a nervous catch in his voice.

"We are going back to Lambeth on the drink," said Solli.

"Drink?"

"The water, the river, Ol' Father Thames," said Solli, who was gaining some pleasure from Hector's unease. "Nuthink to worry about, you're going with Patriarch, he's a proper ferryman, Thames pilot 'n' all. He's picking you up, down at Shadwell."

Hector was trying not to turn green at the prospect. Memories of the bobbing boat and the vertical ladder of Spike Island stirred and plucked at his quiet confidence and his growing curiosity. The Thames could not be as choppy as the sea, he thought. The ladders to shore not as high. Nicholas turned and stared at them without a smile. It was time to go.

Outside, away from the music and the limelight, the world had dimmed and become much colder. Snow was falling in uncertain flurries and the sun was tucked behind unfallen tons of deep grey cloud. The odd party made their way diagonally across the eastern outskirts. Hats and scarves held tight against the approaching cold and the eyes of strangers. There was some rivalry in the lead. Solli was darting, stitching his way across the smoke-filled streets, congested with industrial traffic. He stopped and started, always looking back to check on the safety of his charge. Nicholas was gliding forward, unaware of anything or anybody. He could have reached the boat blindfolded. Hector had never seen him like this. It was fascinating and unnerving. By the time they reached Shadwell the snow was falling evenly and the sounds of the city were being swallowed alive. They stopped by a derelict wooden door with "Moses Kessler, Pilot" daubed on it with green paint. Solli ducked in and the others followed onto a dripping wooden path that ran between the tarred warehouses and turned into a broad sturdy jetty.

"Kessler's pier," said Solli proudly.

The Thames stretched out from it in an equally solid muscular expanse of brooding water. It stank and the disappearing light gave it a proportion of despicable indifference. One of Solli's henchmen reached behind a thick tarpaulin and pulled out a battered squat bugle that had been hanging there by its leather strap. He wiped the mouthpiece on his woollen scarf, put it to his lips, and gave a few off-key squawks across the water. Some minutes later a dark shadow moved alongside the pier. The steam launch had been built for endless rough service and it had none of the faux doomed gaiety of the small passenger boat that Hector had been terrified on before. It was called the *Cromwell*.

Solli's men held the ropes, and while the others boarded, standing on the tarred deck and looking around, a man lighting a paraffin lamp was suddenly there beside them.

"Season's greetings, gentiles," he said.

Nobody knew what he meant.

"How many going?" he said to Solli.

"Just the two, Patriarch."

"And coming back?"

"Just the one," said Solli, pointing at Hector.

It had not occurred to him that only he and the Erstwhile

would be travelling this mournful river. He had become used to the company of the gang.

Solli's taciturn abruptness appealed to him. He was beginning to have an attachment to this younger opposite of himself. He liked having the rabbi's danger on his side.

Suddenly the boat sounded empty, unworldly, and cold, and the journey back would sound worse. In his doubt he looked towards Nicholas for comfort and saw the wafting snow breaking against his now-remote profile. The general strangeness of the man seemed a million miles away and Hector wondered what the job, the task before them, was to have removed him so far from their company.

"Let's go, gentiles," said the gruff captain.

"Thank you, Patriarch," said Solli with respect in his voice.

"Tell your father I will see him when the 'festivities' are over."

Solli nodded and climbed onto the pier, his men throwing the untied ropes back on the boat. The engine groaned louder and the boat moved away from the solid shore into the middle of the solid water. The three sticklike figures did not wave and looked like structural details as the boat pulled farther into the dark water. The captain lit another lamp and put it behind its green starboard shade, the falling snow dancing against its movement. He then opened a double door and stepped down into a tight warm room that smelt of coal, oil, tobacco, and men.

"Here you are, gentiles, snug as a bug in a rug. It will take us just over an hour on this tide. Make yourselves at home. There's even some yuletide grog down there, but save some for me, mind."

"Is it Christmas?" said Hector, surprised at his own question.

"Where, old father, have you been hiding for the last weeks?" said the captain. "Tomorrow is Christmas Eve. You people should know that."

"I am not a gentile," said Hector.

"You're all gentiles to me," said the captain. "If you need me, I'll be up in the wheelhouse with me son." And with that, he hoisted himself up the iron ladder at the end of the wooden cabin, through a hatch in the ceiling. The engine cleared its throat and accelerated, throbbing forward into the twilight and the drifting snow.

"Nicholas . . . Nicholas, I know that what awaits in Lambeth is important . . . more vital for you, because I have never seen you so distracted before."

There remained a numbing silence, cupped in the oak cabin above the pulse of the boat.

"Please tell me of the anxiety that grips you so, and that we must face together."

The snow fell white through the grey sky into the sullen grey waters that heaved against the timber skin of the speeding craft.

"It's so sad," Nicholas said after a long pause.

"What, my friend?" said Hector, almost without voice.

"I saw many things there."

"Where?" said Hector.

"In that wonderful place, the Pavilion. I saw wonderful things there. I saw the great Madame Feinmann die onstage. I saw her faint and rise and faint again. I saw her agonies before us all, after taking poison. I saw her torment the last fifteen minutes, while the audience stopped talking, stopped crunching peanuts, and became like undropped pins. The only sound being their tears falling onto the thick-carpeted floor. Which only I could hear."

Hector said nothing; there was nothing to say.

"And then when the curtain fell and she came back to life, I had to put my hands over my ears because of the explosion from the audience, their applause. And now it will all disappear, all be gone in a few more years. As if it had never been. It's so very sad."

Nicholas stared into the space of another time and remained speechless.

Sometime later the wooden room slowed and Hector remembered he was on a boat. The captain's head appeared through the hatch in the ceiling.

"There's a still in the change of tides, you might want to see this, very rare."

Nicholas arose and opened the door onto the deck. It was dark now and they adjusted their eyes. The water, the millions of tons of it, was stationary like a millpond. Hector could only guess that this unusual phenomenon was due to the incoming coastal tide changing into the outgoing one and that a strange point of stasis had been achieved during the exchange. But the stillness of the water became a secondary feature to the movement of the snow. It fell straight down into its own reflection on the mirrored Thames, the depth of the reflection rising up to meet it. Each flake fell from a black sky and fluttered up from the river's black bed to meet its twin and become one in a second before disappearing, every particle of snow weaving the same way above and below them. They all stood in amazement. Nicholas began to smile again.

Nobody spoke; the world was holding its breath.

Without warning the river suddenly rolled back into action, the boat lurched, and the captain was quickly back in the wheelhouse shouting at the helm. The engine roared and everybody grabbed on to something solid as it turned into the shifting massive tide. The snow became normal and they continued on the last part of their journey. Big Ben awoke sullenly in the moment and sounded seven o'clock as they approached Westminster Bridge.

"We're here, voyage over," called the captain as the boat

slowed and slid alongside a jettied pier. By now darkness was everywhere. The snow gave the only light blinking around the calm bobbing dock.

Hector was greatly relieved to find that the climb up onto land was insignificant and easy. Nicholas led the way. They thanked the swaying captain, whom they couldn't really see, and waved him away from the gently rocking Lambeth shore. After he had vanished into the snow and tide they heard, "Good night, gentiles."

"Isn't he going to wait?" asked Hector apprehensively. "I thought his moorings were here."

"No," said Nicholas slowly. "Patriarch has no moorings. He will come back when he is ready."

Hector was puzzling at this strange answer as they started to walk from the edge of the Thames inland. His next question was erased by Nicholas saying, "I am sorry that I did not tell you that tonight we must stay until dawn. It is a night of semblance and later we will rest in the plural."

Hector was trying to understand, concentrating like a listener in the high wind to a man who only whispers.

"Did you not see back there on the water, feel bits of time hold their breath?"

"You mean in the stillness of the tides?"

"The Thames gave a barometer show. Fluids have that way about them. Did you know the oceans are the memory of the world? But I deviate and lose points. What you saw was the river demonstrating what is happening all over the city tonight. Semblance comes now in the game and shakes the normal out of its current time and gives the before a while to sit back cosy where it used to."

Hector was lost. They were moving away from the river, Nicholas with his collar turned up, and the old man tightly muffled in his thick scarf. A hesitant wind eddied the snow in all directions except down, and the frozen slush creaked under their feet.

Nicholas continued. "That's why we come here tonight. To visit the old place, remembering during the semblance."

"What old place?"

"My ol' man's place," said Nicholas.

They walked quickly forward while Hector was remembering.

"Oh, Wilhelm Block!"

Nicholas stopped and peered down at the shivering stranger. "I mean William Blake."

"You are cold, my friend," said Nicholas. "Don't worry, the work will warm you."

They entered Hercules Road and walked along its emptiness until they reached the house with the plaque on its front wall. Ivy grew from just beneath it and cascaded down, almost obscuring the front door and lower window. Their portals had been trimmed to allow light and egress to occur but not enough to let a tall man in without stooping. The snow dappled their shuddering movement. A rustic wooden gate completed the metal-spear-pointed railing that enclosed the modest front garden. A single small light could be seen at the back of the house. Nicholas placed one of his hands over his heart. With the other he touched the gate and felt it move. He bowed his head and said something under his pluming breath. He then raised his hand and made a movement over his head, circling his flat palm.

"It's all right, you are safe," he said.

Hector looked sheepish and uncertain. Nicholas left the gate and walked along the fence to the side of the house, where a narrow alley marked its contour. Towards its end was a wooden door, also bedraggled with ivy. Nicholas clicked its latch and walked into the scruffy garden. It was dominated by two closely planted trees. He stopped and held out his hand towards Hector and, like a child without a moment of thought, the old man extended his hand into the warm waiting grip. They walked in the gentle snow to stand under the trees. The warmth of Nicholas's hand changed to a tingling pulse and Hector remembered the same sensation while in the presence of Hinz and Kunz back in Heidelberg. The sensation that had healed him and turned back the years and scars in his brain.

"You are to write a message here," Nicholas said, casting his other hand over the ground under the trees.

"How, what am I to write?" said Hector, looking at the scrub grass and pebbles under the snow.

"With the fingers of your right hand. I will tell you what to say. It will take all night to complete."

Hector had a million questions, but none of them could find their way to his voice, which seemed hidden and ineffectual. Instead he tested the ground with the tip of his shoe. It was rough, uneven, and looked incapable of receiving anything but a crude ploughing scratch.

"I don't know if this is going to be possible," he said to Nicholas, who was no longer there. Hector looked all around and paced the garden. The door was shut and the house looked impenetrable. Nicholas had vanished. For a horrible moment Hector thought he might have buried himself again. But the ground was evenly carpeted by untouched snow; only their footprints delineated its surface. Then from above Nicholas said, "Write."

He was in the tree, or at least his voice was. Hector looked up. A colourless, elongated shadow moved under the white leaves, which did not move, shake, or lose their icy covering.

The first words fluttered down and filled Hector's mind, then shunted into his stiffening moving arm. He knelt and began scratching at the frozen earth.

The cold that filled the garden bit hard into the tree and shabby grass; it ignored Hector and his labours as he did, working unaware and in a fit of purpose. The warmth that filled him and guided his hand came from the shadow in the tree, whispering in between the frost, the darkness, and the impossibility.

The weak yellow sun slid into the garden as the old man stood up from the finished text. He tottered a bit, as if his legs had remembered his age. He was stiff but warm. His clothes should have been saturated, but there was only a slight dampness, more akin to humidity than crawling in wet snow. He stepped carefully backwards to his starting place under the tree. He began to read the words before the pale sun stole them. As he stared, he saw a movement inside the letters themselves. At first he thought it must be an optical illusion brought about by fatigue, which he was beginning to feel. Or the disintegration of the ice particles, but as he looked more closely he was amazed to see that the whole text was infested with ants. Thousands of them. Their dark bodies weaving in between the ice and earth, stitching the crystal and the stones together. Surely there should be no ants now. Didn't they hibernate or die each winter? Certainly they didn't become active on such a night. But this enormous colony was determined and feverish in their commitment, making the words become darker and agitated. Hector started to read the words that he had no knowledge of.

"Do not read it, it is not for your eyes," said Nicholas, who was now standing by his side. "Your task is achieved, top marks." He clamped his tingling hand on Hector's shoulder. "Now you must rest. I will take you back to my room where you may sleep."

Professor Schumann did not much relish the idea of sharing Nicholas's bed. But they were a long way from anywhere else and his tiredness seemed to be growing exponentially. They left the seething text without looking back and walked out of the garden and down the alley into a brightening crisp Christmas Eve morning. They followed the alley at the back of the house, the snow laden with yellow light, tingeing with red and the first sounds of the birds waking to sing against the cold. Hector looked back as they shuffled and skidded away. The house was gone. All the houses on the south side of Hercules Road were gone. A rough building site contained behind a temporary hoarding was all that could be seen. Broken ground and irregular frozen puddles scattered around the untouched trees.

"Nicholas," said Hector.

"I know, don't look back at it. It must look like the Somme back there."

"The Somme. Have you been there?"

"No, but I know many that have."

The snow was holding back and they made quick progress through the empty streets to the hospital. Nobody noticed them as they strolled through the sleeping corridors.

"Would you like a chair?" Nicholas asked as they passed a corral of wheelchairs.

"No thank you, I can walk," said a tired but determined Hector.

They turned the corner into the seclusion of the Erstwhile's narrow room. Nicholas pulled the bedcover back and plumped the lifeless pillow.

"Please make yourself comfortable, you need deep sleep, lots of it if we are to make the plural. I will return when you are refreshed."

Hector frowned and nodded, incapable of speech. He was greatly relieved that he was not expected to share the bed with this strange unearthly creature, and the reassurance of a lone undisturbed sleep made him ready to drop instantly onto the waiting bed.

"One other thing," said Nicholas. "Please don't touch my radio."

And with that he was gone, and four minutes later so was Hector.

CHAPTER THIRTY-SIX

Ghertrude had been trying not to think about her father. She had seen him rushing in the crowds at the station and he had ignored her. He must have seen her sitting in the conspicuous limousine at the entrance. The not-thinking was eating her away, as was her grief and frustration. If the Kin had told her the truth, then her father was implicit in something so huge and shapeless that it was impossible to hold it in her understanding. She had decided to confront him with it. Last night's fiasco had convinced her that she must discover where Ishmael had come from. It might be the same place that Rowena had vanished to.

Deacon Tulp was in a quandary. He had sent his family away. His wife and younger children had all left for South Africa, where they had family friends. They had the last of his savings and a promise that if Fleischer's plan failed, he would join them very soon. He had been sluggishly preparing his own departure when the news came of the return of the Limboia. If they could be controlled, then the industry would restart and his place in the city would be restored. For the first time in months he was feeling optimistic.

As Ghertrude climbed the office stair, she heard him whistling and shuffling papers in his room above. The carpet had been removed from the wooden flight and now her footfall sounded hollow. Like one who was not there. He was packing the last bulging briefcase of files when she walked into his office.

"Ghertrude, how nice to see you. Have you come to see me off? I am not sure I am going now. Your friend might have saved all our bacon."

"No, Father, I have come so you can tell me the truth."

Her tone froze his hands over the briefcase and there was almost a hiss of his extinguished sanguinity.

"Tell me about the creatures that live in my house, that you and the guild have worked with since before I was born."

Tulp slumped. He found a chair by touch, like a blind man, and sank into it.

"My dearest child, I—"

"Tell me the truth, Father."

In a very small voice he said, "I cannot. I am sworn to secrecy."

"Even to me?"

"Especially to you."

She came closer so that he could not avoid her presence. "Is Ishmael my brother?" She had no intention of being put off that easily.

He shook his head and glared at her.

"Who is Rowena's father?"

"This is very difficult for me," he said wearily.

"But I must know," she shouted.

"Stop now, child, before it's too late."

"I will not, I am your daughter and you must tell me. You have always told me everything. Trusted me to do things for you and to have my independence. You must tell me, I am going mad imagining all kinds of things that might be fact or fiction. Sometimes I think I am dreaming my life and that Rowena was never there at all. It's all becoming a nightmare of uncertainty and I must understand for my own sanity. The only thing that I really know is that you are my father, we share the same blood. So please tell me."

"No we do not," he said with a very firm quietness.

She was breathing heavily.

"Do not?" she asked, with tears behind her eyes.

"We do not share the same blood. I am your guardian, you are my adopted child."

She moved slightly, lowering herself to see his wet down-turned eyes.

"I don't know how or where you were born. I fear we are not the same at all."

She quietly folded before him, softening inside her clothes and shrinking. Sitting in a pool of her past. Her mind now totally empty. And so was her mouth, there being nothing else to ask. Everything started here, this was the wellspring of all the streams of her life that had flowed into the magnificent river that had been her life. She walked across the room, retracing her steps of arrival. Her skirt catching a corner of a desk and dislodging a pile of papers that slid gracefully to the floor. She did not see or notice them; neither did the man she left in the office slumped and confronting his own portion of woe. Ghertrude unwound herself down the stairs and found her way to the street. She was dazed and walked in the wrong direction, locked in the delirium of a truth that she wished she had never upturned. Why couldn't she learn to leave things alone, to not open doors and pry? She wanted to wind the time back to before all the questions had blossomed in her capricious brain. Why must she always be like this? Others weren't; their lives and loves were simpler, less tangled. Why was she so cursed? The great tides in her had never tasted doubt this deep and they started to waver, sending eddies and undercurrents that had never existed before. Her eyes were flooding and her milk was flowing and a cold perspiration was making her expensive clothes cling to her flushed skin. She stumbled in a gutter and splashed her delicate shoes. Then the stink of the place awoke like smelling salts. The old reptile brain becoming erect and dismissing thousands of years of evolution in a second. The genius of the frontal lobes turned off. She was in danger, her nose told her so. Where was she?

Only one place in Essenwald stank like this: She was in the Scyles. And no woman of her class and high race ever came here, unless it was to debauch her swollen identities. She wiped her eyes and looked around. Men and only men loitered in the shabby doorways of ancient structures. They were all watching her. Some exchanged comments, and one was making lewd gestures with his filthy hands. Were all men like this? What had been her father and what had been her lover Ishmael? Were they the same? Their lies and corruption capable of anything? Crime, murder, rape, and kidnapping. The sudden thought of the lost Rowena became the flint that sparked the iron of the old hind brain and ignited a flame that set ablaze a jackal fury. She would skin them alive for touching her child, no matter who they were. She turned on her heel. She had not finished with her father yet. He was going to get Rowena back. No man was going to stop her now, and all those on this street understood that and slunk back into the shadows, not wanting any dealing with this creature with flames in her eyes.

CHAPTER THIRTY-SEVEN

Sholeh had found a room in the Scyles where she could live and Ishmael could visit and stay whenever possible. Somewhere that the higher classes of Essenwald would never wander into. Sholeh's inquiries led to many rat-holes and subdued palaces. But none was more perfect than the two small rooms above the Skinners House. A place avoided by many for all sorts of reasons. The most obvious being the owners.

Gotfrid and Taphath Droisch were opposites in everything except their business and their marriage. He was very white, stringy and dry, just under two metres in height. She was very black, permanently damp and spherical. He had "gone native" and married a local a month after he arrived in Essenwald at the tender age of nineteen. One of a flock of wide-eyed innocents imported from the old country to widen the gene pool and beef up the colonial power. He had always desired a black woman, from the first pictures he had seen in one of his uncle's dubious "geographic," "peoples of the world" magazines. He found their bare-breasted exuberance to be entirely opposite to the laced-from-the-ankles-to-the-neck females of his puritanical kreis. He grabbed the opportunity to leave and change worlds with both hands. To see if the pictures were true. And they were, to some extent. But it was Taphath who floored him. She was the epitome of his wildest and most extravagant dreams. The most round, most protuberant and abandoned of them all. She had been in the city only a year, a daughter of the Moon Hearth People, who were legendary trappers and hunters. Their homelands skirted the southwest contours of the Vorrh, an area rich in game and many species of larger animals that were greatly prized for their pelts. The expanding trade between those lands and Europe was channelled through Germany, Leipzig being the skin hub of the rest of the world. Essenwald was perfectly placed and connected to develop the growth. The marriage of the Droisches was a perfect blessing to that trade. For twenty years their business had been growing and now the couple were prosperous and continually busy. Their wooden house, factory, and shop were in one of the oldest quarters of the old town. Gotfrid's hobby was an obsessive determination to crossbreed different species and thus produce a unique new pelt. He had no scientific skills and a very shabby understanding of natural history, and even less of basic genetics. But he did have persistence, no moral code, and an abnormal interest in sexual organs. His little workshop was well worth avoiding. The odours and sounds that emanated from it were spectacular.

That is why the small set of rooms above it was so very cheap. Tenants did not stay very long and they were generally of a secretive kind. So when the beautiful young dancer with the scarred face applied for a short lease, Gotfrid was overjoyed. Taphath less so, but she knew he would behave himself. After all, it was she who did the gutting and skinning downstairs. Part of their success was due to Gotfrid's enthusiastic adoption of the Moon Hearth People's ritualistic practices. Some said that Gotfrid even had his own altar in his factory workshops, surrounded by caged mutations. Three times a year they both would attend a four-day trance sacrifice in the homelands, and that is where they were now, which meant that Sholeh had the entire building to herself. She could light more incense sticks and be less concerned about her dress on the stairs. She could play at homeowner in this strangest of homes, while they were away, naked in the jungle. The timing was perfect. Everything was cleaned and perfumed, the candles lit, the entrance unlocked.

The Moon Hearth People were two days into their sacrificial offering. The dancing would last all night and on into the next day. As the crescent moon rose into the new twilight, Gotfrid Droisch staggered behind the drums. Naked and white, he looked like a dead tree creaking in a forest of blue-black undulation. Clouds of fireflies stitched the trees with green luminescence and for a few seconds tinted his ridiculous foreignness into something vaguely exotic.

➡

Sholeh lay in bed and he came in through the expectant back door. Put his small but bulky bag down on the bottom step of her stairs and undid his shoes. The incense from above made his anticipation sharpen. He removed his shoes, picked up his bag, and climbed the creaking stairs. It was dark and the only light was a faint glimmer under her door. There was no real need for such caution tonight because the nosey couple who ran the pelt shop beneath were away somewhere performing rituals to their hairy gods. He crept nevertheless. The landing outside her door groaned and he knew she must have heard it, if she was still awake. He opened the door. The perfume was overpowering, and mixed with the scent of her body it became intoxicating. A simple night candle was burning in a small metal holder. From a tin spur built into the holder dangled a suspended ring, a tiny rudimentary chandelier, and from it hung crudely cut flat metal angels. The heat of the flame caught the blades of the ring and spun the angels around and around. The light of the flame sent their silhouettes dancing and bobbing on the walls. He took off his topcoat and put the bag down at the end of her bed.

She moved in the silken sheets and said, "I have been waiting for so long."

"I too," he whispered.

He undressed and tiptoed to the bed. Lifting the sheet and sliding in next to her.

She giggled and stretched out her tattooed hand. The moment it touched his clammy skin, she choked and flinched back. Sidrus clamped one hand on her throat and one on her groin and slowly brought his bulbous looming face to within inches of her terrified eyes.

➤→

Hours later Ishmael came in through the open back door. Put his small but bulky bag down on the bottom step of her stairs and undid his shoes. The incense from above made his anticipation sharpen. He removed his shoes, picked up his bag, and climbed the creaking stairs. It was dark and the only light was a faint glimmer under her door. There was no real need for such caution tonight because the nosey couple who ran the pelt shop beneath were away. The smell from their shop nearly overpowered the incense. He crept up to the landing outside her door and it groaned. He knew she must have heard it, if she was still awake. He opened the door. The perfume was overpowering, and mixed with the scent of her body it was intoxicating. But under its high pitch lay the sweet blank smell of rawness.

A simple night candle was burning in a small metal holder. From a tin spur built into the holder dangled a suspended ring, a tiny rudimentary chandelier, and from it hung crudely cut flat metal angels. The heat of the flame caught the blades of the ring and spun the angels around and around. Their silhouettes dancing and bobbing on the walls. He took off his topcoat and put the bag down at the end of her bed.

He saw her form in the bed.

"I have been waiting for so long," he said.

He undressed and tiptoed to the bed, lifting the sheet and sliding in next to her. His hand extended for the first ravenous delicious touch. The bed was wet and his fingers touched something that was not the exquisite smoothness of her skin. He jumped back, repelled. Something moved under his hand in a motion that was not human. He slid from the bed onto the floor, breathing deeply. He eventually stood up shakily and bumped into the small table where the candle burnt. The slowly spinning shadows became skew-whiff and the clumsy angels cavorted violently about the walls. On the table was a small bread knife next to some food, a bottle of wine, and two glasses. He snatched it up and pulled back the sheet to find out what manner of beast had crawled in there. Had this followed him from the Vorrh? He nearly screamed as he crashed back into the table, sending it and its contents spilling onto the floor. The light was extinguished and a hideous guttural sound came from the twisting sheets as he grabbed at his clothes and bag and bolted the room, falling badly on the stairs, head over heels, spilling his possessions in the darkness. Vomit was in his mouth. He snatched his things together and fell into the outside night, naked and bruised. He yanked on his shirt and soaking trousers and ran through the streets wanting the light, wanting this to be no more than the worst nightmare he had ever had.

Halfway home he was violently sick. Twenty minutes later he stumbled through the back gate and staggered to the washhouse, where he lit a lamp. He and his clothes were saturated with blood. He pulled them off and threw them with disgust into the firebox of the boiler. It was still smouldering from the evening laundry. He drew some tepid water and washed all the blood off his shivering body. Would this never end? His world was always stained with blood; thank God at least it was not his own. The clothes suddenly ignited and made him start. He was seriously unnerved. The repulsive skinned and truncated thing that somebody had tied down in Sholeh's bed was still writhing in his mind. He needed a drink. He found a towel, wrapped himself in it, and crept up to the library. He lit the lamps and poured himself a very large whisky. Outside, the rain started again and he found its pattering flow soothing and oddly cleansing. He guessed who had played this foul trick to scare them and hoped that he had not hurt or terrified the girl too much in the process. Perhaps this was the work of some other malicious agent who wanted to scare them. He and Sholeh would make a list of all those who bore them grudges and he would use his new power to find the culprit and all the others. The clock in the living room struck three and he remembered his meeting with Quentin Talbot later in the morning. This could be the most important meeting of his life and he did not want to attend it exhausted. He poured another whisky and slunk off to one of the guest rooms. Cyrena heard him moving about and a bedroom door close and she was relieved that he was not returning to her.

Why would anybody want to have a meeting at such a god-awful time in the morning, especially one as important as this? If he was going to be invited to join the directorship of the guild, then it should at least have been over a long lunch. It was raining again and Cyrena had agreed that he should be driven to his appointment. He was still tired and anxious from a restless, disturbed night. Images of that thing tethered in the bed, of anticipation crashed and haunted in queasy regularity. He would find Sholeh after this meeting and they would report this atrocity to the authorities together. They would listen to and obey him now. The car was waiting outside the house and he checked his appearance in the mirror again. Cyrena was standing on the staircase, watching him in an irritating manner. At least she could offer good luck, he thought. He went to the hall stand to retrieve his hat and froze. The double pearl necklace was laid out on the polished wooden surface. He said nothing, left his hat, and hurried to the car. The rain fell continuously and he fretted about what she knew. This was a hell of a time to confront him like this. He could not think about it now and forced it back into a corner of his mind where it sat next to his waiting hangover.

He was on time and expected. One of Talbot's menials showed him through the illustrious but surprisingly sparse outer offices. Talbot stood beaming in his crafted sanctum. Everything was made of wood. Elegant, simple, and unusually styled. He offered Ishmael a seat and ordered coffee. They chatted over trivial things until it arrived and was poured. Talbot again thanked him for taking over Fleischer's planned expedition and for the successful conclusion. He talked about the "terrible cost of lives" and how the families of the fallen men would be compensated. This was boring stuff and Ishmael wanted to move on to his future in the guild.

"Now tell me something about yourself, Ishmael."

This was a most unwelcome change of direction.

"I know you are a great friend of Mistress Lohr and the Tulp family, but I know nothing about you and your background. Pray, do indulge me."

The key in the ignition of Ishmael's lost hangover was turned and a dull thudding started inside his brain.

"Well, I . . . I . . . I am a stranger to these lands."

Talbot made a small genial laugh.

"We are all that," he said pleasantly. "Are you from the old country?"

"No."

"Where, then?"

Ishmael shifted uncomfortably. "Is my background that important now?"

"No, I don't mean to pry. I understand that many in these lands have started new lives, begun new identities. I offer no criticism or judgement. I and the guild would like to know a little more about you before we work together."

At last, thought Ishmael.

"Anton tells me that you fought in the Great War and that you were rewarded for your valour."

His mouth felt like the Sahara and the pounding was now in a quarter of his unprepared brain. How could he have guessed things would have gone this way? He could have invented a whole sheath of fabrication if he had known. Fucking Fleischer, yabbing like a housemaid. He had to think on his feet, claw back the lost ground.

"I don't like to talk about or even remember those times. I was very young and my injuries are recollection enough."

"Quite so," said Talbot, in the first stages of embarrassed retreat. Ishmael saw it and pushed harder.

"Every day I see this face I am back in the trenches, back with my men. Can you imagine what it was like for me, fighting again for you and the guild?"

That did it. Talbot shifted and straightened.

"Please forgive me, Mr. Williams, I did not mean to distress you. It seems I am making matters more complex than they need to be."

Ishmael dramatically gulped at his coffee; half his head was pounding, but he tasted victory. He put the cup down and looked directly at Talbot with his good eye.

"Herr Talbot, I am sorry for being so frail. It's not my normal condition. The truth is, I am still a little fatigued from my time in the Vorrh. I am sure you know of the consequences of a prolonged stay there. And the sadness about Urs has affected me greatly."

"Yes, yes of course," said Talbot.

Then Ishmael remembered a gem, something that had totally slipped his mind.

"There are other matters that I cannot speak of. I am consoling Ghertrude Tulp through a very difficult and traumatic time."

Of course Talbot knew of the abduction. Half the fucking city probably knew about it now. And if they didn't, one look at Ghertrude's miserable countenance would have told them.

"Yes of course, and I respect your candour. Let me come to the point, Mr. Williams."

At last, thought Ishmael.

"We, the guild and I, are very impressed by your actions in the Vorrh and how you constructed a rapport with the workforce. Your organisation of their return was masterly. So we would like to offer you a position inside the company."

Ishmael rose to his feet, taller than he had ever been before. He smiled at Talbot.

"We would like you to accept the position of the new overseer of the Limboia."

The pounding now filled his brain and made his ears ring. He must have misheard what Talbot said. He stared at him in disbelief.

"Overseer," he said, and it tasted like cancer in his mouth.

"Yes. You seem to have an affinity with them. An authority that they respect."

"The Limboia?"

"Yes. With your help we could have them back to work in no time. We will discuss the salary later and I can arrange for you to view the warden's house."

"The fucking Limboia, you want me to be their fucking keeper? Is that all you think of me?"

Talbot was visibly shocked by this outrageous behavior. He walked around to the other side of his desk. "I think you are unwell young man." He pressed a buzzer on his desk. "I think we should have this discussion another time."

"It's Cyrena, she has done this. She's been talking to you."

"I don't know what you mean. I think tha—"

"I mean that . . . that cunt has done this, turned you all against me."

Talbot pushed the buzzer again.

"You owe me more than this," shouted Ishmael, tears streaming from one of his eyes.

The secretary was at the door, her hand to her mouth. Two uniformed men stood behind her.

"It's the police, sir, they want to speak to Mr. Williams."

They were brusque and uncommunicative and had the simple duty of arresting him. When Ishmael flounced out of their grip they tightened their iron fists on his bruised arms and he yelped and faded. He was collapsing inward, towards the roar of his thunderous headache.

The holding cell was narrow and very hot. He sat on a low hard bench and waited for the commandant to stop reading his notes.

"Okay," he said, "you know why you are here?"

Ishmael shook his head and wetly whispered, "The pearls?"

"What pearls?" asked the impatient commandant.

"Cyrena's pearls, it's a misunderstanding," he said in a daze.

"I know nothing of pearls. You are here because of what we found in the Droisch house."

Ishmael looked up. "What?"

"The house of the skinners Droisch."

It took him a few moments to understand.

"Oh, the thing in Sholeh's bed. She called you in. I was going there next."

"Were you?"

Ishmael wiped his face with his hand.

"It's been a horrible day, I want to go home, can you take me?"

There was silence in the holding room, a squat perspiring silence full of grit and mosquitoes.

"You ain't going nowhere."

"Is Sholeh here?"

"No, but it's why you're here."

Ishmael was confused and angry. He could smell his own sweat, which seemed to be escaping in bucketloads. His face ached, his head rocked in pain, and the commandant was ignoring him.

"Get Sholeh and we will find out who put that horrible thing in her room."

"That's going to be difficult," he said nastily. "That horrible thing *was* Sholeh."

Talbot had always admired Cyrena Lohr from afar. Even, and perhaps especially, when she was blind. How was he ever going to tell her that her friend—and he really hoped that was all Ishmael was to her—that her friend had been taken by the police? That was bad enough, but the disturbing and repulsive behaviour Ishmael had demonstrated earlier really troubled Talbot now. How could anybody, no matter what their mental state may be, say such revolting things about Cyrena Lohr. Talbot was worried about her safety and happiness at the hands of this abusive ruffian. He would have to tell her himself. Such delicate issues could not be conducted by a messenger. But first he needed collaboration from one he trusted, so he sent for Anton Fleischer.

Anton had recovered and the fearful memories had been overridden by his defeat and the miserable triumph of Ishmael's return. He sat in Talbot's office a fraction of the man he was before, a glass of water held in both hands. He had just told his side of the story through the lens of his defeat.

"But, Anton, it was all your plan from the beginning." Talbot's kindness seemed to be matched by his unwavering belief. "It might have been this Williams person would have sat in splendour on the incoming train, but it was your careful planning that guided the expedition and selected him to be its guide. The fact that he sustained only trivial injuries, while all else around him died or sustained terrible wounds, is in itself a matter of some anxiety."

"Yes, yes, I suppose it is."

"And who was this 'shadow' person who so abused you? Not a creature of the forest, I think."

It had never occurred to Fleischer that the creature who had stolen Urs and removed all the other men, before abusing and humiliating him, leaving him naked in a tree, might be one of his own party.

When had it all occurred? How far away was Ishmael? What was the monster's motive?

"I think with all that we have learned since Mr. Williams's return, that we should be very cautious handing out any more laurels. And his involvement with this butchered prostitute must never be spoken of within the guild or near the delicate ears of overly generous friends whom he has taken grievous advantage of. I think it is time that we all celebrated the true architect of the 'Return from the Vorrh' rather than an unknown upstart with no respect."

Talbot then put his arm around the frail young man in a gesture that he had never practised before and had no intention of ever doing again.

CHAPTER THIRTY-EIGHT

*H*ow the ants found their way down there he never questioned. His pain bleached all details other than what he was told. He sat exhausted, holding his hand that he had bandaged with the scraps of Modesta's torn dress, while the ants fed on the message that he did not understand. They fed more deeply because his blood mixed with the sugar water gave them a richer tastier nutrient to devour. Modesta had placed a rectangular wooden box at the far end of the cave chamber. It looked like a pencil box but three times the size. After the ants had erased the ink, they filed into the box until not one was left. She closed and sealed its lid and then turned her attention to him. After losing the nail, a tip of bone poked through, but she still would not let him stop until the message was written and the first joint of his index finger was becoming exposed.

"It will soon heal," she said, squatting next to him. "You must be strong for your journey."

He barely heard her; the throbbing in his hand was in unison with the waves below and the stump of his bandaged finger was pointing upwards to the stair and the fading square of light above.

She held his other hand and gave him what remained of the ink to drink. Her warmth dazzled him and he glanced at her beauty. Something not unlike the honey that he had been experimenting with before passed through his veins; it soothed his finger and opened his mind.

"Where am I going?"

"To the Sea People." She looked deep into him. "To my father."

"But your father is no more, is he not dead?"

"He is waiting. Waiting for you and this box."

"I don't understand."

"You don't need to. You only need to walk. To deliver this and return, then your function will be over."

"You mean I will die then?"

"No, just that your tasks in life will be over. I will be here waiting for you."

"But Carmella said that the seraphim would be coming to guide you."

"It will, but not before I know that my father has this message." She stood up, lifted the box with care, and pointed at the stairs. "You must go," she said.

Modesta and the old woman let him sleep for a time he never understood, in which his dreams attempted to unravel any meaning that he might recognise. He saw himself giving the box to the legendary Bowman, with the ferocious Sea People watching. He saw her nakedness climbing the stairs into flickering light. Her movement still agitated but changing; the staccato frames were softening, becoming graceful, and matching the first softness and care that she had ever shown him. And now he knew that he had never been there to protect her, that that had been a lie. The voices had lied to him. He was an instrument for her growing and contacting her dead father. "Instrument": The word rang familiar. Who had used it? He tossed in his sleep, the bandage falling away from his wrecked finger; it twitched and wrote the word "instrument" in the air.

When he woke he knew it was Lutchen who had said that his brain was an instrument.

There are clarities and visions in waking that are often fleeting, vapour-thin, and momentary. The dawn chorus or a sneeze can shred them. Their vividness dulled by the intrusion of the ordinary. But on this morning, after so much interference in his life, something had woken up to make a clarion outside of all manipulation. It was bland in its saying and sincere in its objectivity: There were two meanings to "instrument," one with a dignity and the other without, fundamentally different in the way they were understood. One was a device or an agency of purpose, with an integrity that reads and measures an indicator or a gauge, a compass. The other was a duller mechanism, a hollow that is played: a vehicle, a puppet.

He had hoped to be the first but now knew he was the second. He lay in the bed of twisted sheets and ran through everything the voices had told him, everything they had told Carmella, and everything that Lutchen had advised him. A discrepancy separated, like oil in water. By the time they arrived to help him prepare to be on his way he knew that he would not go to Essenwald on his journey to the Sea People, that the water and advice Lutchen had sent to him was not blessed, and that the only truth that had been spoken was by Modesta and it had been hard and uncaring, and that his little place in the world did have only one direction. And if there was a balm in Gilead it would be with Modesta, when he brought her news of his successful mission.

They escorted him to the edge of the village. The box and food were snug inside his satchel and he had been given coins and cubes of salt and tobacco to pay for whatever he needed on his way on the long coastal journey. Modesta again explained that they would wait on the seraphim and that his duty was to return to her after the ants had spoken to Oneofthewilliams, not the cyclops, the one who was hiding deeply in the Sea People's domain. Deeply hidden inside another man's body and soul. He told Carmella that he would obey, but she must promise him that if he did not return she would take Modesta straight to the forest and not pass through Essenwald. She agreed, but said it was ultimately in the hands of the seraphim. They said goodbye as he climbed up onto the track. She even waved at him as he walked out of the village towards the sea. He no longer had the kernel of pain, anger, and frustration, only a biting sense of loss, because some part of him feared he would never see them again.

CHAPTER THIRTY-NINE

*H*ow did you know this girl?" asked Cyrena. Ishmael had been rehearsing such a scene for weeks, but the circumstances had drastically changed. He now needed Cyrena on his side. Her position and wealth aligned to pick the lock and set him free. He would have to be very careful now that nobody in the room believed him. They just stared and waited for more.

"She, like I, was a patient of Nebsuel the healer. He sent her to me with a message. The old man is a great surgeon, you can look at our faces and see his identical handiwork, the same processes of folding and stitching."

"Not anymore we can't," said the commandant.

Ishmael closed his ears and wrestled with the brief image he had of what was left of the thing's face flapping in bloodied blurs. He did not even think it human then. The idea that it was Sholeh made him retch and shudder. Sidrus must have cut every stitch and undone every fold; again he saw the truncated stumps of her limbs, black from the cauterizing that sealed her blood and ensured her consciousness. He had run away in disgust and dread when her shredded vocal cords must have been calling to him.

"What was her message?" asked Cyrena calmly. Ishmael was a rat in a wheel, running hard in the spinning cage of lies.

"She brought a warning that an old foe of mine would be coming. Clearly this is what happened. I believe this man is Sidrus."

"Sidrus the forest warden?" asked the commandant, suddenly taking a new interest. "I know the man, he was a most trusted officer. But he's been gone for years. Killed in the Vorrh, some say."

Ignoring this line of enquiry, Cyrena continued with her own questions.

"Why were you visiting her so late?"

"I had not seen her since my return and she was leaving the next day, and I had brought some money to help her on her travels," he lied.

"Money," said Cyrena with a smile, "what money?"

He was painting himself into a corner, he had to twist or tilt the containment in his favour. "I had to get money for her so that she would go away. I had to get it any way I could because if she had stayed, she would have come between us." He looked at Cyrena, both his eyes working overtime in different directions.

"How would she do that?" said Cyrena, with polar exactitude.

"She would have told everybody of my previous physical condition. She would have told your family and friends, and they would have never understood. She would have hurt you and saddened our union. I could not let that happen, so I paid her to go."

"You mean she was blackmailing you?" asked the commandant, who was now really interested.

"No, she was desperate and unscrupulous. She was not an evil person, just one who needed help and guidance away from a dishonest background."

Cyrena's expression was unreadable. The commandant was scratching his head and Ishmael was steering forcefully over very thin ice. His hand mercilessly frozen to the tiller. His knuckles white as snow.

"She sounds like a deceitful selfish bitch," said Cyrena.

"Yes, in many ways she was, but it had been a savage family history that robbed her of her compassion and humility. She could not be totally blamed," said Ishmael generously.

"Indeed," said Cyrena. After a thoughtful pause she continued, "How then did she find the time and inclination to do charitable deeds for the poor and disposed of this fair city?"

Ishmael frowned at her, having no idea what she was talking about.

"I have met this girl, this Sholeh, in the blind home," said Cyrena. "She was caring for two sightless street urchins. Beggars really. She had brought them there for treatment. What do you suppose was the ulterior motive for that kindness, from a person bereft of compassion?"

Ishmael almost laughed. She had gone mad, he thought, trying to conceal the glare growing behind his eye. Trying to hide his anger and the slap that he so wanted to administer. Cyrena was finished, she went to the door of the cell and waited to be let out. The commandant barked an order and rapped on the metal door. The bolt was pulled. Before she left, she addressed the officer as if he were the only person in the sweating room.

"I will of course pay for all of *Mr. Williams's* daily needs until after the trial. I do not want to receive any more messages or communications from him. This matter is now entirely out of my hands. Do I make myself clear?"

"Yes, madam, perfectly," said the commandant, and escorted her out of the dumbfounded cell. He gave her a suitable amount of time to leave the building before he charged Ishmael with the murder of Sholeh. "If it was up to me, I would carve you up the same way."

The trial was brief and matter-of-fact, and the outcome inevitable. Witnesses proved that Ishmael was one of the few, if not the only person who knew Sholeh since her arrival more than a month ago. The Droisches confirmed that he had been the only regular visitor. Their comments about the two scared strangers mating in their home had to be restrained by the judge. Some of the clothes found on the stairs were easily identified by the fine workmanship and customer number of Cyrena's expert tailors. Cyrena's evidence was inconclusive about the whereabouts of the accused that night. He was certainly not in her bed and there were other rumours about him being seen half naked and running near the crime scene. Anton Fleischer's testimony was supposed to be on the good character of Ishmael, but its weak and uncertain delivery suggested further doubts about Ishmael's conduct and motivations. The ambition and stealth of the young Fleischer had been removed and replaced by directions of thought and memories engineered by Talbot. The prosecution, led by Jacobus Klimt, made short work of Anton's vague uncertainties, and seemed to produce new evidence against the accused. Any notion that Ishmael had been a war hero was quickly rejected, Klimt revealing with a flourish that no war record could be found for the man calling himself Williams and matching Ishmael's description. Indeed, no record of his existence could be found at all. The most moving and compelling testimonial came from blind Sergeant Wirth, who told of Ishmael's valour and humanity in saving him and some of the other wounded men. But all of that was absorbed by the brutality of the crime, which Klimt explained in sickening detail. Ishmael's story of the vengeful forest warden was dismissed as nonsense. No trace of the man called Sidrus could be found. He had vanished from the city years earlier. Everything Ishmael said sounded like lies. The police mentioned "the pearls" and he was forced to lie again. There was little doubt of the outcome and it took the three judges only forty minutes to come to their verdict.

———

Execution techniques vary widely, and taste and cultural prefer-
ence do not always travel well. So was the case in Essenwald. The
twentieth century's fashion for enclosing the act and making it
clandestine and elitist was not well received among the ancient
tribes of the African continent. They wanted, demanded something more theatrical, lavish in its spectacle, and democratically
available to all. This was, of course, perfectly acceptable for the
execution of slaves and black-skinned criminals but was abhor-
rent in the case of European felons. No civilised man should be
expected to face a savage non-Christian mob, no matter what
his or her crime. The first time a white condemned man was
dispatched, it was behind canvas screens and there was a near
riot. The denial of the public ritual was stronger than the sense
of racial injustice, but one amplified the other. Four died during that night of outrage that so threatened the tenuous stability
of the far-flung empire. Two days later the demanded spectacle
had returned and the wooden platform of the scaffold shook
with the impacts of the eleven murderers receiving their pun-
ishment. These were followed by a series of delicate and vital
debates between the colonial overlords and the tribal elders.
Even some of the distant kings sent representatives. This was
a very important matter and the balance of empire had to be re-
addressed. The unspoken acceptance and continual cooperation
of subject and master had to be verified in the importance of
execution. The deadlock lasted a tense week, the potentates and
militia sweating under the wheezing fans.

One day was dedicated to the discussion of the means of
execution, which drew attention away from the vexed argument
about accessibility. It was during this exchange that the force of
visual ceremony was recognised by all. The most popular device
ever employed in this outpost was the guillotine, which arrived
with the fifth wave of settlers in the young Essenwald. Nothing
like it had ever been seen. The aboriginals marvelled at its inge-

nuity and mechanical elegance. Of the wonder of elaboration; a distinguished gin to do in prolonged minutes what a man with a sword or a rusty knife could do in seconds. The operators of the machine behaved with polite indifference, performing their tasks in remote reverential authority. No human hand would touch the neck or the blade and the divided body would be instantly slid away as if it had never been united, or even existed at all. The barbarism astonished them and left them in awe. Truly, these white beings were a terrifying new species.

The guillotine had existed in mainland Europe and the British Isles for centuries. The sharpened head axe or crushing weight had scuttled down between its long verticals to messily separate life in all manner of different forms and variations. Its distinctive profile reached into many dark and gloomy skies long before it obtained the lasting nomenclature of the good Dr. Guillotine, who, seeking a fast and humane method of dispatch, unwittingly signed his name in blood forever to laws allowing the use of an instrument of fearsome horror. Its dramatic simplicity came to represent the revolution's repetitive slaughter, turning it into the dripping icon of the Terror. Germany had a part in the French prototype—a highly skilled harpsichord maker named Tobias Schmidt crafted the pencilled designs into functional reality. Some say the gleaming, oblique, forty-five-degree angle of the blade was his own personal refinement. The speed and efficiency of the new "gin" or engine was infamous. With its endless supply of clients, a new manner of operation was needed. An almost industrial, conveyor-belt mentality that kept it overstocked. These earnest labours of the rational matter-of-fact instigated even greater performances of bizarre fact and elaborate fiction to dance around the juddering leaky basket, which Dumas tells us had to be changed or mended every three days because the wicker bottom would be chewed out by the growing number of furiously chattering heads that thrashed in their narrow containment. Better-documented but equally weird accounts tell of numerous experiments carried out to ascertain the consciousness of the severed minds. The most elaborate being conducted by two young doctors who waited at the foot of the engine, ready to receive the falling head. Once grabbed it was rushed to their nearby carriage and attached via its arteries and gutta-percha pipes to a pump that, in turn, was connected via more tubes to a living dog, strapped to the carriage floor. The horses were geared up and sped towards their laboratory, the cobbled streets sending loud shock waves through the passengers, who swayed and steadied themselves while frantically hand-pumping the dog's hot blood into the flushing head. All the while shouting the victim's name aloud and slapping his cheeks over the deafening noise of the hard wheels and the whimpering dog. Some success was recorded, a partial opening of the eyes, a shudder of the lips. Even "some slight agitation" one hour and a fresh dog later, when the head was decanted to an attic laboratory.

The model that had been imported to Essenwald to deal with criminals and runaway slaves was based on the Hamburg Fallbeil, a much more sophisticated device than its Parisian ancestor. Prior to its celebrated arrival, hanging and garroting had been tried, with little enthusiasm or effect. There was something about the dignity and slow preparation of the Longfellar, as the Fallbeil became known, that caught the public's attention. It took several executions to clarify the cause of its popularity. Like so many things around the Vorrh, it was a manifestation of paradox. The aboriginal and drifting tribes had experienced and relished all manner of prolonged and excruciating ceremonial murder. The rawness of the event being the clarion of its rightness. The Longfellar did the opposite; it enfolded its victim into its structure and asked them to wait in its bed of death, becoming implicated in its process. When the blade eventually fell, the corpse instantly disappeared through the floor, the head tumbling down a canvas chute. This and the waiting is what gave it its heightened sense of conjurer's magic. The illusionist's flourish. The very fact that the blood was almost concealed heightened the barbaric mystery. For a society that saw everything, that lived with life and death hourly, and that witnessed constantly all the traumatic stages in between, this obscuring was a fetish of great power. So that when the first white felon's death was screened off and the magic conducted in camera, the crowd felt cheated and excluded. Only hearing the sounds was not enough. Disappointment turned to anger, which turned to crime. So the talks went on and it was reluctantly agreed that unless a satisfactory substitute could be found, then the next white execution would indeed be conducted publicly and given to ol' Longfellar without the canvas screens. The militia and the Timber Guild sent out discreet requests for suggestions to solve the problem. A new thought or compromise was needed. Because they had no real intention of displaying the death of the superior race. That might lead to much sterner and undermining problems. They waited months but nothing much came back, except from the fanatical ravings of the lunatic fringe and a pedantic three-page letter from a French intellectual. When a possible solution did arrive, it was from the most unlikely source of all.

Of course it was the Valdemar brothers who created it. No more commissions came after the cathedral and the Chapel of the Desert Fathers. There were no more windows to be made in Essenwald. It was not the money; their meager needs were still being fed by the cathedral stipend. They wanted a project to get their creative teeth into. It was art not poverty that was chewing at their long days. They designed some small machines and fanciful bridges, but nothing challenged them. They wanted a cause, something original to interpret, and wring pathos and meaning out of process and invention. Ernst was sawing in their workshop and Walter was crossing the street to fetch beer, cheese, and bread for a late lunch. The usual itinerants and beggars hobbled and shouted their way down the street. This sector of the old town was famous for its bizarre assortment of human detritus. It had been affectionately known as St. Giles by the Christians, even though no church stood in its precincts. The Africans here were almost all exiles from their tribes, outcasts and offenders in every shape and form that the continent produced. The whites were equally squalid and deranged. Personal histories did not exist and nobody was foolish enough to ask. Over the years the name St. Giles had collapsed like everything else in the narrow confine and had now become the Scyles. Some of the oldest dwellings were rotting away here, mended and re-mended huts from the original village. Even the more recent small warehouses had a dilapidated and defunct feel about them. They were the cheapest in the city. In other words, the Scyles was perfect for artists, the dispossesed, and those whose essential calling had curdled.

Walter Valdemar nearly collided with Father Lutchen, who was standing stock-still in the bubbling street. "Good morning, my son," he said. "I have something to show you."

Walter nodded towards the other side of the street and both men pushed their way into the dark entrance. Once in their workshop, the food and drink was laid out on a table covered in tools and sawdust. Lutchen took out one sheet of paper and pinned its curled stiffness down with a chisel and a hammer.

"I have brought something that I thought you should see. It is not your usual kind of work, it's a little grim, but it's got potential."

Ol' Longfellar was to have a companion. And the genius of the Valdermars provided it. A symbiont that would connect to its erectness whenever called for. This deus ex machina took two years to build, during which time the magisterial system showed great leniency towards white criminals, if forced labour alongside the Limboia could be seen as lenient . . . their brains and willpower rotting after the first three months. The mechanism was kept in felt- and camphor-lined boxes, away from changes in temperature and humidity. It was made entirely of wood. A combination of ebony for the finely engineered mechanism and black walnut for the outer claddings. An articulated tree with highly stylized branches was bolted to the left-hand stanchion of the guillotine. It shared its uprightness and stretched its branches over the height, touching the release mechanism of the blade in the process. Many of the hundreds of wooden leaves of the tree were hinged and articulated. Connected through their slender stems to the branches and then to the elegant trunk. Beneath its canopy, and leaning slightly against the trunk, was a life-size manikin of the imaginary Adam. It stood directly on the planked floor of the scaffold. One of its hands touching its chest, the other holding the apple of disobedience. The detailing of the figure seemed adequate but unremarkable, its rough-hewn outer casing giving the impression of skilled but rustic craftsmanship. Its face bore small signs of satisfaction and its downturned eyes seemed focused on the apple. The true genius of the sculpture was hidden in the layers of sliding mechanics that filled its head, limbs, and trunk. Beneath the scaffold with the waiting body sack were a series of dangling weights, each on a taut cord wound around a wooden drum. These were the power source for the figure's movements and expressions.

The first customer of the novelty was a child killer called Ralf Beisner. It took all night to set up the contrivance. Flickering lights active behind canvas screens. At dawn a great quietness fell over the platform. When the cathedral clock sounded eight the screens were removed and a sigh arose from the gathered crowd. The guillotine had been loaded with the condemned man. At least it was assumed to be a man. Every inch of his body was covered in a suit of wood, a flexible, tight shimmering layer of pale lustrous Abachi. But that is not why the growing audience gasped. Nor was it their first view of the black tree, with its thin strong leaves moving in the light breeze that crossed the stage, and the standing ebony man sheltering beneath them. It was not that which made their eyes pop and their tongues freeze. It was the fingers of the timber Adam that made them point. On its chest they tapped gently as if drumming time. The other hand turned the spherical wooden apple in its flexible fingers. A bite could be seen missing from its solid body. As it rotated and passed into Adam's gaze, his lips and jaw moved. The layers of oiled wood that made the muscles of his face move slid into a hard sneer that twisted into a look of horror. Suddenly the fingers and the facial expression slowed and stopped. As did the leaves. The wind held its breath and the entire mechanism ceased, awaiting the next shift in atmospheric pressure. During this lull some agitation could be seen in the prone condemned figure. A struggling against its restraints, creaking against the resistance of the bascule. A few minutes later the breeze picked up again, followed by small irregular gusts. The leaves became agitated and flapped with a sound not unlike that of the keys on a mute piano. Adam again became engaged with the apple, his sliding face looking even more perturbed. Word had spread and the crowd was now double its previous size, those at the very front of the scaffold being forced against its hard surface and losing an overall view of the proceedings. Those who had just arrived were being told by those already there exactly what was happening and how the wind passing over the leaves encouraged the wooden Adam to move and face the consequences of his forbidden action.

After an hour or more, during which no lack of attention had occurred, another movement was seen in the trees. A carved spiral appeared from within the foliage and wound its way along one of the straighter branches. This hitherto unnoticed element progressed as it revolved, and the greatly excited audience pointed furiously at the slinky serpent's motion. When it reached mid-way there was a sudden and sonorous click. Not from the tree or from Adam, whose head had started to turn towards the direction of the noise. But from the uppermost part of the guillotine. The crossbar, which contains the grab. The jawed mechanism, which holds the heavy mouton and blade in place. Adam's head had now entirely turned with every one of the crowd's, whose fixed attention was on the razor axe. The wind dropped again and the wooden flurry of clacking leaves was still, as was every-thing else, save the bound figure below, who still clenched him-self taut against his restraints. The eerie quiet was broken by a pox-faced youth in the front of the crowd. He started to blow at the tree, in the manner of one attempting to extinguish a distant candle. Then out of the stunned silence others joined in, until the entire audience was violently puffing at the stage.

A few leaves twitched and the excitement increased. They blew harder and harder, some turning scarlet and purple with the effort. Then a great breeze came, spinning out from the Vorrh, as if it had decided to join in the sport. The tree rattled and a further stressing could be heard in the latch of the blade. Suddenly, and with great force, Adam's head sprang back to con-front the crowd, his arm and hand holding the apple shooting up to his mouth, where it embedded. His other hand had grabbed at his chest. The snake had now twisted along the entire length of the branch and come to a halt, its head clearly visible, glaring at the crowd. There was a sharp cracking sound as Adam began breaking his head from his body and wrenching open his chest. The grab of the blade parted and sent the splitting axe rattling down. Adam's chest flew open, exposing all the inner organs in a bright array of varnished colours. Beisner's head could be heard scuttling down the canvas funnel into the unseen sand-box below. The bascule tilted and sent his shivering wood-clad body noisily following it through the trapdoor. Adam's head was now completely off, attached to his hand via the apple, as if the jaw had locked onto it. Slowly, and with sedate deliberation, the internal organs began to slide out of the chest cavity, where a thick viscous substance had kept them in place. They started to slither forward from the tilted figure, gaining a heavy momentum against the honey-thick slime. Gradually they tumbled and fell languidly onto the resounding hollow stage, a long stream of mucous-like jelly bridging the floor and the open body. Gleaming in the morning light and now providing the only movement in the jaunty breeze. Because the leaves and all else moved no more.

The audience, some still frozen in the act of puffing, stared in disbelief. Their eyes like saucers. The spell was broken by the discreet snake spiralling back into its position of invisibility. The crowd went wild. They bellowed, they whistled, they clapped and hooted. They all started talking at once, explaining to one another what they thought they had just witnessed. Some tried to climb the scaffold to collect a souvenir or just to touch the carved bright heart or the varnished white lungs. They were quickly repelled by an armed guard, who entered the stage with five other men, who carried and unfolded canvas screens to shield all the apparatus from view. The crowd dispersed to bars and shabby halls and continued to celebrate all day. Behind the screens the business end of the guillotine was doused in buckets of water. Adam's organs were lovingly collected, cleaned off, and put in their holding case, as was his body as it was gently taken apart. The brilliantly engineered head was cleaned and reset for next time. The remnants of the snapping bar of brittle wood, which had produced the horrible sound effect, were removed from his neck and thrown away. The tree was fastidiously disassembled, its fragile inner moving parts padded and locked down against damage in transit. All the individual parts of the machine would be polished and oiled before they were bedded away in their camphor-smelling cases. They all worked with diligent attention for the next two hours, while below the wooden suit was stripped from the corpse. It would be hung empty and bloodstained by the city gates. There for the birds to lovingly pick and splinter until all sustenance was gone. The remains of Ralf Beisner were shovelled into a thick canvas sack and dragged to an unmarked grave, half full and thirsty with lime.

During the trial of the "hero of the Limboia" there was a great division of the city's opinion. One half thought that leniency should be given to such an important murderer. After all, it was only the life of a vagrant whore dancer. What was that compared to the salvation of the city? The other half wanted a strict settlement that demonstrated that no man was beyond the law, even the most admired. And after all, he was not of old family or significant wealth. Just another drifter, without any history, who had made good. All the opinions were influenced by the fact that they wanted to see Adam and ol' Longfellar function again.

Ishmael sat in his cell and tried not to sleep because that was the cruellest time. There was escape, mistake, and salvation there, determined to sweeten reality until awakened, when the truth bled back black, doubtless, and without a trace of mercy. He knew now that his greatest mistake was wanting to be human, to be accepted by these freakish twisted-eyed, divided-brained monsters. Nebsuel had been right all along. He was unique, a living legend from a potent mythical time. He should have stayed as he was and dealt with these samelings from there. If only he had commanded instead of inveigled. He planned it differently next time and was again swindled through the razor-wire hoop of hope. No one spoke to him. The guards mumbled only about food and latrines.

It was all gone, everything. All that was left was the sparse hot cell and the pain of memory, the butchery of hope. Ishmael had given up trying to suppress the fictional projections of future events. They came no matter what. The struggle to keep them at bay exhausted his last hours and tortured his dreams. So he gave in and let them flow. A giggling torrent of vengeance, apology, and redirection flooding against his eroding stone of being, which in itself was transforming into a softer version of his obstinacy: his eye. The eye he should have trusted all along. In the head it was designed for. His present face was a travesty, a blasphemy, as Nebsuel had told him before Ishmael forced the old man to operate.

He was not allowed a mirror in the cell. But he looked long and hard into the narrow water of his tin washbowl. He looked at the other eye seated in the skilfully puckered scar tissue and pinched stitching of Nebsuel's delicate surgery. Maclish's eye. The eye that lived without blood or any other nutrient. Scooped out from the Scotsman's undead body before he was eaten alive by the anthropophagi. Ishmael wondered how long it would survive in his decapitated head. If it would still twitch in his hollow skull after it had fallen inwards, into the rotted nest of his erasure. No one had told him about the lime.

The living eye became an affront to him, a symbol of the alien world that had stolen his uniqueness with its demands for constancy. A destructive compromise living in his living face, then in triumph continuing after he was cold mutton. "If thy eye offends thee . . ."

It was two days before Ishmael's meeting with Adam Longfellar. The chief executioner, who was always masked in a grey silk hood, had visited him again with the wooden-suit maker. He said nothing but just stood with a guard while the carpenter made final adjustments to the smooth white shards. No more visits were planned after this. His so-called friends would not come again. They had already given him up to the waiting machine. It was gnawing at his heart when he saw the nail. It had come off the carpenter's shoe. He stood up and moved during the fitting, complaining of a cramp. The other men looked at each other and the hooded man nodded approval. Ishmael put his naked foot over the nail and put all his weight onto it, squashing it into the hurting flesh. After they left he retrieved it and hid it beneath the canvas straps of his uncomfortable bed. He was not going to let the eye live. He would kill it before they strapped him into that hideous suit. He would die the way he was born, a cyclops.

CHAPTER FORTY

Sidrus returned to his former home in Essenwald after he had chastised Sholeh. He hadn't been near his bolted rooms since he was cursed to live in the illusory bogland. Now he stood before the door that he had designed and gradually remembered the sequence of its ingenious lock. Which was fortunate, because if he had not placed his fingers in the precise keyholes, then the small sprung blades would have removed the tips of his totally healed hand.

Everything was the same as the day he left, and the memory of it settled on him like clay in water. He sat still and let it happen, a haze of former connections knotting spidery dendrites about him. He opened all the modest rooms, the bulky cabinet and concealed drawers. He handled all the tools and weapons. The charms and talismans. They tingled in anticipation. He washed for hours, admiring his body and celebrating his success. Nebsuel's apprentice Ishmael was taken care of, he would be cloven apart by Adam Longfellar after days of hideous anxiety, for a crime he would never have had the guts to commit. Sidrus had enjoyed his time with Sholeh, remaking her body through agony so that she would live just long enough to appall and sicken Ishmael. He wanted to stay for the trial and execution. Stay and watch it, relish Ishmael's last moments of miserable despair. But the police were looking for him; his name had been mentioned.

Questions were being asked. He must not undo what he had so beautifully manufactured. Best to leave and let the fools who had celebrated Ishmael bring him down and cut his life away. His next target was more important. He wanted Nebsuel and needed his slow death more than his own life. That night he slept in the sweet solidity of the best, most profound rest he had ever had. No drugs, no demons, no other worlds to soothe him. Just his own: perfect, cruel, resilient, and unstoppable.

The next day he meticulously packed his implements. Dressed in clothes he had bought in the market. He japanned his new hair and set foot back towards the perimeter of the Vorrh and Nebsuel's hidden isle.

The Sea People had heard distorted tales of impossibilities. Of Williams eating a child, and of the white people needing his sacrifice. Feeding him to a black original whose hunger for his breath was so great that he would open his own chest and pull badly at the seams of his head. The solution was simple: They needed to intensify the calling charm. The child that carried the bloodline of the first Williams being needed to give more than his previous offering. It was time for his little life to be lovingly mashed over the shrine.

Neither man saw nor sensed their balance change in the wilderness of trees, but the half-awake Williams who hung badly folded in the concealment of the body and soul of the creature named Sidrus harkened and began to glow. A warming. A light, dim as a candle in a bottle, bobbing in a nameless midnight ocean. The call that travelled out from the Sea People's dripping altar shuddered in the wind and grew in momentum under the mottled sun. When it found and awoke its beloved Williams inside Sidrus, he started to unfold like the first shift of an exhausted slumberer. A stretching of intent. An outer waking long before the mind floats to the surface and dawn suckles it. He was becoming aware of the confines and textures of the vessel that held him. Sidrus felt only a series of aches, small displacements of ease that travelled from his cerebellum to his toes. Pins and needles that he thought might be more signs of his growing vigour but in fact were thousands of tiny lesions and detachments. Something deep inside the monster was coming away.

Some of his instinctive tuning was being warped, so that days later when Sidrus was travelling south the first real signs of his cleaving became apparent. He was moving quickly in a recently acquired pencil-thin canoe with narrow, sleek outriggers. It was faster that way and he was not forced to cross the painful pathways of his previous journey to and from Nebsuel's rotting isle. He savoured his arrival so much that he did not notice the oddly nudging tides, the slant breezes, and his own imbalanced rowing. It was as if one side of him had a greater strength and made the paddle dig deeper. A curve was being performed. A biding rhyme that pulled him closer and closer to the lands of the Sea People and farther from the twisting lower lip of the estuary. Even the stars and the great full moon that lured him to travel by night were in league with the calling. The fair hair and the smouldering bones of the blessed child that once carried the genes of the first Williams performing the first stages of dissolution. The Williams in Sidrus rowed with the night and against the obvious day. Towards separation, vengeance, and benediction and towards the Sea People, who had awaited his return for generations. Some of their priestesses had predicted that he would be enwrapped in another man, for safe passage and nutrition. Because everybody knew that it was a long journey from the another world, especially when travelling backwards. The speedy road of death was an easy one; every man, fool, and sage would do it at least once. But its reverse took great courage and an indomitable will. Only a sacred being like Oneofthewilliams could achieve it. The signs had been gathering. The tides had been changing. Umbitippa of the Lamprey tribe said that he had caught a mermaid in his net, but it had bitten though its restraint and swum into the estuary. Visions of the Black Man of Many Faces were being reported every week. And the Desert Fathers said that a live voice was travelling towards them from far along the coast where no black people lived. There was a great excitement in the air and the knives and hard grass were being sharpened. The Sea People had been practising their skills and experimenting with new techniques of surgery and physical magic with great success. In their villages there were many walking examples of astonishing fusion and separations, and those who could not walk crawled, hopped, and slithered with great pride at the achievements. Oneofthewilliams was coming and everybody was waiting to celebrate.

CHAPTER FORTY-ONE

Everything that had been touched by Ishmael now needed to be cleansed. Cyrena's natural warmth had been compromised. Her trusting love defiled. She had never had such a negative reaction to anything. All memories of their time together, even the first ones, were foxed and bitter. The pity she had for his weakness had turned to disgust and contempt. And even that was not enough; she railed against her own gullibility. How could she have let all this happen, not seen what so obviously was rotting under her delicate nose? She systematically removed every trace of him from her house. The idea of a torturer's touches everywhere made her feel unclean. She dared not even contemplate the murderous hands caressing her body, probing inside her. She imagined his single eye, glaring and abnormal. Nausea struck continually and she wanted to flee, to sell up and begin again with an unsoiled body in a sanitary house in an uncontaminated land. At the same time her anger argued for her to stand her ground, show her strength, shrug off this little unpleasantness, and get on with her life. Maybe the whole incident had been a wakeup call for her to change her existence and put it to better use. At the absolute bottom of the pit was her blindness. When she locked the doors and coiled her overly washed body deep in her new bed, it came to greet her like an old genderless friend.

She would go to the execution. Use her beautiful, perfect eyes to see every detail. To be sure that he was gone forever. She asked Quentin Talbot to accompany her, to arrange a discreet but total viewing. He had happily agreed, concealing his brimming pleasure beneath a sincere commitment to help. He knew "the perfect place," rooms belonging to the Timber Guild. He would book them for the day of retribution and nobody would disturb her witnessing.

The stiff cleanliness of the new sheets folded about her as she gave up all her plans of this world and entered a place that she prayed would be kinder. She stretched her luxuriant body against the tautness of the white and let her strength go. She was asleep in five minutes and her dreams were quick to catch up and take her through her garden below directly into the forest that was growing darker with every silent footfall. Dark beyond comparison. Dark towards sightlessness.

She was dreaming blind again and the space around her doubled. All the nails and pins of detail vanished, leaving a rich volume that she deeply understood as it welcomed her home. She was blind in joy and she almost wept in her sleep. She understood so much more and the forest was helping her. The white sheet became jet-black and as powerful as the night. The Vorrh showed her its secret, one she had always known but could not speak. It was there for all to see and read.

But sight gave humans blindness, especially about their own species.

When she awoke the sentence was on her triumphant tongue, but there was nobody to speak it to.

Ghertrude had shut herself up in Kühler Brunnen since the confrontation with her father. Or rather, the man who had pretended to be her father throughout her previously happy life. He had been the stability in her existence. The proud rock to please and build upon. Mistress Tulp had always been her father's little princess, the light in his eye. Or so she had thought. Her granite confidence had moved, being no more than a blemish on the vast tectonic plates of a will-less world. She was more akin to the Bakelite machines that hummed under the house than to the gaggle of strangers that she had been tricked into believing were her family. Both she and her daughter had been bred by someone or something that she had never met. Never dreamt of. She now knew nothing of her womb, or her mother's womb, and she feared even more for the womb of her daughter. They had all the properties of someone else. Ishmael the cyclops was more like her than anybody else. No wonder she had always felt a freak, a child aside. She pondered his astonishing growth. That once she had taken him from the cramped confines below, he grew and gained maturity in abnormal time. She wondered if the reverse might also be true. Why should the constant and irredeemable rules of normal life apply to her? Perhaps she might go into the cellars and find smaller and smaller spaces to shrink into. Wind her life back into nothingness, each diminishment erasing painful experience until she receded into mindless gel. She spent some grudging time with the Kin, trying to ask more about Rowena and when she would return. Infuriatingly, they claimed no current knowledge, saying that all they knew was that she was calm, happy, well, and looking forward to seeing her mother. When pressed, they meagrely explained it was part of her well-being. A period of adjustment before she entered the world completely.

Ghertrude had confronted them with the facts that her father had finally divulged. They remained aloof and impartial to the new situation, saying only that she should not have been told. But it made it easier for them to explain that both she and Ishmael had been through the "tempering period" along with many others, and all had come back stronger and more secure in their world. When questioned on the exact meaning of "secure" they clammed up or diverted the subject. There were long interludes of angular silence. Occasionally she would hear one of them switch automatically into stasis mode, a slight shift in the emphasis of their continual hum. Apart from talking or being with her, they had no other purpose now that their teaching duties were over or suspended. During one of these stubborn silences she asked almost in whimsy, knowing the answer must be negative, "Did you ever teach me?"

They all bristled and Abel clicked back into active mode again.

"But if you had taught me like you did Ishmael, then I would know, I would remember."

No sooner had the words left her lips than she knew this was part of the secret. Part of the answer. A thing she was not supposed to comprehend.

The conversation was disturbed by the front doorbell ringing high above. The Kin looked up.

"You have a visitor," said Luluwa.

Ghertrude said nothing. The bell rang again.

"I don't want visitors."

"It might be about Ishmael," said Luluwa.

The bell rang again. She stomped out of the room and climbed the stairs into what used to be the real world. Nobody else was in the house today, so she went to the door herself and yanked it open. Nobody was there. She stepped out and looked about. There was a ringing and a muffled pressure in her ears. As if she had been swimming or stayed too long underwater in the bath. She stepped back into the hall and closed the door. The sound happened again. It was coming in chunks and waves, pressures. Then something brushed against her hand and she jumped back, startled and defensive.

"Why can't you see me?" bellowed Meta.

Ghertrude covered the touched hand with her other and stepped back.

"I am here about Rowena, I think I know where she is."

Ghertrude heard her child's name and clamped her hands to her ears to keep her sanity from leaking out. But instead of muting her troubled mind, it made the words clearer and seemingly spoken in a different voice.

"Stop it," she said.

"But I know where she is."

This time there was no mistake; she knew the voice.

"Meta?" she said.

"Yes, mistress."

"Are you . . . are you a ghost?"

"No, mistress, I am alive and real and standing a few feet before you. Why can't you see me?"

Ghertrude flushed and stabbed a hand out before her. It struck solid warm matter and she yelped with the shock.

"You can feel me," said Meta.

"What? You are very faint."

"You can feel me. Here is my hand."

Meta slowly brought her hand forward as Ghertrude unclamped hers and again probed before her. Meta let her touch her fingertips before seriously engaging, as one might do with a strange dog before stroking it. The weight of their hands came together and this time Ghertrude did not flinch. She let the girl's fingers unfold hers and then gripped back in response.

"Why can't I see you?" said Ghertrude.

"I don't know."

"Don't shout, Meta, I can hear you now. When I touch you I can hear you." She brought her other hand forward to hold Meta's other hand, but she missed and touched the girl's abdomen by mistake. The air changed around them. Meta stepped back slightly and Ghertrude saw the movement. Not as a person but as a tremor, a ripple in the air. It was greenish and dispersed when she stood still. Inadvertently her hand stayed in contact with Meta's belly, a seeming act of familiarity that was strictly out of place between heterosexual women. Especially between mistress and servant. In fact, the intimacy had accidentally bypassed the body completely. Ghertrude's hand was perfectly placed over Meta's solar plexus. Both women had frozen, feeling the sensation pass through them. Their attention was dislodged by another movement. An iridescent line of energy was looping the length of the hall. A fast delineation of great poise and beauty was drawing fluid aerobatics in three-dimensional space. It held its inscription in both time and space, a crystal linear sculpture woven before them. They both turned their heads to watch the wonder and Ghertrude could see Meta's face floating in the air, its expression of delight rippling in pale viridian waves. The line spun and returned again over their heads and then stopped on the lampshade above them in a squat black dot. A fly. Which had entered unseen with Meta. Only a fly, a debased irritant scavenger had drawn the most exquisite thing that either of them had ever seen. Ghertrude removed her hands and nothing was there. The fly was a fly and Meta had vanished, not even a wisp of her dented the air.

"Meta, I don't understand any of this. I don't know whether I am dreaming, hoaxed, or spellbound. But I think you are here with me as you were with Rowena before. Please help me find her. Please let me touch you so that I can find you again."

Her hand was brushed and she reached out and found a mesmerizing place where the world seemed reassessed and hopeful. Where she might recover Rowena and all the malicious stirrings, all the devious manipulations were neutered and replaced by positive opposites. Where a fly was not a fly but a beautiful signature of flight.

Meta settled back into Kühler Brunnen, resuming her previous hours. A special chair was placed close to Ghertrude's in the upper sitting room, a small card table next to it with a silver bell. Thus Meta could announce her presence in a less alarming manner than touch. Anybody watching their communication would have received a very false impression of the content. They sat huddled close together. The older woman pressing the abdomen of her friend while continually moving her head and staring in a strange shortsighted manner at her face. The younger woman seemed indifferent to the ministrations and just talked normally. They talked about Rowena, about her abduction, the warehouse and what lived there and why Meta was invisible to only one person. Sometimes their conversation would be halted by moths or dust. By the rain outside and once by shadows. In each of their sessions Ghertrude seemed to become stronger and more perceptive. Meta noticed something about her mistress, which she found puzzling and faintly alarming: She had none of the channels of inner perception that had been so strong in herself, so strong before they were defiled by the monster in the warehouse. Meta always knew they were weaker and thinner in others, but she had never met a person who had a total absence of them. It was as if she had been born with the subtle stenotic antennae solidly blocked or simply not there at all. It would explain her confidence and her lack of intuition. It might even explain, in some way, her lack of vision.

Ghertrude thought long and hard about telling her about the Kin and their residence below, but she did not want to frighten her off or set the Kin against her. But she did remember Mutter had told her that Meta felt the abduction rise up through the house "from below."

She decided to confront them again early the next morning before Meta arrived. She stepped with ease and anticipation through the locked doors. They greeted her with their usual politeness and over-interest, their engaged concern, which she no longer believed. They sat together and told her all was well with Rowena and that she would be home soon. Ghertrude waited to hear their mode change. Their gearshift of security, letting some of their unused mechanism shut down. When she heard it in two of them she aimed her question.

"I want my maid, Rowena's nanny, to know about you. She is called Meta and I think she should know."

The Kin shifted back into alert agitation, all standing up and displaying a hitherto unseen tremor.

"It might not be a good idea to involve Meta in our business. We exist entirely for you and she might not be able to understand that. It is best to keep the business in this house to ourselves," said Aklia.

Ghertrude noticed a different emphasis between the words and could not place its uneasy pace. She decided to push further. To use this uncomfortable question as a pry, a wedge to see deeper beneath their carapace.

"I don't think you understand. I am sure Meta would not be disturbed by you. After all, she has visited the library of crates."

There was a knocking of bodies as they moved closer together, which added to the agitated concern in their speech.

"You mean Meta has been to the w-w-warehouse of substance?" stuttered Seth.

Ghertrude had never heard any of the Kin falter in their clipped and resolute speech.

"Yes, she had an unpleasant meeting with some sort of creature who lives there. After that, I think she will find you rather mild."

"It is not necessary. She does not need to know of our existence no matter what she has seen before. Ghertrude, we think it is best for all if she is kept to the upper floors. We can provide all you need or desire," said Luluwa.

"I was thinking of bringing her down here this afternoon."

Their bodies were now pressed against one another, the heads shaking in disapproval.

"If you did that, then we would have to hide. To not be here," said Seth. The word "not" was spoken by them all in unison. At this point their posture and speech became clear to Ghertrude. It was not a vexed concern about being seen by a stranger or the unquestioning enforcement of a taboo. Or a spoiling of the unique relationship that they kept insisting they had. It was simpler than that. It was fear.

"Why are you afraid of her?"

The response was instant and unexpected. They turned off. Bodies still touching, staring at her. They switched into inert. End of conversation. Ghertrude waited for more than ten minutes. She even had the nerve to tap on Seth's head.

"Anybody home?" she said. Then, getting no response, she retreated to the door, looking back one last time for a glimpse of movement. There was none and she climbed up into what used to be the sensible world to wait for Meta.

The rainy season was over, and while the last few drips were wrung out of a cloudless evening sky, Ghertrude looked for the key to the garden, which was overgrown and full of life. She had Mutter clear a path through it and make an island where the bench and table stood. She told him to leave the rest for careful clearing another time. She well understood his slash-and-burn mentality. The subtlety of gardens, even wildly overgrown ones, was beyond his sensibility. She and Meta would sit in its private enclosure and watch the afternoon turn into night. The early twilight that they enjoyed the best. Holding hands for sight and touching Meta's belly for vision. All manner of winged creatures left their crystal traces. The scarlet dragonflies were the most exciting. Flying in pairs, dipping and swirling in wild irregular orbits that repeated continually until they moved on to sport elsewhere or were hurried away when the bats arrived. The interlacing of fluttering furrows was truly breathtaking, each tiny nuance of their double-paired wings etching the air into the finest intricacies. There were larger dragonflies that collided and ran with wings spluttering together like Japanese fans, but their trail, although beautiful, lacked the diamond-point scorings of the scarlets. They sat enthralled, sometimes squeezing each other in their new joy of closeness between the gap of loss and anxiety. When the bats came, the show increased. The high riffled sky drawings of the swallows became underpinned by the bat's solid ricochets of twisted light. It was during these times—unbeknownst to either of them—that their friendship deepened, exposing a nearly raw seam of love. Proximity of bodies can be ignited only by proximity of souls. All else is meagre, momentary lust. Which at that moment was beyond their wildest contemplation.

The scraps of joy, the enthrallment, and the sadness were being woven into a single text:, a scroll of yarn, a fabric that already had weight and colour without them knowing. In the little island, amid the weeds and exotic foliage, they were becoming one. Firstly in the place where one was missing, and later fusing in the depths of themselves.

The days ran warm again and they became inseparable. Occasionally Ghertrude ventured below to see what was happening and maybe continue her enquiries. But it was not possible. The Kin were set in the same position as before, shut down and huddled together like arctic musk ox locking their bodies in defence of frozen winds and wolves. It was an astonishing act of denial, if it was true. Ghertrude doubted their fidelity. She imagined them wistfully unlocking the moment she was gone, going about their normal obscure duties. The second she turned the key in the basement door they fled back to form their inert cluster before her foot touched the lower stair. She examined them close up, seeking signs of vivacity beneath the polished brown shells. There were none. The idea of them permanently in stasis like that began to appall her, the encroaching image even trespassing into her unique space with Meta. After eleven days she had had enough, she would give in to shake them out of her head. She went below again and confronted the irritating tableau.

"Very well, you win, I will not tell Meta about you."

Instantly they came apart, regained their previous postures as if the film had simply been wound back.

"Good. Then we won't have to leave here. We want to stay close to you," said Seth, as if he had not even taken a pause for breath or thought before continuing his speech.

"Sometimes you are very childish," said an infuriated Ghertrude.

"A condition that we have never ourselves experienced," said Luluwa.

Ghertrude listened for sarcasm in the clicking rattle of her speech but realised that none existed.

Two days later, Cyrena arrived unannounced. To her great surprise, Meta opened the door.

"Hello, Meta, I did not expect to find you back here. How are you, my dear, after all these horrible incidents?"

"Very well, madam," answered Meta.

Cyrena caught something in her sparse answer and her body language that made her curious.

"Is Ghertrude home?"

"Yes, madam."

There was something about the way that her diminutive figure was filling the door.

"Then may I come in?"

"Of course, madam," and she moved aside.

Ghertrude had heard the bell and Cyrena's voice at the door and hurried to meet her friend in the hallway. They hugged and smiled and went arm in arm into the drawing room, leaving Meta still holding the door and the brightness of the outside world. She had never really felt jealousy before, and its bitterness rose inside her without comparison or control. She closed the door and moved closer to what was being said.

"Yes, Meta and I are getting along famously. She is keeping me company in these difficult times."

"Difficult?" said Cyrena in an incongruous way.

Ghertrude ignored it and continued.

"We have been planning what to do on Rowena's return."

She made an inclusive gesture with her arm, which indicated that Meta was nearby. Meta saw this from outside the room and scurried towards its friendly corral. Cyrena saw it too. Nothing ever escaped those sharp clever eyes, and a sightless history of understanding positioned by emphasis of the voice. How many people were present when only one spoke?

"Come here, child," she commanded to the approaching Meta. Who was halfway across the room.

"She is here now, Ghertrude, you may continue."

"Er . . . I was saying that we are planning . . . planning to . . ."

"You still can't see her."

"What . . ."

"You can't see her, can you?"

Ghertrude looked panicked, her eyes skating the room.

Meta moved quietly to her side and touched her hand. She instantly gripped it, looked down, and became more settled.

"We . . . we . . ."

"What is going on?" demanded Cyrena in a less-than-friendly tone.

Ghertrude was intimidated and tongue-tied by the force of the question.

"Please, madam. Mistress Ghertrude can see some of me and hear me when she touches my hand."

Cyrena looked at the pair, who were now desperately holding hands, her friend giving imploring looks back and forth between her and the maid, who was staring in concern and admiration at her mistress. It looked like a scene from a melodrama or a grimly sentimental Victorian painting. Cyrena choked on a tiny suppressed laugh.

"What are you talking about?" she said in an equally theatrical voice.

"It's true, I can only perceive her when we touch. And then almost as an afterthought," Ghertrude said. "Can you see her now?"

"I can see both of you, and a very pretty picture it makes. Ishmael is about to be executed. There is no trace of your lost daughter. You haven't set foot out of this house for weeks and now I find the pair of you sitting like lunatic old maids in a storm. What are you playing at?"

Cyrena had not meant to let loose this flood. But the strain of the trial, with more and more harrowing details coming to light, was taking its toll. And Ghertrude hadn't once so much as contacted her or been to visit Ishmael.

CHAPTER FORTY-TWO

*T*hey had come to get Hector. Compton and three others entered Whitechapel on a Sunday morning, shielded and disguised by the visiting hordes to the Petticoat Lane and Club Row markets. Just another bunch of punters seeking a good deal, a last-minute grab the day before Christmas. Crossing the boundaries and the centuries to barter with biblicals and yids for a cheap killing. The snow lay thin and scattered. The crowds pushed in overcoated resolve to comb every inch of the festoons of battered goods. The traders stamped the cold out of their static pitch and tried to absorb the heat and the money from the swollen tide of the pushing mob.

Compton and his band entered the markets at the south, coming up through Aldgate, crossing the congested streets into Whitechapel proper. His face was still heavily bruised and one of his teeth was loose and squeaked when he touched it. From his meeting with Hedges. It was disgusting, he thought. Doctors, educated men should never behave like that. After Hedges's immediate reaction to his questions, he and his men had been arrested by military police and questioned for three days. But they had nothing on him and let him go with a warning about setting foot on military property again. He had to be more careful with his questions in the future. So here among the poor scum of the ghetto and the market he would make softer, more cunning enquiries about his old friend recently arrived from the fatherland. It would be easy for him to beguile and corner this riffraff, most of them did not even speak English properly. In the faster road between the two markets he thought that he had let his little questions about Heidelberg academics fall casually on dim, unsuspecting ears. He thought that his subtle hooks about escapees from Bedlam were missing their targets. Landing on innocent, shrugging costers who knew nothing about such things. He was disastrously wrong. They had all been primed, and his questions and his identity had dominoed before him, fifty minutes in advance of his plodding step. Solli's gang was waiting at the end of the market, where the traders cranked down to dishevelled old men selling the leftovers of poverty. Lovingly laid out on scraps of carpet, scarves, or dishcloths. Each a prized treasure: old dentures, used candles, bent forks, smuttier and pissed-upon remnants of remnants. A perfect place for Compton to ask his final question. The old men with their diseased droppings stood in a line opposite the old bathhouse and the Repton Boys Boxing Club. They hugged themselves against the freezing weather and many had water dripping from their red pinched noses, where icicles threatened to form. A few had mugs of hot sarsaparilla that steamed from their cupped gloves into their haggard faces. Solli and his lithe gang waited across the road, dispersed enough to look like strangers.

Compton had cast dozens of small nets and found nothing squirming in them. He was forced to purchase a few goods to keep up his subtle masquerade. Also forced by the mischievous guile of some of the canny traders, who saw him coming and marked his passage with ridicule. He had bought and his men behind him had carried: a lampshade (torn); a gross of assorted room deodorisers, the kind where you pull the green wick out;

a cloth warehouse coat; and a tribal deity (which amazingly had once been a much-prized icon of the True People). They stood behind him trying to look both invisible and intimidating while holding the array of ludicrous objects. Behind them in the last street arrived another three khevre of Rabbi Solli. They looked far from ridiculous, being young, poised as wolves, and happy to be tooled up and ready for a bit of chiv and skirmish. In his final round of subtle questioning Compton actually said the word "Jew." What a clever boy!

Solli was standing behind him.

"You don't mean an old kraut yid wid funny hair, do ya, mister?" he said with great comic timing. Compton turned to confront the grinning street scum who was half his size.

"Exactly," he said. "Recently arrived."

"From Krautland," finished Solli.

"Eh! Er, yes."

"He's over there, sleeping in the back."

Compton was overjoyed, he had found him, and these idiots had given him up. They all crossed the narrow road, grinning, and went in the back door of the looming vast warehouse that ran adjacent to the boxing club. They walked through the ugly compressed spaces of piled carpets and blankets, colourless and worn by age. They came into a far corner where the building had shrunk into a once-white tiled room with a closed gate onto an outside yard. Without anything being said they all stopped and waited. Compton's men felt it first; they started to put down their armfuls of tat. Lenny, the biggest one, moved quickly to Compton's side as he said, "Where is he, then?" Looking straight into Solli's grinning face. Lenny leaned over him, ready to start punching the smile out of this cocky little tyke.

The razor came up and across his face in a second and then fell back to Solli's rigid side. One single movement. As simple as sneezing or swatting a fly. Action, then back to a standstill.

Nothing happened for ages. Then Lenny's face burst open. Solli laughed and his khevre moved out of the shadows and tore lumps out of Compton's fleeing gang as they frantically bolted though the labyrinth of musty piled rags, desperately seeking the door and escape.

Compton stood dazed at the sight of Lenny with half of his face in his hand, panting, and then running away in a spray of tears and blood.

"Got a message for you and your pals back in Krautland."

Compton looked up.

"They got a new kinda cross, ain't they?"

Compton tried to understand.

"Looks like this, don't it," said Solli as his stiff arm and the barber's razor flashed in the air and carved a sun wheel into Compton's face before his hands could react.

They dragged him and one of the others who had not escaped outside, kicking them towards the old men who were shovelling up their false teeth, broken cups, torn postcards, and other priceless possessions because the market was closing and the pubs were open.

Compton fell between them, some of his blood splattering onto the tea cloth that a wizened aged man was daintily folding up, his gnarled hand trembling from six hours of frozen penniless exposure. A long icicle of snot hanging like a spinal pendulum from his red ice-clad nose. He stepped back, wiped his nose with the back of his hairy hand, and kicked the open wound of Compton's face with as much force as his frail bones could muster.

"Fucker," he spat, and gently retrieved his treasure.

Compton was now crawling away on his hands and knees. Solli stood over him and slipped a few coins into the hand of the old man, who winked and rapidly dispersed towards the warmth of the closest pub.

Compton was never heard of again and the furious Himmelstrup never received his last communication.

➤—→

Hector knew none of this, high in his attic room above the layers
of hectic business that hours before had bobbed and thrived in
the streets below. He had returned after a deep dreamless sleep
in the core of the house of the insane. Nicholas had been there,
motionless and smiling, sitting on the end of the bed when he
awoke. He had escorted him from the weird security of his room
through the vast hospital that was being decked in garlands and
strings of coloured-paper chains that the inmates had lovingly
made weeks ago. They passed the Christmas tree that sparkled
with the new and highly questionable electric candles. Outside
the snow was holding off and a weak sun insisted on trying
to add colour to the passing day. The *Cromwell* arrived at the
dock at two. Nicholas and Moses's son carefully helped Hector
aboard.

"Your first two tasks were magnificently achieved," said
Nicholas as the old man bobbed up and down on the deck, gripping the rail of the boat with both hands. He had entirely forgotten about his night in what once was Blake's garden. He was
about to say something, or so he thought, but it was unknown.
His mouth and vocal cords waited to catch it, but nothing
arrived as the boat pushed out into the thick water. Nicholas
waved at the diminutive figure as it headed towards St. Stephen's
Tower and Westminster Bridge, which had managed to hold on
to some of the low sun's light, giving it just enough radiance to
muster a whisper of the poet's glorious London.

"Dear God, the very houses seem asleep," said Nicholas
quietly.

Hector heard him, heard him above the sound of the boat
and turned around to look at the bridge. Its little glow filled

him with an unexpected joy. He turned back to wave thanks, or friendship, or communication to Nicholas, but he was gone. The old man smiled and gripped the boat in a different way. He knew that Nicholas had gone back to help and encourage the inmates with their festivities and that later he would return to the rumpled bed to listen to the voices on his radio.

He actually enjoyed the voyage back to the East End, relished the view of London from the cold stout wooden deck. Occasionally he was aware of the captain or his son looking from the wheelhouse to make sure that their precious cargo was still there and comfortable.

The post-market streets were desolate and emptier than ever before.

He climbed the cold stairs to his room, still feeling the Thames sway in his tight and trembling legs. There was no sound from Mrs. Fishburn's door as he crept past its immaculate sleeping step and climbed the last flight, key in hand. He quickly lit the fire and boiled the kettle, humming an old tune under his breath while he watched the steam and the smoke take hold. He became shocked by the happiness that throbbed inside him. Like that cold bridge, it had accumulated warmth and transformed all else. Up here with his few possessions and the hum of a new security he felt the eerie growing belief that what the Erstwhile had told him might just be true, and that he did have some part to play in a future event. Not bad for a man who had given up on life a few months ago and settled into a regimen of gentle crumbling back in the Rupert the First Retirement Home. Heidelberg seemed remote, like a fiction from another century. He had forgotten most of his previous life, which was a good sign. He had not been touched by God's "kindness enzyme" that Nicholas had insisted arrived at the beginning of dotage, where only the past existed and the deceasing elder slid backwards to meet its glowing embrace. For a moment his thoughts drifted back to the garden in Hercules Road. He tried to read the text through the lens of his memory, but patches of it were missing or refused to focus. Then the garden tugged away, leaving a sense of fulfilment, a job well done.

He heard Nicholas's words until the sounds from the city or the river filtered up and mixed them with the nightly hum from the rooftops, a low reassuring resonance that came from all of London and was compressed by the heavy clouds that were laden with snow. He sat close to his small but intense coal fire, his tea and whisky comforting his hands, looking out the floor-to-ceiling window that dominated the room. The first flakes of the day fell slowly, as if against all the sound below. The great engine of London was turning even on this day. Restless and endless. The landscape looked different in the snow. The balance between the areas of open land and the buildings had changed, had shifted. The snow had worked like a lens to magnify the obvious. The buildings had encroached on the grass and trees, even in the short time he had been living there, the pattern had tightened. Human symmetry now had the upper hand. It turned his mind to what Nicholas had said about the trees and the collective "mind" of a forest, of the possibility of a retaliation from nature should man's greed become overbearing. He had referenced the great jungle called the Vorrh, thinking it only a fiction before. But there it was on the maps, a great fist of vegetation in the centre of Africa, its proportion immense. To understand it more he had a cut out an oval of paper to the same size and covered the area of the Vorrh with it, his intention being to make a calculated estimate of its magnitude. He was just about to retrieve the cut paper when he saw the map a different way, suddenly it jumped into something else. With the central bulk of its shape removed, the map of Africa now looked like a perfect question mark. The serendipity of the image rocked him. Another question mark had raised its ghostly head. More enigmas in life; he was brimming over with them.

He sat back farther in the ancient chair and thought about that odd discovery and about the strange night, and about the ultimate enigma that was Nicholas. Much of what the Erstwhile said was beyond him; his shifting persona and its accents and the obscurity of it left him confused. He also felt he was being tested, that many of the questions Nicholas posed were there to define his boundaries and that most did not have simple answers. Except of course the one that he posed backwards by giving him the answer and telling him that he had to find the question. The small fire crackled in Hector's room and he scanned the piles of books that had been sent to him, casually making equations with their titles. The majority were about Judeo-Christian mythology, the Old Testament, and the story of Eden. From them he summoned the archetypical image of the garden, with all its suggested symmetries and purposes, and then he saw the answer again and suddenly he knew what the question was. It was so simple and so devastating. For the first time since he had met the occupant of room 126, he wished he was what he originally thought him to be: a deluded lunatic, rambling nonsense in an asylum. Because if there was any truth in what had just been revealed, then the understanding of the world had just been turned upside down.

God's last act of creation was to place the tree of knowledge at the centre of the Garden of Eden. Adam was told not to touch it. The angels were placed there to protect it.

Question: So if the tree of knowledge was not meant for men and angels, who was it made for?

Answer: The trees.

CHAPTER FORTY-THREE

*T*he crowd was enormous. They pushed and elbowed their way into position long before the sun rose and the screens came down. By nine the entire square was a compacted mass of heaving, sweaty humans. Some had been there all night. Some had to be shooed off from trespassing on the raised scaffold by the armed guards with fixed bayonets. Adam and the tree arrived in their cases with their technicians at midnight, who waited for the canvas to be erected around their precise deliberations. By two, he and the articulated tree had been jointed back together, ready to test the intricate mechanisms. The executioner arrived much later to oil the blade's bearings and grease the running table of the bascule, the trapdoor, and the restraining brace. He waited for the artificial forest and its occupant to be fully bolted on before he and the other men tested the release mechanism. He hardly ever spoke under the silken hood. The blade had been removed and sharpened two days earlier and he grunted when he tested its edge with the back of his thumbnail.

By the time the buildings had warmed and the breezes of the day had gathered momentum they were finished. The executioner disappeared, moving quickly towards the holding cell, where Ishmael was being morticed into his wooden suit.

Crows and ravens circled above the tight geometric square. There would be no pickings today. But the scent of blood was already vivid, exhaled in ghosted anticipation by the mob below. The slender rod that connected the twin spires of the cathedral was straining against the hour, concealed inside the silver bridge. Straining in its inert control. Wanting to shunt the demand of the hour from the clock to the bell.

Cyrena sat framed by the casement window of the third-floor room owned by the Timber Guild. She sat bolt upright on a gilded chair, half on the balcony and half in the shaded room. The view from there was uncompromised and theatrical. Quentin Talbot stood behind her, immaculate and resolute. Nobody else was allowed to use the room that day. He had seen to that. He had blocked all attempts, even Krespka's. The old man had been furious, pulling rank, age, and authority on Talbot, but to no avail. He would have to take his whores elsewhere.

In all the bilious turmoil of recent days, in all the spinning contradictions and emotional churnings that had kept her from sleep and soured every waking hour, this place paradoxically felt safe and calm. Even with the rabble boiling beneath and what was about to expose itself on the stage before her, there was tranquillity high on this shelf. As she watched in operatic isolation, Talbot tried not to look at the nape of her majestic neck. He was here to help and protect her, not to be aroused by her sad beauty. Or the thought of his plan so perfectly fulfilled and that she would watch it innocent of his contrivance in the destruction of this Ishmael creature. The only man who had ever touched and mated with her. The image of that excited and sickened him and he quickly banished it. Thinking like this would make him no better than the despicable Krespka. And that might possibly show.

On a side table he had arranged cooled water and glasses, and a discreet starched pile of delicate linen handkerchiefs, which he had chosen and bought for today. There was also some pale French brandy. In his pocket were smelling salts, just in case.

Mutter was in the crowd, standing on a high step and eating a pork pie the size of the hub of a small cartwheel. He noticed Mistress Lohr in her royal box and grinned. The congealed fat of the pie jellied out of the corner of his tipsy mouth. He was thinking about her fucking the condemned freak, whom he had never liked or trusted. He choked in delight, bits of crust shrapnel spraying over the heads below him, making some look around. He coughed and then laughed again.

Anton Fleischer and Deacon Tulp were in the dignitaries' enclosure to the side of the scaffold, looking uncomfortable in their duty of witness.

Eight streets away Ghertrude and Meta sat holding hands, trying not to hear the noise from the square. The Kin did the opposite. Each one of them had their heads knocked hard against the basement windows. Straining for the sound through the foxed glass and their Bakelite shells.

At nine the bell awoke. Its hammer jerkily yanked back, ready to strike, resentful and amnesic of the thousands of times it had done it before. The note sounded through the air and collided with every particle of matter in its path. An unnatural quiet fell over the crowd and the circling birds heard their dry feathers against the resistance of empty space. The distance below them was the same as the distance to the next toll. Mutter stopped chewing. Talbot made a tiny unseen faltering of balance behind Cyrena, who was stiffening in the chair. The iron ball of the second blue-grey toll rolled across the platform of the scaffold and the workers there removed the canvas screens. The crowd inhaled, and with the third note exploded with a great roar of approval. Adam Longfellar and his forest were ready for action. The black wooden man stood poised and ready again to contemplate his terrible disobedience and to pay the consequences.

The forest of trigger leaves waited to count the wind towards the conclusion. The condemned man struggled in his pale suit of white wood, already strapped into place. His tugs and wrenching against the restraints could be felt through the planked floor and into the stern uprights of the guillotine. One of the carved leaves fell back against its hinge, like a sleeping dog's ear that had been previously folded. Some of the crowd saw it and gasped, thinking it was the beginning of the ceremony. Fathers pointed, explaining to their children—some sitting on their shoulders for a better view—how the mechanism worked. Fleischer, from his privileged seat, saw the brightness of blood on the headpiece of the pale suit. He nudged Tulp and whispered. The executioner made one final adjustment, removed the brake, and left the stage, closing the door behind him. He had work to do below. It was important that the drama occur without any other human being involved. The stage was the condemned man's alone. All eyes were now on him, the machines, and the responsible wind.

Just before the first bell, when the executioner was above and only a single guard was outside Ishmael's cell, he had removed the offending eye. He dug it out from its pristine sutures with a rusty nail. He felt no pain as he winkled out the split orb in three soggy pieces.

The guard, sensing the quietness of concentration below the crashing waves of excitement, turned to look into the cell, seeing the first blood on the prisoner's hand. He called to another and they rushed into the cell, taking the weapon out of Ishmael's hand. He had been wearing the body section of the wooden suit. Drips and splashes already stained its subtle pale lustre. A few hasty words were exchanged and one of the guards started ripping the thin hessian sheet off Ishmael's bed. The other restrained his limp and resigned body. They sat him down, the new wood creaking badly with the strain and small ruptures of sap escaping through the sandpapered surface. The bleeding was much less than they first imagined. The hasty bandage stopped the rest. This was all a terrible mistake, and if discovered before the event, the executioner would have them whipped. They knotted it tight around Ishmael's flaccid head and quickly started to pull the masked headpiece on, concealing the wound and the dressing. Making sure that none of the rag was visible or causing an obstruction to the naked gap in the suit between the head and shoulders. They were so intent in their labours that they did not hear the grey hooded figure enter the cell behind them.

The wind tickled the fine scalps of the bouncing infants held aloft by so many proud fathers. It measured the square and buffeted the balcony, making the small hairs rise on the perfect curve of Cyrena's neck. She unwittingly brought up her slender hand to touch them and Talbot shuddered. The first three leaves rattled. The dog was awake. The crowd gasped as the sculptured forest quivered over Adam's head and his fingers moved and his eyes began to slide open, the offending apple twitching in his grasp.

The actual time of waiting from the unveiling and the departure of the executioner to the dropping of the axe, the spilling of the wooden guts, and the shunted corpse into the sacks below was never known. True, everybody knew the wind fluttering the trigger leaves made the action occur, and the strength and direction of the wind gauged the time it took. But what they did not know was that there was a seasonal adjustment control box under the stage. Only the executioner and the makers of the mechanism had keys to it. In the box were a series of slides that balanced a summer day against a monsoon against a mistral and the doldrums. The whole business would be ridiculous and self-defeating if it ended in a few minutes or dragged on for days. The average duration was just over three hours, which gave the

crowd time to gather and keep the tension engaged. To give
the impression of random control, a few executions had been
manipulated to heighten the unpredictability. For example, that
of Adolf Bühler, which lasted a full six hours and had the crowd
anxious to leave the arena to relieve themselves during the last
moments of Adam's movements. Or that of Constance Zembla,
the infamous vampire, who it was claimed drank the blood and
sipped the bone marrow of a dozen people. Some of them white.
Her execution was triggered in twenty minutes during a par-
ticularly savage and unforeseen storm. The spectacle was very
dramatic, with the leaves clattering frantically, a few wrenching
themselves off their constructed boughs. Adam's face grimac-
ing to the full extent of its mechanical expression and the mad
woman screaming loudly in her wooden suit, having chewed
through the muffling gag. Even with all of that, such a short
time was considered unfulfilling, especially by some of the mob
who had not arrived or settled yet. But it did prove the point that
the procedure was outside the control of men.

Ishmael's dividing had already lasted 186 minutes when the
first click of the blade restraint was heard. The crowd pushed
closer and Cyrena at her upper window bit her lip and covered
the action with her trembling hand. Talbot moved behind and
closer to her chair, his hand shuffling in his trouser pocket,
presumably with the bottle of smelling salts. Mutter stood on
tiptoe and nearly lost his balance from his high step. Tulp and
Fleischer were becoming really concerned about the amount of
blood now seeping from the wooden hood of the condemned.
Tulp stood and moved closer for a better look. The gap between
the shoulders and head was bright red. He was about to call back
to Fleischer that something was wrong when he heard the second click high above him and the great weight and the gleaming
blade rattled down the oiled shafts and cut the red section in

two. In the front of the stage, Adam was performing his final formal throes. The headless body thrashed and was tilted into the hole in the stage. Adam's slithering innards bounced on the stage and a great uproar came from the crowd as the severed head tumbled down its sticky canvas chute.

"Ishmael," said Cyrena, his name cupped in less than a sob.

ACKNOWLEDGMENTS

Enormous gratitude to my editor, Timothy O'Connell, for his enthusiasm, sensitivity, and skill.

Great thanks to my brilliant agents, Jon Elek and Seth Fishman.

THE VORRH

Prepare to lose yourself in the heady, mythical expanse of *The Vorrh*, a daring debut that Alan Moore has called "a phosphorescent masterpiece" and "the current century's first landmark work of fantasy." Next to the colonial town of Essenwald sits the Vorrh, a vast—perhaps endless—forest. It is a place of demons and angels, of warriors and priests. Sentient and magical, the Vorrh bends time and wipes memory. Legend has it that the Garden of Eden still exists at its heart. Now a renegade English soldier aims to be the first human to traverse its expanse. Armed with only a strange bow, he begins his journey, but some fear the consequences of his mission and a native marksman has been chosen to stop him. Around them swirl a remarkable cast of characters, including a cyclops raised by robots and a young girl with a tragic curiosity, as well as historical figures such as writer Raymond Roussel and photographer Eadweard Muybridge. Fact and fiction blend, the hunter will become the hunted, and everyone's fate hangs in the balance under the will of the Vorrh.

Fiction